GRANTING KATELYN

THE SWEET VALLEY SERIES

BOOK TWO

S.E. REICHERT

5 PRINCE PUBLISHING

Published by 5 PRINCE PUBLISHING & BOOKS, LLC

PO Box 865, Arvada, CO 80001

www.5PrinceBooks.com

ISBN digital: 978-1-63112-319-1

ISBN print: 978-1-63112-320-7

Cover Credit: Marianne Nowicki

F07172023

For my girls.

May you always be strong and loved.
May you always know the difference
between being admired,
and being valued.

ACKNOWLEDGMENTS

Thanks to my family and my amazing daughters, the brightest, funniest, most complicated and kind people I know. You've taught me so much about love and patience, and embody the kind of lead characters I want to see in the world. This life won't ever be easy, but I hope you navigate it with strength, grace, and the kind of self-worth, all women should carry. I will always have your back.

To my local writing group (Writing Heights) and your supportive and inspiring members. You are the resource that made me a better writer and gave me the courage, confidence and skill to make it this far.

To Rebecca Schwab-Cuthbert: You've encouraged me through some of the darkest nights of my soul and I wouldn't be able to do this writing thing, or this living thing, without your friendship.

To my beta readers, Misty, Kristine, Heather, Lucinda, Jean, Heidi, and Jessie; thank you for taking the time to read and give me feedback. You make a better book and you help make me a better writer.

Thank you to the fantastic team at 5 Prince Publishing. To Bernadette Soehner who has given me warmth, laughter, opportunities and encouragement since the first day I met her. To Cate Byers who takes my rough work and makes it so much better, with a level of talent and kindness that is unparalleled. I am so grateful for your support and help.

To all my readers, thanks for continually picking up these books. Thank you for sticking with the characters and for believing in their happily ever afters. May we all find a little of the same for ourselves.

GRANTING KATELYN

ONE

THE SUN WAS HOTTER THAN HELLFIRE ON HER DUST AND sweat-covered skin. Muscles in her shoulders tensed as she tightened her core and narrowed her eyes on the target ahead. The angry bull charged the group of riders and Katelyn Sullivan dug her heels into Dakota's sides, her hips nudging effortlessly and thighs contracting as they flew, one being, over the expansive field. Dakota's nimble and honed muscles responded to Katelyn as if the same neurological impulses were shared between them. The bull dodged right, Dakota anticipated, and responded. It swerved left and tripped in the rush to evade horse and rider, then turned a semicircle around a clump of sagebrush.

"Son-of-a-bitch," Katelyn growled. "Go get 'im!" She took the rope into her calloused right hand. The thunder of the bull's hoofs against the clay-packed ground shook through and across the field, and Katelyn leaned into the chase, raising her hand above her head while guiding Dakota with the other. The loop began large and easy, as Katelyn slowed her breathing and focused on the twin tips of the horns ahead. While the world sped by at a breakneck pace, it faded in Katelyn's brain, and her focus narrowed.

"Ease up, babe," she spoke softly in the palomino's ears. The mare was attuned to her voice. The bull cantered to the right, as Katelyn anticipated it might, to avoid the approaching fence line, and her nimble fingers tightened the loop and sent it through the dusty air with a whispering hiss. It ringed around the bull's right horn, and before the slack could disappear and cost her a finger, Katelyn wrapped the end around her saddle horn and pulled Dakota up with a lean back and a soft "Whoa." Without taking the bull to the ground, and gently turning its head in the direction she wanted it to go, she safely secured it to Dakota and led it back to the open fence, where it had come over to romance the heifers of Bar Nunn's only-for-show herd.

"WOW!" ONE OF BAR NUNN'S GUESTS GASPED, MOUTH hanging open. "Does she work for you?"

The hired hand being asked could barely keep his own horse from bolting at the excitement.

"Uh, no."

"Make that, *hell* no," Katelyn said as she passed by and tipped up the bill of her ball cap to the yaw-mouthed male guides as she passed. "Ladies."

"Who is that?" a man at the back asked tersely.

Another guide at the back of the group chimed in. "Katelyn Sullivan. All-state barrel racing champ."

"Sullivan? Like the baked goods they deliver to the resort?"

"That would be her sister, Elle."

"Quite the horsewoman," the terse man said and watched her pass by the group, spine straight and riding just as effortlessly as if she'd been born on the horse's back. He hadn't been able to keep his eyes off of her from the minute she'd jumped the palomino over the fence and taken after the bull upon hearing the guest's screams from one field over. She certainly was a take-charge type.

"She's also an equine therapist. She's worked with a couple of our own," the guide remarked as his agitated horse tried to follow Katelyn. "Including this one," he grunted.

"His name's Otis, Joey, and if you'd take a minute to actually get to know your horse, he might do what you want him to," Katelyn grouched as she passed by. "I'll send you a bill for my services," she called over her shoulder and escorted the bull back to Garrett's ranch down the road.

"Therapist, huh?" The interested older man watched her go and committed her name to his sharp memory.

"She's good with horses, but a bit crass," the first guide sneered.

"You mean she doesn't put up with bullshit?" the man said. "I need to speak to that young lady," he whispered to his wife. "I think a mutual friend of ours could use her help."

"Maybe even help his horse, too." His wife wiggled her eyebrows.

KATELYN MAY SULLIVAN HOISTED THE WESTERN SADDLE up and onto the fence with little difficulty. She wiped the sweat from her neck, just below her ponytail, and looked out over the cottonwoods into the setting sun. It grazed the bright green shuddering of leaves and left semicircles of shadows at her feet.

"That was some decent riding," came an older man's voice from behind.

Katelyn turned to the couple approaching the small paddock at the back of her parents' house. She recognized them from the Bar Nunn group this afternoon and eyed them with caution.

"It was all right. Nothing that any decent rider couldn't have been able to handle. Sorry you didn't have better examples with your 'dudes'." She turned to wipe the saddle down.

"I'm Jim Parsons and this is my wife, Sharon."

Sharon nudged in front of him. "That was the best thing I've seen all week," she said and held out her hand. "Should have seen their chins hit the dirt when you roped it in a single throw. Serves them right." Katelyn took her hand with renewed interest and a warmer smile. "Many moons ago, I won Sheridan County Fair in calf roping."

"I bet you did, Sharon," Katelyn said. Jim cleared his throat and Katelyn turned to shake his as well.

"What can I do for you two? I assume you don't need real riding lessons." She smiled. Jim put his hands on his hips and Katelyn felt like she was about to get roped into something herself.

"I hear you're an excellent equine therapist as well as a helluva barrel racer."

"My reputation might have been exaggerated."

"Humble is fine too," he said, and nodded. "I have a proposition for you."

Katelyn looked across the paddock to the small stables where Dakota had finished her dirt bath and was now swishing her long blonde tail at the water trough. When Jim didn't go on, she turned back to look at him.

"I'm afraid to ask what that might be," Katelyn said, disliking the hanging question in his voice. Sharon sighed, threaded her fingers together, and leveled her eyes on Katelyn.

"Have you ever heard of Tennyson Stables? The horse racing facility in North Carolina? Ian Tennyson owns one of the most promising bloodlines of thoroughbreds in America."

Katelyn leaned back on the fence, took off her gloves, and tucked them in her back pocket. She looked back to the burly and hardworking quarters her family had bred. A long way from the best thoroughbreds in America.

"Can't say as I've heard of them." Truth be told, that world clashed with the ideals of her heart. She'd seen too many case studies of racehorses and the damage done to their bodies for the sake of a payout.

"Grant Tennyson, Ian's son, is a friend of mine. When he came over from the UK about ten years ago, it was his first experience with that kind of work. I helped him get Tennyson Stables up and running. He's managing the facility himself now." Katelyn could read the slight change of tension in Jim's voice.

"Okay?"

"But he's had a rough go of it lately, especially with their breeding program."

"So—what's the problem, exactly?"

Jim smiled and leaned on the pole fence next to her, studying Dakota. "Well, it's their prize stallion, Hugh Dancy McFinnegan O'Shea."

Katelyn snorted. "Jesus, that's a hell of a name."

"Yeah, pompous, I know," Jim said.

"So? What happened to McFinnegan Sir Prance-A-Lot?"

Sharon stifled a chuckle. "Hugh was in an accident last fall and he's not performing as he should be."

"Well, that I'm sorry to hear," Katelyn said. "Surgery?"

"They flew in the finest equine surgeons they could find and, initially, it went well, but he's not responding to the recovery program." Katelyn watched Jim's body language. He seemed reserved, holding back the whole truth.

"Surely Tennyson can find a closer and more experienced therapist—"

"Well," Sharon interjected, "Grant is a—" She cleared her throat and looked out into the red-soil paddock.

"What?" Katelyn scowled.

"Grant isn't good with people. He's fired most of the therapists assigned to Hugh."

"Uh...golly, that sure sounds like a fun job. I don't think I'd be a good fit."

"That's just it," Sharon interrupted. "Jim and I, after seeing you ride and deal with the ranch hands this afternoon? Well, we both think you might be exactly the right person for the job."

Katelyn looked at Sharon sideways. "On account of my charming personality?"

"On account of you seem like someone who doesn't put up with bullshit, and this job requires a bit of fearlessness."

Katelyn didn't respond. She sighed with a troubled scowl set between her brows. Her brain turned the idea around and around in her head. She liked a challenge. She didn't put up with bullshit. And lost causes *were* a specialty of the Sullivan clan, her father had always said.

"What kind of injury?" she asked.

"He took a bad fall. Down an embankment. He was being pushed too hard over rocky terrain. Pulled a tendon in his chest, tore ligaments in his forefoot."

Katelyn nodded and thought. "I've seen something like that before, when I was younger. We had a gelding, Sal, who fell down a creek embankment. My grandma Em was able to help him recuperate nearly altogether."

"So, you think there's a chance Hugh could make a full recovery?" Jim asked.

Katelyn sighed. Thoughts of helping her dad bring in the summer hay and working with this year's foals fell away while the chance to work with a thoroughbred and help free it from pain and immobility pushed them aside. The added bonus of working in a new place, with high-end stables, no doubt a beautiful arena, and getting out of Sweet Valley for a spell, did its own work on her stir-crazy brain.

"Could be," she whispered.

"Great! I'll make a few calls this evening and have it arranged," Sharon said resolutely and shook Katelyn's hand again.

"Uh, oh—okay?" Katelyn stuttered. "Is this Grant guy gonna be upset if I just show up?" Katelyn asked. Jim smiled a charming grin and winked.

"Don't worry, Miss Sullivan. I don't think he'll stand a chance."

"Well, I don't know what that means."

Sharon smiled, and a slight blush rose in her cheeks, flashing her mischievous blue eyes. "I'm sure he'll love you."

"Uh—I'm not very—loveable," Katelyn said awkwardly.

Jim and Sharon laughed together, and Jim gave her one of his cards.

"We'll be in touch."

They walked away, hand in hand, and whispering excitedly to one another. Katelyn sighed. It wouldn't hurt to take a look.

Two

GRANT WOKE, COLD FROM SWEAT AND FISTS SWINGING into the empty air. His muscles shook the bed springs beneath him when he sat up against the sharp memories, still vivid in his brain. He could hear Hugh's echoing, terrifying scream, as though he knew he would die, but lacked the power to stop the fall. Dazed, Grant looked down over the side of the ostentatious bed for the horse that had fallen into the ravine; for the woman he had tried to get back to.

He gasped and ran his hands through his hair. With no longer the body of a young lad, his once-dislocated shoulder ached at the memory. His left leg throbbed where the femur had suffered such unforgivable damage. Grant willed the muscle to stop seizing beneath the scar. A knock at his door focused reality. Jeffers, the old, graying butler, peeked his haphazard-haired head in through the doorway with a night lamp.

"Are you all right, sir?" he said in his stoic British voice. The hint of concern made Grant shy away, just as with any warmth.

"O' course I am. Wha wouldna be?" Despite having lived in America for the last ten years, shades of his childhood Scottish burr filtered in through the weakness of fatigue and fear. Jeffers stepped into the room in his plaid bathrobe and gave him a knowing once-over. Jeffers had been present for many of his sleepless nights, from boyhood on.

"I heard screaming, sir. That is to say, *you* were screaming."

"Don't be ridiculous, Jeffers. Old age has made you delusional. Get out, before I call the hospital and have you committed for senility," he said harshly, the cultured sound of his years in English boarding schools reasserting itself into his voice. Jeffers frowned.

"As you wish it, sir," he rolled his eyes with a nod and turned to leave. "Shall I wake you somewhat later than normal?" he said, turning at the door as the thought occurred to him.

"What? No, don't wake me at all. I'll get up myself." Grant said, a toddler in the throes of asserting his independence whilst trapped in the sizable man of forty-two.

"As you wish, sir." Jeffers smiled, as he might with a toddler and left. The silence that followed the click of the door startled Grant, and for an instant he felt the same sadness he always had as a child when Jeffers would leave his room. That empty and crushing sense of darkness surrounding him. Being all alone.

"Fool. You've always been better off alone. Always," he argued, throwing himself back into bed and forcing his eyes closed. He hoped he wouldn't hear the horse scream again. Hoped he wouldn't hear his mother cry, or the beep of hospital machinery that failed to keep her alive, or the million other rotten memories that surfaced in the dark nights he spent alone.

"I dinna..." he yawned and tears escaped the corners of his eyes, "...need anyone." Exhaustion fell heavy and silenced his protest. He imagined fingers through his brown, softly curled hair, gently lulling him to sleep. So little comfort was left in his life, that he didn't apply his overriding sense of reason to stop them.

"North Carolina?" Melissa Sullivan said over the phone. "But Katelyn, what do you even know about these people?"

"They're from Pinedale. But I guess Jim used to work with Tennyson Stables, helping them get set up, and this Grant is a friend of theirs."

Katelyn paced in the airport, as far as the payphone would let her. She'd gathered her things that morning and left for the Laramie airport to catch her economy flight out of Denver. She was a grown-ass woman, managing the Sullivan's herd, working in her father's vet clinic, and by all accounts grown up. Still no one could nag like her mom.

"Look, I talked it over with Dad."

"When?"

"Before I left," she scratched at her ponytail, "this morning."

"Katelyn!"

"It's just, this is a really interesting case, and I don't think it will take me more than a couple of weeks, maybe a month, tops. I should still be home by the end of summer." She shifted the olive-green canvas bag over her shoulder.

Melissa sighed, no doubt regretting that she'd ever fostered Katelyn's independent nature. "Well, fine. Did you arrange for someone to cover your hours?"

"'Course I did, I wouldn't leave without covering things. I already talked to Blake, and it's not like the clinic is that busy, Mom."

Her mother only sighed in response.

"I guess this horse is a real prizewinner. They think two of his sons have a chance at the Triple Crown." She tried to put a spin on it that would make her mother more interested.

"Pomp and circumstance." Melissa waved her off. "Probably only good for looking pretty and breeding. And who knows what kind of abuse they suffer."

"I know," Katelyn sighed. "Probably a lot more than they

should. But the money is good and there's a chance I can help this horse. He's been through something awful Mom, and I just—well, you know I can't not help a horse in need," Katelyn said. She could see her mom shaking her head in her mind and already felt a twinge of homesickness.

"I know, Katie May," her mother sniffed on the other end. "You could never stand by and watch an animal be hurt."

"Just a few weeks," Katie reassured.

"Okay. But you hurry home as soon as you can. And you'd better call your sisters."

"Yes, ma'am. When I land."

KATELYN DIALED ELLE FIRST AFTER SHE'D GOTTEN OFF the plane. The response was the same. *What in the hell did she mean she was in North Carolina? How long was she going to be there?*

"It's only for a few weeks! Holy shit, Elle, Mom already got on my case." Katelyn had expected her middle sister, Eleanor, to be a bit more relaxed. Maybe motherhood turned you into a tyrant.

"When you left this morning you mean? With no warning except to tell Blake he was working the next few weeks for you?"

"Well, he said okay." Katelyn argued.

"Katelyn. The last side job you took turned out to be over a month, and the one before that was almost two. What's up with the wanderlust?"

"Maybe I just need to get the hell outta Sweet Valley once in a while."

Elle sighed on the other end, knowing that as the younger sister, Katelyn had upheld the weight of the family ranch. "Okay. I'm just jealous, and besides, Laney needs someone else to boss around and Emilee is getting so big that you're gonna miss out on it." Elle's guilt trips were a thing of beauty.

"Firstly, I took more than my fair share getting bossed around by Laney, and secondly, you can't use the baby, that's just not a fair fight." Katelyn argued back.

"But we'll miss you." Elle's voice softened.

"I miss you back, you crazy kitchen wench. But I think I may be able to earn enough from this thing to help with the hay shortage this year and the bum foaling Dad had last winter."

"Katie May, it isn't your responsibility to save the ranch single-handedly."

"I know. But we all gotta do our part, don't we? I still can't believe you saved Gran's place and the back forty with nothin' but a goat herd and some pies."

"Well, it took us a bit more than that," Elle scoffed. "I suppose Blake helped, a little."

"Blake's a keeper, but don't tell that little asshole I said so." Katelyn smiled over the phone and Elle laughed.

"Little? He's a good six inches taller than you."

"He'll always be a little asshole to me," Katelyn said wryly while she looked out at the lush, green fields beyond the airport. "Listen, I should go, I'm supposed to be meeting the owner and the ranch manager this afternoon."

"I thought you already knew them."

"I've never actually met either of them. I'm contracted through an interested third party. The ranch belongs to Ian Tennyson, but his son, Grant, is supposed to be running the thing."

Elle giggled. "Grant Tennyson sounds like somebody Laney would write about. *Grant had a brutish manner and a chest like steel*," she added lowly before bursting into laughter. Katelyn's heart sang to hear it. Only a couple of short years ago, it was a herculean effort just to get Elle to smile.

"I'm pretty sure he's a portly, middle-aged accountant," Katelyn said. "I don't think it will take long, if I can get everyone on the same page about the recovery. I just need them to stay out of my way and let me work."

"Well, I hope Steely-Chested Grant gets on the same page for you, but if not..."

"What?" Katelyn said after too long a pause.

"You know what can happen when handsome men start butting heads with us," Elle said.

"He's not handsome."

"You don't know that."

"Oh, shut up! Who are you? Laney?" Katelyn rolled her eyes.

"What if he isn't a portly, middle-aged accountant?" Elle led. "What if you finally get to roll in the hay?" she giggled.

"Stop!" Katelyn could feel the blush spreading up her neck to the line of her golden hair. "I hardly think my virginity's gonna be lost on this job."

"Well, if you keep traipsing all over the world to exotic locales—"

"North Carolina isn't exotic—"

"One of these times, you'll find someone who's gonna make your knees buckle and your panties fall." Elle burst into a fit of giggles.

"You are a bona fide asshole sometimes, you know that?" Katelyn grouched, now glowing from embarrassment.

"Maybe that's why Blake and I get along so well. We keep praying for you," she sighed dramatically.

"Praying I'll get laid?" Katelyn asked with an eye roll.

"Hallelujah and pass the wafers," Elle giggled.

"Asshole." Katelyn nodded to the Lyft driver, who pulled up alongside the airport curb and took her one bag up over her shoulder. "Listen, I gotta go, I'll call you later. Take care of that baby and ol' what's-his-name," she smiled.

"Alright, I'll let what's-his-name know you still think he's a punk."

"Thank you."

"Love you, Katie May."

"Love you too, Elle." They hung up and Katelyn opened the

car door herself when a subtle clearing of a throat sounded behind her.

"Ms. Sullivan?" Katelyn turned and her bag swung off of her shoulder. Behind her stood a small, gray-haired man, very dapper in his coat and driver's cap. His tie was impeccable, his shoes shined and neat. He nodded and tipped his cap. "I am Jeffers, Mr. Tennyson sent me to fetch you."

"Fetch me?" Katelyn asked, scowling. "Uh, I don't need fetched. I am perfectly capable of handling myself."

"Allow me to take your bags," he nodded, ignoring her protest.

She tightened her hand on the strap and continued to stare at him suspiciously. "I appreciate that offer, Mr. Jeffers, but I was under the impression that I was an independent contractor. There's no need to—"

"If you please, it is just Jeffers, and if the young miss would allow an old fool the honor, I would be most happy to take you to Tennyson Stables myself."

"I hardly think you're a fool, Jeffers. If anything, I think you're the kind of man who knows how to get things done, by the look of you."

"The young miss is too kind."

"The young miss prefers to be called Katelyn, if it's all the same."

"Miss Katelyn, if you would permit, I will take care of the rest of your bags."

She studied Jeffers. He was her height, slight in the shoulders, and getting on in his years; yet she could tell from his posture that he was wiry beneath his suit and probably stronger than men twice his size.

"I wouldn't permit, and this is the only bag I have."

Jeffers looked over the old, camo duffle bag with concern. "Surely, you have other items."

"Nope, and don't call me Shirley," she said with an odd grin. Jeffers scowled in return. Katelyn cleared her throat awkwardly.

"We doing this or what?" the Lyft driver grunted between the two short but strong-willed characters staring at one another.

"Miss Katelyn," Jeffers nodded.

Katelyn turned to the driver and smiled with a nod. "Sorry. I didn't realize I had a ride arranged *for* me," she said it with an air of annoyance. Jeffers nodded to the man and offered him a stack of bills.

"For the trouble, and any fare you may have missed."

Katelyn stared at the money. "Did you just pay that guy for not doing anything?" The Lyft driver gave Jeffers a mock salute and left.

"You'll find, Miss Katelyn, that greasing the wheels allows for less conflict." Jeffers said and reached for her duffle once more, thinking her distracted. Katelyn turned her shoulder and stepped out of the way. Jeffers missed and scowled at her.

"I'm not a woman afraid of a little conflict. Or in need of greasing," she said. Jeffers's stoic mouth frowned. "I get the impression that's new for you."

"Please follow me." He acquiesced to let her carry the bag and weaved through the crowded airport drop-off zone. Katelyn followed with a scowl.

What kind of circus had she signed up for?

THREE

THE DRIVE TO TENNYSON STABLES WAS SMOOTH AND quiet in the back of the upscale Lincoln Town Car. Katelyn sat uncomfortably, with her legs tucked close, in fear of getting her 'simple' all over. The leather was brushed soft, and it smelled like unlit pipe tobacco and money. She tried to shake the discomfort of a world so far removed from hers by staring out at the lush green that lined the road.

"I trust that your flight was comfortable," Jeffers said from the front. She looked up at the rear-view mirror.

"I suppose. As comfortable as coach can be."

"You flew—*coach*?" One might have thought she'd said she'd sprouted wings and flown in like a butterfly for the disbelief in his tone. Katelyn snorted.

"Uh, yeah? Don't we all?" She watched his eyes dart to hers and then back to the road. "Okay, well maybe *you* don't, and I'm sure the Tennysons don't, but normal people do."

"Surely you were offered better accommodations?"

"Surely I was not. I would have preferred to fly myself, but I don't have enough to rent a plane for that long."

Jeffers' curious blue eyes darted to hers in the rear-view mirror.

Looking like he knew he shouldn't, he asked anyway. "Do you fly, Miss Katelyn?" Jeffers voice had changed and Katelyn detected something less cold. She leaned forward in her seat and stared at him in the mirror.

"I do. I had an uncle who was a crop duster back home, and he taught me the summer of my senior year."

"And, are you still current?" he asked. Katelyn smiled.

"You talk like a guy who knows his way around a pre-flight check."

"Her Majesty's Royal Air Force, Miss Katelyn," he said humbly. "Forty-third division, the Fighting Badgers." The joy and pride in his voice seemed to come from a strange and distant place, as if he'd nearly forgotten that life all together.

"Well, I am impressed, Jeffers! You fellas must have had nerves of steel. I'm sure that's come in handy with your current position," Katelyn said with a twinkle in her eyes. Jeffers turned his gaze back on the road and his smile fell away.

"How often do you fly? What ratings do you have?" he asked as he turned right into a tree-lined county road.

"I've kept current. Though I can't really afford to just go jetting around whenever I want. I usually work out some sort of trade to keep my training up. So far, I've gotten my single-engine, private, instrument rating, multi-engine rating, and some high-altitude training. I would love to work on a seaplane rating someday. It's all for the fun of it really, I don't think I'd ever make a living at it. I think it would take the joy out."

"It would indeed," Jeffers said. "Should you ever like to dust off the propellers, Mr. Tennyson has an extensive hangar and multiple aircraft that are in need of a good run up."

"I would love to take you up on that offer, Jeffers." Katelyn smiled at him in the mirror.

"I shall see what can be arranged, Miss Katelyn."

Katelyn, feeling much more comfortable, looked out of the window and saw a worn woman, one leg-tugging kid on either side of her, walking down the dirt drive of a dilapidated farm. She was hauling jars of honey and sorry-looking bushels of corn and beans to a run-down overhang of a shed beside the road. A baby was tucked safely in a carrier at her chest. She looked crestfallen but determined, and as the Lincoln sped past, Katelyn noticed her threadbare clothing.

"Who's that?"

"That is Mrs. Sutter, of Sutter Farm. It lies adjacent to Tennyson Stables."

"Adjacent? She's your neighbor?" Katelyn looked back and pulled her hand away from the posh wooden inlaid armrest. Jeffers cleared his throat as if he could read the direction her thoughts were taking them.

"Her husband has been out of work, and she's been keeping up the tax payments on the land with sales from the farm."

"Those baskets look pretty empty," Katelyn said with a lump in her throat, understanding all too well the harshness of trying to live off of the fickle grace of the land.

"Indeed. It has been a hard year with the drought last spring and the rash of bee deaths in the valley." Katelyn looked back over her shoulder.

"But Tennyson Stables hasn't suffered?"

"Oh no. Mr. Tennyson has things somewhat tightly wound, around here," Jeffers said, smirking.

"Tightly wound? Grant?" Katelyn asked.

Jeffers chuckled but hid his amusement in a cough.

"*Mr. Tennyson* prefers not to be called by his first name. Especially by the staff, Miss Katelyn."

Katelyn lifted her eyes and a small, mischievous smile spread on her lips.

"Oh, he doesn't, huh?"

Jeffers stared at her for a moment and something twinkled in his eyes so briefly that she couldn't tell if she'd imagined it. He slowed the car as they approached a turn.

"Does *Mr. Tennyson* actually work with the horses at all, or just the bottom lines?" she asked as they turned down the packed gravel drive to the most ostentatious 'ranch' house she'd ever seen. "Holy horseshit," she whispered. Jeffers cleared his throat. "Sorry, just, Jim didn't really prepare me for—whoa!" she breathed again. The perfect green fields lay sprawled as far as she could see, partitioned into neat paddocks with white fencing. A large indoor arena sat in the middle of the fields, white with a kelly-green tin roof, and a thoroughbred weather vane cresting its highest spire.

The arena must have been a quarter mile round at least. Beside it, stretching out in front of the circular drive was a collection of stables in the same white and green combination, housing at least twenty individual stables and a second story for god knew what else. The main house was a ranch style, though not like any ranch house Katelyn had seen. Where the small house she'd grown up in had been cozy and a bramble of add-ons and bedrooms, Tennyson Manor was pristine white, with green shutters, partitioned into three main quarters, an office wing close to the stables, the main house that was a two-story colonial feel, and a third wing that, Jeffers explained, was Ian's private quarters.

"The whole wing?"

"Yes, miss."

"What the hell does one man do with so much space? Just live there with Grant?"

"*Mr. Tennyson* doesn't live with his father. He rarely leaves the east wing."

"So, he lives in his office?" She smirked as she opened her door before Jeffers could do it, bringing out a scowl in the old butler.

"One could say so."

"Real party animal, huh?"

"Party? No, Miss Katelyn," Jeffers said, unsuccessfully trying to wrestle the bag from her arm. Katelyn turned away, surveying the rest of the land and turned back to him.

"Just animal, huh?"

"The staff has been known to call him the—" Jeffers stopped and his eyes fell.

"Well, you can't stop there. What do they call him?" Jeffers began walking to the main house, nodding for her to follow.

"Jeffers, come on now. You and I are buddies, I'm not going to rat you out."

The old butler blushed over his shoulder. "Buddies?"

"Any man who can fly a Douglas Boston in the heat of gunfire is surely a friend of mine." Jeffers stopped. The truth of his warm nature shone through as he looked at her. For a moment, Katelyn was reminded of her own father.

"They call him 'the beast,' Miss Katelyn. On account of his temperament and size."

"Size?" Katelyn asked and resumed her path behind Jeffers.

"Grant, unlike his father, was blessed with a far more brutish constitution."

"Huh," Katelyn said, curiosity piqued. A big, grouchy number cruncher. *As long as he didn't have a chest of steel*, she snorted.

"Perhaps, you would like to get settled first?" Jeffers asked over his shoulder as he led the way to the large house. Katelyn stared distractedly around, her eyes lighting on the large stable.

"Actually, Jeffers, if it's all the same to you, I'd like to take a look at Hugh."

"The staff is unaware of your arrival, miss. They would not be prepared."

"I'm not here to study the staff. I think it would be best to catch Hugh on the fly."

"On the fly, miss?"

"Yeah, sort of in his 'natural habitat'," she said, her eyes followed the thirty or so horses that were out in their pens being groomed and trained. Some of the wranglers in the pen seemed to know what they were doing. Others, not so much.

"With all due respect, and with your safety in mind, I must inform you that Hugh has a propensity for aggression, Miss

Katelyn. It might be best to wait for one of the stable hands to be available."

Katelyn gave a disgusted snort. "Jeffers, please. I'm not scared of some pampered thoroughbred."

"He's quite belligerent, miss."

"My favorite kind of horse." She smiled at Jeffers. He sighed and shook his head. Just like with the bag, he was learning there was little use in arguing with her.

"As you wish, Miss Katelyn. Hugh is usually kept by himself on the north side of the stables on the far end. Just by the large magnolia tree. I shall tell the young master that you've arrived."

Katelyn nodded distractedly with her eyes fixed on the stables. She walked across the pebbled lane, up the groomed walkway, and off the path to circle the stables from the back side. The pen beneath the giant magnolia was empty. The water trough was filled but the side of it had been kicked in. Buckets were overturned in the paddock, bridles and lead ropes scattered and bitten through.

She noticed mane hair stuck in joints along the fencing. She dropped her bag beneath the tree and jumped up on the railing. The door to the stable was open and the white-painted frame had been pawed at and damaged. From her high position, she studied the hoof patterns in the dust and mud and found evidence of agitated pacing along the fence that corresponded to the hair that had been left behind.

Hugh wasn't a happy camper. Harder depressions from his forefeet meant he was stamping and rearing, showing aggression, but not deep enough to suggest he had the power he should have. The right foreleg print was less pronounced; he was favoring that side.

From inside the stable she heard him pacing. She made a slow, soft whistle in his direction. The horse huffed, then stamped the ground inside. She whistled again. Quicker than she'd anticipated, Hugh stormed through the door, ears down, nostrils flared and gunning for where she stood on the fence. Katelyn watched calmly, even as her heart thundered in her chest. She stepped off the railing as he knocked into it with his side, turning away at the last second.

"Is that so?" she yelled. Hugh pranced, circled back and came again. This time, Katelyn wasn't surprised, she was curious. He was a beautiful, dark bay stallion, the chiseled features of his nose and jaw spoke to his high-born genetics. Powerful legs, well-balanced and athletic. He stood nearly seventeen hands high, if she had to wager a guess. He was beautiful, but there was something irrevocably broken about him. She studied the way he walked towards her, leaning to the side, opposite a very obvious scar. But the true measure of his injury was in the wildness of his eyes and the panicked breaths he huffed out as he charged again.

At her unshaken response he slowed, pranced away, huffed and circled the ring, keeping an eye on her, ears perked in her direction. The third approach, he changed direction, and she studied the way he hitched into the turn. In those moments, she made no judgments, but allowed her senses to build a picture of him.

No wonder they were so insistent on his recovery. He was a champion; maybe the most beautiful horse she'd ever seen, and his value was evident. But more than that, she could tell his personality was unique. He was hurt, and he hated it. She stayed calm and quiet, leaning on the fence for a few more minutes, as his pacing slowed, his breathing deepened, and he started to make softer, nuzzling sounds as he observed her in kind. Finally, Katelyn took her booted foot off the fence, hooked her fingers in the belt loops of her pants and paced along the boundary of his pen. She nodded in thought.

"All right, well, let's get to know each other." She dug into her bag and pulled out a light jacket that she wouldn't be using in this heat. She tied it to the top rung, careful to not let the arms dangle in the wind. Lifting her bag over her shoulder, she turned and walked back towards the house.

The deep voice struck hard through her thoughts.

"Just what do you think you're doing? This is private property!"

Katelyn looked up from the grass-lined path to see a large man storming, with a slight limp, towards her.

The sunset silhouetted him in the fading light. He was built like an impenetrable wall, and Katelyn's heart stopped. His chestnut hair glinted with hints of gold and red, and it curled at the base of his thick neck. His brown and golden-flecked eyes flashed below heavy brows, and a slightly crooked nose flared its nostrils. Beneath, his lips were thinly stretched around clenched teeth. She watched the muscles of his jaw twitch as he approached. His shoulders were broad and uncomfortably shrugged in his crisp white dress shirt, tucked into pressed gray trousers.

He was not, much to her surprise, an old, portly accountant.

But he was tightly wound. Katelyn shot her eyes back to his and she read more than just annoyance and threats that lay in them. His angry march to her cost him; his shoulder dropped briefly, and the side of his body that he'd favored hitched. Pain flashed for only a second across his face. Katelyn's gaze softened; her lips parted. She put her hands up and stepped back.

"Whoa, there. Easy," Katelyn whispered while her heart spiraled up into her throat and fell back down.

"Do not shush me! Who the devil are you? What are you doing on my property?"

"I'm Katie— Katydid—Katelyn," she stuttered breathlessly as if she couldn't remember. The trepidation in her own voice angered her, and she shook herself out of the spell he'd cast. "Katelyn Sullivan. I agreed to consult."

"I made no such agreement!" he demanded with a light Scottish burr that added an interesting roll to the *agrrreement.*

"I'm here because Jim Parsons asked me," she returned and stood her ground as he came within a foot of her. Grant faltered at Jim's name; his eyes darted over her with fast and hard judgment. Katelyn had to look up, her neck straining, to meet his gaze.

"I wasn't informed of this. Why didn't you check in with me first? What exactly are you doing here? What purpose did Jim think I would have for someone of your—" he paused and looked down at her, "stature," he fumbled.

"Oh, I'm sorry; is there a height requirement for Tennyson Stables?" Katelyn quirked a smile and caused him to scowl even deeper.

"Why are you here, Mrs. Sull—Mrs—"

"Miss. Just—ugh, just call me Katelyn. I'm an equine therapist. Jim and I met in Wyoming and he asked me to come out and take a look at Hugh."

Grant's jaw twitched.

"You must be Grant." She held out her hand. He stared down at it as if he'd like to swat it away.

"You'll address me as Mr. Tennyson. Whatever Jim might have seen in you, I highly doubt a woman of your age could possibly have the experience necessary to deal with one of the most valuable horses in the Eastern United States. Why else did he hire you?"

"Look, asshole—" Jeffers, who had approached sometime mid-argument, cleared his craggy throat strongly to stop Katelyn from being fired on the spot. "Just what do you think this is?" she demanded. "Because I'm young and short, I couldn't possibly know my way around a horse? All titles and worthless accolades aside, that puffed-up show pony is no different than a half-wild quarter—"

"Show pony? Quarter—" Grant bristled.

"I don't know what you've been doing to him, but it's not working. He's going bonkers in the solitary confinement you've got him in. Why hasn't someone closed his door? What's with his paddock? It's dirty as hell! How often is he getting worked? Why is his scar not healing? Are you even doing anything to address his left flank compensation?" She fired off the questions as if it were her own horse she was defending.

Grant sputtered. "Solitary? He's not trapped, you dinn—you dinna ken a feckin thing about—"

"Then why's he acting like he's being caged? Why's he so aggressive?" Katelyn saw Grant's eyes fall and felt a sudden rush of emotion. Her anger melted away. Grant looked to the far side of the stable where they could hear commotion coming from Hugh's pen as he pawed at the walls and screamed into the darkness.

"Because he's a danger to the other horses, and to himself." Grant paused, softer. "No one can help him."

"Except me," Katelyn returned, self-assured and calmer. Grant crossed his arms in front of his broad chest and looked down at her. She was distracted by the golden-red hair on his thick forearms. She blushed and quickly crossed her own arms, closing off herself to him as well.

"Two weeks," he said definitively.

Katelyn shook her head.

"Six, at least."

"Three weeks and *dinnae* argue wi' me." he said tersely.

"Five weeks and *don't* bully me!" she returned angrily and leaned in. Grant inhaled and his eyes dropped to her lips. He leaned away and his tone deepened, sending shivers up her spine.

"Four, and nay one day more," he growled.

"Fine," she seethed through clenched teeth. He huffed, turned, and stormed back towards the house.

"Asshole," she muttered under her breath.

She stared after him long after he'd left. What a jerk. What a bullying, condemnatory, asshole of a jerk. The insults circulated around and around in her brain. She'd never met someone so bristly or difficult. He wore his anger out like some personal barrier. Like armor. Like he was...Katelyn stared at the side door of the house that slammed behind him.

Hurt. Grant Tennyson was hurt.

Why? She quirked her head and uncrossed her arms, cocking her hip to the side as the strange epiphany lessened her anger towards him. When he'd stormed up to her, he'd been in pain. He'd pushed it away. He'd hidden it.

"Why's that my problem?" Katelyn said under her breath. She didn't have to get along with him. She didn't have to even talk to him. She was here to help Hugh, that was all. But something about Grant; the broken pain in his eyes, the way he hunched up and tight-fisted every action to stay guarded; unsettled her. She blew a stray strand of her hair from her eyes.

"Miss?" Katelyn turned to see Jeffers still standing stiffly behind her. "I'm to attend to any needs you may have, and to get you settled into your room." Katelyn nodded and remembered to breathe again.

"That's awfully generous, but I was under the impression that I'd be making my own arrangements."

"It is customary for contractors to be given lodging during their term at Tennyson Stables. I've set aside one of our best rooms for your comfort. I can also point you in the direction of the dining room. It is usually the insistence of the senior Mr. Tennyson that guests choose their own meals, so whatever you desire for dinner shall be planned for and made."

Katelyn looked at him as if she'd been unexpectedly thrown into a Disney movie.

"Jeffers, are you real?"

"When last I checked."

"I mean, I'm willing to pitch in and cook a night or two if you need, but you don't need to wait on me. I'm not really a guest." She turned to look back where Grant had disappeared. "Least not a welcome one. My concern is Hugh. I don't care what happens in the kitchen. If I'm hungry and you're already making something, I'd be happy to join you."

"As you wish. Dinner is at eight," Jeffers said and nodded before leaving.

"Oh? Wait, but—" Katelyn stuttered and Jeffers halted. "Am I supposed to dine with him?" she asked and nodded to the window where the curtain was pulled back. Grant's face disappeared quickly from view when he saw her look his way. Jeffers watched with curiosity and turned back to Katelyn.

"The younger Mr. Tennyson ought to be made aware of Hugh Dancy's daily treatment and progress. Over a meal is the easiest option, as he is very busy throughout the day dealing with the finances and management of the property and horses."

Katelyn looked back to the house and away again. Why would she put herself alone in a room with that guy? Especially when it seemed that he didn't think she'd make any progress with Hugh to begin with. She couldn't imagine having to sit across from him and defend herself, while trying to eat.

"Tonight, my brain's a bit too busy for food," she lied.

"But, Miss Sullivan—"

"Jeffers, please don't make a fuss over me. Besides, I don't think 'young' Mr. Tennyson is willing to dine alongside a *commoner* such as myself."

"Miss Katelyn, you are no such thing."

"It's okay, Jeffers, don't worry. I'll make sure to write detailed reports and deliver them to Mr. Tennyson. If it's all the same, I'd prefer to find my own accommodations." Katelyn looked into Jeffers eyes. He nodded, perplexed.

"Yes, Miss Katelyn, as you wish."

"Thank you," Katelyn breathed and squeezed his arm affectionately before returning to the stables.

———

GRANT WATCHED HER MARCH BACK TO THE BARN instead of coming to the house. Her proud chin rising as she left. Grant pulled the curtain closed. At first, when he'd seen her coming from the stables, he'd thought she was another one of his father's prospects for a future wife.

How many had he seen traipse through the grounds on some

private tour of the facility in the last ten months? Rich breeders' daughters, the high-society elite princesses, casting coy glances his way, blushing and accommodating his foul temper, sighing and feigning distress when he raised his voice or made snide judgments. Twittering around him like beautiful and useless birds, acquiescing to his temper, and cowering at his raised voice. All fodder for his father's plans to find a suitable woman to marry.

Now there was *that* girl.

The idea that she could be a candidate in his father's matchmaking scheme, was quickly dismissed when he'd gotten closer. From her well-worn boots, jeans, and t-shirt, to the honey-blonde locks in a disheveled ponytail, it was obvious she would not have been an acceptable choice of Ian Tennyson's. Grant peeked through the curtain once more to see her leaning on the railing outside of Hugh's pen, watching as the horse danced in painfully clipped circles on the other side. He wasn't charging the fence like he had with the others. Grant studied the relaxed sway of her hips, her unclenched hands and lowered shoulders. The breeze blew a lock of her hair out of its ponytail and the sunlight lit it like golden wheat.

Jim Parsons had sent her. Grant respected Jim. When he'd first come to America, broken hearted and lost in the new world of managing such a large facility himself, Jim had helped him learn the basics of the daily operations and had helped him see the bigger picture, for long term success. Jim was an investor for Tennyson Stables, but he had also been one of Grant's first real friends. He and his wife, Sharon were down to earth and friendly, despite their financial success. A paradox Grant had never witnessed in his own life. Grant liked them.

A loud whinny broke him out of the thought, and he snapped his gaze back to the paddock, where Hugh Dancy was now nuzzling a jacket she'd hung from the top rail and shying away to prance and offer truncated and pathetic pounces in defiance. She spoke firmly, words that he couldn't understand, but his spine straightened from the tone and he thought back to his own mother's voice when he'd misbehaved.

Hugh straightened too, and Grant watched in fascination as he seemed to calm himself at the sound of her softening tone. She headed into the stables, presumably to the inside stall doors. Maybe she *was* a therapist.

The rest of the workers were leaving for the day. She would be alone. What if Hugh charged at her? God, the insurance and nightmare of a lawsuit alone made his stomach turn. He looked back to the work spread across his desk and decided not to take the chance. He told himself it had nothing to do with her safety. Nothing to do with Hugh, and wanting to know if he was safe and well-cared for. Nothing to do with the rising curiosity of what skill she might possess that dozens of other therapists did not.

He took a quiet stroll, glancing around for any stray stable personnel, but the day shift staff were already gone. He ducked in through the side gable door, and kept quiet, hoping to see what a simple, rural girl thought she could do that all his experts could not.

He watched her reach for the latch of Hugh's stall and he moved in nervously closer, keeping his bulk behind a small hay cart, until she was inside.

KATELYN HAD NO TROUBLE FINDING HUGH'S STALL from the ostentatious, impeccable hallway. It was the last on the right, across from a dark mahogany office where paperwork was strewn across the desk and filing cabinets lined the wall. A crystal decanter of scotch and glasses sat atop a small table by the green leather guest chairs in front of the desk. She looked farther through the doorway into the warm and homey office and suddenly could picture a gruff, old, stable manager leaning back in the comfortable leather chair with a glass of scotch at the end of a long day of riding. There was even a pipe laid on its side, small tendrils of tobacco peppering the desk, and a dilapidated pack of matches nearby. It might have been Ian's, but she felt for sure it wasn't. She remembered the slight tinge of pipe tobacco, leather, peat, all things warm and earthy that had wisped from Grant as he'd barked at her in the driveway.

Katelyn sighed and turned back to the stall. Patiently sorting through her own nerves at the door, she took a deep breath and opened the latch, stepped inside and closed the half-door behind her. Hugh recognized her and stopped his rooting at the wall to turn around. He huffed out a huge breath and made to lunge at her, fury and anger in his eyes and nostrils flaring. Katelyn watched the way he pounced towards her, how he lowered his head in challenge. She stood her ground.

"Alright, ya feisty son-of-a-bitch," she growled and centered her body in his path. "Stop!" she commanded. Hugh paused at the sound, his forelegs bearing the weight of his inertia flung forward.

"Knock that shit off," she said and put her hands on her hips, staring him down. Hugh swung his head to one side and then the other, prancing backwards at the unexpected reaction.

"See what you did there?" she said, in a softer tone and walked to the right, studying his chest. "You gave yourself away. Why you you're nothin' but a big ol' faker." She watched as he reared up and blew out a snort of protest. She held out her hand. He shied until the soft and sweet sounds came from Katelyn's lips, like a song, soft across a prairie. Her words were gentle and deep.

"They can't fix the injury because the injury isn't the real problem, now is it?" She stepped closer and her hand touched his long velvet nose tentatively. "You've a hitch in your giddy up, that's for sure, but I think—" Hugh nudged her with his nose and his breath quieted. He pranced away one step and lowered his head. "I think the real wound is deeper, isn't it?"

Katelyn thought back to what Jim had said. He hadn't given her much information except that Hugh had gotten into an accident. Only Grant could give her the whole story. She frowned. The chances that man would open up to her were highly unlikely, unless she could prove she was making progress.

"Might have to renegotiate on those dinners after all, old man," she said as Hugh dipped his head to nudge her chest. "You're a fast learner." She smiled and offered him a piece of oat and apple cookie from her shirt pocket. She'd snagged a few from the tack room on her way by. Hugh took it and stepped away, chewing it with slobbery exuberance.

"Okay, poser. We'll get to work tomorrow." Katelyn continued to talk in low and soft tones to him until he was calm and leaning into her voice.

———

HAD HUGH SEEN THE BIG MAN STANDING JUST OUTSIDE of the stall, looking in, he would have continued his tirade. Had Katelyn seen Grant, she might not have been able to keep herself or the horse calm. But he stayed in the shadows and was allowed a secret glimpse into the strange new beginnings of her friendship with his horse.

Grant stalked into his preferred office across from Hugh's stall. He closed the door and drew the blinds. He'd nearly jumped over the door to keep Hugh from trampling her. His heart raced and his throat had gone tight when Hugh had screamed and the hoof beats had shaken through the barn.

Then...her voice.

Strong and solid, but not angry, cut through the air, and the stomping stopped. Grant listened as her tone went from firm to gentle and Hugh's breathing slowed. He had peeked in, ducking low, and watched her gently soothe the stallion with her strong hands and her loving but indiscernible words. He had to give her some credit. She hadn't run away on the first day, and that was more than any other therapist had done.

Four

THE EARLY EVENING SETTLED ACROSS THE LANDSCAPE, and Katelyn felt worn out by the trip and the stress of her new position. She could have accepted a room at the Tennyson's. It would have been more efficient. Her pride said she couldn't take the offer of a rich landowner, who might hold the favor over her later down the road.

The Tennysons might not have been like the big ranch owners back home, but they were at least kissing cousins. She gathered up her notebook, tucked it in with her other belongings, and shouldered her bag. Maybe one of the ranch hands could give her a ride into town. The memory of the harried mother she'd seen earlier that day flashed in her mind. Living just up the road and struggling to make ends meet while Tennyson Farms had extra spilling over their tidy knot.

She reached the gate of the Sutter Farm after the sun had already set over the rich line of trees separating the two contrasting properties. Here, the fields were patchy in places. The irrigation seemed to be off from what Katelyn's trained eye could tell. The fence was falling down in places. The barn was in poor shape. The old bunkhouse seemed to be in need of paint and some repairs.

The chicken coop could use a couple more rooms from the sound of the clucking that greeted her as she came closer to the plain gray house settled towards the back of the property.

Without reservation, in true Katelyn style, she knocked on the door and waited with her hand tucked into the strap of her pack. The sound of two or three dogs barking and a baby crying reached out in muffled tones behind the door. A woman in jeans and a button-down shirt opened the door with a shotgun tucked under one arm.

Katelyn backed away, hands up. "Mrs. Sutter?"

The woman lowered the gun and closed her eyes with a sigh.

"I'm sorry. I'm sorry. I thought you were from collections." She swallowed and put her wrist to her forehead.

"No ma'am," Katelyn said with a small smile.

"What can I help you with?" the woman said, distrustfully, not stepping back to admit her. Katelyn cleared her throat and shuffled her boots.

"My name's Katelyn Sullivan, Mrs. Sutter. I just got hired on at Tennyson's for a month or so, and I was wondering if you might have a room to rent."

The woman looked at her sideways with hardened green eyes. Her dark brown hair was in a messy bun above the collar of her threadbare shirt. She was thin as a rail and her collarbones stuck out from the gape in her shirt. A young boy toddled up in his diaper and cowboy boots and clung to her leg. Katelyn smiled down at him.

"Why would you want a room here? We don't have room here. Why aren't you staying there?"

Katelyn rolled the dice and chose her words carefully.

"I could, I guess, but all things the same, Mrs. Sutter. I don't want to owe Ian Tennyson anything."

"Jasmine," the woman said. "My name is Jasmine." She put the gun safely up on a high shelf by the door. "I'm sorry, Katelyn. We don't have space here for any boarders."

"I was actually wondering about your bunkhouse."

"Bunkhouse? Nobody's stayed out there since before the last drought. We haven't been able to afford any hired help since then," she admitted. Katelyn nodded.

"I see your fields are still trying to catch up." Before the icy distrust could come back into Jasmine's eyes, Katelyn spoke. "My dad and mom had a similar problem two summers ago in Wyoming. I think it's a matter of adjusting the irrigation trenching."

"Oh? You know about that kind of thing, do you?"

"Well, I was raised in a dry state, ma'am." The young boy was now toddling towards Katelyn. Jasmine scooped him up before he could grab onto the strange girl's jeans.

"Cowgrill, Momma! Cowgrill boots," he slurred behind new teeth that were still trying to sprout and pointed down at Katelyn's well-loved boots. Jasmine looked down, and her expression changed. She studied Katelyn more closely.

"I don't expect to be long at Tennyson's, probably not more than a month, and I can't afford to pay you much, but I'd be more than happy to help out around your place. I'm pretty handy. I can fix fences, help out with the chores, I'm good at painting, and barn repair, and any animal care you might need help with—" Her voice died away at Jasmine's change of expression. Katelyn knew the look. "I'm not saying you need me. I'm not saying you're doing anything wrong here. Just, I don't want to stay at that freak-show down the road and I'd feel a lot better helping out at a place that feels well, like home. You can call my mom if it makes you feel better," Katelyn stuttered. Jasmine didn't say anything so Katelyn continued with some desperation.

"I don't mind cooking, or cleaning, or watching babies if that's what you need. Hell, I've never met work that I was too proud to do. And I can stay outta your way too. I'm fine with whatever state the bunkhouse is in."

Jasmine looked as though she might cry, and for a moment Katelyn thought she'd insulted her.

"Well, that would just—I suppose that might be okay." Jasmine held back her tears. "Since my husband lost his job, he's been working whatever odd jobs he can find in town and I'm, well, I hate admitting it, but I've been having a little trouble keeping things up. The two older boys are in school, but I can't have them stay home to help out. I don't want them to miss out on their classes. Much more important that they get an education, you know?" she stuttered and swayed with the toddler in her arms. "Colin here is just two, and his little sister Bethany is just barely six months." As if on cue a baby cried from a bassinet somewhere further back in the house. "I can't find someone to come from town to watch them that doesn't charge an arm and a leg, so it's hard getting things done around the farm."

Katelyn came a stitch closer.

"It's a lot of work for a someone who already has a full-time job being a mom. Grant Tennyson expects me to be working most of the day out there, but I think I'd still have time to help out in the mornings and evenings," Katelyn said.

Jasmine's eyes shot back to Katelyn's. "You're working for Grant Tennyson, the son? Doing what exactly?"

"I've been hired as an equine therapist for their stallion."

"Aren't you a little young to be a therapist?" Jasmine's head swung back around to the sound of Bethany's calls. Katelyn looked towards them too.

"Look, if you need to get her, you should. I know my niece Emilee doesn't stand with being ignored for too long."

Jasmine sighed, mouth skewed, and begrudgingly stepped back.

"Come on in then." She put Colin down and raced for the baby. "Colin, you stay there!" she yelled over her shoulder. Colin, only slightly put off by being put down in favor of his louder, younger sister, looked up at Katelyn.

"Cowgrill."

"Heya, short stack. I like your boots," she said and knelt down to Colin's level. He grinned his wide-spaced smile and clapped his hands.

"Imma cowboy."

"Yes, you are." Katelyn nodded and tipped her ball cap at him. He eyed the open door and freedom beyond and made a beeline to pass her. Katelyn, not new to the Houdini-like speed of the under-three crowd, quickly closed the door and cut off his escape. Jasmine came back with a red-faced and red-haired baby girl in her arms. Her tiny hiccups were punctuated by sobs that were subsiding in the arms of her mother.

"Colin, did you try getting out again?" she said, assessing the closed door and Colin's frustrated grunting as he tried for the handle.

"He's got business to do," Katelyn laughed. "I don't know how you do it, he's an awful lot of work just on his own," Katelyn said, something tugging on her heartstrings as she watched the young cowboy give up on the door and run for his stick horse in the center of the comfortable and clean, but sparsely furnished living room.

"You don't have to worry about meals or anything for me, but I can cook a few for you if you like. That'll give you some nights off a week." Katelyn sighed and shifted her pack as she stood up. "What do you think?"

Jasmine took a deep sigh.

"I think, yes. Okay. If you're okay with the bunkhouse. And I don't think it'd be right to ask you to work more than ten or so hours a week just for an old rat-infested bunk."

"Any place not near Grant Tennyson is worth whatever you wanna ask," Katelyn said.

"Yeah." Jasmine eyed her suspiciously and bounced the baby. "I don't see a girl like you being comfortable with a man like him. I mean,"

She leaned in closer, while Colin took his horse for its fifth lap around the living room. "The way I hear it, that man is a bear. Grouchy, demanding, harsh. He's always got some pretty model type 'visiting' the stables. But he loses more employees than any other business in town. My husband is too afraid to even ask for a job, even though he's a good worker. Grant's reputation has the whole valley running."

"Oh? Huh," Katelyn said and stood in thought. "Well, he is a prick." She looked at the kids, "Prickly. He's prickly."

"Our neighbor to the south, Mavis, she's a little old beekeeper next to the river, says she's seen him once or twice in town, mostly at the county assessor's offices or the BLM. I guess he's quite handsome."

"I hadn't noticed," Katelyn said. A knowing grin came over Jasmine's face.

"Well, I kinda like you already, so just be careful around him." Katelyn saw in Jasmine a glimmer of the love and protection her own sisters gave her. "I'm not gonna sugarcoat it, that bunkhouse and the bathroom in there are filthy, so for tonight you can use our bathroom to clean up."

"That's not necessary."

Jasmine looked at her hay-dusted jeans, dirt-crusted nails, and dust-coated cheeks. "No honey, it's necessary."

"Yes, ma'am." Katelyn smiled.

Katelyn showered quickly, careful to not dirty any towels in the process, and changed into clean clothes. The babies were put to bed and the older brothers were tucked in. Jasmine met her at the door with clean sheets and blankets and they walked to the bunkhouse together. The lights flickered on in the small wooden cabin.

The south wall had an old wood fireplace and cook top. There was an old refrigerator and a short counter with a sink, over which sagging shelves were hung with dust covered dishes and cooking pots and pans. The windows were clouded with dust and the curtains moth eaten. There was a small couch and chair by the woodstove and a row of bunks along the far wall.

"I know it's not—" Jasmine began.

"Not bad at all." Katelyn nodded and smiled at the cozy retreat. She was pleasantly surprised. "Beats the heck out of a dirt floor covered with hissing cockroaches the size of your hand," she said with a smile and remembered her brief stay in Costa Rica as a counselor at a riding camp.

"Oh god, that's *horrible*." Jasmine looked at her with a scowl. "Why would you stay in a place like that?"

"'Cause the cockroaches *outside* the huts are as big as your arm," she chuckled. Jasmine's lips broke into a smile that turned into a full-blown, disgusted laugh and Katelyn loved happiness on her.

"Well, get settled in, as best you can. In the morning, we'll take a walk around and see what you can or want to take on."

"Sounds good."

"When do you need to be at Tennyson's?"

"Uh—" Katelyn stumbled, realizing that in all of the confrontation, they hadn't discussed her actual hours. "I think around eight or so?"

"Good, we're early risers. Meet me at the house at six?"

"Yes, ma'am." Katelyn nodded. Jasmine nodded too and left her to the quiet and musty cabin that still felt more like home than what she imagined the pristine and cold halls of Tennyson Manor would be.

She made up one of the bunks and settled in for the night with an old Louis L'Amour book she'd borrowed from Laney. She usually fell asleep after a few pages, so it was taking her a while to make it through. It made her realized that she'd taken on two jobs when one would have done just as well. She never did shy away from work, but apparently, she'd taken on another full-time job, just to avoid Grant Tennyson.

GRANT SAT HUNCHED OVER THE COMPUTER IN HIS office. The facility was finally not bleeding money, but they needed Hugh's recovery if they wanted to boost the reputation and sales of their thoroughbreds. Not that Ian cared. His father had always been well-off, and as a result, he was looser with the purse strings than Grant was. Sometimes ordering Jeffers to offload stock and properties for a song, just so he could be rid of them.

Growing up in squalor, Grant had learned early to be careful with money. His mother, a secretary at Ian's Edinburgh office, had been fired after a brief affair with Ian, which had resulted in Grant's birth. Knowing the man Ian was, she'd never wanted Grant to have any contact with his father. But when she knew she was dying, she'd had little choice, and Ian had begrudgingly taken the eight-year-old Grant in, and promptly sent him to one of the finest boarding schools London had to offer.

When Grant had turned eighteen, he'd joined the British Army, more out of respect for Jeffers' time in the service than anything. But as soon as his contracted time had ended, Ian pressured Grant to return to school and paid for his business degree, but Grant, again, found a way to irk his father by obtaining an agricultural minor.

It seemed if there was one thing Grant was consistently good at, it was disappointing Ian. Grant suspected that Ian hated him for the simple fact that he was an unplanned mistake. That he was not raised 'correctly' for his formative years. That his mother was a common secretary. That Ian was, in some way, obligated. It became clear, very early on, that Grant would always be indebted to his father. And Ian liked that.

But when Grant went to school for business, what he really wanted was to learn about was land; how to survive on it, tend to it, make the most of what little he was given. He studied herd management and animal husbandry, and Ian never failed to make him feel less the proper scholar for it. Only common people wasted their degrees on agriculture. He might as well have thrown Ian's money away as far as his father was concerned. But Grant loved it. It was one of the only reasons he now tolerated being at Tennyson Stables. Besides the business part of it, which he hated, he also had a say in the field and crop planting, herd dynamics, breeding, and land management. The only saving grace of working under his father was the land and horses.

He loved the horses. He loved their spirit and their strength and the uncanny way they could read you even without words. Especially, he thought with pained regret, Hugh. He turned back to his work, to the ledgers showing his efforts that had put Tennyson Stables in the black after nearly ten years of Ian's former team mismanaging it into the ground. With Jim's help, Grant had been able to undo the damage of the previous management. They had all been all rich, well-to-do, prep school dandies. Much more concerned with their polo weekends, international vacations, and model mistresses to be concerned with what type of hay they should be planting in a field long overused. They'd never had to worry about money wasted.

But Grant still remembered being hungry. He still remembered the way his mother had wept when she couldn't provide enough food. He remembered when she couldn't afford to miss work to treat her cancer. Living under Ian's care had given him enough to eat, but never enough love. Even on holiday, or parental visits, it was Jeffers that came to check in on Grant, or take him on excursions. Jeffers had always been more caring of Grant's needs than Ian ever had.

It wasn't until after he'd graduated, and had taken a top position in Ian's office that he finally felt secure. But even that was not guaranteed for long. When Grant had met a young florist and fallen in love, Ian sensed a mistake about to happen and threatened to cut Grant off. Hunger, poverty, these were tools Ian knew would always work to sway Grant back on to the path he deemed worthy. No matter the consequences to others. No matter if Grant had to break the woman's heart in the process.

Grant's heart rate shot up, his breath quickened, pain shot through his leg and his body broke out in sweat.

"Dinner, sir." Jeffers' voice cut through the memory, and Grant turned with anger at the older man.

"I'm busy," he gasped, trying to slow his heart and massage out the cramping muscle.

"As you like, sir. I can have it brought here, perhaps?" Jeffers said, unmoved by the briskness of Grant's tone. Grant shuffled through the paperwork on his desk, dabbed at the sweat on his brow and looked over the calendar on his computer. Dinner was blocked out for a consult for the next six weeks.

"Am I supposed to be having dinner with someone?" he asked, trying to dredge up anything but what he had just remembered.

"Ah, yes about Miss Katelyn—er, Miss Sullivan."

"Sullivan?" Grant asked distractedly. *Katie, Katydid, Katelyn.*

"The equine therapist? Jim Parsons recommended her?"

Grant looked up and heard her voice in his head. *All right, you feisty son-of-a-bitch, stop.* A soft smile broke out and it felt foreign on his face. Katelyn Sullivan didn't come from money. No prestigious school had groomed her.

"Is she waiting?" he asked.

"Ah, no, sir. She is *not* waiting for you." Jeffers smirked, and his tone was pointy, bringing Grant back to the present.

"What? What do you mean, she's not waiting for me?"

"She's retired to her own accommodations, down the road."

"What do you mean her own accommodations?" Grant barked. Jeffers showed no sign of impatience with Grant's surly attitude.

"Miss Sullivan insists on simple dinners if she eats here and I believe she is staying at the Sutter Farm, down the road, for her accommodations."

Grant stopped and looked at Jeffers with confusion. "But that's nearly a mile away! How did she get there?"

"I believed she walked, sir."

"She walked?"

"Yes, sir. She thanked me for the ride from the airport, asked if I could use help with the dishes, and took her leave. I offered to accompany her, but she said my time would be better spent attending to your—how did she put it?—maintenance." Jeffers' lips twitched, in resistance of the smile.

Grant had no response. *What did she mean 'maintenance'?* He sat back in his chair, mulling over the insulting remark she'd made about his helplessness.

"I'll take dinner in here, Jeffers," he said.

"Yes, sir." Jeffers nodded.

"And don't expect me to help with the dishes!" Grant barked at his retreating back. In the quiet, Grant had a hard time remembering his train of thought. He'd been fuming over his father, missing his mum, regretting his lost love, then thoughts of Katelyn had short-circuited the normal spiral into pain and regret. He looked out the window. Jane would be back; in his nightmares, just like always.

"Doesn't do any good to dwell on her," he said harshly to himself. "Can't ever have her back," he whispered before his throat closed.

FIVE

KATELYN WAS UP THE NEXT MORNING BEFORE THE SUN. Like the rest of her family, she was unaccustomed to sleeping in. The youngest of the three sisters never tired of work on the ranch. While they all did their fair share, Laney, the oldest, often found her solace and free time in between the pages of books. Elle, the middle girl, had loved helping their grandmother in the kitchen. But Katelyn loved trailing her father around the ranch, never bored of the hay-bale swinging or ditch digging that went on. But her favorite, by far, were the horses.

By the time she was four, she was riding. By the time she was seven, she was in her first rodeo. She won state barrel racing five years in a row and earned scholarships towards her two-year degree as a veterinary tech. But school was confining and too much time spent indoors. So, she decided against following her father's footsteps towards a doctorate, and interned anywhere she could learn the art of the horse. She completed an equine massage therapy program in Colorado and came back to work at her father's veterinary clinic. Even at the age of 26, her years of dedication gave her experience that not many other therapists had. Above all else, Katelyn made the most out of every day.

So, when her internal clock woke her before dawn, she got up, threw on her baggy sweats and ran a loop around the Sutters' property. While still grubby, she scoured the bunk house bathroom down to an acceptable shine, cleaned the kitchen, dusted the shelves, and stripped the curtains in hopes of washing them later that day.

Katelyn took a shower after letting the rust run out from the unused pipes, dressed, and walked across the backyard just as the sun was beginning to rise over the eastern horizon. She knocked and was greeted by Jasmine, who pressed a finger to her lips and nodded to the back rooms, where the kids were still sleeping. She handed Katelyn a cup of hot coffee and motioned for her to go outside.

Katelyn drank the coffee and told Jasmine what she'd seen on her run that morning and what she thought they could do in the coming mornings and evenings to get the fields back on track. When they came back in, she helped with breakfast, fed the chickens and cleaned out their coop, and managed some minor repairs to the front steps before heading off down the road to Tennyson's. Katelyn could almost detect the slight warming of Jasmine's smile as she waved goodbye.

Most of the horses were getting let out to pasture, but she didn't see Grant anywhere among the staff members. Katelyn snorted; that guy probably didn't dirty his hands with the mundane tasks. She stopped the stable hand who was pacing outside of Hugh's stall.

"What's the plan?" she asked, thumb in her belt loop and hip cocked to the side.

"I've got to get this evil bastard out to the pasture."

"Oh?" she asked. "Doesn't he want to go?"

"He doesn't want to do anything. If I can get him out without getting trampled, we have the worst time getting him back in. Catching him takes half the day."

"Well, then, let's not today," she said with a nod.

The boy looked at her with a disbelieving scowl.

"But Mr. Tennyson says—"

"Yeah, I'm sure that a-hole is always saying something. Listen, I'll take the heat for it. Hugh's my case for the next month."

The stable hand had no desire to argue and handed her the bridle before heading out to help with the other horses. Katelyn heard the hoofbeats pound against the door and she opened the top section. Hugh paced inside and when he saw her, he screamed and bucked, kicking the sidewall.

"Keep it up asshole, I got all day. You're not getting out until you show me some manners," she said and took a bite of an apple that Jasmine had sent with her. The sound of it, the crunch and smell, caused Hugh to pause his ranting and his ears to perk up.

"Uh huh. I know you smell that," she said. "You calm down and we'll see about getting you one of your own." As if on cue, Hugh bucked and squealed and knocked over his water bucket, smashed a small stool beside the door and pawed at the straw in his stall, scattering it around.

"Well, that's not calm," she said and, making sure he was paying attention, turned her back on him, disinterested. She sauntered out, taking the sweet treat with her. Hugh yelled after her.

She walked beside the grandiose house in her faded jeans and long-sleeved t-shirt. The standard uniform of Tennyson Stables was a kelly-green polo shirt and dark, unmarred jeans. She stuck out and eyes followed her, but Katelyn was too busy thinking about Hugh to worry about it. Her subconscious made observations about the grounds. Most of the windows in the large house were dark, except one. She studied the window and saw the impressive form of Grant Tennyson, pacing the room. He was yelling at someone on the other end of the phone.

"I dinna care if you canna make the deadline, you've known about it for months! You do your job or you'll be out on the street wi' the rest of your crew. I can promise you tha'." When he was angry, his Scottish burr got thick. He looked out the window; their eyes met. Katelyn walked, with her head down, back to the barn.

She filled two buckets of warm water and set them outside the paddock in a grassy area beneath a tree. The summer sun was already climbing its high arch into the sky, and the damp North Carolina air showed signs of its stifling potential. Katelyn adjusted her baseball cap and rolled up the sleeves of her shirt, past her sinewy forearms. She found a spigot close by on the back of the stable, and with the help of a young man named Jake, who was cleaning the stables, she found a hose long enough to reach her spot.

Katelyn took an old tin cup out of her backpack, her lucky cup from her dad and his mom before him, and another bucket of cold water into the stables with her. She paused and took a deep breath before she opened Hugh's stall.

"You sure you wanna go in there?" Jake asked in his squeaky, balls-hadn't-dropped-yet voice. "I wouldn't."

Katelyn turned back and smiled.

"Sure, I'm sure. Let's see how our resident jerk is doing after missing recess this morning." She slid the latch back and heard him shuffling inside.

Same as the night before, Hugh met her by lowering his head, pawing at the ground and leaping, back arched to her. Only this time, she dipped the tin cup into the bucket and splashed his face. He startled, jumped sideways, landed, and looked at her.

"Hey, sunshine," she smiled. He blew a thumping breath out of his nose, spraying the wall with water. When he craned his head around to come again, she threw another at him. He leapt back, shook, jumped, and whinnied loudly at her. "Well? You want to be treated like a gentleman, start behaving like one."

Hugh leaned back on his legs, eyes wide with anger, swinging his head to the side as he readied to pounce. Katelyn dipped the cup in, held it out, not letting her eyes waver from his. Hugh snuffled, un-crouched and stood by the wall, breaking his eye contact and looking at the wall. He hung his head but pawed at the ground in a latent act of defiance.

"Well, there now. There's the fella I met last night," she said and put the bucket and cup down. "What do you say we start this day over?" Katelyn's voice was even and low as she came closer, hand outstretched. His nostrils flared and her scent was taken. Familiar from the jacket she'd left in his paddock the day before, and the treat she'd snuck him last night, he nudged her hand.

"That's a good boy," she said. From her back belt loop, she unhooked the halter and held it out to him to smell. She'd slept with it last night to transfer her scent onto it. He nudged closer. She offered him a slice of apple from her shirt pocket. He took it before looking away. With minimal effort, and no fight, she slid the halter on and gently led him out, slow step by slow step, into the sunshine, out of the gate, and into the shady spot, where her grooming tools and water waited.

Her day was full. After a skittish bath that ended with her soaked and soapy and one bucket overturned in the grass before they'd even really started, she'd led him into an unused paddock away from the rest of the herd, next to a run-down branding chute. She let him wander in the new and unsullied ground, on his own, without the pressure of sounds from other horses or people. Then, she read through Hugh's history, graciously provided by Jeffers. She must have looked through forty pages of records, doctor's suggestions, and surgical procedures, right down to the exact number of stitches. What she didn't find was how the injury had occurred, other than one sparse note from the original vet saying the horse had fallen and a brief mention of an embankment. No mention of a rider or if it was a result of the horse being spooked. What speed he'd been traveling, the angle of the fall. The circumstances that led up to it.

She observed Hugh in the paddock for over two hours, sitting quietly with the paperwork. Not paying any outward attention to him. The horse was reluctant to let her anywhere close, so she sat across from him in the shade of overgrown grass and a tall oak, only glancing up when she noticed his movements in her peripheral vision. She watched the guarded way he held his foreleg. She noticed the way his eyes went wild at the slightest caw or squawk from the branches above.

She watched the way he watched her, curious but distrustful. It reminded her of Grant. Like they both had secrets that they didn't want to share. Secrets that kept them wounded and miserable. She sighed, blew a stray hair out of her face and wondered, not for the first time, if maybe dinner could help clear up some of the cloudiness that was keeping her from doing her job.

"So? How's it going? How's the big fancy horse?" Elle asked a very tired Katelyn at the end of the day, between bites of her leftover lunch-made-dinner that Jeffers had sent home with her.

"Oh, big and fancy," Katelyn said, picking a piece of chicken from her teeth and thinking how horrified it would have made her boss to see such a barbaric mannerism from a female. "He's a pompous douche, but I'm working on it."

"Is this the owner or the horse we're talking about?"

"Ha! They're peas in a pod, those two." Katelyn took a slug of water from her canteen. "I think there's a lot going on that they aren't telling me."

"Wait, haven't you met with, what's his name?"

"Grant." His name felt ripe on her tongue. "But I'm to address him as *Mr. Tennyson*."

"Oh, I see, *Mr. Tennyson*. Shouldn't Laney be kept in the loop here? The guy sounds like a romantic lead."

"Don't let his name fool you," Katelyn rolled her eyes and took another cold bite of chicken coq au vin which, to Jeffers' credit, was quite good, even if it wasn't Elle's fried heaven.

"So, in all your meetings with 'Mr. Tennyson' he never mentioned what happened with Hugh?"

"Uh, well, we haven't actually had a formal meeting."

"Oh, wait." Elle paused to giggle and whispered into the phone as if Blake were in the room. "Are all your 'meetings' informal, between the sheets? Tongues too busy for talking?"

"Jumpin' Jesus, Elle! That's not funny." Katelyn startled the chickens in the coop next to her and kicked at the pile of planks she was using to elongate their home. "I've only met the guy like once, and he was such a prickly son-of-a-bitch that I've made it a point to keep out of his way ever since."

"Well, how will you really find out what happened if you keep doing that?"

"I don't—" Katelyn stopped. "I don't know. It's just that he makes me feel—"

"Makes you feel?"

"He makes me feel things."

Elle paused to take a breath. "I knew it."

"No! Like uncomfortable, and angry—'n kinda tingly—look, it's not important."

"Katelyn honey, in all my years of knowing you, and granted there are too many that are missing, I've never known anyone who made you feel anything that you weren't already feeling. And as far as I know, you've never been uncomfortable and definitely not tingly."

"Yeah, well, maybe this is just me, growing up," she grouched.

"So, big, grown-up Katydid, are you going to bite the bullet and start asking Mr. Tennyson some hard questions? Or are you going to not do your job?"

"Low blow, Sullivan," Katelyn growled into the phone.

"Well, I *am* older and wiser than you," Elle laughed. Katelyn stared at the happy hens pecking at the ground in their pen, and her mind traveled along the unfortunate path she would have to take if she hoped to get to the bottom of Hugh's case. Elle sighed. "Look honey, I've gotta go, Emilee is fussy today. Take care out there."

"Thanks," Katelyn said and wiped her mouth on the corner of her sleeve.

"Don't be afraid of a good tingle. Sometimes those feelings are good to have."

"Speakin' of, gotta go," Katelyn said.

"All right, okay. I get it. There's only room for one pushy sister in the family."

"And we both know that Laney claimed that right a long time ago," Katelyn laughed.

They hung up and Katelyn went back to the coop. She finished the framework and would complete the addition tomorrow morning. She wished Jasmine a good night, skipped a shower to take out all of her old reference material and search out any cases she could find similar to what Hugh had been through. That's where she fell asleep, on top of her open notes, dreaming of a brooding powerhouse of a horse, with brown-green eyes, who reared at her, pawing to keep her at bay, no matter how gently she tried to persuade him.

SIX

THE THOUGHT OF SPYING ON GRANT TENNYSON MADE her nervous. He was, after all, one of the most reserved people she'd ever met. He had a wall twenty feet high around himself, but like most human beings, he couldn't hide the history of his body. She peeked around the stables and watched as he crossed the front lawn with the latest round of investors, escorting them to their shiny black cars.

When the men disappeared into their cars and were driven away, she studied the way Grant's right shoulder dropped almost immediately as if he'd been holding his whole body upright. Maybe in fear of them seeing how much it hurt. He limped, favoring his right leg, and she watched as his hand ran down the length of his pressed pants, stopping mid-thigh to work out a cramp. It was the same side Hugh was injured on. She watched Grant's face contort. The worst part was the way he swung his head around and straightened at the sight of the workers walking by. He nodded at them stoically before stopping to talk to an assistant who'd come up with more paperwork. Boy, would she like to get ahold of him for an hour and see what was going on with that leg.

Imagining his long, muscled thigh exposed in the soft light of a sheltered bedroom and the trail of hair leading up the thick muscle, the way her fingers would slide dangerously close, slip beneath the sheet...his sigh, the rise of his hips, the unguarded desire and softness in those eyes. Heat spread beneath Katelyn's shirt.

The flight of a startled bird above made her jump.

"Shit," she gasped, pulled out of the vision that had stolen her attention away so fully. A young man she'd seen lurking around the last two days stood behind her with his hands on his hips. His smile exposed sharp incisors that reminded Katelyn of a wolf.

"Jumpy?" he asked.

"Uh, no. The damn bird," she said, pointed to the empty tree branch above and put a loose lock of hair back behind her ear. He studied her appreciatively and winked. Katelyn scowled in return.

"You're the new therapist, right?" He sauntered closer and tucked his hands into his clean Wranglers. He was young, Katelyn thought, probably her age. Men her age always seemed much younger. He certainly thought very highly of himself, she thought, by the way he checked his hair in the window before coming nearer.

"Yep, that's me."

"I hear you're from Wyoming, I've never met anyone from there. I imagine you're good in the saddle." Something in the way his eyes looked over her chest and down her thighs made Katelyn's stomach turn.

"I guess I do alright."

"I mean, I've heard you're more experienced than some of the hacks Ian's hired lately. Especially for your age." He smiled and his eyes returned to her face.

"Wow. Thanks."

"You're prettier than the last guy, that's for sure." He leaned his arm on the tree beside her. Katelyn tried to step away, but a bench on the other side of the old magnolia tree blocked her getaway.

"Well, that's," she cleared her throat and faltered back. "kind of you, but I don't really think I'm—"

"Mr. Florence!" A thunderous voice cut off Katelyn's words, and the man jumped back. When Grant Tennyson approached with his hands clenched and shoulders hunched, fear crept into the young man's eyes. Katelyn looked at Grant's typical posture differently, having witnessed his private body language moments before. He either held the tension to ward off the pain, or used it to feed his anger. She watched every movement, barely registering that he was launching into a heated conversation with the young man, seething words like *inappropriate* and *flirtation* and *wasting company time and money*. So deep was her study of the veins in his neck and the tension in the muscles beneath, that she wasn't paying any attention to what in the hell he was so mad about until the tirade was redirected to her.

"And you!" He wheeled around and pointed at her. The young man took the opportunity of Grant's distraction to make his exit.

"What the hell are you mad about now?" She stood up to him, just as angry that he'd interrupted her thoughts.

"No fraternizing when you're on my clock, Miss Sullivan."

"I wasn't fraternizing."

"He was leaning into you."

"He's an idiot who thought I cared how pretty he was."

Grant leaned back. "You and that lad aren't fraternizing?"

"No." She stifled the giggle that rose out of a place she didn't know existed. "I would not fraternize with 'that lad' if he were the last living 'lad' on the face of the Earth."

"I—" Grant's eyes fell to her lips, and he seemed momentarily confused. "It was not my intent to—it's just, a woman with your —" he paused and recentered. "I'm sure you're not lacking company." Grant stammered.

"Listen, the last thing I need is some cocky, narcissistic,

jackass mansplaining to me about how to do my job and expecting me to roll over in the hay with gratitude. Jesus, you'd think I'd be used to it by now, but y'all just can't help yourselves, it seems." Katelyn's cheeks were red with mad. This time Grant stepped back, and she saw a glimmer of humility in him, as if it might have been the first time he'd examined his own behavior in a while.

"I'm—well, that's—I would never mansplain to you, nor expect you to roll in the—why are we discussing this?" he said angrily.

Katelyn crinkled her nose up and stepped closer.

"I think you didn't like him leanin' on me. Maybe you could tell how uncomfortable I felt and, like a decent man or just a good business owner, you stepped in to dissuade him," she said. Grant studied her.

"I run a tight ship, Miss Sullivan and my father gives no allowance to personal relationships between employees. And when Ian sets a rule, it's followed."

Katelyn watched him swallow back the words.

"You've gotten in trouble before," she said, reading his body language and the downturn of his mouth. But instead of dismissing her, he took a deep breath and continued.

"Why do you think I'm here, Miss Sullivan? Why do you think Ian sent me halfway around the world to work a miniscule facility such as this?"

"You think this place is miniscule?" she snorted.

"I broke his rules," Grant interrupted, as if he'd been waiting to vent. "He took me off of his books in the UK and struck my name from the board of directors as a result of crossing him."

Katelyn stared at him, still confused.

"But you get to be *here*, to manage Hugh and the other horses."

"I don't *want* to be here. I was head of the London office. He demoted me." His tone was bitter, a dark sourness on his tongue.

"Well, one man's punishment is another's dream come true. I mean, come on, Grant."

"Mr. Tennyson," he corrected, dark eyes trained on her with fire lighting their depths. Katelyn was mesmerized, as a shiver skidded up her spine and she leaned closer.

"Right. That whole title thing. But, come on, this is hardly a horrible job, you've got here. Which one of the rules did you break to earn a demotion this nice?"

Grant broke his gaze from hers to stare out into the open field. She watched a resignation settle into his features; the relaxing of his jaw, the slight drop of his shoulders. Maybe he wasn't used to someone asking about him, without judgement. Maybe he didn't have anyone to confide in, and her impermanence made her safer to open up to. Katelyn wanted him to open up. He sighed, straightened his spine and turned back to her.

"It doesn't matter what the reasons were. I'm an example. For everyone under his employ; a warning of what happens when you step out of line."

"But you're not just an employee, Gr—" He inhaled sharply to protest. *"Mr. Tennyson.* You're his son. Doesn't that count for anything?"

"No. Ian never allows emotion to muddy the waters of his bottom line, or his ultimate endgame."

"His ultimate what? What the hell does that mean?"

"It's none of your concern, Miss Sullivan. I merely bring it up as a friendly warning to stick to your job and do as you're told."

Katelyn leaned back and raised her eyebrows. "That's friendly?"

"As friendly as I get. You'd be wise to remember that." He turned to leave. She stepped in front of him and he stopped, huffed, and scowled at her. When Katelyn didn't budge, he opened his arms.

"Was there something else?"

Katelyn stared at a curl of hair at his temple. And at the one that touched his ear at the end of its loop. Its playful length betrayed the seriousness of his façade; surely a true professional would have cut it shorter by now. Perhaps there was a bit of a rebel under all that crisp and cold aloofness. The unbuttoned V of his shirt and the freckle by his collarbone that was exposed when he opened his arms made her wonder what other things lay beneath his clothes to explore. She wanted to toy with his hair, spring it between her fingers, nuzzle her nose into the skin of his neck.

"Miss Sullivan? Do we have a problem?" He was staring at her now, and when Katelyn's eyes met his, he scowled back. Katelyn shook her head.

"No, no problem. But I think there's a whole lot more bees in your bonnet than I first thought. And for whatever reason, I think that you *want* to talk to someone, but you're afraid to."

"I do not have a bonnet for bees and I am not afraid of anyone, least of all a stubborn little sprite like you." Katelyn felt her cheeks go hot. "I simply need assurances that you aren't here for some summer romance."

"I'm pretty sure I get the idea, *Grant*," she fired back at his insult to her height. "Two things matter to me: my work and my family. Pretty boys like that preening rooster do not matter to me. If I had to, I'd much rather keep company with a real man— determined and broodier—" Katelyn felt like she hadn't been the one who said it. It was like Laney was putting words in her head.

"You'd rather with—" Grant stuttered. "I don't know what that—" He looked behind him as if there were another more determined, brooding man standing behind him. He blushed and his fists balled back up. "Get back to work."

Katelyn's held breath came out in a whoosh and she watched him storm off, horrified with herself. What had possessed her? She rolled her eyes and put her hands to her forehead before heading to the far pasture to check for alternate places to walk Hugh while avoiding Mr. Florence and Grant.

· · ·

THAT NIGHT, LESS THAN THREE DAYS IN, KATELYN WAS stumped. Hugh still wouldn't let her touch him enough for a full assessment. The second bath that she'd managed to give him was curtailed by Hugh's constant startling. It took Katelyn some time to correspond his reactions to the sound of Grant's yelling from across the grounds while in 'discussions' with workers. She paused and held him steady as Hugh shied away from the angry tirades.

"I don't blame you," she whispered to the horse, who grunted in agreement. She led him back into the stall and spent the rest of the afternoon interviewing all the stable hands—minus the handsy Mr. Florence who seemed to have disappeared—about Hugh's behavior, patterns, and what he was like before the accident.

Whenever she asked how the injury had happened, most of the men shook their heads and clammed up. Either no one knew how Hugh had gotten hurt, or they'd been told not to speak of it. An older woman, responsible for the flowerbeds and landscaping around the house, gave Katelyn the only information that even hinted at the event.

"Two went out and one came back."

"What do you mean?" she asked, looking up from her mud smeared clipboard.

"I mean The Beast took Hugh out one morning, like the devil himself was on their tail. All bunched up and angry. I'd never seen him treat Hugh that way. He's normally very calm when he's riding. But not that day. He didn't spare the poor animal an inch of hair nor hide, whipping him right out the back gate and up into the mountain there." She nodded to the small hills to the south that counted as mountains to people around these parts. Katelyn paused as the information filtered through what she knew of Grant. That he was normally calm in the saddle and that he cared for his horse.

"Did he say anything before he left?" Katelyn felt stupid when the question left her mouth. Grant's mood wasn't her concern, only what had happened to injure the horse. "I mean was he mad at Hugh?"

"Well, I don't know, miss. He doesn't talk to someone like me. He was mad, that's for sure, but I can't say why. I suspect it was on account of he and his dad getting into another fight. He was in a right state though."

"They fight a lot?" Katelyn asked and looked towards the house.

"Oh, yes. Mostly Mr. Tennyson Sr. is away on business. But when he does come back, it's all about what The Beast is doing and not doing and his not being married yet—"

"Married?" Katelyn's head snapped back to her.

The older woman blushed and looked around for prying eyes. "I spend a lot of time working in the flower beds, under windows, miss. Neither of them notices someone like me. You'd be surprised what people will say when they don't know you're alive."

Katelyn nodded. "Yeah, that I could believe of them." She sighed. "I'm sorry." The old woman smiled at her and put her gardening gloves into the bucket she'd set down.

"No matter. Anyways, he took Hugh out in that state, and not two hours later that horse came back, saddle gone, bridle dragging. No rider. Hobbled and wild with hurt. It's amazing he made it off of the mountain."

"And Grant? I mean, he obviously came back."

"Well, he turned up but it must have been well after dark, because he wasn't around when I left for the day."

"Didn't someone go out looking for him? After seeing the state Hugh was in?"

The old woman's eyes sparkled as she looked at Katelyn. "I thought you were *Hugh's* therapist." Katelyn opened her mouth and shut it again. That was a stupid question to ask. Her treatment plan wasn't affected by Grant's physical and emotional state after the incident.

"Right. Sorry. I don't know why I asked that."

"Well, beast or not, he is awfully easy on the eyes." The woman giggled and then leaned in. "He has a lovely voice too, when he's not using it to yell."

"You're not wrong about that. I've never known a man who yelled so much." Katelyn sighed and scribbled down the small scraps of information.

"If I were to wager a guess, it was probably Jeffers who sent out a party to gather him. He spent a couple days in the hospital and came back in a brace with a cane. That is, if you were keen on knowing the state of the Beast." Katelyn swallowed. *Keen on the state of the Beast.*

"Thank you, Polly," Katelyn said and walked back to the stables to check on Hugh, account for his medicine and see what he was given, supplement-wise.

When the sun began to set, she filed her notes in her backpack and dropped it outside of the pen before going in, tin cup in hand. Hugh snuffled the hay at his feet, saw her boots and looked up, but did not charge.

"Okay big guy, I'm off for the night. I'll see you in the morning and we'll get to work on that muscle." From her front pocket, Katelyn took out the last slices of apple and some molasses cookies. She didn't come to him but held out the treats. Hugh stared at her and his nostrils flared as he took in the scent. She could see he was weary from the remnants of pain and the fight to keep people away all day.

"You 'n Grant are two are peas in a pod," she whispered and Hugh carefully stepped forward. "Is that how I get to him too? Food, after a long day when he's just too tired to fight with me?" Her soothing tone didn't need to have meaning, the horse understood she was tired and confused, and took her lowering of guard to do a little of his own. He snuck his neck out long and his lips stretched to pilfer a slice of apple. Katelyn held still.

"There you go, baby. That's all yours." Soon, he'd come close enough that she could reach out a hand and gently run it down his neck. He accepted the affection, probably more easily now that the stable was empty and no more yelling drifted over from the house. She gave him a short and light massage of neck, crown and even ears. When he had had enough, which wasn't much, he snuffed at her pockets and, realizing she was out of apples, walked back to the far corner. Katelyn nodded.

"All right then. See you in the morning, you cranky bastard." She left and heard him give a low, agreeing grumble before she stepped out and closed the door.

Back at the Sutters' she had just enough time to clean out the irrigation ditches closest to the house, help with dinner and dishes, and briefly meet Jasmine's husband Jeremy before he turned in after a long week of working long shifts on a temporary road crew for the city. When Jasmine thanked her, Katelyn felt like falling into bed herself, but made it a point to shower and organize her notes before falling to sleep with visions of angry men fighting over her before she stole their horse to run away on. She was nearly just as tired when she woke up, for all the yelling and worry she'd suffered in the dreams.

When the sun peeked through the curtains that Jasmine had repaired and hung while she was at work, Katelyn almost wished she didn't have to go back. She also wished, idiotically, that when she walked down the ostentatious drive that morning, he'd be waiting for her with a cup of coffee and a willing attitude to help. That was like asking for the wind to stop blowing in Wyoming, or for the stars to fall to Earth. Grant wasn't cooperative, he was an obstacle.

SEVEN

"WELL? GIVEN UP YET?" GRANT SAID TO KATELYN'S turned back. He'd stopped on his way to the stable office when he'd seen her bent over in front of Hugh.

"S'it look like I'm giving up? And keep your voice down. He hates when you yell." She grouched at him but did not turn away from her work. It appeared that Hugh was finally calm enough to allow her to massage his injured leg.

"What exactly are you doing?" Grant whispered, startled by how effortlessly he obeyed. Katelyn turned her head to look at him under the brim of her cap.

"Well, duct tape didn't work, so I thought I'd try a method I've actually been trained in," she said, and turned to refocus on Hugh's foreleg. "I'm trying to break up some of the scar tissue to increase his mobility."

"What the hell does that mean?" He drew nearer.

"It means it's gonna to take a bit more time. More if I'll be getting interrupted every twenty minutes. Between you and your horny staff of boys runnin' round, it's amazing a girl can get any work done."

"My horny staff?"

Katelyn burst into a fit of raucous laughter. Grant rolled his eyes and did not join in on her immature response, though he felt the warmth of her joy.

"Look," she cleared her throat, all-business again, "he didn't acquire all of this scar tissue and muscle entrapment overnight; he won't be better overnight." Grant quietly moved into the stall, still far enough away that Hugh remained calm, but close enough to inspect her work. Rather than shy away, as he thought Hugh might, the horse nickered from over Katelyn's shoulder.

"More time? More money you mean." He crossed his arms. Katelyn finished the stroke she was on with a sigh, and released some of the fibrous tissue. The horse made a pleased grunt and swayed into her, nuzzling her with his mouth.

When the thoroughbred attempted to groom her blonde ponytail and she chuckled back, something below Grant's gut tightened. His eyes fell to the curves of her bottom, hugged in jeans. She was muscular, and the Wranglers did everything to accentuate thighs that were used to gripping the sides of a beast much larger than herself. Grant's breath quickened.

"All right, baby. I know. That feels better doesn't it?" She stroked the long muscles of the stallion's neck and Grant watched her capable hands glide the length of Hugh's muscles. It was erotic, and the sunlight from the window lighting her golden ponytail made his body warm. He'd never wanted to be a horse so much in his life.

"We don't have to discuss payment until there's marked improvement."

"I'd feel better if we discussed it now," Grant demanded, off-kilter. She turned and he watched her quirk her luscious lips into a frown.

"Fine, have it your way, as usual." Tension steamed between them and Hugh stamped one foot to the ground. Katelyn took a deep breath and gave the horse a soft shushing cluck of her tongue before turning back to Grant. "You really piss me off, you know?" Her tone was soft but her cheeks showed the color of her anger.

"*I* piss *you* off?" Grant said in a hushed whisper, unaware that she'd brought his volume down with her own. "You're the most stubborn, arrogant woman I've ever had to deal with." Grant's voice rose.

"Well, seeing as most of the women you know are useless, daddy-bought-me-a-pony-I-don't-ride princesses, I'll take that as a compliment."

Hugh stomped both forelegs and bumped Katelyn with his chest. He threatened to rear, and she placed her hands against his neck, over his face, down his long nose. Her quiet voice calmed, and Grant imagined those same fingers on his own jaw, calming, comforting, caressing. Her voice in his ear, lips grazing. She patted Hugh's neck and picked up her tools and grooming kit.

"Let's discuss it outside. No sense in you undoing all of my good work with your temperament."

"*My* temperament?" he said to her back as she walked out of the stall. When they reached the outdoors, heavy with the promise of an afternoon rainstorm, she turned to him.

"Two gallons of milk, a five-pound bag of potatoes, apples and a fifty-pound bag of chicken feed. The use of your trencher and three days of your best combine."

"What?"

"I want two gallons of milk, potatoes, fruit and the chicken feed every week, until the treatment is done. And sometime in the next two weeks I need to borrow the combine and trencher. Oh, and are you using all of that leftover timber and sprinkler pipe I saw laying in the junk pile? 'Cause I could use that too."

Grant stared at her for a moment suspiciously. "That's ridiculous."

"Why?"

"You live in a one-room bunk house, where in the hell are you going to store that kind of food? And do you even know how to run that equipment? And what in God's name would you do with the leftover scrap from Tennyson Stables? Build a fort for you and the rest of the under-thirty crowd?"

Katelyn's cheeks turned pink and she scowled up at him.

"Of course I know how to run that equipment. Just because you've probably never built a goddamn thing with your own hands doesn't mean you get to discredit me for being able to. And it's not for you to worry about what I do with it all. You wanted to discuss payment, and that's what I want."

His jaw tightened, and his eyes fell to her lips. Heart racing with anger at her words and the truth behind them, blood rushing to his brain and body. He wished he could shut her up. He looked at her mouth and wondered what she would do if he kissed her right now. If he backed her up against the barn wall and bit her neck, tongue tracing up her throat, lifting her just where he wanted her. The flash of heat spread quickly to Grant's body.

"Idiotic!" he stammered, quelling the fire. She quirked her eyebrow at him. When she refused to respond, he clenched his teeth. "Fine."

"Great."

"Brilliant. Should I just have all of it waiting for you on that dilapidated cabin's front steps?" he seethed.

Her eyes hardened. "You can deliver it to the Sutters' front door."

"To the family?"

"Yes. You know, your *neighbors*, who need help." Katelyn pointed north. "I know it's a stretch of the legs for you, but you can deliver it tomorrow morning."

"What do you mean *I* can—"

"Oh, that's right, you don't do menial labor," she huffed and turned away. Grant's mouth went dry.

He'd heard that Jeremy Sutter had lost his job in the coal mine two months ago. Rumor was that the family's farm would soon be lost to a land developer. The family, with four children, was hanging on by threads. Grant's stomach fell. It reminded him too much of his childhood.

"What good is this payment to *you* then?" Grant said, coming up behind her. She turned back around and wavered as he approached. Looking down at her, eyelashes fluttering over pink cheeks he was struck by the delicate laugh lines just beginning to show.

"It does us all good, to watch out for each other," she said and her eyes met his. "We never know when we'll be the ones in need. And you can't build a community if you're walled off in some lonely old castle."

"You aren't part of this community, Miss Sullivan."

"You are," she whispered and turned to walk away, taking with her the light and warmth. "The first payment, by tomorrow morning. The rest within the week. Prove you can be a man of your word, Tennyson."

Grant wanted to yell. Instead, he growled in frustration and kicked the dirt. He turned back to the house and stormed inside. What a ridiculous woman! It didn't make sense. If she didn't make money, how would she pay for her lodging? How would she make enough to survive? If she didn't accept payment, how would she feed herself? Idiotic.

"Fine," he said to himself. "She'll starve to put food in the mouths of strangers, then that's just fine. Her choice. Her stupid, stubborn choice." He went to the den to fill his pipe up with the brown strands. As he stared out into the lush paddock, his heart stilled. The honesty in her eyes still cut through him.

He saw Hugh wander out from his pen and begin to prance slowly around. Grant stopped puffing for a moment, struck with awe at the agile way his thoroughbred was striding around the arena. One lap down, he stopped and hitched his right foreleg up a bit and slowed down. Grant's eyes filled with concern and his brow furrowed with thought. He picked up his phone.

"Jeffers!" he yelled in his trademark way.

"Yessir," came the prompt reply.

"I need two dozen eggs, the largest rib roast we've got, two gallons of milk, ten pounds of potatoes, a bushel of apples and a hundred pounds of chicken feed sent to the Sutters' tonight. And see what you can do about sending over a couple of the lads with irrigation equipment. Tell them I'll pay them for three afternoons of work out there."

"Sir?"

"Do it. Care of, Katelyn Sullivan."

"Yessir. Of course."

"And Jeffers!"

"Yessir?" Jeffers answered confused.

"See if Jeremy Sutter would be available to interview for a position for stable management," Grant added.

"Of course, sir, but isn't that job Mr. Florence's?"

"And fire Mr. Florence, effective immediately, for harassing a contracted employee." Grant barely breathed.

"Y—Yes sir, I'll see what I can do."

"Don't *see* what you can do, just see that it's done."

"Yes sir," Jeffers answered.

Grant dropped the phone on his desk. Not knowing exactly why the commands he'd issued had come so easily. Or why they felt so right. Only that his heart felt less constricted, and he could breathe deeper. Maybe it was the words she'd spoken.

It does us all good to look out for each other. You can't build a community walled up in a castle.

Grant looked at the giant desk, the office, the accolades on the walls, the pictures of Ian breaking ground on his expensive buildings and other uncared-for businesses. Though he'd been subjected to the cold influence of Ian's selfishness and reminded constantly that kindness set one's own prospects back, that was not how he had begun his life. That was not the way Jeffers had treated him when he'd first come to live with Ian. Grant felt the war between the boy he was and the man Ian had tried to make him into.

"It doesn't have anything to do with her," he grumbled. They had been in need of a new manager for the stables the past two months. Jeremy Sutter was close by and had little excuse to not be on call when needed. Desperate men made for complacent workers. Desperate men with sweet, hard-working wives, and joyful children who, often times, Grant would see playing in the yard as he was chauffeured into town for budget meetings. Tossing balls, and failing at kite flying, riding around on stick horses, and building rivers from the leaky hose water, floating tiny boats along tepid muddy banks and imagining water sprites at the helm. They reminded him of himself as a boy. Of Katelyn, in her own way. Muddy and daydreaming. Grant stared blankly at the paperwork in front of him.

Tomorrow, the Sutter children would wake to a warm breakfast. Bellies full for school. Something deep and fierce gathered inside of Grant, and the unmistakable pain of his lost childhood reared its ugly head to the power he now had to help someone else.

"It does us all good to look after each other," he whispered.

What *was* it about her?

"Katelyn Sullivan," he said softly. Katie—the endearment stuck to the roof of his brain and he repeated it. "Katie." Her name felt delicious and sweet on his lips. She would feel just as good under his lips, he had no doubt.

———

THE END OF THE DAY BROUGHT KATELYN THE BLISSFUL exhaustion. When she got back to the Sutters' bunkhouse, she went with Jeremy and helped him fix their back pasture's fence. Then, she'd helped cook dinner with Jasmine. After a simple but filling dinner all together with the children and their laughing accounts of the antics of the day, a sharp knock came at the door.

Jeremy looked into Jasmine's nervous eyes, stood slowly, and tilted his chin up. He answered the door as if there might be an actual wolf there, waiting to steal the land from underneath them. Instead, it was the short-statured former Royal Air Force pilot, in his off-hours tam, and an expression that Katelyn could tell was a horrible attempt to appear aloof. The warmth of pride betrayed him. Jeffers delivered the heavy basket into Jeremy's arms, laden down with milk, eggs, fresh bread, a large rib roast, and cheese. A second basket of various fruits and vegetables followed and Katelyn helped him set the chicken feed on the porch. Jeffers righted himself with a huff.

"Care of Miss—"

"I think," Katelyn interrupted and shot Jeffers a hurried glance. "Grant Tennyson sends his regards." Both Jeremy and Jasmine looked from Katelyn to Jeffers in stunned silence, their mouths hanging agape.

"Wait, Tennyson? Mr. Tennyson?" Jeremy stuttered.

"The Beast?" Jasmine asked before covering her mouth and staring at Jeffers in horror. "Please don't tell him I said that."

"Of course not, ma'am," Jeffers said reassuringly and shook his head.

"But why?" Jeremy asked, not taking the basket.

"I believe Mr. Tennyson was just talking the other day about how rough it's been for people in the area this year. Right, Jeffers?" Katelyn asked, leading him. Her eyes pleaded, and Jeffers nodded with a sigh.

"Quite right, Mr. Sutter. He also sent me to ask if you had a resume and references. A position has opened up at Tennyson Stables, as a stable manager. Your work ethic has been commended, and I've heard from some of the stable hands that you were once employed by Willow Hills and managed their boarding. You come highly recommended," Jeffers said. A pin could have would have raised a ruckus in the small living room after the words were spoken.

"I," Jeremy paused. "I appreciate his thinking of me," Jeremy stepped away. "But we don't need his charity."

Jasmine stomped her tiny foot.

"Jeremy! Thank you, Mr. Jeffers. We are very appreciative and my husband will deliver his resume tomorrow," she said. Jeffers tipped his hat and smiled. He winked at Katelyn in acknowledgement before he left.

Katelyn's heartbeat careened out of control with something strange and foreign. She had the urge to run down the road and bang on Grant's office door, rush into his mahogany fortress of solitude and leap into his arms, kiss his face and reward him with her warm body pressed to his. Instead, she walked back to the bunkhouse under a blanket of stars; aware that he was only a mile down the road, probably still up and crouched over his desk.

Tennyson Stables swam through her thoughts. The beautiful greenery and acres upon acres of fenceless fields to roam in. Hugh was showing improvement, and she'd hoped to take him out for a ride in the next couple of days. That was, if *he* would allow it. Katelyn washed her face and fell into bed. As soon as her eyes closed though, pictures of Grant filtered in and out of her brain. *Broody and stoic, on the back of Hugh, barking out commands and getting the respect he felt he was owed. He came down off his horse, walked slowly to her, his hand reaching out to touch her cheek. Hazel eyes softened; the hard line of his mouth eased into a smile. A smile that opened her own, just before he kissed her. Hard and deep, making her knees buckle.* Katelyn writhed in her empty bed.

"Damn it," she whispered. Her body hummed in response and she closed her eyes harder, letting her mind wander much farther than it should have.

GRANT SAT BEFORE THE FIRE. JEFFERS HAD LONG-SINCE retired for the evening, and he was left alone again with his thoughts. Nights like these, when he'd exercised even the least little defiance against Ian, he would sit and stare into the flames and think of Jane. Her perfect, delicate features and thick dark locks. She used to smile when he brooded. She'd cluck her tongue and pull at his hair.

"Don't frown so, love," she'd say. "You'll be an old man before your time."

Eleven years nearly to the day, and still it hurt. He sipped his scotch and stared wistfully into the flames.

"I miss you so," he whispered. He laid his head on the chair back and felt through the years for the memory of her touch against his skin. It faded more with every passing year. When he closed his eyes and tried to picture the exact curve of her chin, it had faded too. His body relaxed into the warmth spreading from the fire and his fingers loosened. He fell into dreams as the glass fell quietly to the carpet, spilling the last drops of amber.

He walked through the fields. The soft fog of early morning hugged the gentle slope of the land. His hands touched the tips of the tall grass growing up alongside the path. The brush of someone's legs hushed ahead and her delighted laugh beckoned. Grant's pace sped and his heart beat in his chest so rapidly that he thought it might burst. He climbed the far hill, came over the crest and saw her facing away; staring into the sunset of a green valley.

"Jane," he whispered. When he reached out, she turned and his eyes met blue instead of brown. Katelyn smiled, crinkling her freckled nose at him. Grant's brow drew in and he scowled.

"Katelyn?" Her full smile made him dizzy and drunk. She turned in his arms and reached up on tiptoes to kiss him. His body responded. He wanted her. He needed her. The soft taste of her mouth, moist and cool, made him thirsty. Far from Jane's willowy frame, Katelyn's curves fit against him in ways that made his whole body shake.

"I don't understand," he breathed.

Jane's voice whispered from far away. "She will teach you to be strong. She will show you the man you can be." The fading tenor of her voice pulled the fog from around them. Katelyn faded too.

"No! Wait!" Grant reached out to the darkness of his study. He fell back, heavy breaths in his chest, and aroused. He stared into the blurry glow of the softening fire. "The man I can be?" Fingers dug into the arms of the chair. "I already am the only man I *can* be," he argued. "I don't need to be shown." Then, looking into the erotic dance of the flames, he remembered what Katelyn had said to Hugh that afternoon.

All right, baby. That feels better, doesn't it?

He groaned and touched lips that still felt her softness there, as if they'd really kissed. He looked down into his lap, his body still strained from excitement.

"Damn you, Katelyn," he grumbled before leaving the study and stomping down the hall to bed.

Eight

It was a muggy and stifling day. Hugh was antsy, pacing back and forth without a limp about him. Katelyn watched his motion after their morning session of assisted stretching, which was designed to break apart the scar tissue. Now, he was butting against the confines of his pen, testing for a way out. She leaned over the rails and studied his gait. He'd done well with their ride in the corral yesterday. When she had worked on his foreleg this morning, he'd been stiff but not hurt. What she wouldn't give for a water tank. Hydrotherapy was useful in the rehab process for humans, dogs, and even horses. She screwed up her mouth in a frown.

"Is everything all right, Miss Katelyn?" Jeffers said from behind her. Katelyn jumped at the quiet approach. She swung down from the fence.

"All of this fancy land and I just wish Tennyson had a swimming pool." She wiped the sticky moisture from the back of her neck. Jeffers raised one gray eyebrow and his bright eyes, full of mischief, caught hers.

"There's a small pond on the north side of the property. Very secluded this time of day, in case you don't have a suit," he whispered. "I won't tell The Beast if you don't."

Katelyn laughed. "It's not for me, Jeffers. I was thinking it might be a good way to loosen Hugh up." They both turned towards the stallion that continued to pace. Jeffers nodded.

"It is not a far ride. Seem likes something the young man could use."

Katelyn blushed, thinking of Grant naked, wet and walking out of the lake towards her. Of course Jeffers meant Hugh. But, it probably would be just as good for Grant. That man could use some loosening up to be sure.

"I think that's what we'll do. Still, maybe we shouldn't tell Mr. Beast," she said from the corner of her mouth. "You know, lest he think I was slacking off on company time."

"After all you've done for Hugh and what you do every day for the Sutter family, your work ethic could never be questioned. And he'd be a fool to say otherwise." Jeffers put his gnarled hand next to Katelyn's on the metal rail. She reached over and squeezed it.

"Many men are not as good as you, Jeffers." They sat silent while the still and heavy air draped over them like a thick blanket.

"Well?" Jeffers said. "Best go on then, before he's back from town."

Katelyn smiled; a kid about to play hooky from school.

"Yessir." She took off her cap as she ran into the tack room and shed her long-sleeve shirt and her heavy boots on the floor. She wanted to feel what Hugh's body was doing, and for that, she needed fewer layers. In her white tank top and jeans, she gathered his tack and met him on the inside of the corral. He nickered when he saw the bridle.

Without struggle, he let her put on the bridle. Katelyn checked around the stable for Grant's hulking frame but only found the buzzing of flies, clicking of grasshoppers, and the quiet fullness of a sizzling afternoon. He was in town today. Sweat beaded on her brow. She wiped it away and led Hugh from the stable.

She could feel Hugh's hot breath, huffing in and out, over her shoulder and down her neck. Elated and nervous at once, just like she felt. With assured strength, Katelyn mounted. Like in the days past, he stood still, and she sat patiently with him, breathing deep until they both relaxed against each other. With a slow but steady gait, they crossed the north pasture.

Without the saddle as a go-between, Katelyn could feel the movement of Hugh's rib cage, the residual tightness on his right from the injury. She could feel a slight pull in his left side from compensating. She looked ahead and directed him up a small hill, to test the strength of his muscle and how the incline affected the gait. They stirred the hoppers as they brushed the tall grass. He snorted but didn't fight the climb.

After they crested the hill, she stopped and held him steady. From up here she could see the house and stables behind them, the trees between and the small glimmer of a lake to the north. Beyond it, the tallest hill she'd seen in North Carolina. The gardener had called it a mountain. The same one Grant had gone up with Hugh. She frowned. Today certainly wasn't the day for that.

"Want to go for a swim?" she whispered as she looked back down the long path to the lake. Hugh's ears pointed forward, and he seemed to share her thought. He rustled, pranced, and made a pleased grunt, pushing forward against the reins. "All right then," she laughed. "Quick, but don't tell Dad."

GRANT WAS MISERABLY HOT. THE TRIP INTO TOWN HAD been tiresome. He had waded through the contracts, yawned during the presentations, and daydreamed during the question-and-answer sessions. Mostly, his thoughts turned to her. The dream he'd had. The kiss he still wanted. The sound of her laugh and the way she'd touched something deep inside of him. He couldn't let his mind wander too far down those paths. He did have to stand up, after all, in a roomful of people. He cranked the AC in his car as high as it would go as he sped down the winding road back home.

Would she be in the stables? Sweat-slicked and dusted with corral dirt? She even smelled good when she sweat. He thought of kissing her salty neck, biting at her chin. Throwing her down in the rugged sweet hay, like two uncontrollable beasts. He shifted in his seat, breathed out, and looked out the window. Something caught his eye and caused him to swerve into the median. He slowed down, checked behind him, and turned the car around. This was the northern border of his property. The sign on the fence warned as much, and yet...

He stopped the car, squinted through the trees, and saw something white dangling from a branch 100 meters in.

Feckin kids, he thought, *sneaking into my lake.* He drove a short distance, and pulled off the side of the road near the two-track access, barely noticeable from the highway. Grant grabbed his rifle from his trunk with the intent on scaring the crap out of the trespassers. Never mind that he himself, as a young lad, had snuck into plenty of lakes. He hadn't been so brazen to do it in broad daylight, but that was the stupid nature of youth.

Jane would have smiled, pulled him back to the car.

Let them have their fun. You wouldn't want to be interrupted in the middle of a tryst, would you?

But Jane was gone. And he was alone. And he didn't want anyone trysting on his property.

He hiked through the thick underbrush until he'd come to the side of the lake closest to the road. He continued to trace its shore, keeping just out of sight, until he came within twenty yards of the shirt he'd seen from a distance, hanging on a branch. Grant turned to the water and saw her.

In only her pale pink underthings, Katelyn was frolicking at the water's edge with Hugh. The horse pranced along beside her and she laughed as they ran deeper in. She held him by his bridle and stayed close under his neck as he swam out, his nostrils flaring and huffing. Grant sunk onto his heels and watched from behind a tree. Her hair was free of its braid, dark blonde and wet down her back. When they'd swam out twenty-five meters, she directed Hugh to the shore. She clung to his neck as they swam back, water dripping off of the tip of her nose and eyelashes. Her full pink mouth was moist. Grant's fantasies of the afternoon paled in comparison to that moment. He stared at the hard tips of her breasts as she found the shore with her feet and stood. She looked up and turned to where he waited.

"Busted," she said to Hugh and walked, with utmost confidence, towards him. "Aren't you supposed to be in some big important meeting?"

Grant stood and scowled at her, trying to keep his eyes from her muscled thighs, the whisper-thin material of her underwear.

"Aren't *you* supposed to be working? Four weeks is a very short time." The gentle tone of his voice caused a visible shiver to run through her.

"I am working," she said and reached over his shoulder to grab her white tank top from the tree branch. Water dripped on his arm. She dried off her hair with her own shirt but made no move to put it back on.

"Naked?" He flared his nostrils. Katelyn blushed and put her wet shirt to her chest.

"Well, I'm not naked."

"Close enough," he grumbled.

"Close enough?" She smiled and leaned closer. "Darlin', there's no close enough in naked. You either are, or you aren't." Grant stumbled backwards.

"Close enough to be indecent," he corrected, and took a wide berth as he walked around her. He inhaled and tried to hide his reaction by keeping his back to her.

She snorted. "There are billions of bodies in this world, Mr. Tennyson. Not a one of them indecent. Just humans attaching antiquated judgements on 'em." She continued to dry herself. He turned to face her, studying her body and absorbing her words. "Besides, its hotter than sin out here. You can't blame a girl for wanting to cool down."

Grant thought of hot sin, and his antiquated ideas about sex and duty, and nearly lost all sense of control and reason. Hugh had gotten out of the lake, and was rolling on the muddy shore. His beautiful coat matted down with the cool and sticky muck. Grant looked over her shoulder at him.

"Ugh, just look at what he's doing!" He took a step towards the happy stallion. Katelyn put a bare arm across his chest.

"Let him be," she ordered. "It's a hot day. It'll keep him cool." Her touch on his arm, just below the rolled-up sleeve of his dress shirt, made him recoil.

"Don't," he snapped. "Don't touch me."

Katelyn stepped away with a strange hurt in her eyes.

"Okay, I'm sorry. Don't worry about him, it's not a big deal, I'll get him groomed this evening. He's just enjoying the day." She leaned in closer and said, quieter. "You gotta unwind when you've been working hard, or you won't wanna work anymore." Grant, who had been watching the horse in an effort to not look at her, felt his jaw muscles tighten. His arm was still cool where she'd touched him.

"Is that some sort of personal jab, Miss Sullivan?" Grant looked down at her. A small leaf clung to her collarbone. The presence of it was unsettling. It didn't belong. It made her even more a watery naiad, bewitching and sensual. He reached out to peel it away. Katelyn stood still. His fingers were warm on her cooled skin as they traced down to the small indent below her throat.

"Why's it okay for *you* to touch *me?*" she asked.

"Is it? Okay?" he said, still staring at his finger on her skin, the wet leaf, now forgotten.

"I can't say I mind," she whispered. "Lord, I think you could use some unwinding." Her words were softer and punctuated by a nod of her head.

"Oh?" He stared down at her with eyes, deep and mesmerizing. Katelyn looked at his mouth. "You think I'm tightly wound?"

She leaned in; her breast brushed his shoulder and his cheek twitched as he closed his eyes. He dropped his hand to his side with a tightly clenched fist.

"I do," she said. He wished she'd undo his buttons, pull off his shirt and lead him to the water.

"Well, maybe I don't want to unwind. Maybe I'm happy, just as I am," he grumbled, his body trying to fight the urge to lean down and kiss her.

"But you aren't happy." She shook her head, eyes never leaving his mouth. Her body shook against his in a nervous, expectant way. He looked down at her silence and saw her lips, her skin, trembling. The dream of kissing her flooded his mind. Hugh nickered, and she glanced away to see him trotting along the soft edge of the lake.

"Hey!" she yelled, and the moment shattered. She dropped her top in the sand and ran after him. Grant watched her speed after the horse, strong legs and backside striding easily through the mud and up to the horse. She'd caught up with him down the shore and grabbed his bridle. He watched her give the horse a stern talking to, still in her underwear, and Grant wanted to hold back a laugh. By the time she'd made her way back to him, he'd had enough time to remember how mad he still was. He stooped and picked up her shirt.

"I don't want you taking him here again." He threw her shirt at her. She caught it.

"What? That's not your decision. This is good therapy for him."

"You obviously can't control him." Grant grasped at straws and wished she'd put her shirt back on.

"I'm controlling him now!" She leaned into the argument and he looked away. She was controlling a lot of things.

"Put your clothes on and get back to the stables. I won't tell you again." With that, he grabbed the rifle he'd dropped when she'd come up to him.

"What were you going to do with that? Shoot me, like I'm some kind of trespasser?"

"You are a trespasser. From now on, this lake is off-limits to you." He turned around and stalked back through the trees to his car. Katelyn watched him go, Hugh nudged her.

"GODDAMN IT, HE'S HARD TO GET A READ ON," SHE seethed. "Why's it even matter, Katie May? Do you really need to read the book of Grant?" she asked herself out loud, as if it were the most ridiculous notion she'd ever come up with. But it was the answer she puffed out in response that startled her most.

"Yeah, that's a story I need to read," she said, and stared after the crunch and crash of a beast in the woods, headed back to his high-priced Town Car. Katelyn swore under her breath. That book was locked down tight.

She reluctantly dressed and walked Hugh back, quietly in thought. She thought of the way Grant's eyes had caressed her, the way he'd shied from her touch, but then touched her himself. She used to pride herself on being able to read people, but she just couldn't understand him. One minute he was hot and oozing desire, the next shut down in disgust. She couldn't tell if it was disgust at her or himself.

She thought about Hugh's accident. They'd both fallen. Which meant pain stood as much between them as between Hugh and his healing. It might help her get to the bottom of Hugh's injury if she could help heal the rift between Hugh and Grant.

She stroked the horse's neck as she climbed on. She could tell they'd been friends once, by the way Hugh had reacted so strongly to Grant. She could tell by the slight glint of pain and regret in Grant's expression when he saw the horse cringe away from him.

She rode slowly with no stress or strain to Hugh, a quiet meander through the forest in the late afternoon. When she reached the barn, she dismounted into the still-hot dust, and led Hugh straight to where the stable hands had provided fresh water and hay.

"Where is your uniform?" An unfamiliar voice startled Katelyn. She spun and faced a man, tall and thin, piercing green eyes and gray hair swept from his forehead. With hands clasped behind his back, he was severe in his Italian shirt and slacks.

"Hello, Mr. Tennyson," she said, not needing an introduction. She saw traces of Grant in his height, and in the worried brow. The now-gray hair was probably once burnished brown. "I don't have a uniform. I'm a temporary therapist for Hugh," she held out her hand "Katelyn Sullivan."

Ian stared at her hand, but did not offer to shake it. "Why is he so filthy?"

"I took him to the lake for some hydrotherapy."

"I see—and who were you with at the lake?"

Katelyn felt the menace. Saw the hawklike stare that seemed to question her very soul. Fraternizing with the staff was forbidden. It didn't matter that all they'd done was fight. Her hands tightened on Hugh's lead.

"Just Hugh and I."

"Oh? Anyone else?" He wouldn't be asking, if he didn't already know.

"Grant stopped by to yell at me, per usual."

"Did he?"

"I don't reckon he knows what to do with someone like me and my rehab methods," Katelyn said and chanced a glance at the closed blinds of his office window. Ian followed her gaze, and something sinister lit his smile for just a moment.

"I'm sure you're right about that. Grant hasn't yet found a therapist he trusts with Hugh and he certainly isn't used to dealing with women who get their hands dirty. You must seem quite the novelty."

"Well," Katelyn stopped. "I don't know what that means."

"Is there something I should be apprised of? More than just yelling? Any crossing of lines? I'm sure you've been made aware of my policies on—"

"Fraternizing with the help? Yeah, I've heard."

"So you and Grant?" His strained voice spoke worlds to her well-tuned ears.

"Of course not! I took Hugh to the lake. Grant thought I was a trespasser, flashed his rifle and sharp distaste for my therapy, and then he left."

Ian looked pleased. "Good! Grant has prospects, serious ones, important lines to maintain."

"I didn't realize *he* was part of your breeding program," Katelyn said with a sideways glance. Ian stiffened under the scrutiny. Katelyn read the bristling and salvaged her opportunity to help Hugh.

"Look, your business is your business. I'm not interested in being a fling for anyone. I'm here because Jim Parsons asked me to help Hugh. I'm here for him. Nothing else." Katelyn tugged on the lead. Hugh snorted into Ian's face as he passed.

"This place is more of a shit show than I thought," Katelyn said quietly, not looking back to see Ian's cross and still stunned expression. She didn't look to Grant's office. She just looked ahead. To the barn, to the safety of a world she understood. To go and be surrounded by horses who, especially after the events of the afternoon, were the kind of people she preferred.

"ARE YOU AND THAT HORSE GIRL BECOMING INVOLVED?" Ian led with the accusation before even stepping into the office. Grant scowled over his computer screen at him.

"Who?"

"Katelyn Sullivan."

"No." Grant looked back down at his work. "Not that it would be any concern of yours if I was."

"It would be very much my concern. You should know that I've already had a conversation with her about my expectations for your future." Ian said testily, and slammed his fist down into the soft back of the leather chair across from Grant's. Grant looked up with one eyebrow raised.

"My physical relationships are hardly your business."

"You are my only son. The last of the Tennyson line, you have an obligation."

"To breed with only the finest mares?" Grant asked tensely.

"I will not have you belittle the seriousness of the matter with vulgarity!" Ian shouted back. "We have an agreement," he said in a low and vicious tone. Grant's shoulders pulled higher towards his ears. "If you want even one scrap of this facility that you've prided yourself on saving, you'll—"

"You needn't remind me, Father."

"I think it's important that I do, given Miss Sullivan's attractiveness and that she looked as though she'd been skinny dipping."

"She was not naked," Grant responded resolutely. *There's no 'close enough' in naked. You are or you aren't.* "And I don't find her attractive." He turned his eyes away from Ian and back to his screen.

"Let us not forget what happened last time, Grant, when you let your cock do your thinking for you."

"Who's being vulgar now?" Grant said over his deep frown. "And you don't need to worry. I won't ever forget," he said lowly and looked at his father as if he could burn holes into his chest with his eyes. Ian glowered at him.

"I have a meeting with Archie Langston this evening at the club. We are discussing his daughter's interest in your future well-being."

"Cecilia?" Grant said with an unchecked air of disgust. "I hardly think she has any interest, whatsoever, in my well-being. Unless it's directly tied to my bank account."

"She would make a suitable match. She's more than attractive, intelligent, composed, and doesn't rock the boat," Ian said, jabbing at his son's lack of conformity in past years. Grant ran his hands through his messy hair.

"She isn't *unattractive*," Grant acquiesced.

"We're settled then," Ian said resolutely.

"Settled? I hardly think fair looks are enough to build a relationship on."

"Marriages have been built on less, Grant. You are running out of time and options. Make a choice now, or have it made for you," Ian growled and left the room. Grant clenched his teeth and directed his attention back to the screen. The muscles of his shoulders and neck burned with stress, and he could feel them winding themselves tighter towards his ears.

"Tightly wound," he said, the words finding themselves on his lips. He lost track of the numbers and stared blankly down at his hands, clenched against the chair's leather arms. *You could use some unwinding*, her voice was in his head.

He got up, threw his latest pile of paid receipts into the trash and stalked around the room until he could find composure. Cecilia Langston was a bona fide bitch. What she lacked in genuine affection, she made up for in calculatingly successful business deals. She was beautiful and cold. No wonder Ian thought her the perfect wife.

Grant stopped to stare out of the window. He closed his eyes, and remembered Katelyn coming out of the lake, warm pink curves and wet. Saw her smile, heard her laughter, shuddered and felt his groin pull. Cecilia wouldn't dip a toe in an unchlorinated pool, let alone swim half-naked with a horse, through leech and bug-infested waters.

He opened his eyes and caught a glimpse of Hugh dancing around his pen, still caked in mud and happy as a lark.

NINE

"WE NEED TO TALK." KATELYN'S VOICE CUT THROUGH the numbers and drew Grant's glazed-over stare from the screen. He sat up, took in a quick breath, and looked, disoriented, around the room before settling on her in the doorway.

"Don't you knock?" he grouched.

"The door's open, it's working hours. If you don't want to be disturbed, close the door," she said and strolled in. The last time they'd spoken, she'd been in nothing but her delicate underthings, dripping wet on the banks of the lake. He rubbed his eyes, scowled at her again, and turned back to the screen.

"What do you want? I'm busy."

"We need to talk," she repeated.

"Finally come to your senses about payment, have you? Tired of digging ditches and taking out trash for the Sutters? Ready to actually get ahead for yourself?" he said.

"No, but I—" she started.

"Is this about the lake? Because that's not open for discussion."

"Wow, that really bothered you, didn't it? Seeing me in my

underpants?" She leaned in closer, and her eyebrows lifted. "Or was it the leaf?" she whispered. Grant blushed.

"What d'ye want?" he said and his fists clenched on the desk.

"I need to talk to you about—"

"Whatever my father said to you yesterday is also not open for discussion."

Katelyn cocked her head at him.

"Well, I didn't realize you two chatted about his telling me 'the rules'. I didn't come here to talk about your sex life. Hardly my business. But if it *were* my business, it wouldn't be any of *his* business."

"If it *were* your business?" Grant's voice rose. Katelyn barely registered what she'd said.

"Well, I don't mean we should make it our business. I mean I'm not opposed to the idea, I—that's not what I was—shit," she breathed out heavy and Grant watched her with a small smile playing on one corner of his mouth. "Look," she said, "it was awkward yesterday for him to bring it up. I can only assume it's because I'm a young woman. He'd never treat a man that way I'm sure. Anyway, that's not why I'm here either."

"Then what, pray tell, are you doing in my office, Miss Sullivan?"

"I'm here to talk about Hugh." She uncrossed her arms and leaned on his desk. "More to the point, we need to talk about the accident."

"What accident? Where's Hugh? Wha've y'done?" Grant's voice rose, and with it, his Scottish accent. Katelyn threw her hands in the air and turned to close the office door.

"Settle down, I'm talking about square one. About what happened with you and Hugh, how he got hurt in the first place."

"And how'd ye know it was me?"

"I figured it out, genius. You have similar injuries on the same side and you hold your body to protect it, and I noticed."

"You noticed aye?" Grant pulled away. "You and Ian seem to

know a lot about my weaknesses, then don't you?"

"What do you mean me and Ian?"

"Well, why don' you ask my father, since you seem to be on good speaking terms? He's the expert on practically every failing I have!" Grant raged. Katelyn didn't budge, just stood in front of him calmly.

"Maybe you're not used to honesty, but here's a little taste, Grant. I'm *not* on speaking terms with your father. I know you've almost single-handedly saved this place, and that's not a failure. I sure as hell don't think you're weak, but I do think you've been hurt. And I want to hear about what happened from you. The only story I care about is yours. So, dinner, six o'clock. If you aren't in the dining room, I'll come and get you." She turned and walked out.

"But I—" he stuttered at her retreating back.

TWO HOURS LATER, AT SIX O'CLOCK, GRANT SAT resolutely at his desk. No woman, no *hired* hand, was going to tell him what to do. He sat in his chair, going over the same numbers once more, just to have an excuse to not be in the dining room.

"Come and get me indeed. I see how much the honesty of a hayseed, farm girl is worth—"

Katelyn strode in, knocking as she opened the door.

"Sorry I'm late. This goddamn house has too many rooms. I must have found seven different offices. Dinner. Let's go," she said, nodding to the door. He stopped his words, perplexed.

"I'm not hungry, and I have work to do."

"Course you're hungry—"

"Really, Miss. Sullivan, I hardly see how a wee lass the size of a hobbit could make me," Before he finished, she pulled him by his wrist to the door. Her small hand was a shock of warm strength. Touch. So long withheld, so rarely given, stunned him into complacency.

"Hobbit? Having pretty small feet, I take that as an insult," she continued without missing a beat. "Jeffers and I made a nice meal. It's been a long day and we're both tired and hungry. There's nothing on that computer that can't wait an hour. Hell, I even showered just for you."

Grant, curious to see for himself, leaned in closer and his nose brushed her hair. She smelled like tart and sweet apples. She'd left the golden-brown waves of it free and out of the normal ponytail. He wanted to touch it, but his hand was currently useless.

"Will you unhand me!" he said and tugged at his arm. Katelyn stopped and looked up at him. She stepped closer instead of pulling away.

"That depends. Are you going to behave like an adult or a child?" she asked. Grant glared down at her. The question left him little choice. If he refused, he was being childish. He relaxed under her hand.

"Fine. But this isn't some friendly get-to-know-each other dinner. It's strictly about Hugh's recovery. It's just business."

"Has it ever been different between us?" she said and let go. Grant followed her down the dark-paneled hallway and to the formal dining room. Katelyn walked past the ostentatious table and chairs and through the swinging mahogany door of the kitchen. There, in the softly lit kitchen, on the preparation island were two plates, a shepherd's pie between them. A basket of crusty bread, and an iced bucket filled with cans of Boddingtons.

"What is this?"

"Dinner," she returned.

"In the kitchen?"

"I thought this would be more comfortable."

"I dinna want to get comfortable with you," he grumbled.

"Yeah, I know. But you're gonna have to if you want me to help Hugh and get the hell out of your life. I think you *do* want that."

Grant shot daggers into her shoulders when she turned away.

"Plus," she added, "I heard that this is your favorite and that you don't get to have it often because your dad says it's *too common*." She said the last words in her haughtiest British accent and grabbed two forks from the drawer beneath the large sideboard. "And I helped make it, so I'd be insulted if you didn't at least try it."

Grant stared down at the fork she offered him and back at the lightly browned, potato-topped dish, steaming on the table. The smell was divine, hearty and warm, and he felt his resistance fail. It *was* his favorite. Jeffers had remembered from when he was a boy. He'd asked for it often, and whenever his father was away on business, Jeffers had always acquiesced. Always. It filled Grant with an emotional tug of nostalgia for the old butler, who had shown more kindness for the past thirty years than his own father.

"Jeffers," he whispered.

"He cares an awful lot about you. You should be nicer to him," Katelyn said and sat down. Grant followed, unaccustomed to the tall stools at the counter. He sat down awkwardly and looked around, as if he wasn't sure if he could balance and eat at the same time. He leaned over the pie, inhaled and sat back with a sigh. Katelyn opened a can of Boddingtons and split it between their glasses. He watched the nitrogen-induced cream swirl in the glass.

"Now, normally, I'd prefer a Guinness, but since it's been so hot out, I thought this might be more refreshing."

"Refreshing, aye?" Grant felt a smile come to his lips.

"Not as refreshing as a skinny dip in a forbidden lake, but yeah, refreshing." She smiled and lifted the glass to her lips. A small bit of white foam topped the pink sweetness of them and he wanted, with a strange urgency, to kiss it away.

"Are we discussing your indecent trespassing at this business dinner?" He scowled to remind her she hadn't gotten past any of his high walls.

"Nope." She dug into the first bite of pie. "Let's talk about the day of the accident."

"I fail to see how that will help."

"What kind of ground were you covering? How fast were you going? Was it just you or was there added weight?" Katelyn fired off the questions. Grant put his hands on the table as if to leave but she grabbed his fork. "Here, try this." She put a bite into his mouth before he could even get off his teetering stool.

The moment it touched his tongue he sat down. The warm, savory sauce, ground lamb, herbs, peas, carrots and the soft buttery fullness of the potatoes stopped him. He sat down, closed his eyes and moaned. His stomach gnashed with hunger and he grabbed the fork from her. He shoveled another steamy bite into his mouth and his senses exploded with pleasure.

"Good?" she asked.

"Aye," he grunted and dug in. The food hit his empty stomach and filled more than just the space there. His heart warmed, his senses filled with contentment, and he spoke before he could really think.

"I took him out last autumn. Was the anni—" Grant stopped, mid-bite and looked up at Katelyn who had just licked potatoes from the back of her fork. She blushed.

"What?"

"An afternoon I'd had a row with Ian," Grant stuttered. Katelyn studied him. He cast his eyes down to the table. She understood he was omitting something. The bread broke open with a satisfying crackle between her hands and she passed him a large piece. Grant took it, avoided her eyes, and continued.

"I took him to the trail south of here, up Maker's Peak."

"On the old logging road?" Katelyn asked.

Grant looked at her. "That's right. How do you know it?"

Katelyn froze—the gardener had told her. She didn't want him thinking the staff was gossiping behind his back. "I've looked at some maps of the area, and saw it on my way to the lake." Mentioning the lake had the desired effect of distracting him.

"What happened then?" she pressed.

"I was upset. I needed to get away. I dinna ken if you can understand that, but I had to leave this place. I couldn'a stay on the grounds, anywhere Ian owned." Katelyn noticed the way Grant, again, called his father by his first name, and had slipped further into his burr in the comfort of the kitchen; telling details of a time he was upset. "I ken well that it doesn'a make any sense," he sighed as she stared at him.

"I understand it better than you probably know," Katelyn answered. "My mom says I'm a bit too wanderlusty." Grant's eyes snapped up to hers, distracted. Katelyn buttered the bread and popped a bite into her mouth.

"Why did you take Hugh out? Must be twenty other horses in that stable," Katelyn asked with her mouth full. She filled his bowl and his glass again, as most of it had disappeared between breaths. Grant watched the steam rise up and the potatoes sink into the brown gravy.

"Hugh is my father's pride and joy," Grant said. "That bonny lad is the one thing he cares about most on this estate."

"More than you?"

Grant didn't answer.

"It wasn't his fault. I pushed him up the hill, faster than I knew he should go," Grant bowed his head, looking ashamed. "I dinna mean to hurt him. I was," Grant sat back from the table, wiped his mouth and sniffed. "I was in too much pain to care what happened to him or me."

"Why were you in pain?" Katelyn asked and her hands moved to reach across the island before she withdrew. Grant slugged down the beer and cleared his throat. He ignored the question.

"Hugh caught a rut, stumbled and fell forward off to the right. I tumbled off, o'er his head, as we both went over the edge. I must have rolled sixty feet down into the ravine before I was stopped by the underbrush. By the time I'd crawled up the hill, he was gone, run back down the mountain. I dinnae ken how he fell, only forward and right, and I dinna ken how far down he went—not as far as I, nae doubt. He was in the stable when I finally made it back that evening." He paused to shake his head. "They attended to his injuries promptly. The finest specialists were called."

"For you?" Katelyn asked, her eyes narrowing. Grant's head snapped up.

"For Hugh," he said with disbelief at such a stupid question. "They didna give a shite about me. Not then. Not now. And why should they? I'm but the bastard son of Ian Tennyson." He finished the rest of his dinner and tossed the fork into the empty bowl with a clatter. "All that make sense? Clear enough now?"

His angry tone didn't seem to sway her. He knew she saw through it, to the tender hurt lying beneath. Katelyn lowered her eyes to meet his. When he looked into them, he knew she didn't buy his dismissal of the painful event. He looked away.

"Well, I guess it'll have to do," she sighed. Grant rose to leave. "Hang on." She stood up, turned to the counter, and picked up a plate of warm cookies. Grant looked at her, then down at the plate. His eyes went soft before he pulled his feelings back in and scowled.

"What's this?"

"You have to try them; it's my sister Elle's recipe, and they'll knock your mad right off."

"Knock my what off?"

"Yep."

"I like my 'mad' where t'is."

"Aye," she teased, "of the very little I know of you, that's for certain."

"Are you making fun of—"

"But I don't think it's doing you much good. Give it a rest for tonight. Here." Katelyn shoved the plate into his hands. "Thanks for taking the time out of your busy life for dinner with me." He wasn't used to genuine gratitude; not even for some great gift or expense, but certainly not just for his company over a simple dinner. His heart trembled.

"Oh? Had I a choice, then?" His tone now teasing.

"Och! The mean wee lassie made me eat a warrrm, delicious meal, actually listened to me, and sent me to bed with homemade cookies. My life is so harrrd! I dinnae ken how I can endurrre such torrrment!" she said in a mock burr and rolled her eyes. Grant's mouth twitched, and he was unable to stop the smile before she saw it and smiled back. His stomach settled into the warmth of the meal and he felt drowsy and full.

"Thank you for dinner, Katelyn." He stumbled on the unfamiliar words and hurried back to his office. He sat down at his desk and placed the full plate on top of his paperwork. The warm cinnamon smell, hearty and sweet, made his mouth water.

"Maybe just one," he muttered. "It would be rude not to at least try them, after she went to the trouble," he reasoned with himself, and picked up a cookie between his fingers. He bit in just as she opened his office door with a tall glass of milk in hand.

"Here. Can't have a plate of cookies without at least one glass of milk," she said breathlessly and set it on his desk before leaving. "See you in the morning," she called behind her and shut the door.

"See—yes—tomorrow?" he fumbled with a mouth full of cookie. Its flavor cascaded through him like a warm hug. He closed his eyes, and let the evening play through him. The pain of remembering. The shame of being forced to relive it. The beauty of her honest eyes staring, nonjudgmentally, into his. The warmth of the moment, the pleasure of the food, and her company. He reached for the milk and the combination sent euphoria through his brain. He wanted to hug her.

He turned to look out of his office window, hoping to catch a glimpse of her as she left for the evening. Within moments he saw her check in at the stables before walking down the graveled road for Sutter Farm. He shoved another cookie into his mouth ravenously and looked at his finished work.

Grant couldn't wait for the next day to start.

TEN

"RISE AND SHINE!" KATELYN SAID SUNNILY, JUST BEFORE she pulled the curtains back and the brilliance of the morning sun exploded into Grant's sleeping face.

"What the devil!" Grant shouted, sitting up, shirtless, and shielding his eyes. Katelyn turned from the window in well-worn jeans and a tank top, covered with a zip-up hoodie. She scratched at her tousled locks, tied into a messy bun on top of her head. She watched him, breathing heavy with his strong hand still over his eyes.

"Mornin'," she chuckled.

"How did you get into my room? This is sheer insolence!"

"It's a what?"

"I'm not decent," he snarled. Katelyn stared at the broad expanse of his chest, a light sprinkling of hair trailing down into the sheets tucked at his waist. Katelyn felt a hungry smile play on her lips. Her cheeks warmed.

"Well, I'd say you were better than just *decent*." The words slipped out. Her eyes shot up to meet his. "I mean that you, well, you're nice to look at. Uh, I mean, you have a really big—damn it, I'm not supposed to notice things like—sorry."

Grant was watching her. When she met his eyes again, he chuckled.

"Can you tell me, Miss Sullivan, why every time indecent thoughts cross your mind you turn into a cursing, bumbling virgin? Surely you've seen a man without his shirt before?"

"Well, ha! It's funny you should mention that," she fumbled.

"What are you doing here?" He pulled the sheets away and stood. Katelyn watched, fascinated, as he walked closer. His gaze traveled over her body in a way that made her shiver.

"Um, here for therapy?" she stuttered as he came closer and his body heat engulfed her. He didn't seem angry. Quite the contrary, his anger at being woken seemed to be replaced by curiosity.

"You're *my* therapist? I think you're out of your element. I'm not a horse," he said, with a seductive smile. Katelyn backed away and raised her hands to his chest; Grant took them softly in his and gently dropped them to her sides, holding her there.

"I—I know that. I know you aren't a beast...horse," she stuttered.

"Then why *are* you in my room? What therapy are you providing, Katelyn Sullivan?"

A cute and nervous snort came out of her. "Only my mom uses my full name." Her breath came in shallow gasps as she stared at the angry downturn of his mouth.

"What would your mom say if she knew you were visiting men in their bedrooms at such an hour?"

"Probably *way to go?*" Katelyn laughed weakly then swallowed her nerves. She'd never felt so unbalanced as she did when Grant's body leaned into hers and she melted against him. The heat of his bare chest against her, his heady, clean scent that sparked something primal in her senses. She didn't know his body would be so hard, like a wall, or that certain parts of him could seem so... eager. She closed her eyes and felt his excitement press into her stomach. Her breath quickened, and she looked up into his eyes losing herself to the brown and tortured depths.

"What are you doing here, really?"

"Water therapy." She paused and inhaled. "It's bath time," she said and gazed at his mouth.

"Are you going to give me a bath?" he said in a dark and husky voice. His hands loosened around her wrists, his fingers trailed lightly up her arms, past her elbows, delicately touching her neck, up under her ears, sinking into the mess of her hair. Katelyn's head fell back into his hands and she gasped. Her voice was stuck in her chest where the blood pumped harder, and the heat spread in waves down her belly and making her wet and needful. She shook her head no.

"Then why are you in my room?" This time Grant seemed breathless, as his lips gently came closer. He bent down low, inhaled the scent of her neck, his nose grazing her chin. Katelyn shook and made a small seductive sound in the back of her throat. He nudged her thighs apart and pressed closer to her. Katelyn pushed away, Grant let go, and she moved to the other side of the room.

"You're giving Hugh his bath," she managed, took a full, deep breath and tried to calm down. Grant turned away from her.

"What in the hell is wrong with me?" he grumbled and put his hands to his head. Katelyn took his words to heart.

"Well, I guess you've just been too long away from affection," Katelyn said, as she straightened her clothes and scowled. "Why else would you be interested in somebody like me?" Grant turned back to her with disbelief in his face.

"You don't think that I find you attractive?"

"Why would you?"

"What kind of a daft girl—"

"You're helping groom Hugh today," she interrupted. "Then, you're going to be my shadow in his therapy." Katelyn backed away towards the door and kept her hands crossed over her chest.

"That's a horrible idea." Grant said. He rummaged through

his armoire and slipped on one of his expensive, crisp shirts. Katelyn quirked her mouth into a frown.

"No, that shirt's a horrible idea. Don't you own anything rough and ready?"

"What the devil is *rough and ready*?" he fired back.

"Something that can withstand some work? Something that you're not going to care if it gets dirty?" Grant turned away with a grunt and harshly pushed away at his costly line of dress clothes. In the back was his old University of London rugby shirt. He touched it, his shoulders dropped. Katelyn noticed.

"That'll do. Put that on," she said from behind him. When he hesitated, she leaned across him and took it out. She slapped the shirt and hanger against his chest. "Meet us out by the magnolia on the east side of the paddock." She walked away.

"He hates me. There's no way he'll let me near him." Grant yelled to her back. Katelyn slammed the door behind her and took a few deep breaths on the other side of it.

God, she hadn't known. She hadn't known her body could feel so much, want so much. She didn't know how she'd had the wherewithal to stop the situation. Her hands shook. Grant was right; this was a terrible idea.

SHE MET HIM ON THE OTHER SIDE OF THE PADDOCK, in the shade of the old magnolia tree. The morning sun was already heating up the ground, but the shaded space stayed cool. Katelyn took time, while Grant dressed, to settle herself, reprioritize, and gather her nerve. If this was ever going to work, if she was ever going to be able to leave Tennyson Stables in good conscience, then she had to pull it together and keep the boundaries firm.

Last night's dinner didn't help, watching him from across the kitchen island, eat with such passion. The satisfied grunting, the way he licked butter from his fingers. Her thoughts had been a tormented daydream of what she'd like him to do to her, ever since last night. And then this morning when Jeffers had let her wake the Beast, as he was in no mood to be on the receiving end of Grant's temper himself, she was sort of intrigued to be let into his inner sanctum. It hadn't been his temper she'd gotten; she blushed and relived his hard body pressed against her stomach, of his nose on her chin, his breath, his hands in her hair, wanting to kiss him so badly she nearly cried.

"Damn it." She shook her head. "You got weak boundaries, Sullivan," she berated.

GRANT ROUNDED THE CORNER OF THE STABLES. WHEN Hugh, who'd been tied securely to the tree, saw him, he shuffled nervously.

"See?" Grant stopped moving and stood, arms out and menacing, staring at Hugh. "I told you this was a bad idea. He hates me." Grant kept his threatening stance and Katelyn looked between the two of them.

"Well, of course he does. You came around that corner looking like some mean ol' grouchy beast." She scowled and stroked Hugh's neck. The horse still pranced.

"I don't know what you're talking about."

"Here," she said and came to Grant. He shied away. "Will you just—" She sighed and took his hand in hers. "I'm not gonna hurt you, you big baby."

Grant scowled but allowed her strong fingers to run the length of his forearms and back down to his wrists. She pulled his arms down to his sides, pushed his shoulders down away from his ears and back, and nudged his legs together. She shook him by his shoulders until his confused muscles let go of their tension. She took his hands in hers and kneaded them until all the tension fell away and he took in a deep breath.

"There now," she soothed. "The two of you are just like a

couple of brothers who got into a bad fight. You can't come at each other ready to brawl. You gotta come to him ready to forgive."

"Forgive?"

"To say sorry. Sorry I hurt you. Sorry I was hurt," Katelyn whispered and took Grant by the hand. She led him to Hugh. "Keep your head down," she whispered. "And your eyes. Be humble."

"Humble? He's just an animal. And I don't do humble." Katelyn's fingers tightened around his and Grant sighed, annoyed. "Fine." He approached Hugh with a solemnity he rarely had elsewhere and stumbled along beside Katelyn. At first the thoroughbred neighed and backed away. Katelyn slowed their walk. She nudged Grant towards the bucket next to Hugh and placed both of their hands on Hugh's back, staying still for a few moments.

"Now," she said and handed him a currycomb. "Nice and easy."

Grant's fingers flexed into the warm flesh of Hugh's back. He was transported back to the day, and his teeth clenched. Hugh pranced away as Grant's energy changed and Katelyn quickly wrapped her arms around Grant's back from behind. She stepped in closer and wove her fingers into his and wrapped her other arm around him, holding him close to her body. She could feel his heartbeat quicken through his back. She felt the tragedy of the memory coursing through his blood and raising his temperature. He tensed in her arms.

"Grant," she said softly. "He didn't do anything. Whatever it is that Ian's done to you, Hugh had no part in it," she whispered into his back. "He's just something else that Ian thinks he owns. He's nothing more than a possession to your father, a sign of his wealth, a symbol of his success. But to you, he's a companion. He's your friend." Grant's body warmed, relaxed, his fingers opened, and she held them to Hugh's skin even as she swallowed back tears. When she pulled away to look up at Grant, his breathing had slowed and he was staring at Hugh, perplexed and shaken, tears in his eyes.

"It's not his fault. Whatever happened on that mountain? It wasn't his fault. And whatever happened that drove you up that mountain, was not yours." She reached her hand out, steadied Hugh. "Now, both of you, say you're sorry." She put the comb back into Grant's hand, and together they brushed the fine hair in rhythmic waves.

Grant's shaking fingers felt more relaxed with every stroke. He'd never groomed the horse before. His father would have a meltdown, thinking of him doing such common work, but Grant felt grounded and calm. The earthy, slightly sour smell of the dust and horse punctuated the warm morning and transported him miles away from his desk.

Katelyn gave gentle whispers of direction and he watched her hand glide along with his, listened to her words until he could feel what she felt, until he could begin to read the lines of Hugh's muscles. The story of his body. It was fascinating and true. His hands, hers...Hugh, were all connected in the morning, with the birds twittering above them and the quiet stillness of the land.

The hair flew in flurries, and the dust collected on his arms and fingertips. With deliberate slowness, they set to work on Hugh's mane and tail, threading through the dark hair with a comb, untangling the snarls and hay and a bit of debris. Grant gently picked out a stick that looked like it came from one of the lakeside bushes. He smiled and turned to Katelyn with a mock scowl.

"I believe this belongs to the lady of the lake." Katelyn's expression turned from embarrassed to pleased at his smile. They continued to work quietly for the next half hour beside each other. Katelyn felt better for being in the cool breeze with him, especially now that he was distracted from the morning's encounter and his breath and body were calm. Grant stared at Hugh with wonder and sadness and as the horse started emitting pleased grunts.

"Oh, he likes that. You must have good hands," Katelyn said

with a chuckle while she rinsed out the dirty bucket and filled it with fresh water. Grant looked back, his hands still resting on the calm stallion.

"You didna seem to mind my hands on you either, if I recall," he said without thinking. Katelyn's face flamed, and she looked away.

"I'm sure that was an accident. You're not the kind of man who fraternizes with the help."

"I didn't touch you by accident. I very much meant to," he said and doused the brush in the bucket before returning to his task.

"But why?" Katelyn said.

"You underestimate how beautiful you are. How," Grant paused, at a loss for what it was exactly about Katelyn that drove him insane. "Maddening."

"Well, lord knows you don't need to be any madder."

"I mean, you get under my skin."

"I don't mean to," she scowled.

"All the more reason you do."

"I'll go get more soap," she said and avoided his eyes as she left.

GRANT WATCHED, A WICKED GRIN ON HIS FACE. HE liked that his insinuations seemed to be the only thing that could shake her cool exterior. When he looked away as she entered the stalls, he noticed a small crowd of stable hands watching him with surprise. How long had their eyes been on him? On Katelyn? On the two of them, together?

"Shouldn't you be working?" he glowered. They all scampered away.

As if his transgressions were already known, Ian's Town Car pulled up in the far drive. Heavy lead sunk into Grant's gut. What if he'd seen them grooming Hugh together, laughing? What if he found out about this morning? What if Ian could sense the change between them?

Grant's hands turned tense, as the stress built in his shoulders. Ian probably had plenty of ears to the ground. Eyes watching him. Making sure he stayed in the lines. Katelyn wasn't part of his plan; she was a distraction. He knew what happened when he strayed from Ian's grand scheme towards distractions. The last two days of warmth and discovery made him feel torn and confused. Hugh backed up beneath his hands and whinnied.

"Easy, easy," Grant growled. Hugh pranced and bucked. Katelyn came out and dropped the soap in her hurry to step in front of Hugh as he reared and pawed at Grant.

"Damnable brute!" Grant yelled. One of Hugh's hooves scraped down his forearm. He backed away.

"Okay, okay," Katelyn said firmly, stepping between them and taking Hugh's lead in her hands. "Take it easy," she commanded. Hugh settled down, his nostrils still flaring.

"What happened?"

"You mean, what did *I* do wrong?" Grant barked with his shoulders drawing up. Katelyn scowled and shook her head.

"You aren't responsible for his behavior, but he can feel your stress."

"This was a terrible idea. I shouldn't be here," Grant deflected and turned away.

"What? You can't quit now." Katelyn argued. "It's not gonna happen overnight."

"I have to go. I have important work to do." Grant said over his shoulder coldly and trudged back to the main house.

"This is important." But he was already stalking away, nearly out of earshot and he didn't want to give the crowd that gathered more to talk about later.

. . .

"WELL—WHAT—WHAT WAS THAT ABOUT?" KATELYN whispered to Hugh. She ran her hand over the horse's nose and calmed him down. She looked back at the main house and saw Ian's car parked in the drive. Grant's demeanor had changed, his trauma triggered, like a switch. She had every inclination to believe that his father was the cause. Maybe more than just his father, maybe it was in the small but important changes that had taken place in the last few days without Ian Tennyson. Maybe Grant was afraid if Ian saw them together.

Katelyn sighed and finished grooming Hugh, her heart confused and sad. She'd never really been with a man. It wasn't for lack of trying on the part of her prospective boyfriends. She'd just never felt the spark. Sure, she'd been attracted to men before, but for all her self-assuredness, she felt awkward and unsure around the idea of sex. It seemed like such a hassle, and a mess of feelings and expectations that she just didn't want to wrestle with. But something had happened in Grant's room that morning. Something had changed; she'd wanted him.

Grant probably understood the trouble it would bring. A young, common woman falling for him when his father expressly forbade it? Lord, she didn't want to cause that kind of damage. She just wanted to help Hugh and go home.

Didn't she?

She scowled as she finished Hugh's grooming routine. She did want those things, *and* she wanted Grant. Naked in her bed, preferably.

Katelyn sighed and put away the cleaning tools. She walked Hugh to the paddock, where she slid the blanket on his back and then the saddle.

She hoped Grant would get to ride him today. But, like she'd said, it wasn't going to happen overnight. She walked beside Hugh, around the ring, both directions and with figure eights over low poles, monitoring every hitch and stumble to more accurately pinpoint the areas she'd work later in the day.

At the end of her day, she helped one of the stable hands feed the horses and clean out the last stalls. She'd hung up the shovel and rake and walked outside. Her eyes naturally fell to Grant's open office window. She saw Ian facing him at his desk and heard the tense yells that followed. It occurred to Katelyn that Grant's injuries from the fall were nothing compared to the repeated devastation that Ian Tennyson inflicted on him on a daily basis.

"I willna!" came Grant's strong disagreement.

"You will," the steely menace of Ian's voice cut through the open window. "And what are you wearing? Why do you reek of the stables? Go shower for God's sakes, Cecilia is waiting!"

"Let her wait! I don't have to explain my appearance to her or anyone else."

Deathly low tones followed and Katelyn leaned farther out the doorway, but still couldn't tell what Ian was saying. Grant's rumble of acquiescence followed, and she watched him storm from the office to the main house. The arch of his shoulders, the way they nearly touched his ears. The ball of his fists. He looked in her direction and then disappeared into the house.

Eleven

Grant tugged at his tie and missed the rugby shirt immediately. How could a few hours with Katelyn make him remember how comfortable he could be in his own skin when he was allowed to live in it? He sighed and adjusted his cufflinks; his jacket seams popped as he stretched his broad shoulders.

What a goddamn mess. He turned his face to the ornate door of the restaurant, half-hoping someone would walk through and claim some emergency to take him away from the contrived meeting, but there was no escaping.

Cecilia Langston cleared her throat from across the table, her brilliant blonde hair perfectly coiffed, her slender figure displayed in a low-cut white dress. Grant picked up on her genteel cue to pay attention to the physical attributes she laid before him like a window full of sweets. She was engineered to be beautiful. From her manicured nails to her perfectly shaped brows, her appearance spoke of money and good breeding. She even smelled like she came out of a Vogue magazine. Bathed in some high-priced perfume, chemically constructed to make him think of luxury and sex.

She certainly didn't smell of sweet hay or fresh apples, and he was positive she wouldn't be caught dead in a t-shirt. She smiled, leaned forward, and flashed the curve of her breast before sipping her wine. A move that even three months ago might have set his mind on the cold and disconnected sex they could have in the back of her limo. But in this moment, staring at her perfection, he was bored out of his mind. She smiled with painted lips.

"Enjoying the view?" she purred and uncrossed her legs. Grant looked away and nodded to the waiter.

"Scotch, your best, double. On ice, please." When he looked back, she was waiting for the proper response. Her blue eyes pierced his, a perfectly defined brow arched and gave her the look of a viper ready to strike. "You look lovely. You always do. Is that the correct line in this show?"

She scoffed at him and rolled her eyes. "You're so dramatic."

"Doesn't every woman want to be told she's beautiful?"

"Every woman wants you to *believe* she's beautiful."

"Every woman?" Grant said distractedly and looked over her shoulder, out the large windows at the magnolia tree-lined drive leading up to the restaurant. He thought of Katelyn. He thought of the unkempt softness of her honey brown hair, her unpainted and freckled cheeks. How when he said he was attracted to her, she fumbled and blushed in disbelief, and wondered about his agenda. He looked back at Cecilia. Speaking of agendas.

"We both know you're beautiful, Cecilia. Though I suspect you're more assured of it than anyone." He adjusted his tie again.

"Are you uncomfortable?" She crossed her legs and sipped at her chardonnay. Grant stared at her slender fingers wrapped around the delicate stem of the glass.

"I could think of other places I'd rather be." Visions of Katelyn, in his bedroom this morning, her lips moist and her body strong and willing in his arms. Smelling like earth and apples, pliant and warm. A woman who liked being touched.

Cecilia, he suspected, didn't do anything that wasn't calculating and moved her towards the future she'd written in her life planner. She probably had the date of her wedding, first child's birth, and appropriate age to die written in down in stone. No wonder Ian liked her so much. She was all business, and didn't mar the pot with unpredictable feelings.

"Grant?" Cecilia tapped her wineglass with a sharpened nail.

"Hmm?"

"Would those other places include the bedroom?" she purred.

"Bedroom?" He adjusted his collar. "I don't know what you're talking about."

"Don't you?" Her hand slipped beneath the table and ran up the length of his thigh. Grant recoiled, crossed his legs and sat back. Cecilia also sat back in surprise.

"Or was it not me you were thinking of?"

"I was thinking about my whisky," he said tightly, nodding to the waiter, who set the drink in front of him. "Send over another, my good man. The day's been long," he said.

"Poor Grant." She smiled and sipped her wine demurely. "In your expensive office, managing those big accounts. I know you must be under a lot of stress."

"You do, do you?" He glared over the edge of his glass.

"You need a wife."

Grant swallowed half of the whisky in the first gulp and set the glass down on the pristine white tablecloth. He cleared his throat.

"So my father keeps telling me."

"A wife would help carry your burdens," she said pointedly. Grant glared.

"Carry my burdens or my wealth?"

Cecilia chuckled. "Oh, darling," she leaned forward, "your burden is your wealth. Without a wife, at least one your father approves of, there won't be any wealth, will there? Surely, you don't want that. Not after what happened with Jane." The name was laced with venom and Grant sat forward, grabbed her wrist, and pulled her across the table. Cecilia gasped, but Grant wouldn't let the pressure ease until their faces were inches away from one another.

"You listen to me—"

"We can help each other," she said. "You don't want to be out on the street. I want breeding rights and Tennyson Stables. I know you don't love me, and you know that I've never been sentimental enough to expect or want that." His hold loosened. "Marriage is really just business. It doesn't have to be more than that. You can keep your precious memories of little Jane safely tucked away and still keep your father happy."

"Are you suggesting that we build an entire life around a lie?"

"It's not a lie if we both go into it with the understanding that it's more of a merger than a romantic relationship." Grant let her go and sat back with a huff. Cecilia checked to see who had witnessed the intensity of their conversation.

"What about the children, Cecilia? There's to be no romance in that process either?" His voice thickened with the next drink. "And surely you wouldn't want to damage your delicate," he waved his hand indifferently at her body, "stature."

Cecilia didn't feign disgust. She merely adjusted the napkin on her lap, took a stout pull of her wine and looked at him squarely.

"Ian wants an heir. I understand that. It would be part of the arrangement. I am fully capable. That's why they have drugs, C-sections, nannies, and boarding schools."

"So you wouldn't have to get your hands, or anything else, dirty?" he said. Cecilia scowled and Grant's thoughts turned back to the grubby girl with hay in her hair and horse dust on her hands. What kind of parents had she had? The loving kind, no doubt. A woman like that, with so soft a heart and so hard a spine didn't come from parents who didn't care. His stomach clenched; his gut twisted.

"There have been worse parents. Surely, you'd agree with that," she said. "Along with a child, I would bring my inheritance, my horses, brood mares, grounds and trainers. We could build the biggest thoroughbred empire on this side of the U.S." Now her eyes lit with excitement and Grant saw that her passion was not for his heart, but the handfuls of money she expected to make. The fame, the wealth.

"Well?" she asked when he didn't respond.

"Where's my drink?" Grant asked and clinked the ice against his empty glass.

"Grant—"

"That's quite a lot to digest, Cecilia, my dear," he said in his accented voice. "Seems like you've got our life all planned out to the letter."

"All you have to do is say yes, Grant. I think any idiot would see that I'm giving you the best possible solution." The waiter deposited his drink and took away the empty glass.

"Bes' possible?" he slurred and raised his glass to the quick-on-his-feet waiter. "A loveless marriage, a distantly placed child, and all the horse-fucking I can stand?"

"Lower your voice." Cecilia hushed over the table as the other patrons shot disapproving glances their way. "This is not your stable or some damn Scottish pub!" Her icy tone was tense between them.

Grant, whose head felt light in the wake of the whisky and the dizzying circumstances surrounding him, smiled at her. He looked down at the foie gras in its molded form, the tiny corners of toast, the elegant spring salad consisting of three leaves of arugula and some damn reduction of Hungarian quail piss for all he knew.

"No, Cecilia, this is not a pub." He shook his head and remembered the warm highland pie, filling his belly.

"You don't want to throw it all away. All of Tennyson stables? All the work you've done? Hugh? Surely, you don't want to lose him. You know what Ian has planned for him, should he fail to perform? He needs you," she said, but her pout was more menacing than sympathetic. Grant's smile fell.

His father had mentioned that a slaughterhouse was Hugh's next stop if he was past his usefulness. The horse didn't deserve to be punished for Grant's refusal to comply. It wasn't Hugh's fault. Cecilia saw the weakness in his armor and moved in for the kill.

"Now you're getting a better picture of things. Why don't you," she paused to reach across the table and tighten his tie against the thick circumference of his neck like a noose, "just enjoy dinner and we'll see how this plays out, shall we?" Her innocent tone was bolstered by her fake, beauty-queen smile. Grant's hand clenched on the table and felt the threats mounting all around him. He lowered his eyes to the fancy fare before him and realized that his choices were growing fewer by the day.

THE HEAT HAD BEEN UNBEARABLE AND THE WORST OF IT was that Grant had been picked up by a limo last night for dinner and Katelyn hadn't seen him since. Today, his office window had stayed closed. She wondered what he'd been required to do, and how much it had cost him. She knew she had no right to worry for him, but couldn't help the feelings that rose in her chest.

All day long, Hugh had been temperamental and edgy. She'd done physical therapy, brought him a ball to play with in his pen, and had talked to some of the stable hands about their knowledge of a well-mannered goat in the area who could serve as a companion animal to keep him calm and give him company until he was acclimated and healed.

Jasmine met Katelyn at the front gate that evening with a nervous face. She dried her hands on an old towel and fussed with her hair, smoothing back the brown-turned-gray hair behind her ears, pacing out front of the house.

"Everything okay? Is it the kids? What's wrong?" Katelyn asked, rapid-fire.

"Did you do it?" Jasmine asked, angry, scared and hopeful.

"What?"

"Did you send him?"

"Send who? What's going on?" Katelyn returned.

"Grant Tennyson," Jasmine replied in a strained whisper and gestured towards the house.

"What? No, I didn't! I haven't seen hide nor hair of him all day. Jasmine, you have to believe me. I didn't send him." Katelyn insisted. Her heart raced in her chest and she glanced furtively over Jasmine's shoulder to the house. "What does he want?" Katelyn asked with worried fingers gripping the handrail.

"I don't know. He said he had business to discuss, and Jeremy sent me out with the kids so they could talk in private. You don't think—you don't think he's going to try and buy us out of our land, do you?"

"Hold up, I don't think he'd do that, would he?" Katelyn asked herself more than Jasmine.

"What if we have to move?" Jasmine stared off into the distance and watched the children run through the newly green fields and catch fireflies in the dying light. "I don't want to go back to the city. I can't make them grow up in that city."

"Okay, okay, just hang on," Katelyn said and bit her lip. Her heart tore at itself. She wanted to rush in and stop Grant from hurting them, especially if he was doing it to retaliate against her for complicating his life. But she also wanted to trust that maybe he was in there, doing something good. She wanted to know that the spark of potential she'd seen in him, the ability to love, wasn't a lie.

"I'll go in." Katelyn took a deep breath and started up the stairs.

A raucous noise came from behind the door, and Katelyn froze. The two men came out, shaking hands and laughing. She fell back two steps and stared in fascination at Grant's genuine smile.

"I'll have the lawyer draw up the paperwork and send it over tomorrow," he said. His eyes fell on Katelyn.

"Thank you, Mr. Tennyson," Jeremy said. "You sure you won't stay for dinner? Jasmine makes a delicious roast."

"Of that I have no doubt, Mr. Sutter," Grant said and turned his eyes to Jasmine, who blushed and looked back, unflinching. "You've a lot to discuss with your family over dinner and I—" He looked back to Katelyn, whose whole body seemed rent with anticipation. "I've a lot of work to catch up on tonight."

"You don't wanna stay?" Katelyn asked. Grant's eyes softened and his shoulders dropped.

"Thank you, Miss Sullivan, no. I expect we both have busy days tomorrow. Goodnight." He passed by her, without touching, and walked to where his Jaguar had been parked next to the old farm truck. Her eyes lingered on his broad back and her heart lingered on him, long after he'd driven out of sight.

"What happened?" Jasmine asked. "Is he gonna take the land?" She picked up the baby and the other children raced back up the porch steps inside. "Is he?"

"No, Jasmine, my love. No. He's not." Jeremy came to her and put his arms around her and the baby, kissing Jasmine's forehead. Katelyn looked away and back down the road to where Grant had disappeared. "He offered me a job. Stable manager. Seems the last one, Mr. Florence, got caught harassing one of his workers."

Katelyn's head snapped back at Jeremy. "Harassing?"

"Yeah, I guess the guy was harassing a young lady working at the stables and he, Mr. Tennyson, needs someone reliable who can start right away. Friday, in fact."

"Stable manager? Not hired hand? Not bottom rung of the ladder, barely scraping by?" Jasmine said, elated.

"No, a good job, steady. He promised me full benefits, vacation, health, even retirement. And I'll be close by, I can even come home for lunch and help out more—Jasmine, don't cry! This is good news." Jeremy held her tighter.

Katelyn shook her head. She hadn't known the position that Jeremy was applying for was the same one once held by the overly-friendly young man. She didn't need Grant standing up for her. Or was it something else that caused him to fire the boy?

"He also told me he'd been thinking a lot about the community lately and that it does us good to look out for one another. I think I may have misjudged him," Jeremy said, and kissed Jasmine's forehead before turning to Katelyn. "You okay?"

"He said that?"

"Yeah," Jeremy chuckled. "Something's changed that guy. I don't know what it was, but" Jeremy studied Katelyn, "something must have got to him."

Katelyn blushed and turned to look down the empty road.

"You coming in for dinner?" Jasmine asked, a new lightness in her voice and a glow from inside.

"Yeah, I'll be along. I've just got a few things to do," Katelyn lied and walked to the bunkhouse. Katelyn couldn't make sense of the pounding of her heart. The heat that swelled inside of her. The need she had to see him.

Was this a tizzy? She'd never been in one, so she wasn't sure what was involved, but with thoughts of him now occupying every space in her brain, feeling fevered and breathless, it must be what her sisters had deemed in their high-school knowledge, as a tizzy.

He'd helped a family. Given them a chance. He could have offered the job to the next stable boy in line. He could have probably delegated the duties to the underlings and saved himself and Tennyson Stables the money, but he hadn't. He'd chosen a good man, a hard worker, and given him what he was worth. He'd stepped up and done something good for someone else. He wasn't his father, and she felt like he wanted her to know it. Katelyn opened the bunkhouse door and flopped down on the worn couch. The events of the day flooded her mind, and she retraced her steps.

IAN HAD CORNERED HER WHILE SHE'D BEEN OUT IN THE paddock that morning, taking notes and assessing Hugh's ability to be ridden by one of the willing stable hands. Feeling and watching were two different things, and since Grant was nowhere to be found, she'd had to make do with the young rider she'd met on the first day. He'd remained calm, she thought in part, because he trusted her when she'd given him the reins.

When Ian had strolled up, a hawk-like look in his hazel eyes, she'd resisted the urge to stand at attention, and instead looked up calmly beneath the bill of her ball cap. He didn't say anything, knobby hands behind his back, as he watched Hugh, mildly impressed. All Katelyn could think about was how he'd treated his own son; how little he'd cared that Grant had been hurt too. The animosity that lay between them, given her budding affection, was most certainly Ian's fault.

"I see he's progressing." The words were pinched and Katelyn nodded without looking at him.

"He's stopped being such an asshole, that's for sure," she grumbled, and Ian swung his head to her. "And I can feel that we're getting through the scar tissue in his medial pectoralis that seems to be compromising the facia of his right foreleg," she added, and offered her clipboard to him. Ian refused to touch it, as it probably was coated in dust and horse snot, but he looked over the neatly hand-drawn diagram of his horse and the various angles at which she'd been measuring his progress and range of movement.

"I see," he said, belittling the in-depth understanding of the horse's mechanical and physical structure. "Speaking of that, I will need you to come to a meeting with some of our shareholders."

"Uh," Katelyn snapped her head away from Hugh and stared at him. "I'm probably not really qualified."

"If Hugh doesn't have investors for his future breeding rights, then he's no good to us, and all of your work here is for nothing. He'll be sold off to the highest bidder or the closest glue factory as far as I care, unless you can convince the men with money that he's back in the game." Ian cut to the chase in a manner so efficient and cruel that Katelyn was left speechless.

She shook her head and looked up to watch Hugh prancing

carefully around the paddock. His keen eyes sought her out. When he found her cowing beside Ian, he stopped, despite the boy's insistence that he continue. Without reserve from rein or command, he trotted over and nuzzled her shoulder, as if he could sense her distress. She reached up and cupped his jaw lovingly and he nudged her.

"So, that settles it, I suppose. I will see you on Friday promptly at seven in the main house. And try to take a shower first. I recommend something other than this—" he stopped to give her a glaring once-over, "attire you're currently in. A dress if you own one. Don't make them think I hired Shit Creek's Rodeo Queen." He said it so flippantly and without remorse that Katelyn's eyes shot up and she opened her mouth to give him a stout 'fuck off' but Ian glided past her, away from the paddock, and to a waiting Town Car on the edge of the field. She tried to see Grant in him. The height, perhaps, but not the build. The eyes, but not the mouth or the jaw. The anger...

"But not the heart." Katelyn startled herself back into the present.

GRANT HAD HEART; HE HAD PROVEN IT THIS EVENING. She had been so angry and worried when she'd come back to the Sutters', that seeing him laughing and being admirable made her even more sad that he was under Ian's thumb. She would go to the investors party, she would put on her best face, she would save Hugh.

It was the least she could do, she thought, before scrubbing her face and going to bed with an empty stomach and heart, after all he'd just done.

TWELVE

"WHAT THE DEVIL DO YOU THINK YOU'RE DOING?" Grant's voice cut through the hallway Friday evening as Katelyn stepped out of the main house's powder room. The incomparable sight of her in a dress shocked him silent as his eyes traveled down her legs. The curves of her calves were accentuated with the heeled sandals. Her feet were distinctly un-hobbit-like. He looked back up to her flushed cheeks and moist pink lips. He'd never seen her in makeup or with her hair curled. Her eyes were deep like ocean waves, beneath full black lashes, so big and wide, staring at him in the dark of the hall.

"Uh, getting ready for the party? I had to come straight from the stable, it was such a big day getting Jeremy up to speed and helping him adjust that I nearly forgot about this...whatever this is, and had to borrow something from Jasmine," she grunted breathlessly, as she adjusted the top that was a little too tight across her more generous breasts. His eyes fell there even as she continued to fuss.

"Probably doesn't surprise you that I don't have anything fancy to wear, so she loaned me some makeup and this get-up. Then by the time I got Hugh settled it was 6:45, and I had to—"

she bent to adjust the strap on her heel and balanced on his bare forearm "change in the shitter," she grunted. Grant scowled down at her.

"Sorry, *powder room*." Katelyn rolled her eyes. Grant's eyes fell to her hand, still on his arm. She pulled away. Men's muffled laughter came from the den down the hall.

"You aren't going to that party. That's for investors. Important people."

Katelyn glared at him. "Jesus, Tennyson, that was low. Even for you." Her voice was husky.

He rubbed his eyes, adjusted his tie, and put his hand back on his hips. "It's no place for a hired hand."

"Well, upgrading me from unimportant to a hired hand isn't exactly gentlemanly either."

Grant leaned in, nearly nose-to-nose. "You've no business in there. It has nothing to do with you."

"Ian thinks I should—"

"They aren't kind men!" Grant interrupted. Katelyn leaned back at the veiled care in his words. "And I canna watch you be judged by them."

"Do you think I *wanna* get thrown into that shark pit? I'd rather deal with a stable full of acute equine diarrhea than spend all night hob knobbing with your pompous, highbrow cronies."

"They're not *my*—"

"Grant!" The sharp voice made Grant physically recoil. Katelyn watched as a small boy's eyes shone from under his angry brow. His shoulders hiked up into his ears and she wanted to step between them as a shield.

"I invited Miss Sullivan to discuss her treatment and the improvement she's seen in Hugh, along with other experts who have been seeing to his recovery. We need those gentlemen to know their investment is sound."

"In it together, are you?" he growled, too low for his father to hear. His expression fell into coldness and he leaned away from her, as though she'd betrayed him somehow in earning his father's defense.

"What? I'm not in it with anyone. I just—" Katelyn shook her head in protest, but Ian took her elbow in a sharp grip and steered her down the hall. She glanced over her shoulder as Grant angrily watched.

"I don't need to be escorted," she growled and took her elbow away from Ian's grasp.

"If you must serve as a supple distraction, Miss Sullivan, best it not be towards my son." Ian's boorish whisper made Katelyn's stomach feel sick the moment before she was thrown into the room full of pompous patriarchs, all discussing the finer points of white, upper-class maladies. Hungry eyes gnawed at her from several directions.

Katelyn squirmed and wanted to be back in the hallway, getting yelled at by Grant. At least with him, she knew where she stood. She squared her shoulders and wished her dad were here. Or her mom. Or any one of her sisters. Someone who could anchor her and be her solid ground. She took a deep breath and thought about her family. Elle and baby Emilee, even Blake. She thought about Laney and how she wouldn't fail to put this whole room in its place. Without realizing it, her mind settled into the soft hay fields of home. Where the cigar smoke and leering eyes, backed by millions of expendable dollars, weren't on her. She heard her dad's voice.

Just do your job. Be honest. Speak your piece and get the hell out of there.

She gazed in the antique mirror over the fireplace at the face staring back at her. Her mother's eyes, her dad's nose. Her spine, home-grown, all her own.

"Miss Sullivan hails from Wyoming. A real-life cowgirl," Ian bragged while offering her a flute of champagne. Katelyn took it begrudgingly. She felt like a cross between a Wild West traveling act and a mouse in a room of hungry cats.

"Is that so?" one particularly tall and angular man sniffed over his brandy. He smiled, revealing crooked, yellow teeth. "Fascinating. I hear the whole state is rather backwards. Like the Appalachians of our own state."

Katelyn scowled at the man. Grant shouldered his way into the room, tie tightened and lips moist, hair still unkempt despite his efforts to smooth it back. He looked solely at her and ignored the rest. Katelyn took a relieved breath as she stared into his eyes and felt her feet beneath her again. Anchored.

"Well, 'cept we're more educated, have prettier smiles, and don't marry our cousins," she responded. The crowd grew still, coughs sounding over expensive snifters. Grant's eyes lit up and his mouth twisted into something resembling a smile. They shared a brief moment of connection before Ian cleared his throat.

"Yes, well. Miss Sullivan is a board-certified equine therapist, an experienced veterinarian technician and comes highly recommended from the Wyoming State Board of Horsemanship. In addition, she comes from a long line of horse breeders herself. Isn't that true?" Ian prodded her to justify his faith, before consequences would result. Katelyn's eyes stayed on Grant and he nodded.

"For four generations back, sir. My great-grandfather came over from Ireland with ten horses. Sullivan quarters are some of the finest working mutts you'll ever own," she said. "My father doesn't breed them much anymore, but he's still the best veterinarian you'll find west of the Mississippi. And the second-best rider."

"Only second-best?" Grant asked.

"Mom's the first, and she doesn't hesitate to remind him when he gets a little too big for his britches," she returned and Grant quirked his eyebrows. The crowd's nervous silence broke into laughter and the tension cleared. Ian led her to the first group to talk about Hugh's recovery process and put their minds at ease.

· · ·

GRANT, WHO HAD TAKEN TWO MEDICINAL FINGERS OF whisky before coming into the room, was uncomfortable until he'd seen her shared discomfort. Now he was doing his best to be well-mannered, while still keeping an eye on her. She laughed in a more reserved way than he'd seen. Demure even. She spoke with great technical detail. She wowed. She charmed. She was Katelyn in a new light.

The same woman in jeans and a cap who had charmed his horse and wowed his stable hands. The same woman who had the pull of the moon to his sea. He gravitated towards her, listening for the particular rural notes of her voice, only partially aware of the conversations he was supposed to be engaged in.

"If only I could get my son to breed so well!" Ian said loudly from across the room to the delighted guffaws of some men. "Finding a *suitable* mate for that angry beast is more difficult."

Katelyn stopped mid-sentence, drew her eyes away from her conversation and focused on Ian. Her brow creased in anger that a father could say something so offensive in front of a crowd. She looked for Grant, who leaned against the mantel, refusing to look at his father. He downed the drink he had been nursing in one swallow.

"Well," Grant said tepidly in his father's direction. "It isn't easy for anyone to live up to your standards, Father. If my mother were still alive, she'd say the same. So would Jane." The room was thick with quiet discomfort. Katelyn felt a lump stick in her throat and a strange stinging feeling hit her eyes. She could read Grant's pain and felt the gut drop, as if it were her own trauma. She didn't know what to say to break the awful silence, but it had to be something.

"Hey! Why don't y'all come on a tour of the stables with me? It'd do us good to get a little fresh air, and I'd love to show you how Hugh is improving. We can go over his therapy routine," Katelyn broke in loudly. The men looked at her, relieved for the distraction from the delicate situation, and agreed with smiles and nods. She took the elbow of the man she'd been talking to and guided him out the French doors of the large den to the sweet and cool air. She looked over her shoulder at Grant, who was staring heated daggers at his father, before he tore through the opposite door and back down the hallway. She kept her wobbling emotions concealed behind a smile as she led the men to Hugh's stall.

After they had congregated in the warm glow of the stable's lights, Katelyn opened Hugh's pen and stepped gingerly inside. She hadn't been counting on getting dirty tonight in the borrowed outfit, but it was well worth coming back into her comfort zone. The gentlemen raised their eyebrows and smiled to watch her cluck and coo over the large and impressive stallion. Hugh danced beside her; his eyes wild on the crowd at his door. He calmed to her tender touch and sniffed and nudged her neck before settling down next to her.

"As you can see," she began and ran her hand down his right foreleg and pectoralis muscle. "The surgery was a very clean and well-executed procedure. Dr. Williams did a fine job of reconstructing the tendons and repairing the torn ligaments. Hugh had a rough recovery, as he didn't want to sit still and wouldn't work with the physical therapists he'd had before." Hugh tossed his head and gave a shrill whinny. Katelyn looked at him.

"Well, you didn't, you stubborn old bastard!" she said, and he nickered back in agreement. The men laughed. Katelyn felt better with her arm around his neck, and for the first time since she'd arrived at Tennyson Stables, felt as though their roles were reversed. Now she was leaning on him for comfort. The men asked questions, and she answered them, keeping her voice calm and relaxed and stroking Hugh's mane and neck as she did.

"And how is he now? Able to mount? Will he race again?" a familiar voice asked over the edge of his scotch glass. Katelyn met Jim Parson's eyes and smiled to light the night. His tie was loosened and his gray-blond hair was slightly wayward. He looked like this was not his crowd, and he could care less about the formalities.

"Hello Jim," she said warmly. "Yeah, you know as the treatment has progressed, he's now able to trot, canter, and in some cases gallop without any further detriment to his leg. The only way to know if he's able to have his full range of motion will be by trying," she finished with a wry smile. "He's proven to have a superior genetic makeup, healing and recovery has been fast under the right guidance and treatment plan. One would have to hope he doesn't pass on his stubbornness though." Jim nodded, satisfied with her answer.

"How are you doing? Have you enjoyed working with him? Here? Bit different than sagebrush fields and wayward steers?" Jim asked. Katelyn nodded; her fingers wound into Hugh's mane as a wave of homesickness hit her.

"He's a beautiful horse. But like most good-looking men, he knows it. Take away all the fancy paperwork hanging on the wall and he's just another stallion who's in need of guidance. He has a good spirit. Not mean, but not quick to forgive or forget. He remembers things. He holds on to trauma—" Katelyn paused, thought about Grant, blushed and looked down. "That's how I see horses, at least. That's how I can get to know them so well. He's not just a bottom line, he's a companion." The men quieted, and a soft rustle of shame swept through the crowd. Katelyn's eyes fell to her borrowed shoes, coated in dust.

She wished she could see Grant, wished he could know that her thoughts were turning to him, and the unfair expectations he was facing. She looked up and spotted him in the office doorway, across from Hugh's stall. He was watching her, arms crossed in front of his chest. He'd shed his jacket and loosened his tie. She breathed a sigh of relief. When she spoke, she spoke only to him.

"I think we take for granted how intelligent they are, and how sensitive they can be to us, and the world, and the things we ask of them. They should be respected. Their pain should be taken seriously. Our investment in them should be more than just about money and bloodlines. Humans and horses have been living together for hundreds of thousands of years, and that bond is greater than a bottom line," she said.

Ian cleared his throat in disapproval.

"Thank you, Miss Sullivan, for the unsolicited viewpoint." He stepped between Grant and Katelyn. "I'm sure if these gentlemen have further questions, they can ask you after dinner," he hissed, and looked back at his son to show he'd been watching them.

"Now if you'll all follow me; we've prepared a wonderful meal in the main dining room and can discuss the next plan of action." Ian led them away. Some of them turned back to acknowledge Katelyn and shake her hand before leaving. Jim lingered behind.

"It's good to see you again, Katelyn," Jim said and clinked his ice cubes against his empty glass. Katie looked past him to where Grant watched them from the office doorway.

"It's good to see a familiar face," she said and shook Jim's hand.

"Yeah, Ian really threw you to the wolves back there, but you held your own," he chuckled.

"Well, night's not over yet." She swallowed and avoided looking at Grant.

"Sharon told me she stopped by to visit your folks when she was in town and said to tell you they're doing just fine. She said your mother told her the story of how you were born."

Katelyn's cheeks flushed. "Oh, yeah?"

Grant leaned in closer. "Was she hatched or sprouted?" he teased. Jim smiled at the easy humor that he and Grant shared from when they had worked together. Katelyn scowled at him.

"She said Katelyn was so eager to get into the world that she couldn't even wait for the car ride to the closest hospital sixty miles away. Didn't even make it to the house! So, right there, in a spring snowstorm, she was born in the barn with the horses." Jim chuckled and smiled.

"Born in a barn, now that I believe." Grant's eyes never left hers.

"Yeah, laugh it up, Tennyson," she grumbled at him.

"I suppose we'd better go catch up to the stuffy conclave," Jim said.

"It's good to see you, Jim."

"I'll save you a place at the table and keep you away from the wolves."

"I'd appreciate that very much. Thanks, Jim." Katelyn smiled, her shoulders dropped, and she shook Jim's hand like she'd known him all her life. Grant straightened from his lean when Jim turned to him.

"Son, good to see you. I know this is the last thing in the world you want to be doing. Especially with that rat-bastard of a father. But I think you did good hiring this one. She'll set Hugh straight. Hell, she'd probably set the lot of us straight." Grant's eyes fell away. Jim nodded to both of them and walked back to the house.

"Look at you, winning over the hearts and pocketbooks of my father's best and brightest yes men. Even a few who don't feed into his bullshit," Grant said as he watched Jim go.

"I'm just trying to do my job. Just trying to help Hugh," she said wearily. "Are you coming to dinner?" The small hint of hope in her voice caught his gaze.

"No, Miss Sullivan. I don't have an appetite for it."

"Can't say I do either," she admitted and leaned over the half-door to give Hugh a treat from her dress pocket.

"Even in a dress you find hiding places for treats? You spoil him."

"He needs a little spoiling," she protested. "I wish you'd come to dinner."

"Why? So, you can watch me squirm? Does it please you, lass, to see him break me down in public?"

"No, it doesn't," she said. Her cheeks went pink, and he watched them. "Ian's a hateful and cruel son-of-a-bitch."

"Don't waste your concern on me."

"You're not a waste," she fired back, against his cold barrier of words.

"Hurry along, Katie darlin'," he said part kind, part hurt. "You don't want to miss the check signing." He turned his back and shut himself into the office. Katelyn sighed, blew a strand of hair away from her face, and stood at the closed door. She heard the clink of a bottle on glass as she left, heavy in her heart.

She thought back to Ian's cruel words in the parlor and Grant's response. What had happened to Grant's mother? Who was Jane, and what had happened to her? From the way her name had lingered on his lips, she must have been someone Grant had loved, and probably still did. Maybe she was the cause of the 'no fraternizing with the help' rule.

Katie darlin'. His words stuck in the space between her thoughts as she came back into dinner with the subdued crowd. Katelyn watched Ian. Here, at the table, with an investment in the balance, the very failure of his stables on the line, he was shrewd and cruel. Katelyn sipped at her wine conservatively and looked at the clock over the mantel periodically, deciding when the earliest opportunity to duck out might be.

She found it, after the last course of a meal she'd barely eaten. As Grant said, she didn't have the appetite for all of the bandying about, selling Hugh off like he was nothing more than a foal-making machine. She ducked out with handshakes and what she hoped were genuine-looking smiles. She couldn't wait to get back to the bunkhouse at the Sutters' and tuck herself into bed.

A quarter of a mile outside of the property, she stopped.

Had she closed Hugh's pen?

She couldn't remember, with the stress of the night and her newfound sympathy for a miserable man. She sighed and hurried, as much as her shoes would allow, down the dirt road and back to the stables. She cast glances at the main house, where she could hear the loud voices of the men in the den, enjoying

Ian's fine and expensive bribes, cigars and hundred-year-old scotch.

The barn was quiet though. The other horses nestled in and made small noises as she passed their stalls. Hugh's top stall door was still open. If Grant had come out and seen her carelessness, she would have heard about it for sure. Hugh was in the corner, content in a fresh bed of hay; she shut the door with care so as not to disturb him. It would be nice to curl up with him. Have a warm body, and the comfort of someone without judgments or expectations lying beside her. She sighed in her loneliness.

An angry mumble sounded from behind the closed office door. Katelyn stopped, turned her head, and heard it again. She listened at the door and then peeked her head in.

He was asleep at his desk, head down, nearly empty bottle of scotch beside him. She scanned the room. His fingers were still curled around the glass, the ice long-since melted. She quirked her lips in mild disapproval. If she had a father like Ian, she probably would have self-medicated too.

Grant's brown curls fell over his forehead and the stubble on his cheek was tarnish-red in the golden light of the lamp. She sighed and shook her head. He sure was nice to look at. Especially when he wasn't barking orders at her. His shirt sleeves were rolled up and the russet-brown hair sprinkling his forearms glinted in the same tones of his stubble. His breathing was deep and full. She picked up a blanket from the corner trunk and threw it over his shoulders. She shut off the desk lamp and moved the bottle away. When she reached for his glass, prying it from his fingers deftly, he startled and grabbed her hand.

"He'll find you," he grunted, and pulled her body close. Katelyn let out a small yelp before he fell out of the chair and pulled them both down.

"Grant," she grunted as they hit the floor, tangled in the dark, quiet office. For a moment, Katelyn's breath held inside of her lungs. The warmth of his weight on top of her was delicious and satisfying. She'd never felt so safe, so needful. She sighed.

"Stay down, he'll find you," he whispered and nuzzled her, inhaled her scent. "Ah, it's you, my sweet Katie...water nymph." His head tucked in against her neck, as if he was still caught between the dream he'd been having and the reality of her.

His nose grazed her earlobe and traced a light line down her to her collarbone. "God, I want you," he whispered. "Since that ridiculous afternoon by the lake...No, before that even."

He found her mouth and took it hungrily. His tongue, hot and tasting of warm, earthy peat, drove into her mouth, devouring her with reckless want that built up until his ravenous grunts filled the quiet space. He was a man consumed in the fire of her. His hands found hers, and pinned them above her head, while his knee spread her bare legs apart. Katelyn moaned into the kiss, and he broke away. He pulled back and his eyes opened to focus on her as he realized what he was doing. He saw her; pink in the cheeks and breathless beneath him.

"Katie?" he whispered. "You shouldn't be here." His hazel eyes traced her face as if he was touching the delicate skin. Katelyn could feel the steady throbbing of him against her thigh. Her body responded fiercely, and she felt a painful pull between her legs. The words melted something deep inside of her. "It isn't safe," he said, concern in his eyes.

"Ian's busy, and he thinks I'm gone for the evening," she whispered.

"Is that so?" Grant breathed, but made no move to get up from the floor.

"What were you dreaming about? You were talking in your sleep."

"Nothing," he said, and moved to get up, but Katelyn tightened her fingers against his and held him.

"You know I can tell when you're lying to me, right?"

"Katelyn—"

"Kiss me again," she whispered and lifted her lips to his.

Grant took them hungrily. He tasted like warmth and smoky notes and she couldn't stop tasting. His lips found her bottom lip and nipped at it, trailing down the delicate bones of her chin and beneath her ear. She sighed and gasped and arched into him. His hand, needful and strong, let go of hers and ran down her arms to the buttons of her dress. He pushed it aside and his fingers dipped in to caress the soft flesh. He found her hard-tipped breast and groaned. Katelyn inhaled as his fingers teased her. He moved against her, his length pressing in ways that made her body shudder and sigh. His lips left hers with a bite and he trailed his teeth down her soft neck, to the fullness of her breast. He took her tight nipple in his mouth, still pinning her arms down.

"Grant," she gasped, arching to meet his tongue. "Please."

"Please what, Katie?" he whispered, disengaging from her tender skin. "Please stop? You're wise to say so. I wish this were still a dream, then we could do as we wished, and neither of us would suffer the consequences." He hung his head into her neck, body still rent with need and heat. Katelyn gasped beneath him as he pulled away from her and tried to recapture his control. He sat back on his heels and tugged at his hair.

"Please don't stop," she sighed. "Please, Grant. Let's pretend it's a dream," she whispered. "We're in it together and the world is safe here, and the door is barred and only you and I exist." She sat up and kissed his neck, stopping his retreat, and her hands wove into his soft curls to pull him close. He clenched his teeth before kissing her angrily.

She thought of all the pain of loss and heartbreak in his life, of all the want and painful growth she'd put him through, and he still wanted to be here with her. Desire ran through her veins like fire. Katie breathed heavily beneath him, pushed at his shirt, tore his buttons off and bit the hard flesh of his chest. Grant grunted in pleased surprise and grasped either side of her hips and pushed her skirt up. He pulled her panties away and felt the heat and wetness on his fingers.

"Sweet Katie," he whispered into her lips, and Katelyn felt them tremble against hers. She reached down to unzip his pants, and he stilled her hand.

"You can say no," she whispered and nodded her head so their noses touched.

"I'm mad, either way," he whispered.

"Don't let me be a regret," she said softly and brought her hands up to frame his face. Grant looked in her eyes, and he softened, kissed her more gently and she felt like crying.

"I worry for you. You don't deserve the pain that comes from being involved with me." Katelyn had never been a rebel. But right then, she wanted nothing more than to break Ian's rules that held Grant captive and in pain. And for all the hurt inside of him, there was equal healing inside of her.

She tenderly ran her hands through his hair and as he struggled to decide, their breaths stayed heavy and unsure. A moment passed; a soul-searching quiet of two people who shared something deeper than could be denied, and the short opportunity to explore it.

He kissed her again, slower, their bodies pressing together in defiance of Ian's rules.

"I wish I could just be angry with you," he whispered, "and send you away," his breath caught and she nodded in understanding.

"You can still. It's okay, I understand, and I won't hold it against you," she said softly. She reached up, looked in his eyes, and kissed him gently. Her breath caught in her throat and a small cry of frustration escaped. Grant caught her lips with his, aching to fill her need.

"I want you," he said. "I've never wanted anything so much, than to just be with you, Katie," he whispered. Barely had the words left his lips, and Katelyn pulled him back down, between her legs. His hands grasped at her backside as he slowly slid into her. Her whole body tightened and waited, trying to pause the moment and feel everything. Grant's hands tightened on her skin. He gasped into her neck and she felt his body shaking above her.

"Katie," he whispered. "God, are you—" his breath caught, and he pulled back to look at her. When his eyes found hers, now moist with tears, his brow fell. "Why didn't you tell me?" he gasped. Katelyn's body burned with the need to continue. He moved to get up, but she clung to him.

"Because I knew you wouldn't if I did," she whispered. She kissed the hard line of his lips until he kissed her back. He sighed, and his body reacted to her willing warmth. She arched and rose to the rhythm he set, desperate and wanting. His breathing was ragged and pained when she felt his body convulse and he swelled inside of her. She cried out, the pleasure of it overriding any sense of trying to stay quiet. She continued the pace, wanting more, just a little more...

He held her still.

"Stop, stop, stop," he whispered desperately. "I can't. God, I can't." Shivers rolled through him and she held his face in her hands. "Katie—" he paused. "God, what have we done?" He rose, steadying himself on the desk, and turned away from her as he put himself back together. Katelyn stood and felt like every nerve was still on fire. Her bones ached to the core, her knees shook, and she only wanted more.

"Grant—"

"I should have stopped." He wiped his hand across his mouth and pulled at his hair as he stared at the wall behind her. "We shouldn't have." He turned away and shook his head. Katelyn smoothed the wrinkles from her skirt and straightened her spine.

"Why not? We're grown adults. Sex is a normal beautiful part of that. Why do you have to say no to something you wanted? That I wanted?" She stepped to him.

"You're too young to know what you want."

"I'm old enough to know that you can't tell me what I want!" she yelled back. For an instant, a flicker of something in his eyes flashed past the guilt and met her on an even field. Then, it was gone.

"Get out." He pointed to the door. Katelyn's heart stopped, and she kept her eyes leveled on his.

"I'll leave when I want to, not because you bark an order at me!"

"I am not barking—"

"And you don't get to be angry with me because of this. You're not going to suffer regret like some martyr on my account." She stalked out of the room and slammed the office door behind her.

THE WALK BACK TO THE SUTTERS' WAS HEAVY WITH quiet but for the soft sounds of crickets calling, and the chirp of frogs in the low-lying waterways. Katelyn felt cold and empty. She felt sorry for yelling at him. She felt sorry for not being honest. She felt wonderful and wanted to run back to him. But he needed to see that she wasn't some moon-eyed kid. She wasn't.

"I'm not," she said out loud, as if to convince herself. She let out a huff of breath and turned up the drive. She didn't know if she'd still have a job when she came back the next morning. She didn't know if she should just pack up and go home tonight. Maybe she should. Except, Grant.

Leaving him and his horse, two souls she cared for far more than she should, under the abusive roof of Ian Tennyson, without someone to shield them made her throw out the idea. Whether he wanted her or not, she wasn't going to abandon her work, or him. It didn't have to be love, but she had a chance to help him heal. What he chose to do once he could stand up to Ian on his own was going to be up to him. Back at the bunkhouse, she got out the sewing kit under the sink and undressed, changing into a towel.

She fixed the dress buttons that had been pulled down to the end of their strings.

Katelyn pressed the dress to her nose, smelling his warm musk, their love, hay and sweat, tears. Lord, how could she help him and not fall off her own horse? She didn't regret making love to Grant, but she didn't know how people were supposed to act around one another after something like that. It wasn't like they were in a committed relationship or anything. He wasn't her boyfriend.

Were they even lovers?

Katelyn closed her eyes and relived every delicious second, the taste of his mouth, the heat and breath. The pressure and fullness of him between her thighs, the amazing shocks of desire that seemed to fill every nerve, even now. The darkness of his eyes and the remorse in his voice. A man who didn't feel free to be himself, to have what he wanted. To live.

Katie started the shower and let the water run, hot and searing over her skin, and then turned it to cool. She needed to relax, to think. Tomorrow the sun would rise on a new day, and a new purpose.

THIRTEEN

THREE DAYS! IT HAD BEEN THREE WHOLE, GODDAMN days, and not a sign of Grant Tennyson. The first day, she had not asked, only noticed. The second day, she mentioned the empty office window to Polly. The gardener just shrugged.

"Sometimes he does this, takes long trips to meet with other owners around the state. Veterinarians, stables, racing facilities. He usually comes back even more uptight and grouchy." Polly sighed, shook her head, and moved on.

Today, the third day, she'd asked Jeffers when Grant was scheduled to return.

"The young master will be away until at least the end of the day, possibly tomorrow," he'd said, and watched Katelyn. Katelyn huffed, took her cap off and struck it against her thigh, causing a cloud of hay dust to rise up.

"Great," she grumbled.

"Is there something I can do for you, Miss Katelyn? A message perhaps I could relay to Mr. Tennyson?" Jeffers' eyes sparkled while he waited with raised brows. She looked at him, her cheeks blushing fiercely, and she was sure he knew.

"No, 'less you wanna tell him that when he's done being a

goddamn, idiotic coward that I would like to speak to him," she growled and added, under a pitiful guise, "about Hugh."

"Of course, Miss Katelyn. I saw you were working with the Pessoa system yesterday; did it not go well?"

Katelyn put her hat back on and thought of the unused Pessoa equipment she'd found from a past therapist who never made it that far. It was meant to help stabilize and build Hugh's muscles back to pre-injury levels by connecting his hindquarters with his front. He'd actually taken to it well after a lot of complaining. "No, it was fine. His gait is coming back very nicely, and I was able to rig up a wrap with ice that's helping him recover. I was hoping to show it to Grant. He wanted me—I thought he'd be around." She shook her head and looked back to the empty office.

"I'm sure he'd be very interested in what you're working on. He thinks highly of you." Jeffers said with a small smile. Katelyn looked at him.

"I wish," she stuttered in frustration and sighed, turning away from Jeffers, "wish he didn't have it so hard."

"Miss Katelyn," Jeffers said kindly to her back. "Are you concerned for the young master?"

She sighed and shook her head. "No, Jeffers. I—" She turned back to him, frustrated and at a loss. "I don't know." She went back to the stables, to Hugh's pen, and saddled him for an afternoon ride, easy along the perimeter of the grounds. Grant was either truly busy, or running from her, and she hated both. Especially since time was running short.

Being on the back of a horse soothed her. Hugh had a canter that was easy to match and she found, even in the smaller English saddle, that she could easily meld her body to his. The meditative ride was quiet, and the humid field settled heavy around them. She nudged his ribs with her heels gently.

"Let's blow some dust off, old man," she whispered in his ear and leaned in. Hugh grumbled deep in his throat and his canter became a smooth and beautiful race around the grounds, nary a jostle or jolt in his movements. Katelyn held on and felt her heartbeat pounding to the beat of his hooves. They created their own wind, and Katelyn took off her cap and let her hair free. She took him around the acreage and let him dictate the pace. In the settling of the afternoon into evening, she couldn't stop her mind from going back to the night with Grant. His pace, his need, his healing.

Was she ever going to see him again?

ACROSS THE TENNYSON'S PROPERTY, AT THE EDGE OF A long flat field, sat three hangars and the various aircraft used by the Tennysons. Grant watched through the private jet's window as they circled in their descent. He felt no comfort in coming back earlier than anticipated. He felt no joy in this 'home.' He wished the pilot would take them back up and fly him off to anywhere but here. Here, where his father was no doubt waiting for him to come back to propose to Cecilia.

Here, where Katelyn might meet him with lovesick eyes or signs of distress. Or worse, no reaction at all. He couldn't stop thinking about her. Not for the last three days. No matter what meeting he was in, no matter what hotel he had found for the night. Her body was beneath his, the taste of her was on his tongue, her sighs in his ears. When he'd brought along copies of her records to show other investors, his eyes had fallen to her handwriting and diagrams, and he'd felt her soul and eyes on Hugh. He hadn't known how much he could understand the anatomy of a horse until he was able to spend the time reading through her notes. She was an artist. She was tough. She was warm and delicious and all he wanted was to have her in his bed again. And that was something neither of them could afford.

His eyes caught a flash of the stallion from their flight path; the golden hair of his rider. He leaned against the window to watch her moving as one being with Hugh, at a clean and smooth gallop. Nearly healed, with two weeks to spare.

She hadn't left, even though he had. She'd kept working, of course, as only she would. If Hugh could run that smoothly, then her job was essentially complete. Grant's heart hammered in his chest. There would be no more chances for Ian to discover what they'd done. There would be no danger to her. Perhaps now was the perfect time to save her any further madness from the Tennyson name and send her back to Wyoming.

THE DAY WAS LONG, THE RIDE LONGER, BUT SHE DIDN'T mind. Katelyn needed it, and so had Hugh. She groomed him, with great care and detail, wrapped his right foreleg, chest, and shoulder in the ice pack, knowing he'd get out of it by the morning. She fed him a little extra and snuck him an apple from the kitchen. The lights were going down on another day without seeing Grant, and her heart felt sick. Jasmine met her at the front door with a strange look, but didn't ask questions about why she was late. Katelyn had merely said it was a long day with Hugh. She hadn't said she was purposefully taking her time to see if Grant might arrive back. He hadn't.

She helped with the dishes, as she'd missed dinner. When she looked up from the sink, she saw Jeremy eyeing his wife. When a man comes out of a worrisome spell, and looks at the woman who's been by his side all along, something happens. An appreciation. A reawakening. Katelyn knew the look from how Blake looked at Elle. How his dad still looked at his mom. How she wished someone would look at her.

Without being asked, Katelyn took the kids outside to hunt for fireflies. She cleared her throat on her way out.

"Probably take us at least a good half hour or so!" she yelled and closed the door. She could hear Jasmine giggling and rushed footsteps gunning for the back bedroom. Katelyn kept the little ones out, chasing bugs, counting stars, and listening to the owls and creatures of the night, until the baby had fallen asleep in her arms and the other three were dragging their booted feet in the dust. She enjoyed the company of children and felt the pull of regret deep inside of her.

"Come on, cowpokes, time for bed." She made plenty of noise before they came into the house in case anyone still needed to get clothes on. She offered to help put them to sleep, but Jasmine and Jeremy, both looking much more relaxed, wouldn't hear of it. They thanked her with a wink and a smile before she went back to the bunkhouse.

Damn it, she wanted to be the one winking and smiling, and red-lipped and pink-cheeked. She wanted Grant's hands on her, his mouth and teeth and tongue. She wanted...Katelyn sighed, took a shower, and settled into a chair at the kitchen table before picking up her phone. Her sister answered on the third ring.

"Hello?"

"Hey, honey," Katie said, putting a deliberate smile in her voice.

"Hey kiddo! How are you? How did the big, fancy dinner go?" Elle's delight came through the line, but Katelyn could tell she was tired from a long day and probably on her way to bed soon.

"Good! It was real... good." Katelyn got up to pace.

"What's going on?" Elle asked.

Katelyn stayed silent; "It's fine. I'm fine."

"Katelyn May Sullivan, you're a shitty liar," Elle leveled.

"Elle," Katie's voice trembled. "I may have a problem on my hands."

"What is it?"

"I just, well, you know how we—we've been joking about well, broody guys and rollin' in the hay?" Katelyn cleared her throat.

"Katelyn did you—"

"Uh, yep."

"Yep? What in the hell does, 'yep' mean?" Elle's voice rose.

"Well, the world shook, and the panties dropped, and the whole, Laney novel thing." Katelyn tried, without success, to make it no big deal. No words could do it justice, anyway.

"Katelyn! But who?" Elle's shock ripped through the line. Katelyn sighed.

"It was Grant." His name felt like a soft undercurrent with lines right to her heart.

"Oh, Katelyn," Elle whispered. "So, I guess he isn't some sixty-year-old codger, huh?" She giggled. "Oh, shit! Tell me he's not sixty."

"No," Katelyn looked around her empty room as if someone might hear. "He's not sixty." She stopped, knowing he was older than her by more than Elle would approve of. "There's just all of this amazing tension between us and he'd started to, open up and —and all the things he's dealing with and his dad and—well, he was just so hurt and I was just so lonely. And we just sort of found each other."

Elle was quiet before bursting out with a joyful giggle. "Oh my god, Katydid! That sounds amazing. I think I need to meet this guy." Katelyn could hear her sister pacing across the creaking boards of the kitchen back home. "I mean, are you two dating then?" Elle asked.

"I'm not sure. It's complicated." Katelyn thought back to the way she'd left. The look of shame and remorse on his face. How she hadn't seen him all week. "He's complicated."

"Goddamn it, aren't they all?"

"I just wish I knew what he was thinking. He didn't seem happy about it afterwards."

"Uh oh, did you take advantage of that poor man? No means no, Katelyn." Her sister doubled over with laughter.

"Jesus, Elle, could you be serious? I think he's confused," Katelyn interrupted. "It happened sort of fast, for us both, and he felt embarrassed. I think the whole thing maybe caught him off-guard. Like he lost control, and he's not a man who loses control."

Katelyn looked out the window at the darkness beyond her porch light. A set of headlights bumped down the road from Tennyson Stables; some of the late shift going home. She sighed.

"I know it had been a long time for him, maybe not since his... Jane." Katelyn's brain connected the name.

"Who's Jane?" Elle squawked.

"I don't know, and I don't think it was a pretty story."

"What happened to her?"

"I don't know, Elle. I think it had something to do with his father."

"This is some real-life *Dynasty* bullshit," Elle began.

"Kind of, yeah. Grant's dad is putting an ultimatum on him to get married to the right kind of gal and soon, so he can have a grandchild before he dies."

"Before he—just how old *is* Grant?" Laney asked.

Katelyn hesitated. "Forty? If I had to guess."

"Katelyn May!"

"What?"

Elle paused. "That's a little older than you."

"Yeah? And?"

"Fifteen years!"

"Elle, come on!" Katelyn countered. "Age isn't a problem. He's virile." She paused and her eyebrow quirked, thinking of his strong and amazing body.

"It's not that, it's just that he's just done a lot of living before you."

"Haven't I done a lot of living before him too?" Katelyn countered.

"I suppose you have. So what now? Is this serious? Do you think there is something more? Or are you not right-kind-of-gal material?" Elle asked. Katelyn leaned her head against the frame of the window and felt tears stinging the corner of her eyes as she watched the headlights down the road.

Of course she wasn't right-kind-of-gal material. She never wanted to be that. She didn't want to inherit the pain of this messed-up family. It would be better for them both if it didn't go anywhere. She may have been green when it came to love, but she wasn't an idiot.

"I'm not an idiot, Elle," she echoed out loud. The headlights disappeared into a dip in the road.

"Oh, Katie," Elle whispered. Katelyn sniffed.

"I don't regret it, or anything. It was just as perfect as it should have been. He was the right one." She wiped her eyes on the cuff of her shirt and cleared her throat.

"Katelyn, are you sure you're okay?"

"I'm just fine," Katelyn answered sharply. "I'm great. I've only got about two weeks of therapy left with Hugh. I'll probably be home in time to help Dad out at the fair even."

"Did you just decide that so you can run away from this thing with Grant?"

"Elle, please. You know me, I don't run. I miss being close to family, and Lord knows we've got plenty of work to do."

"Katydid—"

"Have you heard from Laney lately?" Katelyn interjected.

"No," Elle huffed. That was another conversation all together, and a good one for dissuading her sister. "I suppose she's all right. She'd call if it weren't, right?"

"The most romantic of us is also the loneliest? Doesn't seem right."

"I know. I wish we could find her a Grant of her own," Elle giggled.

"She wouldn't want him. They'd brood themselves into a suicide pact. She needs someone light-hearted to keep her out of her suffering-artist funk," Katelyn said distractedly, while thinking she'd just heard a car door slam. "I should go."

"All right. Take care of yourself. Let me know what happens."

"Okay."

"I mean it, Katie. I'm your big sister. I will do anything."

"I know. Thanks, Elle. I love you."

"Love you too."

They hung up, and Katelyn sunk down against the wall, deflated. Her stomach rumbled. She didn't want to eat. She just wanted to see him. She wanted to feel his lips on hers again; his teeth. She wanted him in her bed. It was all she could think about. His warm skin, burning against hers.

She closed her eyes to the swirling memory of that night. Soon, she was desperate and hungry all over again. She wanted to run to the stables and camp outside of his office until he came home, whether that was tonight or tomorrow. She wouldn't find any sleep with every inch of her body wanting him. She'd made up her mind. She would go back to Tennyson Farms and wait for him. Even if he told her no, just to be near him would be enough. She stood up and flung open the door.

GRANT STOOD THERE, HAND RAISED TO KNOCK AND silhouetted in the porch light from the Sutters' house. He stayed frozen; eyes moving slowly over her and softening when they landed on her teary eyes. He leaned away.

She didn't let him.

"Where in the hell have you been?" She gripped the front of his shirt and pulled him inside, kissing him with every ounce of pent-up frustration. He slammed the door behind them. Grant grunted and threw his arms around her. His lips were hot and wet, meeting every demand of hers. He bit at her, held her body against his, and gasped in sweet relief. She sobbed in the back of her throat and her fingers threaded into his hair.

"Katie," he breathed. "Sweet Katie. Saints, what have you done to me, lass?" he kissed her jaw and neck. He stopped and set her down to step away. "Hold on," he shook his head.

"Why?" she said with her brow pulled together. "Why?" She

came back to him. He held out his arms and struggled to control his breath.

"You're too much. Don't you see?"

Katelyn rushed him, arms hugged tight around his waist, and kissed the flesh above the open collar of his shirt, her tongue trailing down where her hands undid the buttons. Grant groaned.

"I canna control myself wi' you. For god sake's, listen to me, Katie." He gripped her by the shoulders and pushed her away. Her eyes were dreamy, and deep, and he read every dark thought inside. Every desire. He shook her gently.

"After what happened in the office, you should be running back home." His voice broke and his hands shook. "You're so young and full of opportunities and I'm not free to offer you anything. This will just end up hurting you. I shouldn't have ever touched you." He took a deep breath. "I've spent the last three days away, to try to cool off, to try to distance myself, but I—I well, it seems I'm not doing a good job of that."

"Grant, you've got it all wrong," she whispered. Here, in the safe space, away from his world, his resolve faltered.

"It's been excruciating without you, lass. I should have said something sooner." Grant stared down at their feet. She ran her hands through his hair and felt the tension in his body.

He'd run from her. Run to his job and his responsibilities. He'd run from the way she made him feel, and want, and ache. And now, in her presence, in the simple and quiet bunk house, clean and smelling like apples and soap, he was unsure and torn. His legs felt weak, and he hid his face in his hands, fighting the desire in his heart. He choked on the shame in his throat.

"I dinna ken what to do, except tell you to get as far away from me as possible."

Katelyn pulled his hands away from his face.

"You listen to me," she said sternly and bowed to look into his downcast eyes. "You listen, Grant Tennyson! I'm not some glass doll. You did not break me or condemn me to some kind of punishment. I gave myself to you, willingly." He met her eyes. "I wouldn't change a single thing about that night; except I wouldn't have walked away so easily. I was confused. I didn't—I didn't know what to say that would have made you feel better about it. I've never felt like this about anyone before." Her cool fingers dug into his wrists.

"Och, Katie," he whispered; gaze dropping to her lips.

"Don't shut the door on me." She shook her head. "Don't deny us both what we really need. What we really want. If you really did miss me, if it really is torture being without me, then make up for it. Be with me now."

He paused, and before his walls of armor could rise against her, his hand reached out, took her cheek and drew her closer. His other hand snaked around her waist and pulled her hips against his. He kissed her softly.

He felt hesitant, as though he was trying to remember what it was like to kiss a woman without motive, worry, or regret. Just to kiss her. Her lips trembled. His touch was whisper-light, and she melted beneath him. His hands slid down her arms, up again to lift her shirt over her head. His breath was ragged as he paused his kisses to look at her, the pale skin and full breasts heaving before him. He unhooked her bra and kissed his way from her shoulders down to her breasts. She arched to meet him and threaded her hands into his hair as his teeth teased her nipples into hard peaks.

"God," she whispered, and her hips pressed against his. She could feel his strong length pressing, straining against their clothes. "It was torture being without you, Grant." She swallowed a cry.

Her sure fingers undid the rest of his shirt buttons. He helped her take off the shirt and brought her back closer, holding her bare, warm skin against his. It was heaven, touching her in the soft light of evening like this. She pushed him back to the couch, their lips never parting from hungry exploration of each other. When he toppled backwards to the soft cushions, he made a surprised grunt. She shimmied out of her pants and straddled him.

"Katie," he breathed. The vision of her naked on top of him nearly made him burst. She reached up and let her hair down; it fell in golden waves over her shoulders. He reached up to touch it, soft and mesmerizing.

She stuttered and blushed. "I don't really know what I'm doing." Grant sat up, put his arms around her back and kissed her breasts, her neck, and her chin.

"Oh? Finally, something I can teach you." He smiled. She bit her lip, and he framed her face with his hands. "The things I'd like to show you," he groaned as she reached down to unfasten his pants. "That's a braw start," he whispered. She laughed, and he helped push the fabric down his hips. "Then—" he gasped and guided her hands to the length of him. She sighed in wonderment and curiosity.

She swallowed a breath, and he bit her chin.

He smiled, his ego swelling to watch her fascination. Katelyn's thighs shook, and he pulled back.

"Does it make you nervous?"

"No!" Her mouth was a perfect pink O. "I just want you so much, Grant."

"I'm here," he whispered, and helped her guide him inside. "It will feel different this way," he whispered in her ear. When she lowered herself down, the gasp tore from her throat. Grant watched her with a knowing smile.

"Oh, Grant."

"Aye, my darlin' Katie?" He chuckled and enjoyed the tight feeling of her around him. He wanted to move. He wanted to thrust, pull her down and fill her completely, but this was her time. Her body started to move of its own accord, up and down the length of him, every movement raising a pleased gasp in her throat. He pulled her hair gently back, exposing her throat to his teeth and tongue.

"Oh no," she murmured softly, and slowed her pace.

"What is it?" He sat up and held her.

"I don't know, it's—" She shook her head and her nails dug into his shoulders. Even by slowing his deep strokes, he couldn't stop her body from climaxing. She cried out and her body pulled and tensed around him. He felt every one of her strong muscles contracting and he nearly burst. Her breath was ragged and tears filled her eyes.

"Ah, you *are* a fast learner," he whispered in her ear. She hummed against his cheek and kissed him.

"What did you do to me?" she whispered between gasps.

"Didn'a you like it?"

"Oh, aye, I did." She shivered and clung to him as he rounded her backside with his hands.

"But?"

"But it," she paused, "it felt like I was going to fall off the edge of the world. Or explode. Or—" she sighed, "die." Grant chuckled low in his throat and began to move her hips once more up and down. She shivered and sighed.

"They are little deaths. Beautiful—" he grunted, "earth ending —" His breath quickened, along with hers. "God, Katie—" A shuddering climax rocked them both. She cried out and clung to him, as he bit into her neck. With heavy breath, they spiraled down from the edge together. Grant folded her close to his chest, and they fell into the cushions together. She wound her leg over his hips, pinned him down, and trailed her short fingernails over his chest. Her touch was soothing. She kissed him beneath his ear. Grant closed his eyes and felt his muscles tighten and relax at once as her delicate kisses warmed his skin.

"I came to fire you," he said. She chuckled and her lips returned to his.

"How'd that work out for you?"

"Not well. Seems you're much harder to let go of than I thought." The distant sadness in his voice startled him. Katelyn leaned up on her elbow and studied his face. Her thumb traced over his lips and he turned his tormented eyes on her.

"And that bothers you," she said, as if putting one more piece of his puzzle together.

"Doesn't it bother you? That you're sleeping with the boss? That we've crossed an ethical boundary?" His defensiveness was meant to protect the exposed and tender feelings, but he could tell from her smile that Katelyn recognized the response, typical of stubborn creatures she'd worked with before.

"Not particularly," she drawled, and leaned down to nuzzle his neck. Grant, who meant to tear out of her arms and use the moment as an excuse to distance himself, melted beneath her touch.

"No?" he breathed, while his body awakened to her gentle caress and the warm kisses down his neck.

"For one, you're not the boss of me," she said matter-of-factly. Grant grasped her arms firmly, took her mouth with his, and rolled her into the soft cushions beneath. Katelyn let out a surprised yelp.

"You're right, I suppose. You're under my father's employ. I'm not sure if that makes the situation better or worse," he said, scowling down at her.

"You have just cause to not like that man," Katelyn said in soft understanding, and searched his eyes for some sign of argument.

"What business is it of yours?" Grant argued back.

"Are you, or are you not laying naked on top of me, between my legs?" she said firmly, and raised her head to meet his gaze. Her hands tugged on his.

"I—I am," he stammered.

"Then, your emotional well-being is my business."

"Katelyn, you mustn't get caught up emotionally with this. I know it's your first experience."

"It's my *farthest* experience, I will give you that, but if you don't want my emotions getting in the way of our bodies, then you need to stop confiding in me."

"I didn'a confide in you!" he growled and moved to get up, but she pulled him down, turned them over, and they tumbled off the couch and onto the floor. Katelyn laughed, and Grant grunted. She pinned him down. He could have overpowered her, but her lips found his before he could muster the nerve to throw his strength into her.

"For the record, I don't work for your father either. I'm independently interested in Hugh's case," she breathed as she trapped his hands beside his head and bit his chin. "I haven't accepted any money, and so am not beholden to Ian Tennyson or to you. I'm my own woman," she finished with a small smile. Grant relaxed beneath her, while the rest of his body found the newly submissive position undeniably exciting. He savored her mouth, her kiss, the sweet taste of her tongue as it explored his.

"I want you to confide in me," she said, her breath quickening as her body warmed. Shivers ran through her naked skin in anticipation.

"I've nothing to tell you," he whispered the lie into her neck, wanting to pull his heart back from the edge of her precipice.

"You don't have to be afraid, Grant."

"I'm not. I canna be afraid of something that isna there." He pulled away and looked up at her.

"Suit yourself." She kissed him and slid off. He sat up, erect and panting, and watched her cross the room, throw on a shirt and running shorts and come back to stand above him.

"Tomorrow's an early day," she said and nodded at the door.

"What?"

"It's going to be a lot of work and we're starting early."

"We're? What are you talking about? Come back down here," he reached out. Katelyn stepped away and shook her head.

"Meet me in the stable at six and make sure you have a good breakfast."

"Katie," he tried to reason. She nodded at the door. Grant scowled, peeled himself up off the floor with a groan and dressed. He stormed towards the door. Katelyn stopped him; took his hands in hers and looked down.

"Thank you for coming to see me tonight," she said and reached up on her tiptoes to kiss his immobile lips. "And for the *lesson*." She smiled into his cheek. "I'd let you stay, and let you give me lots and lots of hard, deep lessons," she whispered into his ear and Grant's knees went weak with thoughts of what he could teach her. "But I don't think you're ready to talk yet, so I'll just keep my fingers and knees crossed, that you'll come around." Grant turned to argue but her lips caught his and kissed him, biting his bottom lip and she sighed.

"I don't need your help, sorting through my feelings," he whispered between kisses. "I don't have feelings."

"Of course you don't," she whispered with a smile and bit his chin. "See you tomorrow. Six, and don't make me come get you."

"I'd settle for making you cum again," he groaned and tried to press his body into hers. She allowed it and her leg slid up his thigh. She guided his hands to dip below her shorts to cup her bare bottom. Then she pulled away and slapped his hand. Grant smiled with ragged breath, so fueled with desire and confusion he could barely speak.

"Six," she said and nodded out the door. Grant huffed and turned away. He was halfway out when she leaned from the doorway to shout.

"I'm glad you didn't fire me!"

"Looks like I couldna even if I wanted to," he growled back and left.

KATELYN WATCHED HIM GO AND SIGHED. HER BODY WAS exhausted and malleable. She wanted to chase him down and drag him back to her bed. But if she had any hope of healing Grant, she had to practice tough love and control.

He needed a steady hand, consistent rules, and respectful affection. She closed the door, leaned against it, and thought about all the principles of traumatic rehabilitation she'd learned. Was it wrong to approach this broken man with the same theories of reward and consequence? It was worth a try if it could heal him and help him stand on his own.

If it was one thing Katelyn was sure of, it was that Grant Tennyson had sustained a great deal of pain and injury. He'd erected prickly and impenetrable walls to keep what little heart he had left from being hurt again. It was a layer-by-layer process, and it needed great care and gentle persuasion. Patience. Consistency. Love. She paced the room.

Love.

Could she love him? She groaned and threw herself down on the couch. Katelyn fell into the warm and love-laced cushions, snuggling into the scent of him. Of course she could. She already did.

Fourteen

THE NEXT MORNING, GRANT COULDN'T WAIT TO GET TO work. Last night she'd upended him. And while he'd fallen asleep in a deep and beautiful way that hadn't come to him in a long time, his dreams were of the brazen things he wanted to do to her still. He woke with a smile and the overwhelming desire to see her. He was a man adept in the art of lovemaking. She had shown control last night, holding him physically hostage until he paid a fee of emotional involvement. But today, he planned to make her want him to the point that she no longer cared about his past.

It didn't hurt that Ian had left that morning for a few days respite on St. Thomas. Belmont was coming up the weekend Ian arrived back, but that was days away, and until then, Grant was going to enjoy his freedom.

He woke early, jumped from his bed, and stared at his naked form in the mirror. He ran a hand down his chest, his slightly softer middle, wondering if she thought he was too old. He hadn't cared what a woman had thought about his appearance since he was a much younger man. But Katelyn was young. She was vibrant. She was soft and supple; strong and perfect. Her skin smelled like apples and she tasted sweet on his tongue.

He wondered how she would taste when he ran his tongue over her in the most sensitive places. Grant looked down and saw his fully aroused member pulsing. Just the thought of her. He wondered if she was already in the barn or if he could be there waiting for her. Would she want a private meeting in his office first? He wanted it. He mussed his hair and headed for the bathroom to freshen up. He buzzed the kitchen as he brushed his teeth, demanding coffee and a small breakfast before he was to spend the day in the stable. Jeffers arrived within minutes, before Grant had even gotten a shirt on. He looked at his young charge only briefly before setting the tray on the desk in the corner of Grant's room.

"Are you quite well this morning, Mr. Tennyson?"

"Fine. Better than, why?" Grant said in his short, gruff manner.

"Seems you have a rash," Jeffers said, looking at Grant's neck. Grant spun to look in the mirror and saw the delicate bruises on his neck from her eager mouth.

"It's nothing," he sniffed, and pulled his shirt on. Jeffers looked at him sideways with a smile.

"Will you be out in the stable all day, sir?"

"Possibly," Grant answered, buttoning up his shirt.

"Shall I have your calls forwarded to the stable office?"

Grant thought. He had a lot of responsibilities to attend to, ones he'd blatantly pushed from his mind in his rush to be with her again. His fingers stopped on the last button without fastening it. How could he have gotten so caught up, so quickly? He scowled in the mirror. He wasn't caught up. He was lonely, and she was providing a moment of physical release. His work would only improve, his focus would be better. She was offering therapeutic distraction. That was all.

"It won't be all day. I'm unsure what Miss Sullivan wants from me, but I agreed to accompany her on her therapy schedule for the morning."

"Very good, sir." Jeffers nodded and turned to leave. "Shall I prepare lunch and have it sent out?" he asked.

"No, it shouldn't be necessary. I have other things to attend to today."

"Of course." Jeffers nodded and left.

THE SMELL OF THE OLD BARN WAS COMFORTING. IT made her feel at home as she took up a tangled mess of bridles that a lazy stable hand had piled on a hook outside the tack room. Her fingers ran the length of the leather and she let the feel of it and the smell relax her mind. A thousand happy memories faded in and out, like sunshine bouncing off of a lake. The games of hide and seek, the afternoon naps in haylofts, and the endless afternoons, days even, riding bareback through the paddocks and shabby fields of her home state; the freedom of an uncomplicated childhood. Back when she didn't notice boys, let alone dwell on them.

Boy, was she dwelling now.

The weight of homesickness added itself to the burden of Grant and how she'd ever thought she could save his heart. People didn't change, unless they wanted to. People didn't heal, unless they wanted to. How could she possibly make him want to heal? She was young and pliable, and his life was one near-fatal scar after another, built up into an impenetrable fortress. Katelyn blew a strand of hair off of her face and rolled over the thoughts of Grant and the encroaching time when she would have to leave. Could she reach the center of that fortress by then? It would take a pretty strong force. It would take a family's worth of love to even stand a chance at reaching a man who hadn't had a family. Her brain played with the possibility.

GRANT FOUND HER THIS WAY, STANDING WITH ONE HIP cocked, one booted toe turning in the ground as she fingered the bridle straps and gently untangled them with meditative care. He watched her for longer than necessary, soaking in all of the details that made Katelyn shine. Her hair hung down her back in a plain ponytail, no unnatural hue added to the sun-streaked honey blonde. Her tank top was tight across her breasts and fitted into the waist of her well-loved Wranglers, which hugged her hips just so. Her jaw was relaxed, her eyes cast down the bridge of her slightly crooked nose. How had she broken it, he wondered, bemused, before continuing his study. Her shoulders were toned, and small freckles splashed across them. Her neck was graceful, and the sweetest strawberry mark v-ed into the nape of her hair. Her ears were unadorned, and it made him smile in the secret revelation that she didn't have them pierced. He wondered how many people noticed that.

Grant felt the sudden weight of knowing too much. He needed to focus on the truth. She was his distraction, and he would teach her how to enjoy her body. His study changed; a wolfish saunter down her body, her full breasts, her well-muscled legs and the boots that were scuffed and loved within an inch of their soles. Focusing on her physical beauty took his mind off of how she upended him in other ways. He wanted her, desperately, now. Thoughts of the night before flooded his mind, and he felt them intensely, as if it were moments, not hours, that separated them.

Grant checked over his shoulder for anyone else in the stable, but the crew always began the day with feeding and watering of the horses, not in the arena. They were alone, and his father was gone on business. He was a free man, and Katelyn was his to enjoy. His body swelled with anticipation.

"Can't figure out if you're mad at me after last night," she said without lifting her eyes. Grant jumped; a flush spread up from his collar and he felt like a desperate voyeur, caught in the act. She smiled. "Because you *look* like you're angry, but you're not yelling."

"I'm not angry," he said, and his eyes burned across her body.

"No?" she whispered. "You look angry."

"What you're seeing is a man who wants you," he said.

"I've seen what men—"

"No, you've seen what cocky little lads look like when they're chasing a piece of tail."

"And you're not a cocky lad?"

"I'm a grown man. A grown man wanting you is not the same thing."

"Well, explain that to me." She shook her head. "Because little boys and grown men," she snorted, "ain't much different than a pair of jacks."

He stalked to her and took the bridle from her hands. He pinned her against the wall and lifted her hands above her head. The leather straps of the bridle swung down and cascaded around her heaving chest. He wanted to tie her up with it; or have her use it on him. The thought made his breath quicken, and he nuzzled her cheek and neck. He bit her gently and garnered the satisfying sound of her gasping in response.

"A boy looks for a warm hole and instant gratification, with no care for what you need or want. A man," his hands loosened on hers as they trailed down her body with soft caresses over her ribs and up to her breasts.

"A man looks at you and imagines all the ways he can make you cum. And within each detailed fantasy you ask for, he delays his own satisfaction until you are absolutely witless, breathless and spent in his arms." With each word, his voice sunk beneath her skin and made Katelyn shiver and shake.

"Then, and only then," he continued, tenderly running his teeth along her unadorned earlobe, nuzzling her jaw, and biting her neck, "does he allow himself release." His hand cupped her tight breast and his thumb passed over its hardened tip. A surprised gasp broke from Katelyn and her hips came off the wall. "I'm not angry with you Katie, I'm angry that you aren't in my bed. I'm angry that I'm not fulfilling your fantasies."

"Grant," Katelyn shook in his arms and her hands threaded

behind his head, into his curly hair as he dipped his lips lower. She pulled, but he was determined and lifted her shirt, pulled away her bra and teased her other nipple into a hard peak with fast flicks of his tongue and gentle nuzzling of his teeth. Katelyn felt her thighs shake and her body throb. Her breath came in fast gasps as his hand dipped below the waist of her jeans and his fingers found her. Katelyn writhed against him as he pressed her up against the wall, his mouth still on her breast, his long fingers inside, his broad palm cupping the sensitive bud between her legs.

"God, Grant," she whispered in the still and quiet barn as his fingers continued their skillful stroking. "Oh, God," she cried, louder, as her body shuddered. Grant sighed with her release, lifting his gaze to watch her expression as her world broke open. The pout of her lips, the flush of her cheeks, and the small beads of sweat on her brow. Her hands clung to his shoulders while the world spun. She folded and sobbed into his chest. He hated that he wanted to whisper sweet endearments. He hated that he wanted to offer up something in return.

"Dinna cry, sweet Katie," he said softly and reached around to cup her backside and lift her into his arms. "We're safe here. You're safe with me." Her legs wrapped around his waist, and he nestled into the soft space between her thighs while he kissed every inch of her face.

"That wasn't," she gasped and swallowed. "That wasn't on the agenda for today." She shook her head. Grant chuckled into her neck and brought his other hand, still clenched on the leather bridle, to caress her chin.

"Oh? Had you scheduled to torture me with your sweet body until I confessed some brutal truths to you?" he said and pressed into her. She threw her head back, and he caught it in his hands, studying the tracks of tears down her cheeks. He had to give her something. He wanted to give her something, for the beautiful moment she'd given him.

"What more do you need to know except that Ian hates me

and has since he knew he had a bastard child. What more do you need to know except I dinna have any love in my heart for him either? That's all the story that's in me, Katie."

"It's not," she whispered, sniffed, and dropped her mouth back to his, kissing the corners of his mouth, his chin, the hard line of jaw that held back words between clenched teeth. She undulated her hips with muscles accustomed to maintaining balance and a strong hold, moving in time to his own uncontrolled circles of want.

"And I don't want to torture you into offering up the truth," she said and bit his lip so hard that he pulled back in surprise. "I want to earn your trust," she said and untangled from him. They stumbled. She took the bridle from him and drove him back with kisses and bites, and the confusion of heat, and sweat, and need mixed, until they were in the empty tack room and she kicked the door closed with an ominous slam. She bolted the latch.

"Katie?" The confidence fell from his eyes. "What are you doing?"

"Torture or trust," she whispered against his lips, kissing him. He could taste the tears in her mouth, the subtle change of her body chemistry. "We'll just have to see how you take it."

"Take what?"

"Right now, you're scared. You feel like I'm here to hurt you, leave you, use you, get what I want from you and drop you in the dirt, because that's all you've ever known; someone else determining your worth. Someone else buying your merit. You feel like you can't show what's hiding in there because it's all that's really left to you. All that's left of someone who loved you once. Someone who isn't here anymore." She pushed at his hard and heaving chest that gasped for control even as she cowed him back to the bench beside the windows.

"That isna true." His voice was strangled and afraid.

"You feel like you can't open that lock box inside your chest, but you can. You can here, and you can with me," she interrupted and gave him a final nudge until he was sitting on the bench. Katelyn knelt down in front of him, unbuckled his belt and unfastened his jeans. "But you have to want to," she said and looked up at him, kneeling, in apparent submission. But Katelyn was not submitting. She was in control.

"Ah, Katie." His eyes closed as she took his hard cock in her mouth and ran her wet tongue in circles around it, her full lips pressing in delicious waves that made him dizzy and desperate. "Please, stop." He reached down to lift her, but she caught his hands in the bridle, tied them together, and made him stand.

"Do you want me to stop? I will."

Grant didn't answer. He was captivated, and drunk, and he thought his body might explode. He didn't want to stop. He wanted to let her read all of his secrets, but he was scared she would break him. She bent down and pushed his pants to his ankles and ran her hand up his injured thigh as she stood. The pain that shot through his body was confused by the pleasure of her touch, and he shook.

"You tell me, when you want to stop. You tell me, when it's too much. But if you want me," she whispered. "If you want someone to tell, it's just us here. Sometimes it hurts to get past things, but it's okay to be in pain with me."

"Katie," he breathed.

"You were hurt," she whispered into his chin. "You were hurt and you think nobody cared. But that's not true. I care. Hugh cared. He could have run away to anywhere, but he ran back here. So someone would know you were missing. Jeffers cared, and he saw to your recovery in the hospital. You aren't alone," she whispered. Grant wanted to leave, but his hands were still tied and she held them while the other hand expertly stroked his throbbing cock.

"Katie, stop...stop!" Her hand stilled.

"Admit I'm right," she breathed against his chest, keeping her body close to his.

"No!"

"Admit I'm right, and I'll reward you." She gasped and turned away to press her full bottom against him. She lifted his tied hands over her head, her back pressed to his chest, her strong backside cradling his arousal. "Admit it, Grant."

What did it matter what he confessed to her while they were alone? As long as he got to have her.

"Yes," he whispered.

"Say it." She slid her jeans down her hips, naked and trembling heated skin, pressing against his. "You're not alone," she whispered.

"I'm not—not alone," he groaned and thrust into her without reserve. She gasped and sighed at the pressure and newness of the position. "I'm not alone. I'm—God," he groaned.

"You're not alone. You're cared for," she gasped between his frantic thrusts.

"I'm not alone. I'm cared for," he grunted and she bit into his forearm, arched her back, took him fully as his body exploded. Her own body responded and tightened in waves.

Their loud breathing broke the quiet of the room, where leather straps and crops, saddles, and ropes surrounded them in potential, waiting. Quiet dust motes danced in the light of the morning sun, and Grant felt the sweat on his back drip down as she released his hands from the bridle. He kept his arms wound tightly around her; his head collapsed onto her back with a groan of surrender.

She stepped away, righted her clothing, and came back to him as he slowly did the same. His head hung, and a tear made its way down the outer edge of his cheek. Katelyn took him by the hand, tested the fight in his hold, and led him to the bench. She pushed him to sit, crawled into his lap, smoothed his hair from his face and watched his downcast eyes lift to hers.

"That—" He cleared his throat. "That didn't mean what you think it meant."

"Do you think you can ride today?" she said, not acknowledging the weak structure he was trying to put back in place.

"Again? Christ sakes, lass," he sighed and his head fell back to the wall. She laughed and kissed the corners of his smile. The first real smile she'd seen on his lips.

"No, someone much bigger and hairier."

"Uh, I dinnae ken how far your idea of torture extends, but I assure that I'm just fair and fine with your size and smooth skin, sweet Katie."

"Come on, darlin'." She giggled and nipped his chin before bouncing off his lap and to the door. Grant sighed. He felt a lightness from his shoulders as he followed her into the arena. She took his hand and led him to an older gelding, a former champion, that he'd managed to save right from under Ian's nose.

"Scotty," Grant whispered with relief. "Where'd she find you, old man? One hoof in the grave, I wager." He laughed to see the docile giant. Katelyn didn't interrupt the exchange, but saddled the horse with ease and grace. Grant watched and noted that she did so with more hesitation than he'd seen before.

"Do you need help, horse whisperer?" he chided.

"English saddles and I are new friends. I'm always in the midst of learning something." She quirked her eyebrow over the back of the large horse and Grant came closer.

"Oh?"

"I call it, being a perpetual idiot. My sisters agree." She tightened the straps and Grant continued to watch her.

"How many sisters?" he asked.

"Two. Laney June is the oldest. She's a writer and teaches at the University of Wyoming. Elle, Eleanor Augusta, is the overlooked middle child who's the best damn baker and cook you'll ever meet."

"Ah, so you're the baby?"

"I'm grown enough," she said back, irked by the slight to her age.

"Laney June, Eleanor Augusta...so, what is your middle name, Katelyn? Let me guess. October on account of you being scary as hell," he teased. She smiled.

"Tell me yours first."

"That's a strange middle name," Grant said. Katelyn scoffed and threw the stirrup over Scotty's back, almost hitting Grant's beautiful, smiling face.

"Lachlan. Grant Lachlan Tennyson, formerly Blackwood, before Ian made me change it." His mother's last name was a long time from his lips, strange and full in his mouth, and he whispered it again. Katelyn watched him, not missing the subtle sadness in his eyes.

"Blackwood is a fine name," she commented.

"It's no Irish mutt like Sullivan," he snapped.

"Ha! Mutt! All the Irish are mutts. Tough, long-lived, cagey bastards, every one of us," she said with a light in her eyes and a brogue of her own, and he smiled over the horse where she'd bent down to check his hooves. "That's what my granddad would say, least."

"Ah, I see."

"The Scots and Irish, we have no beef, you know. If it weren't for the Brits, we'd get along fine," she said. Grant was not so dull as to miss the dig about Ian.

"Katelyn December, on account of your cold, cold heart." She broke into a fit of laughter and patted Scotty's foreleg and chest while whispering how good a boy he was. Grant heard the same purr in her words to him.

"Katelyn May. Born in May—"

"In the middle of a freak snowstorm in the hayloft of a barn," Grant finished, remembering the story. "You've been around horses from the very start." He studied her.

"They comfort me. More than people most days."

"Aye, I ken that," he said, and nodded. The moment was soft and tender. He reached his hand across Scotty's back and grazed the back of her hand with his fingertips. Katelyn's heart was lost, and she felt the sudden, inescapable fear of knowing she might very well lose him. She looked away.

"Okie dokie, Grant Lachlan Blackwood, get your arse on this horse."

"I havena ridden in a long time."

"Well, that's not true," she winked. "But, I think *you* should hold the bridle this time," she whispered over Scotty's back.

"Katelyn," Grant's hand went instinctively to his right leg.

"What? You need a boost?"

Grant scowled. "I dinna need a feckin boost."

"Well, then get on the horse," she said back. His leg ached, pain shooting through in remembrance of the fall that hadn't killed him. His face went pale.

"Ugh, you're such a baby," she sighed and groaned. "Come here."

"What?"

"Just," she sighed, patted Scotty's great russet nose as she passed, "trust me." She offered him her knee to step up on.

"I don't see the point to this. We're not even working with Hugh." He scowled and deflected the trauma surging through his veins.

"You aren't ready for Hugh, and he's not ready for you yet. You want to ride him again? You need to prove to me you can handle it."

"I dinnae need to prove a feckin' thing to you."

"Get on the horse, Grant." she yelled back, somehow not angry.

"Och, you wretched lass." He mounted without help, with a grace that she hadn't expected, and swung his long leg over the back of the complacent gelding. Without so much as a nod in her direction, he took the reins and set off with Scotty on a canter around the arena.

"STUBBORN IDIOT," HE BREATHED, AND STOLE GLANCES over his shoulder to where she watched him, as if she were trying to find his hitch. He sat up, but the rhythmic hoofbeats and the movement below him made it difficult to stay stiff. The gentle jostle was not at all like Hugh's lithe speed. Soon, he wasn't thinking of Katelyn at all, only the feeling in his body, the pull of his legs, and the tightening of his core as he found balance.

He didn't know how much time had gone by, but people filed into the arena in slow waves, and soon, most of the staff was there. Some with smiles and approving nods, some with sheer disbelief. They looked to Katelyn, who studied Grant's body and reaction time. He took Scotty on a short course over low jumps and in graceful figure-eights. When he felt his right quad start to shake and pull, he turned back and stopped Scotty just shy of where Katelyn stood, arms crossed in front of her chest and a knowing smile on her beautiful, pink-kissed lips. He dismounted.

"There? Happy?"

"Well, don't ask me; you know I enjoyed the ride." She smiled and raised an eyebrow. "The only thing that matters is how you feel about it." She offered Grant a few pieces of molasses treats, which he gave to the contented horse. Grant took a few moments to give Scotty attention, and stroke his thick neck while he thought.

"How is your leg?"

"What?"

"The femur that you broke, right side. If I had to wager, it was probably closer to the hip than the knee." His head snapped back to hers. "Plus, I saw the scar in the tack room," she whispered, not subtly covering her mouth.

"It twinges."

"I bet it does."

"What do you intend to do about that? Give me a massage and feed me cookies if I comply with your treatments?"

"Well shit, that sounds like a really good deal. Why would you be mad about that?" Grant opened his mouth to berate her for treating him like a horse, when a quiet clearing of throat cut through their discussion.

"Excuse me, sir, your father is on the phone. He says it is quite urgent. About Belmont next week, I believe."

"Did you tell him where I am?"

"No sir, I said you were in the middle of a training call. I did not mention the nature of your business," Jeffers said with a kind nod. Grant's heart slowed.

"See, you are loved," Katelyn whispered. Grant scowled down at her.

"I should go."

"Probably." She nodded.

"Thank you," he said and wanted to lean down and kiss her, but held back. The arena was full of prying eyes.

"Thanks for showing up this morning. Good luck in there, Blackwood," she added under her breath. Grant turned back and shook his head at her before following Jeffers out of the arena and back to the world he was committed to.

Katelyn sighed. Her body was still throbbing from their encounter, her brain busy with all that he had said, and hadn't. She groomed Scotty, put away his tack in the room where, not an hour before, they'd made the most incredible, passionate progress. She only had two weeks, if the imposed time limit still stood. It wasn't a matter of Hugh being well enough, it was now a matter of helping Grant to find some peace.

Taking Hugh through his normal routine, warm-up, massage, riding, more massage, a look at his dietary log, and a good steady grooming was just what she needed to keep her hands and mind busy. She stretched her time out in the corral with the staff and other horses. The honest work was good for her mind and distracted her away from how hard she was falling for Grant. She focused on practicing on the English saddle, and offered to teach some of the team what she knew about Western style, including a short lassoing lesson. It made the day go by, and before she knew it, the stable was emptying out.

Katelyn checked all the stalls, gave nightly goodbyes to the horses and the few stable workers still there, and walked out into the cooling air. She heard Grant's voice cut through the din of crickets and katydids.

"He's practically healed. His speed is improv—" Grant paused, his shoulders back up to his ears as she watched through the window. "Yes, I suppose she is. Well, I'd have to discuss that...I gave her six weeks to—well, if you're so damn concerned a—" He paused, the person on the other end cutting him off finally for good. "Yes, Ian. Of course." Grant hit the button and tossed his phone onto the paper-crowded desk before pulling at his hair. He turned to look out the window at the stables and saw her staring. He shook his head, in a strange sort of defeat, and closed the blinds. Katelyn scowled, screwed up her mouth in a frown, and took her own pause to breathe.

"Slow and steady wins this race," she whispered to herself. "Today was a big day, and we've got years of unwinding to do." Without looking back, she gathered her gear from the stables and made the long and lonely walk back to Sutter Farm.

Fifteen

Katelyn put in an arduous morning, helping Hugh get reacquainted with some of the herd. There was a young filly he had taken an interest in, and she thought it might be an opportunity to test his abilities. Then again, if the horse wasn't on the books as one of the best possible mates, she could get in trouble. Katelyn stopped the train of thought that led to her and Grant, rather than Hugh's recovery.

Jim stopped by that afternoon to see how things were going with Katelyn and the job. They talked for a good half hour and Jim visited with Hugh. To Katelyn's great delight, the horse immediately took to the older gentleman.

"You know, if you want to see what all the fuss is about, Sharon and I have box seats this year at Belmont. We'd love to have you join us." Katelyn watched a grasshopper whisk away beneath the morning light, its red underwings clicking loudly in the space of the conversation.

"I've never been to a race. I mean, not like that. Rodeos and whatnot, when I used to barrel race, but nothing like that."

"It's a helluva lot more pompous and cleaner than a rodeo, unfortunately, but I know Sharon would love to see you, and we've got a jet that needs some hours put on it—you just say the word, yeah?"

Katelyn nodded and hugged him before he left. She was daydreaming about getting some flying time in her logbook, when she rounded the corner of the stable doors, and her eyes fell to a pair of shiny black riding boots. Katelyn raised her eyebrows in disbelief at the outfit, and the woman who wore it.

"What the hell—o? Hello," she stuttered and tried to mask her reaction at the ridiculously tight, tan pants on thin legs, designer white blouse, and perfectly styled, shining blonde hair. Katelyn reached up self-consciously and pulled a piece of hay out of her own, and dusted her hands off on her even dustier shirt.

"And who are you?" the woman sneered.

"Who's asking?"

"Cecilia Langston, Grant Tennyson's fiancée, and the future owner of this facility." The woman narrowed her eyes on Katelyn, who hoped her surprise was kept below the surface of her scowl. Fiancée? He'd told her there were expectations and duties to fulfill, but he'd never mentioned an actual fiancée.

"Katelyn Sullivan. I'm the equine therapist working with Hugh." Katelyn held out her hand. Cecilia stared down at it with disgust.

"Ew, no. I just washed my hands."

Katelyn dropped her hand back to her side. Normally, it didn't bother her being a 'grubby tomboy' in the company of more feminine women. But this woman was different. Maybe because she was so stunning. And Grant's fiancée.

Katelyn's heart dropped, and she wondered why in the hell Grant would stray from such a woman. And what kind of man would have taken on a lover when he was engaged? To be fair, he had tried to end things with her. She hadn't listened. The unfamiliar sting of self-doubt fell like a dark stone in the pit of her stomach.

"Right," Katelyn cleared her throat. "Is there anything I can help you with?"

"I'm riding Hugh today," Cecilia said firmly. Katelyn straightened her spine and her eyebrows rose.

"Oh, really?"

"I'll need him saddled. Get him ready."

"And why exactly do you think I would do that?" Katelyn put her hands on her hips and leaned forward.

"It's your job!"

"First and foremost, if you can't saddle your own horse, you're hardly qualified to ride one. Secondly, I'm not a stable hand. I'm Hugh's therapist," she said again. "Hugh's well-being is *my* job right now, and he's under *my* treatment plan. He's not some fairytale steed givin' out princess pony rides. Thirdly, for your own safety, but more for his, I don't think it's a good idea." Grant stepped out from his office behind Cecilia. From the narrowing of his eyes and his clenched jaw, he certainly didn't look at her like a man in love. Cecilia continued on, unaware.

"Just who do you think you are? Your opinion doesn't matter here. You don't matter. Hugh will be *my* horse, *my* investment."

"Does Grant know you're here?" Katelyn asked, not looking at him.

"What does that matter? It's none of your business when Grant and I see each other."

"Huh, well, that's probably true." Katelyn rocked back on her boots and nodded in consideration. "However, I am in charge of Hugh's recovery and I say he's not ready to be mishandled."

"As though you could stop me from riding him?"

Katelyn looked at the woman's frail frame. "Lady, I don't think you want to test that theory."

"How dare you threaten me. If Grant were here, I'd have him fire you on the spot!"

"Well shit, I guess it's your lucky day." Katelyn said and pointed behind her. Cecilia scowled and turned to see Grant lounging against the office door, an odd smile on his face that sent shivers through both women for different reasons.

"Grant," Cecilia breathed in surprise.

"Ah, my darlin' Cecilia. Was I mistaken, or did you just introduce yourself as my fiancée? Is that something you and Ian worked out without me?" he asked with measured tones falling in the space between.

"Well, I—well, we're practically—" Cecilia stuttered and stepped back.

"Sounds like you two lovebirds have some things to discuss. I'll leave you to it." Katelyn took a bridle from the wall and walked, determined, to Hugh's stall.

THE ANGER IN GRANT'S CHEST BOUND HIS BREATHING. He walked to the distressed blonde with his fists clenched at his sides.

"I never asked you to marry me, Cecilia. So, to find you barging onto my property—"

"Well, technically, it's your father's prop—"

"Threatening my staff—" Cecilia turned her embarrassment and horror on Katelyn's behavior.

"You heard the way she was treating me. I couldn't let her talk to me that way. What kind of woman would let herself be treated like that? Certainly not one who deserves to be your wife."

"You are not my wife! And if you were, and I ever heard you talking to someone like that, I'd turn you out on the street."

"You talk to people that way all the time." Cecilia argued back.

"I *used* to talk to people that way. It's become distasteful."

"Change of heart? Why?" Grant's eyes inadvertently fell behind Cecilia, to where Katelyn had disappeared into Hugh's stall. Her calculating eye didn't miss the momentary weakness.

"Is it because of that little pigpen who's probably screwing every filthy wrangler in this barn?" Cecilia's false sweetness was gone and she looked to where Katelyn had disappeared. Grant's anger flared, and he hit the wall above Cecilia's head with his fist. She startled and dropped her crop.

"You will not malign Katelyn Sullivan," he growled with a deepening Scottish burr. Cecilia's cower lessened and her eyes lit with anger. "Or any of the people in my employ."

"Malign?" Cecilia's anger grew as she straightened. "Are *you* sleeping with that little vagrant?"

"I dinna need to discuss any of my life with you, least of all what I do in my bed." he yelled back.

"Ian would be very displeased if he thought you were—" Cecilia's threat was interrupted by Katelyn, clearing her throat in the hall.

"Hugh's ready, *Ms. Langston*." They both turned in surprise. Grant studied Katelyn's aloof expression and wondered if a lesson was about to occur.

"What?" Cecilia spat.

"You're right, Cecilia." Grant smiled and stepped away. "You should get a feel for your future investment."

Cecilia stood up, looked between the two of them, adjusted her shirt, straightened her hair and regained her composure. She picked up her crop and stormed past Katelyn into Hugh's stall, sniffing disgustedly as she passed. Grant looked at Katelyn with his head turned.

"How 'ready' is Hugh?"

"Oh, he's practically chomping at the bit," Katelyn grumbled. "Besides, I wouldn't deny the future *Mrs.* Tennyson anything. It wouldn't be my place," she finished. Her pert nose turned up as he looked down at her.

"Oh, come now, Katie. You know she's not my fiancée."

"It's not my business who you marry," Katelyn interrupted and dropped her eyes. The way her frown quivered took away his teasing countenance and made him feel empty, and angry, and desperate to explain.

"Katie—"

"Don't...please, don't call me Katie." A sudden shriek from Hugh's stall interrupted Katelyn's fumbling heart. She looked back towards the commotion.

"You probably shouldn't be here for this, if for no other reason than to avoid being an accessory." She nodded her head in the direction of the scuffle.

"Dinna be daft, lass. I wouldna miss this for the world." He chuckled as they walked towards the stall. Pawing hooves scraped the dirt ground of his stall, and hard stomping followed from inside the pen. Grant and Katelyn rushed in to find the saddled thoroughbred cornering a very startled Cecilia against the back wall. Her hair was in an ungodly state of dishevelment. Her pants and pristine shirt had been smeared with horse manure when she'd fallen and tried to crawl away from the angry and huffing beast.

Katelyn crossed her arms in front of her chest.

"Wow! You were right. I guess my opinion about this whole horse thing really *doesn't* matter. I can hardly believe how well you're handling him. You certainly do have a way." She shook her head in awe. "But you know, a pigpen like me is easily impressed," she said.

"Get him away, save me!" Cecilia gasped.

Grant put his hands up and shrugged, trying desperately to contain his glee.

"Save you? But, that's *your* horse!" Katelyn yelled over Hugh's snorting threats. "He's *your* property. I'd better go attend to some duties more of my station. I'm pretty sure there's a filthy stable hand somewhere around here that I haven't slept with yet." Katelyn turned to leave.

"No, wait! You, girl. Help me!" Cecilia cried.

"Girl?"

"Kacey!"

"Nope." Katelyn shook her head.

"Karen? Khloe, please!"

"Lady, if you can't remember my name, I can't help you," Katelyn bit.

Grant chuckled. Hugh moved in and leaned his head down, charging the scrambling woman as she crossed to the other side, crawling through the muck and hay.

"Katelyn, if you please. I think Miss Langston has had enough of Hugh's company for one day."

"Are you sure?" Katelyn looked up at him with her eyebrow cocked. He smiled and her heart flip-flopped. She wished he wouldn't be so charming. Not for a soon-to-be-married man who she had no right to love. She sighed.

"Yes! Katelyn! Please," Cecilia gasped with relief. Katelyn whistled and banged the tin cup on the wall where it hung. Hugh's ears perked up.

"Hey, jackass, that's enough," Katelyn said. Hugh snuffled, blew snot into Cecilia's face and pawed at the ground. "*No*, enough," Katelyn said again and rattled the cup. He turned and pranced away as if he'd just won first place in the Fremont County fair.

"You're such a dick sometimes, you know that?" she said affectionately and scratched him behind his ears. Cecilia came off of the ground, breathing heavily and looking down at her ruined outfit in disgust.

"You're going to pay for this," she growled. Katelyn's hands gripped Hugh's reins, and she looked around his head. Grant put his hand on Hugh's withers.

"It's hardly Miss Sullivan's fault. You stepped into his stall, despite the warning of how temperamental he is. It's actually quite fortunate she was here to contain him."

Hugh whinnied and craned his neck to nuzzle Grant on the shoulder. The small gesture caught Katelyn by surprise. Hugh responded to Grant because they were both relaxed. She glowed with excitement that this could be the major step they both needed to heal. Their eyes locked over Hugh's neck.

"That horse and you, girl. You're both horrible little monsters. Ian will hear about this. My father will hear about this." Cecilia picked manure out of her shirt pocket with disgust and flung it across the room. "Grant, I expect an apology. This is no way to begin our relationship."

"Cannae argue with that. P'haps we just shouldna begin it," Grant said dryly as she came closer.

"Walk me to my car," she demanded with a shaky voice. Grant looked down at Cecilia, covered in manure, with amusement in his eyes.

"Oh, I would, but I just washed my hands."

Cecilia screamed and stormed from the barn, cursing and whipping anything in reach with her crop on her way out. They watched her go. When she'd turned out of sight, Grant turned back to Katelyn.

"Katie."

"Please, Grant. I know I don't have any right to interfere in your business. But please don't marry *that* woman. Any other one, but not her. Okay?" Katelyn shook her head as she stared off to where Cecilia's yells could still be heard. She stroked Hugh's neck lovingly and leaned her forehead into his calm and steady back.

"*Any* other woman?" Grant said.

"I know you've got to, someday soon. But not her. God almighty, the only thing I reckon she could nurture is a pit of vipers."

"Nurture?"

"Isn't that part of your father's plan? Acceptable bride, good breeding, 'foal' to carry on the name?"

"You say it like I'm nothing more than another one of his horses," Grant's voice was tight.

"Well," Katelyn swallowed. "Are you? More than that?"

"Am I?" he questioned painfully back.

"To somebody you are." Katelyn's eyes burned with tears. She held them back. "I—I mean, you should be, more to somebody," she stuttered. They both turned to the sound of car tires squealing away and a dust cloud blew down the dirt road. Katelyn shook her head and led Hugh into his paddock, where she took off his tack and talked quietly to him.

"Well, that's a lot to ask. Arranged marriages rarely begin with love, and besides, who in this world would care what happens to me?" He didn't ask or have to think before helping her unbuckle the saddle and sliding it carefully off of Hugh's back.

"We already talked about this yesterday. Jeffers does. And I do, you dense son-of-a-bitch. I care what happens to you." she said angrily over Hugh's back.

"What? Care about me enough to tell me who to marry? Care enough to see the unfairness of the situation? Is that as far as it extends?" Katelyn paused and fought with the truth on her tongue.

"I'm hardly qualified in matters of the heart."

"The heart?"

"Well? Isn't marriage a matter of the heart?"

"To some people it's just a business merger," he countered.

"Like Cecilia?" Grant didn't answer. Katelyn huffed through her nose in a very Hugh-like manner, and took off the riding blanket.

"Marriage is supposed to make your life better. It's supposed to give you a safe place to land, a partner, a person you can always come home to, who always comes home to you. A marriage is supposed to be a promise. It's not a contract." Katelyn said and hung the blanket up. When she turned back around, he was staring at her, his eyes searching hers. Her mouth went dry, but she didn't back away from his gaze. "And you shouldn't settle for anything less. You deserve someone who'll make you that promise." She bit her lip.

He stared down at her mouth. Katelyn's breath caught. She wet her lips and stood in front of him.

"What?"

"You," he paused, "you never cease to surprise me, Katie May Sullivan," he said. A soft knock sounded and they both looked to the stable door, where Jeffers had cleared his throat.

"Excuse me, sir, if you'll pardon the interruption. Dinner is ready."

Grant watched as Katelyn took Hugh into a different, clean stall for the night. When she had secured the door and given him a final goodnight scratch, Grant held his hand out to her.

"Have dinner with me," he said. Katelyn looked at his hand. She rubbed her dirty fingers down her jean-clad thigh self-consciously.

"I'm dirty," she said.

"I dinna care." His fingers shook with agitation.

"Are you sure?"

"Yes," he interrupted. "We can talk about tomorrow's vet visit, or your sister's novels, or your father's hay sales, or the sugar content of early-morning grass, it doesn't matter. I simply would," Grant paused. "I would very much like your company this evening."

Katelyn stared down at his hand.

"Okay." She nodded, slipped her fingers into his. Jeffers looked back over his shoulder with an approving light in his eyes. "Shouldn't I clean up first?" Katelyn asked.

"No, I prefer you as you are," Grant said.

Prefer you as you are, Katelyn thought with a sigh. She'd never heard a man say that to her before. She'd never been this affected by one.

Sixteen

They walked down the dark hallways of the house, which seemed even more a prison after the warm and earthy smell of the barn. Grant led her into the dining room, pulled out her chair, and Katelyn blushed at the chivalry she wasn't accustomed to. She cleared her throat and took a sip of water from the crystal glass.

"It feels strange in here," she said.

"Aye, the last time you were stuffed into this table with sharp-eyed businessmen," he agreed, and poured her a glass of wine from the bottle Jeffers had opened. "I recall not being able to focus on much else, except you that evening."

"Really?"

"Especially after you shut Cecilia's father up." Grant cleared his throat and continued in an adorable imitation of her Wyoming drawl "'Cept we're more educated, have prettier smiles, and don't marry our cousins.'" He chuckled around his glass of wine.

She smiled. "Well, I guess I know where Cecilia got her charm from." Katelyn took a sip of the wine. "Man, I felt out of place that night," she admitted.

"Aye, that made the two of us."

"What? You?"

"Yet, I felt, maybe for the first time, that—" he paused.

"That what?"

"I felt that you were on my side. That you had my back."

"You did?" she whispered.

"I felt it that night. I feel it when we're grooming Hugh. I feel it when I'm inside you," he said quietly. Katelyn bit her lip and her eyes got dewy.

"Grant, this ultimatum your father has set up and the marriage he's expecting from you, and all the things that are supposed to happen..."

"Aye?" Tension crackled in his voice.

"I just want you to know that I don't hold any illusions about what we are and I don't want to make things more complicated for you. So, I don't know if we should keep testing fate." She faltered, and her hands dropped to her lap, where she picked at her nails. "What are we doing, Grant?"

She felt the strangeness of her uncertainty as her confidence waned. The tremor giving voice to her confusion. But she didn't want him giving her false hope or making promises he had no ability to keep. He took a sip of wine.

"I never thought I'd see you shrink away from anything." He avoided the question and leaned forward. "Did Cecilia get to you this evening? The unshakable Katelyn Sullivan?"

Katelyn snorted. "I'm not invincible, Grant."

"The hell you aren't. I've ever known a woman so strong." Grant's jaw relaxed in an easy smile; his shoulders dropped away from his ears. Finally, at peace; finally, comfortable. "So, how did a heartless waif like Cecilia get under your skin?" Katelyn took a healthy drink of wine and set the half-empty glass on the pristine tablecloth. He thought she was invincible and maybe she had been; but that was before she'd fallen in love. Now everything inside felt tender and exposed.

She sighed and chose her words carefully. "I'm worried for you because of her. I think she has the ability to make things awful difficult. What we're doing could make things difficult."

He toyed with the stem of the wine glass and paused in his own thoughts. Jeffers came in and placed the roasted duck, wild rice pilaf, and vegetables in front of them. Katelyn stared down at the beautiful presentation.

"This looks fantastic, Jeffers." Her heart was in so many different directions she felt sick. If she admitted how much she loved him, he'd probably kick her out. Then she'd never be able to help him. Katelyn knew she'd have to let Grant go someday; she just didn't want it to be tonight. She had to rein in her heart.

"You don't like duck?" he asked after Jeffers had left.

"No, I like it, I just—"

His eyes turned soft. "She really upset you," Grant said.

The opportunity to fool him into thinking she wasn't ass-over-head in love presented itself. Katelyn looked up.

"It's stupid, right? I know. Someone like her shouldn't—be able to."

"She's a horrible person, and she doesna deserve your worry."

"It's just, sometimes, people can make you feel so small. She's so put together and beautiful. She's the kind of woman who knows how to navigate your world." Katelyn looked around the ostentatious dining room. "She knows how to get what she wants, when she wants it. What kind of candle could I even hold against someone like that?"

Grant shook his head once with a sly smile. "You proved you could outwit her."

"Sure, in a barn. But I couldn't broker the huge deals that would bolster sales, or manage the breeding and selling of multiple foals to rich and bored businessmen all over the globe. I'm not cut out for all that. I'm not good enough." The truth bit through. Grant stood up and his chair fell back. He took Katelyn by the hand and pulled her from her seat, and led her out of the dining room.

"Jeffers!" he called.

"Yessir," Jeffers responded, coming through the serving doors as if he'd been waiting for a command.

"Please save dinner. We'll take it later in the study."

"Of course, sir. Shall I cap the wine as well?"

"Yes, please. Thank you, Jeffers." The old butler responded with a smile, taken aback by the new manners. Grant took Katelyn to the other side of the house. His fingers tightened around hers as he led her into his bedroom.

"What are you doing?" she asked in the dimly lit room.

"No one, Katelyn, not me, not Cecilia, my father, or anyone in this world for that matter, has a right to make you feel less than you are," Grant said lowly. His words shivered through Katelyn's body, and goose bumps rose on her arms. He ran his hands up her arms to her neck and cupped her cheeks.

"You call it 'my world,' but it isna the world I chose. It's just the one I have to live in. People like my father and Cecilia have poisoned my life. I have suffered because of them, and I'll continue to suffer under their expectations. But they aren't yours to suffer through. You," He paused and kissed her. "I won't let them ruin you, Katie. Put those thoughts out of your mind. You have so much goodness, selflessness... things that they'll never understand." He smoothed the hair from her forehead and his fingers caressed her chin, beneath her ear and down her neck.

"Well, you have those things too, and I don't want you to suffer either," she began.

"Shh, Katie darlin'. Just," he sighed, kissed her jaw, her neck, and slipped her shirt over her shoulders. "Let's just forget the world outside right now," he finished. His warm mouth and tongue traced down her collarbones to the gentle divot between them. Katelyn gasped, sighed, threaded her fingers through his hair, and kept her mouth and heart quiet. Her body shivered as he took each piece of her clothing off and left it in a heap near his bed.

She helped undress him, and let her mouth wander over the hard muscles of his shoulders and chest.

For the moment, she'd let the day stay behind the closed doors of his bedroom. For this night, she would let go all of the bitterness and drama that was a part of his complicated life. And just be with him. She held on to his shoulders as he lifted her into the bed and slid them both beneath the soft, expensive sheets.

Grant traced his fingers up the outside of her legs, to her waist and up to cup her breasts and tease the tips into taut roses. She gasped and lifted her hips to him, feeling the wet rush between her legs. Grant sighed and settled himself gently between her thighs, but paused. Katelyn writhed and whimpered.

"What is it?"

Grant leaned up, his arms shaking with the effort. "It occurs to me that we havena been very careful, and that's the fault of mine. I've wanted you so much that my judgment was clouded. I forgot that taking care of you is the most important thing," he whispered and kissed her. Katelyn caressed his cheeks and felt warmth for his concern.

"I can't. I can't have children, if that's what you're worried about," she said. He pulled away to look at her. Sadness settled in his eyes, but she shook her head. "I had an illness when I was fifteen. Things were damaged," she said and her voice shook.

"I'm sorry."

"It's okay," she said softly and caressed his cheek. "There's more to look forward to in life than just that." She kissed his jawline, nudging his earlobe delicately until she could feel his body tremble with the fight for control. Katelyn pushed away the strange feeling of disappointment, as if there were a future for them.

Whatever Ian wanted Grant to do in life, in her arms, he didn't have to hold up a legacy he'd never asked for. Grant settled heavy on her and slowly caressed the outside of her thigh. She hoped that him knowing she couldn't become pregnant would ease his worry.

"You are perfect, Katie. Just as you are." He paused in his praise and she gasped as he bit roughly into her shoulder and slid inside of her, holding still for a moment. Katelyn's legs wrapped around him and she lifted her hips with the need to continue. "You don't pay for it, you don't bury yourself in makeup or bend beauty as a weapon, like it's your only advantage. You," he gasped at shivers that rocked through his body, "my sweet Katie, you can be filthy from a day of hard work and still be the most bonny lass I've ever—" he stopped before the word *loved* fell out.

"Ever?" she breathed.

"Ever laid my hands or eyes on."

"Grant," she whispered, before he continued on, a slow and deep pace, deeper than he'd driven her before. Deeper than she knew how to accept without her body climaxing over and over again. Katelyn's world was a flurry, a rollercoaster of falling and whirling, and he was relentless in his drive to pleasure her first, reading her body like a map. She succumbed to him, losing control in his arms.

After her third climax, when she was clawing at his back for the overwhelming sensitivity and sobbing into his shoulder for one more release, he gasped her name like a prayer over the sweat-slicked skin of her neck and she felt the surge and clung to him, letting her arms wind around his waist and holding him close. After moments of heavy breathing, he pressed up and stared into her flushed face, her moist eyes, cherry-blossom lips.

"Three?" he asked. "Or was it four?"

"I lost count," she said, breathless. "How many times can you fall off the edge of the world?"

"I think that might be a record," he admitted with a smile and stood. She felt the cold of his leaving but was placated when he reached his strong arms beneath her soft and pliable body and picked her up.

"What are you doing?" she asked and squirmed against his chest.

"Well, my wee nymph, you're going to have a nice, long bath. You're going to let me wash you, then I'll feed you, and then you're spending tonight in my bed. Wi' me."

"Are you going to use the curry comb and hose?" she asked, her head nudging beneath his chin. Grant's deep and full laugh rumbled through her like an earthquake and she couldn't help but giggle.

"No, love. Not tonight."

That word. Love. Her heart pounded against his chest, but she said nothing. Grant poured the bath in his oversized tub, filling the claw-footed monstrosity with steaming water and scoops of salts from a glass container on its edge. From where he'd sat her on an overstuffed bench, wrapped in a large fluffy towel, she watched.

"What's a big tough guy like you doing with a bathtub like that?" she asked with a smile. Grant looked over his bare shoulder with a raised eyebrow.

"I afford myself very few luxuries."

"Oh?" She wasn't done prying, and Grant turned and walked to her, naked and beautiful in the soft glow of the bathroom's lights.

"I enjoy baths."

"Really?"

"Aye."

"So, the other morning when I came in here and said it's bath time, you were genuinely excited to hear it," she said.

"That I was." He smiled and pulled her towel away. He held her hand while she stepped over the tall side of the tub and into the steaming water. Then he sat behind her, wrapped his arms around her shoulders, sunk in, and grunted with satisfaction. He leaned back, rested her against his chest, and they sat in silence. Katelyn closed her eyes, drifted from thought to thought without reason or purpose.

"This is nice," she said. "I can't remember the last time I had a bath."

"That, I can believe, my grubby wee cowgirl," he chuckled. Her pointed elbow dug into his ribs, eliciting an "Oof!" from him before he laughed again.

"I mean, I always shower. Baths aren't very efficient." She settled back into his chest and enjoyed the warmth that sloshed around them.

"There is more to life than efficiency, Katie."

Katelyn purred and snuggled into his chest, her fingers running up his thigh.

"Why didn't you stay here when it was offered?" he asked. Katelyn looked back over her shoulder, the corner of her glance catching the serious downward tilt of his lips.

"I don't like being beholden to anyone, and I kinda found the offer to be too personal. Then, after I met you that first time, I thought a little space from you would be better."

"Oh? I cannae understand why after meeting me you didn't want to move right in," he scoffed.

"You were about as warm as a frozen prairie dog in February."

"A what? What's a prairie dog?" His low laugh rumbled through her back.

"Kind of like a gopher?" She leaned into him. "You weren't very nice," she said and pinched his leg.

"I'm not nice," he grumbled. "I dinna like people."

"I'm people," she whispered over her shoulder, as if revealing a secret.

"You're different," Grant said, and took soft sponge from the stand next to the tub. With gentle slowness, he washed her back, her arms, hands and neck. He glided down beneath the water and lifted each leg in turn and washed the day from her skin. Her feet entranced him, and he spent longer caressing them. Katelyn watched with amusement.

"Do you like feet?" she whispered. Grant shook his head, his soapy fingers tracing between her toes.

"Dinna ken, I've never really thought about them until I saw yours. They're so delicate. So small. Very un-hobbit like." He glided his hand up the arch, and Katelyn sighed and sat back against the tub.

"Just like my momma's," she said with a quirked smile. "Funny how genetics works. I got the feet, my sister Elle got the height, Laney got the snark."

"I'm surprised that as tough and grubby as you are, you dinna have brothers."

Katelyn opened one eye and looked at him. "You've never met my sisters. They're wicked mean, but nobody's better when you need someone on your side." She sat back and closed her eyes, thoughts of the open wide prairie filtering in and memories of her childhood gurgled up from distant places. Her sisters, her mom and dad, the horses and chickens. Grandma Em, her resilience and love. The boy who'd played alongside them. "I guess we did have a sort of adopted brother growing up."

"Aye?" Grant's voice seemed unreal through the curtain of memories.

"He spent more time at our house than at his own. His parents weren't really there." A frown replaced Grant's smile at the parallel childhood.

"So, you took him in?"

"Momma never refused a meal or a hug to a child. And Blake needed both."

"You must have been close," he said, a spark of envy in his tone. He scowled and put her foot back in the water.

"Sure, we spent a lot of time together when we were younger." Katelyn rose one brow his way and watched his scowl when his fingers dipped below the steamy surface and found her inner thigh. He slipped his fingers inside of her. Katelyn gasped and sat up, her eyes opening in surprise.

"What happened to Blake?" he asked, his dexterous hands stroking and building. Katelyn held on to the sides of the tub and leaned back.

"Grant," she whispered, her body trembling in the hot water. She pressed against the palm of his hand and his fingers gripped her backside.

"Tell me, what happened to that *poor lad*?" he said in a dark voice. Katelyn closed her eyes, air hard to hold in her lungs at the excitement.

"I, uh...I can't," She couldn't breathe, her body shook, she couldn't think. Water sloshed over the sides of the tub as he moved closer. She suddenly knew what this was. He was jealous. She tightened her hands on the sides of the tub and pressed her body closer to his. He wanted to be the only man on her mind and in her bed.

"Blake? What happened to Blake?"

"He married my sister, Elle," Katelyn said breathlessly. Her cheeks were flushed and pink and she squirmed around him. Grant stopped, now settled between her thighs. She saw the darkness in his eyes and stared back curiously.

"What was that about?" she said and ran her hands down his backside.

"Just trying to make sure I'm thorough in my bathing duties."

"Well, my green-eyed beast, you missed a spot," she said and pulled him between her thighs. She rolled him over, straddled him, and sloshed more water out of the tub. With quick and needy waves, she rode him until he yelled out and pulled her down as they both came. Katelyn cried out, and he pressed his lips to her sternum while his breathing subsided.

"Five," she sighed.

"Very aggressive. Have I taught you too well?" he said from beneath her.

"You're the one who was lookin' for a reason to not feel jealous. I gave you one...well, five really." She rotated her hips, and he shuddered.

"Katie, stop." He held her still. She smiled down at him. "Tell me again that there's no chance we could conceive," he said, a sudden worry in his voice.

"Don't fret," she reassured. "The damage was damn complete." She pulled away from him and his eyes followed her for more. "I was up in the Snowy Range at a youth camp, helping teach a clinic on trail riding—"

"At fifteen?" he scoffed. She frowned and furrowed her pretty brow before splashing him with water.

"Jesus, you are something. Yes, at fifteen. I started not feeling so good, sick to my gut and in a lot of pain. By the time they got me down the mountain and to the hospital, my appendix had burst and the infection caused severe scarring."

"I'm sorry," he whispered and caressed her feet.

Katelyn shrugged. "People define their worth by the strangest things sometimes." She paused and shook her head. "You know I never would have let you make love to me, if I thought there was a chance I might get pregnant. I know what it would cost you." Her directness caused him to look torn and hurt.

"I'm starving," she said and leaned over. "Let's eat." She kissed his frown until it faded. Then, on shaky legs, she stepped from the bath and stood, naked and wet, holding his towel out for him. Grant looked up and sighed with his head still resting on the tub.

"Food?"

"That's usually what works when you're hungry," she said.

"I'm not even sure I can lift my body out of this tub. You'll ruin me, Katie."

"Well, I'm trying my best," she said and took his hand to help him out. He dried off his magnificent body. She watched, unapologetically.

They retired to the study. He'd given her his oversized robe to wear and had put on his rugby shirt and a pair of sleeping pants. She liked the way his relaxed clothing hugged his body, his broad chest, the muscles of his legs. She was admiring all of his attributes when he turned from adding logs to the fire.

"What are you doing?"

"Looking at you," she said, putting a decadent bite of duck in her mouth.

Grant sighed as he sunk into the sofa.

"Oh? Trying to find the 'hitch in my giddy-up'?" he twanged and snuggled in with his plate beside her. He stared into the fireplace and she wiggled her toes beneath his thigh. He smiled at the gesture.

"Are you making fun of me?" she said with squinting eyes.

"Just your accent," he smiled roguishly at her.

"I dinnae ken tha' you have any rrroom to talk," she mocked him back in a teasing burr. At this he laughed heartily and leaned in to kiss her lips. When he leaned back, there was a moment of quiet contemplation as he studied her.

"Oh, Katie. I think I'm in trouble," he whispered. "Such, sweet, trouble."

WHEN KATELYN WOKE THE NEXT MORNING, THE MASSIVE bed was empty, and it took a moment to get her bearings. She'd slept so soundly, with dreams of hearth, and home, and pipe smoke in the dark green woods, where she'd walked alone, but not lonely. She could hear the thunder of hooves and the distant sound of his voice rumbling across the fields. She woke to the strong thrums of that voice, its undercurrent laced with anger.

She couldn't tell what he was saying, only that he was stern. She blinked. It must have not even been five. She grabbed his rugby shirt from the end of the bed and pulled it over her head, then lithely stepped down the hallway towards the sound of Grant's voice.

She peeked her head around the corner of his office door and saw him pacing. One hand was tucked into his back pocket, the other held the phone to his ear. He was wearing one of his dress shirts, but rolled up at the cuffs and untucked, and his hair had that sexy, mussed look of a man who'd been in bed. She loved it that way. She loved him. Katelyn bit her lip and fought the urge to run away, and simultaneously, run headlong in.

"AYE, DAN, THAT'S WHAT I SAID. HUGH'S IN EXCELLENT health and he'll be breeding this spring. If you want on the books, you'd best do it earlier than late. We're only looking to seed out a limited number this season." There was a pause in the business-thick tone. "No, not for health reasons! Dan, listen to me. You know my father. You know the reputation of Tennyson Stables. Hugh Dancy is a rare commodity and what Ian says goes. He says thirty, we stick to thirty. Yes—" It was at this point, midway through tugging his hands through his hair, that Grant turned and saw her in the doorway. "I look forward to your decision," he said and hung up.

"Starting so serious this early?" Her sleep husky voice echoed.

"Business." The truth of it was that he'd been up most of the night. He'd watched her until she'd fallen asleep, then he'd tossed and turned, his brain alight with fears and concerns. About her, for the stables, for Hugh, for his future. He hadn't slept well at all, and so, at three that morning, he'd gotten up and decided to do some of his European calls and work while she slept in his bed.

He'd checked on her once. Taking the time to study and memorize the curve of her chin beneath her full lip. The way her golden-wheat hair spread out across his white sheets and fell over her freckled and tanned shoulder. He thought of days she'd spent in sun and snow, outside and working, building up the character of a woman who didn't shy from challenge, who knew herself despite her age. When he'd returned to work on his spreadsheets and quarterly turnouts, he'd thought about her the entire time, a constant warmth in the back of his mind, edged with fear for what might become of her after the affair ended.

"Whoa, you okay? Looking a little green around your gills,"

she said, and sauntered closer. "Are you running out of milk and eggs to pay me in?" she teased as she rested her backside on his desk between him and his work.

"No," he breathed and tried to smile. His hands went around her waist. "I like that you've taken to dressing more appropriately for your position." He smiled wolfishly and kissed her full bottom lip.

"Appropriate for what position, exactly?" She snorted and tangled her hands in his curls.

"You're suited for all positions," he whispered and pushed up the shirt to take her breast in his mouth. She arched into the warm teasing and gasped.

"Are you sure you're okay?"

"Aye, dinna concern yourself," he answered, distracted by her breasts. Katelyn narrowed her eyes on him and pulled him away.

"Dinnae tell me when to be concerned," she answered, and kissed his chin. "I should take that walk of shame. I know you have work to do and I've hogged enough of your time." Her teeth bit into his jaw lightly and he gasped.

"You could kidnap me away from this terrible drudgery," he mumbled incoherently into her lips.

"Aye, that I could," she smiled, "but I'm not getting paid in chicken feed and trenchers to corrupt the boss' son."

"Yet here you are," he teased.

"Darlin', I'll corrupt you for free." She kissed him, gave him a gentle pat on the stubbled cheek and got up. "Thanks for last night." She leaned against the door in a very simple seductive and relaxed way before winking and leaving.

Grant hated that she was leaving already. But Ian would be back tonight. And after that, what? He supposed he had Belmont to put space between them and get his head on right again.

SEVENTEEN

GRANT LOOSENED HIS TIE IN THE HEAT. HE MIGHT DIE right on the spot if he had to smile and shake another hand. But his father's warning glances kept his teeth showing and his hand pumping the future prospects for Tennyson Stables. Women in fancy hats drifted around him, the ridiculous feathers and tufts of fur, large bows and crinkling tulle like flashy displays of a long-gone American era that he knew little about. And here he was, in a 'free' country, still under the thumb of a tyrant. Ian stiffened beside him as if he were privy to Grant's thoughts.

"What the hell is she doing here?" Ian's strained voice hissed in Grant's ear. Grant gazed out over the sea of hats, still a head above most of the people. He saw that Cecilia was in the center of a group of cackling women, her false smile turning ugly at anyone else stealing her light. Couldn't be her. Ian would be pleased to see the canary yellow duchess. Grant swung his gaze around and saw the simple girl in a blue sundress.

Starkly under-pomped for the circumstances, Katelyn's freckled cheeks turned pink with every face that swung her way; still, she lifted her chin. Working the magic that was all her, she shook hands, introduced herself, and meandered through the crowd, unafraid to be the oddity in the room. The color of her dress softened her eyes to deep blue, and her hair was golden and warm in the room of fake coverings.

He fell deeper in love with her on the spot.

"Grant, I swear if you invited her—" Ian began.

"I did not," Grant said tensely and tried to not let the light of seeing her show in his face. Jim Parsons drew up alongside Katelyn with two cold mint juleps and a smile.

"Ah, looks as though someone is playing outside of his marriage bed," Ian chuckled. "Can't say as I blame him. She's a tasty little side chit."

Anger hit Grant in the gut. Of course his father would think that was the kind of thing she or Jim would do. Before Grant could correct him, a woman hailed Katelyn through the crowd. Grant recognized Jim's wife, Sharon, as she wove her way around people towards Katelyn and they embraced.

"Katie! Sweetheart, you look darling!" Sharon doted as she held Katelyn at arm's length.

"I had to go shopping. It was horrible! Thank god for Jeffers, I wouldn't have known what in the hell to wear." Katelyn looked around at the expensive dresses and hats. "Looks like I still might not." Katelyn's eyes darted to Grant.

"Hello Mr. Tennyson," she said to him with a nod. He nodded and tried not to let his eyes fall below her face. She turned to Ian. "Hello older Mr. Tennyson," she nodded at Ian with a sly smile. Ian snorted and ignored her. Grant's heart back-flipped at how composed she seemed. Jim approached Grant, Ian, and Katelyn. He put his arm around his wife.

"Mr. Tennyson, I don't know if you've had the pleasure of meeting my wife, Sharon," Jim said to Ian and handed the second drink he'd been carrying to Sharon. Ian cleared his throat. He begrudgingly shook hands with Jim and turned away to more important prospects.

"It's good to see you again, Sharon." Grant's voice was soft as he shook Sharon's hand and leaned in to kiss her cheek. Sharon smiled and wove her hand into the crook of Jim's arm.

"You too, Grant. You look well." Grant's eyes looked to Katelyn and back quickly.

"I'm feeling well," he said. "Better than."

Jim and Sharon started talking about the roster with one another. Grant realized how close he'd come to losing his temper at Ian for suggesting that she could be sharing Jim's bed. He knew he had no right to defend her, but the inclination ran through his blood all the same. It was one thing for Ian to degrade him. He wouldn't stand him doing it to someone he... the word *love* teetered inside of his chest, new and shaky. Katelyn leaned in.

"Hey? What is it?" she asked, inconspicuously beside him. When Grant didn't respond, she pressed further. "Is it the people? Yeah, it's hotter'n hell in here, and what's with all these dumb fuckin' hats?" Katelyn whispered, and she brushed his shoulder trying to dodge a particularly wide-brimmed monstrosity. "And I keep getting offered gin in various concoctions. Isn't this Belmont? I thought all that stereotypical horseshit was reserved for the Derby." Her lack of filter, the curse words peppered into her demure voice and innocent smile made him realize she was uncomfortably pretending, and he loved her all the more. Yet again, she was his anchor in the stormy world he felt no home in.

"Gin is supposed to be refreshing." He mumbled innocuous words as a barrier from the truth in his heart.

"If you find gnawing on juniper bushes refreshing, I suppose," she grumbled and adjusted a strap on her dress that had fallen off her shoulder. He wanted to lean over and bite one of them, taste her succulent, sun-touched skin, and trail his tongue down her collarbone, lift her skirt, slip a finger down the front of her panties feel her hot wetness and tell her all the ways he'd fallen undeniably in love with her. He stepped away and scowled.

"What are you doing here?"

She looked up at him with a matched scowl. "The Parsons

invited me. I thought it might be a nice way to get out of the stables for a day. Plus, how often does a girl get to go to one of these—," she dodged another hat, but a pheasant feather caught her in the side of the face before she could duck, "shit-shows?" She tried to spit the remnants of the feather out. "I could do with a little less plumage though."

Grant tried to contain it. But he couldn't. He burst out laughing, deep and beautiful. His hand reached up to take the wayward feather from her hair and ran it delicately down her neck. Katelyn shivered, and her eyes fell to his lips. His finger touched her collarbone, and he inhaled sharply. The crowd waned and faded around them. Grant's remnant smile was calm before his brain checked him back into reality. He swung his head around to see if Ian had seen. Katelyn's eyes met his when he turned back.

"I'm making your life difficult right now, aren't I?" Her head tugged towards where Ian was schmoozing a billionaire and his mistress. "I can scoot," she said and threw her thumb over her shoulder.

"I dinna want you to 'scoot'. Don't leave me alone in all of this plumage," he whispered back.

"Grant!" The icy spear of his name soared between them.

"Sounds like a viper in the henhouse," Katelyn said.

"What is that barn girl doing here?" Cecilia demanded as she approached, throwing eye daggers into Katelyn's smiling face.

"Careful, Cecilia, you'll undo your Botox," Grant said. "Katelyn is Jim and Sharon Parson's guest." Katelyn turned on her with a half-cocked smile.

"Well, if it isn't the horse whisperer. Good to see you back on your feet. Were you able to get the shit stains out of your pants? Hugh's and yours, I mean," Katelyn said. Grant was torn between laughing and worry. Jim and Sharon both turned inquisitively towards the conversation.

"How dare you!"

"Cecilia," Grant interrupted.

"Ease up, lady. I'm not tryin' to swoop in on your nest egg," Katelyn said dryly and looked at Grant, who'd been cowed into the background. "But I will tell you one thing for certain. You ever talk to me like that again, and Belmont's gonna get its first taste of a *proper* brawl."

Cecilia took a step back, and the crowd grew still.

"Jim, I think I'd like to try one of those." She nodded to Sharon's drink. "I hear they're refreshing." Katelyn avoided Grant, whose face masked the disappointed pain and overwhelming pride he had inside, and removed herself from the fray. She disappeared into the crowd behind her hosts, and Grant was left with the huffing Cecilia, who grabbed his wrist. He pulled away and gave her a stern look.

"You know how I feel about touching, Cecilia."

"Oh? Is that so? Not five minutes ago you were feeling up that back-country whore." Grant came at her, his face inches from hers.

"Dinna you ever call her that again." Cecilia pulled him in for a biting kiss. Her tongue forced its way into his mouth and she held him there by his tie, breaking away only when she was certain people were watching.

"Oh, Grant! Not here," she gasped and feigned coy for the interested crowd. Grant wiped his mouth off with disgust. "Well, at least now she knows the truth." Grant looked back to see Katelyn staring at them. Her face held something indescribable and raw. He wasn't sure if it was disappointment, understanding, or anger, but he wished he could rush to her and explain. She nodded once in soft resignation and turned away.

"Cecilia, I swear to God, if you don't step away from me right now, I will tell this whole room what happened in that barn. How you begged that 'back-country whore' to save your life while you knelt in a pile of horseshit."

"You wouldn't."

"Get the hell away from me."

. . .

THE RACES BEGAN AND, DESPITE TRYING TO PRETEND otherwise, Grant searched the crowd and faces for where the Parsons were sitting. To no avail. She was nowhere to be seen and between races, when he excused himself from his father and his cronies to use the bathroom, a more thorough search didn't help. Had she left? He sighed. What a fucking mess. He paced in front of the bar where he'd last seen her.

"Do you remember a girl, in a blue dress? Pretty, golden wheat hair?"

The bartender looked at him with a sly smile.

"Blue eyes? Tried to drink a julep but gave up and got out of here before the starting gate? She excused herself from that couple, said she needed a little air." The man said and nodded out the side door.

The whole bloody place was open air, what did she mean by that?

Grant closed his eyes. If he were Katelyn, in a strange and pressure-filled room, surrounded by people and judgmental stares, where would she escape to breathe? He nodded and thanked the bartender. It didn't take him long to wind down the stairs of the arena and into the lower-level stables.

Being a renowned breeder had its perks, and he was able to smooth over the security guards into letting him into the stables. Had they been as acquiescing to her? If Katelyn had asked Grant to pass through, he would have opened heaven's gates. Yet, he recoiled from shame of the truth; he could never be with her. He couldn't let go of the danger they were in, even with the new revelation in his heart. If anything, it made it even more imperative that they were careful.

His long legs strode through the long line of stalls, head swinging back and forth, checking for her hair, the blue of her dress. He'd almost given up hope; maybe she'd left all together. Maybe she had accepted where Grant was headed. He grunted in frustration, kicking at the dusty ground with his expensive shoes.

"Easy there, little cowpoke, you're gonna ruin your fancy duds," he heard her drawl from behind and the fist around his heart unclenched. He sighed and turned to her.

"Who are you to call me little?"

"Oh, I'm sorry. I shoulda said 'wee'." She smiled, and he rushed her, picked her up and swung her around the deserted stable, kissing her neck, her chin, her shoulders. Katelyn laughed and hung on for the ride. Her breath was heavy and gasping when he set her back to earth. She caressed his cheek and tugged on a long curl at the nape of his neck.

"What's on your mind, lad?" she said. "Come to tell me it's all over, that you've been tasked to put a bun in the shriveled-up oven of that viperous she-devil?" Her smile belied the way she'd reacted Cecilia's kiss. Grant sighed with a scowl.

"Katie."

"Hey, listen. It's okay. It's fine. I know you have obligations."

"I dinna want that. I dinna want her!"

Katelyn looked up at him; honesty boring into his eyes.

"Well, then say so."

"I just did!"

"Well, not to me. To your father." Katelyn stepped back and waited for his reaction.

"It's not so simple as all that, Katie."

"Nothin' ever is, is it?" She sighed and looked to the field at the start of another race. The ground beneath them shook with the thunderous might of legs and hearts pounding around a track. "Probably should get back to the Parsons before they worry," she said. Grant wanted to stop her, to find a secluded spot for them, but he could see that she'd been stung. Maybe not so much over Cecilia's possessive kiss, but from the fact that he was so willing to accept his own misery and powerlessness in the matter.

"You best get going too, before Ian does the math and starts thinking you're fraternizing with the help."

"Katie—I—"

"It's okay." She shook her head to brush away whatever lame excuse or worthless apology was building up behind his lips. "I'll see you Monday. I only have one more week to make good on my promise to you. I can't afford to miss a day."

Grant couldn't make his mouth speak, couldn't find a sharp retort, couldn't make his feet move to follow. She hadn't kissed him before walking away, only laid down the law, the line in the sand drawn, and a gentle reminder that their time was limited. Watching her walk away, out of the stables and back up to the hot and crowded, plumage-filled boxes and rich owners, he wished he could just leave, forsake his birthright, accept the assured poverty, and follow her.

But he didna live in a feckin' fairy tale.

EIGHTEEN

MONDAY MORNING BROUGHT A TENSION HEADACHE TO Grant that only came after spending a prolonged time sandwiched between his father and Cecilia, whose cold, skeletal fingers had to be repeatedly removed from his thigh. The after-party and hobnobbing, the knowing glances from Cecilia's father and their respective lawyers, had increased his anxiety. He felt sick to his stomach every time she touched him, ran her hands up his leg, or leaned against his shoulder in a mark of possession. His scars were for Katelyn's hands; his body safe only beside her quiet and unpressured presence. By the end of the weekend, when he and Ian had flown back in their private plane with Jeffers at the controls, he was exhausted.

Had he always felt this way after time spent with Ian?

Or was it only now that he knew something else existed?

He hadn't seen her again at the races. The Parsons' box was obscured from their own, and Katelyn made no further effort to contact him. He knew better than to inquire about their future plans around Ian and Cecilia. He excused himself promptly from his father's company, but was halfway to his wing of the manor when Ian's steely voice cut thickly through the hall.

"I hope now, after spending time with Cecilia, you see it as an advantageous match."

Grant's heart felt odd and strained in his chest, like it couldn't get full.

"I'm sure she'll make someone very rich, some day."

"Best it would be you, Grant. Time waits for no man. And money is time. I'm sure you'd agree."

Grant turned back in time to see his father's knowing smile flick across the otherwise immobile features, before he turned and skulked back to his quarters. Grant shivered and his gut tightened. All Ian wanted was a grandchild. That's all. Just one measly cell from his body. And a viper to nurture it. Only a few months ago, what was not so intangible, suddenly seemed insurmountable. Grant tossed and turned the whole night, visions of Cecilia's sharp teeth tearing through the flesh of his leg, coiled around him and swollen with child. He woke with a start, sweaty and cold, Katie's name on his lips.

The next morning, when he walked to the far paddock, he looked up from his hunched and downward stare to see her gently plying Hugh with soft words and caresses. The stallion looked good. Healthy. Strong. His ears were relaxed and alert and when Grant walked up to them, as she'd taught him, calm and unwound, the horse made a soft and pleased sound. Hugh put his head back down and nuzzled in Katelyn's pocket for a treat. She gladly gave him a few.

"Is that how you keep all the boys in line? Hidden sweets?" he said with a wicked grin. She smiled up at him, tipped her cap up, and he was enamored by her blue eyes crinkling. Today she wore a pink t-shirt that fit tight across her chest and a pair of well-worn Wranglers that hugged her muscled thighs. She smelled clean, and of hay. She held up a small piece of cookie between them.

"No thanks, I had breakfast," he whispered.

"It's for Hugh," she whispered back. "Your treat comes later."

Grant took the cookie from her but made no move to give it to

Hugh. Instead, he watched her lips, wanting to kiss her, but knowing the public display of affection would get relayed by some young stable hand, eager to move up the ladder with Ian Tennyson.

"What's my treat?" he asked and leaned in.

"You'll find out after you get on this horse."

"And if I don't want to?"

"Well," she said and put her hands in her back pockets and touched her breasts purposefully to his chest. Grant inhaled sharply. "I guess you don't hafta. The world is full of choices, Grant. I'd never make you do something you didn't really want to do."

"Is that so?"

"But, it's the only thing left to complete his recovery."

"Complete his recovery?" Grant leaned back.

"Yes sir," she said and watched his face. "If he can go back to everything he was before the accident, he can start over. Maybe even be better than before." Grant looked into her eyes as her words sunk into his brain. She wasn't talking about Hugh.

"What if he can never go back to who he was before?" Grant ignored Hugh's gentle nudges to his back.

"If he's not able to face the pain of the past and know he can overcome it in the present, then it will always hold him back," she said and took Grant's hand in hers. "Pain, even when we can't see it on the outside, even when it's physically healed, leaves a scar on our brain and reminds us that we're vulnerable. We remember so we don't get hurt again. But sometimes we remember too well. Sometimes the memory keeps us from living, and moving, and doing what we're meant to do. So, we have to heal it in our brains just the same as in the body." Her eyes fell to his chest, and she looked back up. "Since he was with you when he was hurt, you're instrumental in his healing process."

"Katie—"

"And vice versa," she interrupted. Grant couldn't pull away;

she'd threaded her fingers into his and held him still. "I think what happened that afternoon on the mountain was not the source of your pain; it just added to it. I think the pain from whatever happened before drove you up that mountain and that you were trying to get away, permanently."

"You've nay right to make assumptions. You've nay right to think you ken what I—"

"Tell me the truth then," she said. June bugs whizzed by outside the paddock. The murmur of their wings died away while Grant stared at Katelyn. Hugh swished his tail contentedly. He looked happy. He looked ready to start over. Grant's scars ran much deeper.

"Gonna get on this horse, or just squint at me all day like you know what's best?" she said, bringing him out of his inner turmoil.

"What if he throws me off? What if I crack my skull open?"

"Then maybe some of your stubborn will drain out."

"Slightly less pleasant than cookies knocking my mad off," he grumbled.

"See? And that worked, didn't it? Goddamn it, how many times do I have to be right before you start listening to me?" she scolded.

Jeremy walked by. "You two sound like an old married couple," he joked, and hurried away when they both glared at him.

"Okay," she said, tightening the stirrup. "Let's get to it." Grant's hand went instinctively to his thigh. Katelyn noticed.

"Yeah, I know," she whispered and came closer. "It hurts, doesn't it?" She ran her hand with firm, even strokes, from his hip down the length of his thigh. The strange and direct touch made him shy away, but her other hand held his hip still. "I don't think it healed properly. It pulls when you're walking, and it's shortened your stride on the right, which means your left shoulder and back are taking the brunt of the compensation." Her hands traveled up to his low back. "Lean on him," she said and turned Grant to face Hugh, his strong hands against the horse's back.

"What are you doing—" Before he could object, Katelyn's fists were pressed into the small of his back, into the ache he couldn't ever seem to find relief from. The pressure shocked him and he stumbled into Hugh, holding onto the saddle with bated breath, waiting for the stallion to rear up in anger. Hugh snuffled, looked back, and settled into Grant's weight. She worked the muscles of his traumatized back, with palms and knuckles, pushing, pulling, stroking deep and even, until he felt heavy and soft.

He looked down; not everything was soft.

"Katie," he said thickly. She ducked under his arms and looked down.

"Amazing what a little improved blood flow can do," she said huskily. "Now," she whispered, and bit his chin. Grant wanted to fuck her against the fence, deep and with the same intensity as she'd massaged him, until they were both gasping and wet. "Get on that horse, and when you're all done, I'll let you ride me." Grant shivered with desire. He bent to kiss her, to try to sway her to forget about him riding Hugh again, but she slipped out of his grasp and took Hugh's reins.

"Well, I can't focus on riding now!"

"That's the point."

"You're going to just leave me like this?" But his tone didn't hold the light banter of before.

"All right." She took the reins and motioned for him to follow. They walked to the indoor arena, and Grant tried to remain stoic as they passed the stalls of workers and stable hands. He felt taller, different, relaxed. Her work had reset something. Her touch, something he shied away from for so long, was exactly what his body needed. When they reached the office, she handed him the reins and stepped into the small space to talk to Jeremy, who was finishing up the records for the day.

"Can we get this place cleared out? Need a little quiet time. Big ride today," was all she said. Jeremy nodded, and without fanfare, cleared out the rest of the people, then gave her a salute as he left.

Grant watched the magical influence of Katelyn rippled through all the people in the arena, the lack of griping or question. The friendly waves, even the kind looks he got when they all realized that he was riding Hugh. It gave him hope and equal amounts of trepidation. She'd been wrong the night she'd discounted her own abilities when compared to Cecilia. She could have easily managed Tennyson Stables—not out of fear, but from the respect and love she'd earned.

"Okay," she sighed, sprung up on Hugh's back lithe and easy, and reached down to take his hand. "Up you come."

"There's not enough room."

She scooted back to sit on Hugh's rump and offered him the stirrup. "Get on," she said.

"Katie—"

She leaned down and whispered, "I'll let you use the crop, and I don't mean on Hugh."

"Jesus." Grant's body responded with a rush of need. He put his foot into the stirrup and swung up awkwardly. As he settled in, he took a deep breath and they both sat still.

"He's going to throw us off," Grant whispered. "We're too much weight."

"You callin' me fat?" she chuckled behind him. Grant huffed. Katelyn reached around Grant, one hand taking the reins, the other finding the hard bulge straining beneath his clothes. "Relax," she whispered into his back. Grant gasped and strained into her capable hand.

"What are you doing?"

"Nice and easy, big guy," she said. Hugh started and Grant's fear response caused him to tense, but the way her strong hand stroked him so assuredly confused his senses, confused his memories, and short-circuited his fear.

"I know you're scared," she whispered.

"You don'," was all he could gasp, as she brought him closer to a peak. "You don't understan'."

"Then tell me."

"I—" The climax came closer, but she slowed her hand and used it to run the length of his thigh as Hugh calmly circled the ring at an easy pace. Grant wanted to cry, and cum, and run away, all at once. He wanted to fall from the horse, take her down with him, and violate her on the dirt floor.

"You?" she led. Grant worked for air, his body coming down from the precipice. "Here, take the reins. I need my hands," she said and placed the soft leather straps in his palms. She used both hands to caress his thighs, massaging the tense muscles. "If you keep tightening up, he'll keep slowing down." On cue, Hugh stopped and turned one ear to her. "Relax. We want a ride, don't we?" The purr of her voice in his back, her hands on his body made Grant realize how hopelessly lost he was. He willed his body to relax, and Hugh, in turn, resumed a comfortable canter. Katelyn's hands returned to his aching body.

"Tell me about that day. The day of your fall." Hugh's increase in speed caused the traumatic memory to surface, and Grant clung to the reins. His body threatened to tighten until she reached inside his pants and surrounded him with her hands. The frenzy of the traumatic memory was cut short.

"I wanted to die," he said suddenly.

"Why?"

"It was the anniversary of Jane's death, and I wanted life without her to just end. I wanted to take Hugh with me. To take away all my father's plans. To ruin him, just like he'd ruined everything in my life. I just wanted to be with Jane again, with my mum. The only people in the world who ever loved me." The words sounded strange and the ideas foreign when he said them out loud. Her hands slowly stroked him, and he could feel her gasp against his back in warm, hot breaths. "I wanted to end it. Take Ian's pride and joy and future away. Just like he took mine."

"He hurt you and you wanted to hurt him back," she

whispered and her hand stroked faster, harder, causing his body to build beyond his control.

"Yes, I wanted to hurt him." He gasped, leaning forward, grasping with his legs, and letting Hugh have free rein until the powerful muscles beneath his thighs tensed and stroked with her own quickening rhythm. The quiet air of the arena was filled with galloping hoofs, gasping breaths, and the memories of the sunlit hill that had almost ended them both. Until she brought him to climax and a deep throaty cry, filled with tears and release.

Grant's body convulsed and her arms wrapped around him assuredly, holding him tight to her as Hugh galloped the circle in ever slowing steps until they were walking the circumference and their breaths began to settle. Grant's body sunk into Hugh's back, his legs found their place, his hands easy on the reins, his chest heaving with his cathartic sobs.

"That's it. You've got it now," Katelyn murmured, her own breath interrupted with contained tears. "That's all it is, baby. Just him and you. You're doing fine. You're okay now. You're okay."

Grant didn't know if he was okay, only that she'd completely upended him, broken his wall down, and crashed inside of his most tender and exposed thoughts. He let her arms hold him, physical affection that he'd long ago prohibited from anyone.

He felt safe. He felt calm; almost relieved. Such a strange feeling in his troubled mind that he fought it, like trying to pick up the broken bricks of his wall and rebuild with no mortar. Jane's words came back, *She'll show you the man you can be.* He tensed and righted his clothing. He slowed Hugh down to a stop.

"Is that all?" she asked suddenly as he dismounted. His knees felt shaky when he stood and he looked up at her, distressed. He saw the tears in her eyes. Strong, unshakeable Katelyn, crying for his pain. A man might think she had fallen in love.

"No, I'm not okay. Not at all." He handed her the reins and walked out of the arena.

· · ·

KATELYN WATCHED HIM GO WITH A SIGH AND THEN leaned down to hug Hugh, her body and mind emotionally spent. Hugh snuffled and whinnied after him.

"It's okay, old man. You did good. You did good," she assured him with a firm pat to his withers before taking him on a few more passes of the arena to clear her heart and mind. She needed to get herself together. If she truly cared about Grant, she needed to find a way to either leave him better than she found him, or to show him that he had options. That he wasn't stuck in this goddamn world he thought there was no escape from. By the time she'd groomed Hugh, set him up in his stable with fresh food and water, she'd thought of a way to open the world up for him. But she would need Jeffers' help.

Nineteen

"I have an idea," she said, coming into his office the next morning without warning, startling the man who had been taking notes via Grant's dictation. Grant cleared his throat and scowled at her. The other man gave her an appreciative once-over.

"Miss Sullivan, you can make an appointment to discuss your treatment progress with me later," he said stiffly. The man looked at Grant.

"It's no trouble, sir. I can come back later," he said.

"No, *she* can come back when we're finished," he directed without room for discussion. Their eyes met and fire sparked between them.

"Sure," she said without lowering her gaze. "I'll just wait right outside this door until then," she said without flinching and stepped into the hall.

Grant watched her go, trying to re-establish the boundary she'd pulled him across yesterday. Since that powerful, vulnerable moment he'd kept himself locked in the office, sending Jeremy dictates for jobs he wanted her to do, paperwork to fill out, anything that kept her busy and away from him. He'd purposefully avoided her, and she hadn't come looking, as though she knew he needed the time alone. It was both a blessing and a curse.

Knowing she was just outside the door though, listening to him, her sweet round bottom pressed against the wall, arms crossed over her chest, strong hands tucked into them. Hands that had so deftly controlled his body on the back of his healed horse. He lost track of his thoughts and stuttered his way through the report he wanted sent overseas. The other man cast curious glances to the doorway. Grant hated the tension she was creating, and hated that she couldn't just leave him alone, especially now when he was so utterly, undeniably weak for her. He finished the report, keeping the insurance agent just a few minutes longer with small talk to delay the inevitable.

"Well, I should be on my way, and you have other business to attend to," the man said, and raised his eyebrows to the doorway.

"She can wait," Grant growled at the door.

"All day, asshole!" Katelyn yelled from the hall. The other man snorted a laugh, collected his things, and left before Grant could turn his anger on him. Katelyn sauntered in.

"Nice power play there," she said, arms crossed over her chest.

"Miss Sullivan, the incident in the arena—"

"Incident? Is that what we're calling it? Okay, I get it. The 'incident' was intense. It was scary for you; I *get* that you're scared," she interrupted. "But I think it's important that you went through it. I think it was good to face it, to share the pain, with," she swallowed, "with someone who cares about you."

"Miss Sullivan—"

"Lord, you don't need to use my last name, not after what we just did." Before he could respond, she went on. "If you'd rather die than live with a man who's caused you such pain, then I think you have cause to explore your choices."

"What?"

"I think you've felt your whole life that you didn't have a

choice, that you have to do what Ian says. And I think he raised you to feel that way, so that you'd never question it."

"You don't know anything about it."

"What happened in the arena wasn't—well, I didn't really plan for that. It just sort of happened. And I know you've got a lot of things to sort through and I've tried to give you time to do that." She took a breath and charged ahead. "But I don't have a lot of time left here, so I gotta," she paused, heart slipped to her sleeve, "get to the point, I guess."

"And what is that point?" he scowled.

"It's that you have choices. You don't have to live like this. You can be whoever you want, you can be with whoever you want and," she faltered and her voice shook. "You can, you c-can have me." Her voice wavered, and she cleared her throat.

"I can't," he argued vehemently.

"I'm right here and I'm telling you that you can. You can choose me." Her resolve stronger now from the desperation in his tone.

"It isna that simple, Katie. Ian has rules. Rules that have to be followed or consequences happen."

"What consequences?" Katelyn yelled across the room. "Why do you let him treat you that way? You deserve—"

"I was starving!" Grant yelled. "When I was a boy. Not just hungry. Starving. I had to dig in the trash behind the shelter, restaurants, other people's houses. I lived most days with an empty stomach. I'd get dizzy in school and I couldna—" he stopped to swallow. "My mum did her best, but she got sick." He choked out the word as if it were filth in his mouth. "Cancer. The virulent kind that hides until, by the time you know it's there, it's everywhere." Grant dropped his hand from his mouth. Katelyn's throat closed, and the stinging started behind her eyes.

"She tried to take care of me, but she was so sick. She couldn't work." He shook his head and turned away to hide his tears.

"Grant—"

"Before the end, she contacted Ian." He shook his head. "She must have known he was worthless, because it took until she lay on her deathbed to admit to needing him." His mouth twisted in hatred. "He didn't even remember her. He demanded a paternity test, and she spent what little we had left on it." He paused, understanding as an adult what he hadn't as a child. "She knew she wasna going to be around much longer and it was the last thing she could give me. Someone who had to take care of me."

Katelyn wanted to hold him. Take him in her arms and keep him away from the memory, heal the great chasm of pain that split his whole being in two.

"When he found he had a son, bastard even as I was, he swooped down and claimed to be my savior. Wasna until I was older that I realized how many strings there were attached to his so-called generosity. I escaped poverty and jumped into Ian Tennyson's feckin prison."

Katelyn came over to where he stood at the window. This giant of a man who had once been a scrawny, malnourished boy, ducking behind dumpsters for scraps of leftover food, scraping away mold and fighting off rats. She wrapped her arms around his waist. He held both of her hands with one of his. She felt her warm assurance help to ease the tension in his body. She put her forehead on his back and listened to the sound of his heart thumping against his spine.

"I've always done as he asked. I've given up dreams he didn't think were good enough. I've given up hopes I had, and choices he didn't think were worthy. I lost the love of my life." Katelyn loosened her grip and waited patiently. "Jane."

"What happened?" she whispered against his back. Grant took a deep breath and pulled away from her, paced to his desk and back again.

"Jane was nothing like you."

"She bathe more often?"

He scowled. "She was sweet."

"Wow, thanks."

"No! Christ, Katelyn—Jane was soft, delicate of heart. D'ye understand? Sweet to a fault. Loving to a fault. She put her heart in my hands." He held them to his chest. "She knew there were risks getting involved with me. Ian was quick to remind her that she wasn't deserving of my station."

"I've heard that about you," Katelyn nodded.

"He insisted that we end our engagement," Grant went on as if in a trance. Katelyn searched his face.

"But you didn't listen." Grant stared over Katelyn's head and let the memory command him.

"I didnae at first. I thought there were ways around it. He was so busy elsewhere; he'd never know. That he would come around when he knew how much in love we were." Grant shook his head.

"He didn't come around," Katelyn whispered.

"No."

"What happened when he found out you were still seeing her?" Grant turned away, paced to the window and refused to face her.

"T'isnae important."

"It *is* important!"

"Why?"

"Because you wanted to die! Whatever he did, whatever happened to her? It made you want to die," she yelled back. Grant, used to arguing with her, thought nothing of rushing headlong in.

"He cut me off! He blacklisted me from getting hired on my own. His reach is so far and so deep that he made sure I would be nothing but the penniless orphan I was when he found me. I remembered starving." Grant choked. "So, I turned my back on her. I was afraid. I told myself it was because I didn't want her to be a part of Ian's life. I thought I was doing the best thing for her, but the truth," a sick look passed over his face. "The truth, Katelyn, is that I was afraid to starve. That we'd both starve."

Grant leaned against the window frame. Katelyn's heart broke to watch him, lost in the pain.

"You said on the ride that you wanted to die. To be with the only people who had loved you," Katelyn paused. "How did Jane die?"

"She took her own life," he whispered. "Threw herself from The Seven Sisters Cliffs." His words stopped, and he squeezed his eyes shut. The room fell into heavy silence until even the birds outside seemed to feel the weight and quieted. Katelyn's lungs were lead balloons, refusing air. Her head ached as her eyebrows drew together and her lips trembled.

"Grant—"

"She thought we'd have a whole life, children, growing old together. She loved me to a point that not being together just broke her." He closed his eyes. "As if I deserved that kind of love. As if I was worthy of it!" Anger rumbled deep in his throat; his eyes burned. "My father spent so much of his energy convincing me that she wasn't good enough for me, but the truth was that I didn't deserve her."

"Grant, listen—"

"No, you listen! So you good and understand the reason I deserve every ounce of pain I carry. I let her go when I should have loved her. I don't deserve to be happy. That day on the hillside with Hugh, was ten years ago to the day she died. I just wanted to get back to her. I just wanted to leave Ian's reach forever. I wanted to die, Katelyn."

She tried to touch his arm, but he pulled away, stalked to the fireplace, and leaned against it. Katelyn watched as the darkness swallowed him. She shivered in the warm room. No wonder Grant hated his father so much. No wonder he hated himself so much. Her heart raced in her chest and her stomach felt sick. She wanted to throw up, or run away, or hit something. Grant snarled a cruel laugh as he turned back around.

"After he found out, he told me good riddance. Told me that's what happens when I get ideas of my own. He had my life perfectly planned, you see. His legacy. I would marry the right kind of woman. Raise children in the proper bonds of his approved, ordained matrimony."

"But you've never married," Katelyn asked.

"This is the last year I have. By the time I'm 43, I have to have a wife, and preferably start a 'family' within the year. Or at least that's the contract if I want to keep Tennyson Stables."

"What happens if you don't?"

"He takes it all. He forces me off the premises and all the work I've done will mean nothing. He'll probably ruin me financially, just for fun, while he's at it. He's threatened to sell Hugh to a slaughterhouse." Grant looked at her, hazel eyes blazing, as if he could burn the truth into her soul.

"You should have never come here. You should have never tried to help me." He choked back tears. "You should have never come into my bed, or looked at me with any hope for a future in your eyes. The best thing you can do is leave."

"Oh, I get it," she said measuredly. "It's been fun, but we need to call it a night, before your dad catches us making out on the couch? Is that all this is?"

"We're a distraction, Katelyn, a detour from his perfectly laid plans."

"Is that all I am *to you*? A distraction? A detour?"

"You know that's not all you are!" he yelled. "But if my father finds out, there's something else, he will destroy you just like he destroyed her."

"I am not Jane!"

"I know!"

"Well, then, fuck him," she said, eliciting a surprised grunt from Grant.

"What?"

"You heard me. Fuck Ian Tennyson. He's told you for so long that you're nothing without him. But you've always been enough, just as you are. You don't have to have all this to be worthy." She gestured out into the expansive land outside.

"Katie." But she came nearer, wrapped her arms around his middle and buried her face in his chest.

"You are enough, Grant," she whispered, her nose nudging his chin. The soft words cut deep into the years and layers of hurt.

"Come on," she sniffed, took his hand in hers and led him from the office.

"What are you doing? Where are we going?" he demanded as she pulled him through the long, dark wood paneled halls.

"Jeffers?" Katelyn said as they passed the kitchen, her hand never leaving Grant's. Jeffers came through the door immediately.

"Is everything alright, Miss Katelyn?" Jeffers asked with genuine concern. "How may I be of service?"

"That thing we talked about earlier, the emergency exit plan?"

"The what?" Grant began.

"Of course, Miss Katelyn. As we discussed."

"How soon can it be ready?"

"Presently, miss."

Katelyn nodded and smiled. "And Ian isn't expected home until Thursday?"

Jeffers looked at Grant with a slight hint of fear. "No, miss."

"Perfect."

"What shall I tell him if he returns early?" Jeffers asked.

"Well, I would hope you would tell him that nothing is out of order. I had to leave on a personal errand, and Grant is away on business." She gave him a smile. "At least, that's what I hope you would tell him."

Jeffers smiled warmly back. "Yes, Miss Katelyn. As you wish."

"Thanks, Jeffers." She turned back and gave him a quick peck on the cheek before pulling Grant behind her towards the garage.

"What's an emergency exit plan?" Grant demanded as she pulled him into the garage and towards the work truck behind the line of high-end sports cars.

"It's what you do to save yourself," she responded.

"Haven't you listened to anything I've said?" he yelled.

"Yeah, I heard. Every word," she said and opened his door.

"Then you know I'm not going anywhere. That *we* can't go anywhere!"

"Can't we?" she said, looking up at him stubbornly. "You say he's taken away your choices, but that's not true. There are always other choices."

"Katie, you dinna ken—" he said softly, his hand cupping her chin.

"I ken plenty. You just have to trust me," she said. Grant sighed, looked down at her, and shook his head.

"I do," he said, "But where on earth can we go that he canna find us?"

"Don't worry your pretty little head, lad." She climbed into the driver's side and tapped at her phone. "I've been keeping a plan on the back burner, 'cause I'm a girl who likes to be prepared. Lucky for us, Ian put the oldest plane in your name, so as to not be embarrassed by it and save on the insurance, I imagine, since you can't fly it."

"But you canna fly it either," Grant scoffed.

"Oh, I'm sure I'll figure it out." She shrugged over her shoulder as they headed down the road at a gravel-throwing speed, towards the hangar on the far side of the property. Grant turned pale and stared, dumbfounded, as she got out of the car, walked determinedly to the oldest shack of a hangar, and manually cranked open the doors. There sat the oldest, most basic plane in his father's possession.

"This is insane!" He barreled out behind her, running to catch up. She stopped and looked back at him with a chuckle.

"Seriously? You think I'd just try to 'wing it?' That's a twin-engine, 300-horsepower Beechcraft Baron. It's not a toy. Well, for some rich guys it was." He stopped and stared at her.

"You're a—pilot too?" His voice echoed between them.

"Oh, I'm just full of surprises," she said, and nodded at the plane. "Do you trust me?" It took Grant a minute to respond, so confused and emotional as he was. He took a deep breath and stared into her eyes.

"Outside of Jeffers? There's never been another person I've trusted more." Katelyn's smile spread and she took his hand and ushered him into the front right seat. He crawled in, uncomfortable in the small cockpit. "When exactly did you make these plans?"

"Last week. It was actually your idea. You asked if I could kidnap you away from all of this drudgery, then I started thinking, what if I could? Jeffers helped. We put in some hours while you were gone." She put on the David Clark headset and motioned for him to do the same. He stared at it.

"He did, did he?" Grant smiled. "So, it's an inside job. This kidnapping?"

"In a manner of sorts."

"Katie, I'm not sure I can do this."

"You *can* get out, if you really don't want to. I *can* take you back to the house and you *can* go on living the same ol' life. We could go our separate ways. It'll hurt, but we'll survive it. You'll always have a choice with me. I understand a thing or two about fear, and pain, and how it locks us down." She held the checklist still, not wavering until she knew what his decision would be.

CONSEQUENCES OF WHAT IAN MIGHT DO IF HE FOUND out be damned. Grant wanted to be kidnapped by her, even if it was just for a little while. He buckled the harness and adjusted his headset. She started the engines.

They taxied out to the private strip, went through the run up, engine check, and weather information. She programed in the coordinates and radioed Charlottesville airport to let them know they were active. Grant listened, awestruck by her. Within minutes, they were speeding down the quiet single runway and lifting off into the air. Grant stared down at the disappearing squares of green and wondered what madness had possessed him.

It was a peaceful flight. On previous flights, Grant had always been engrossed in work in the back of the plane or listening to Ian drone on about investments or country club gossip. His mind was always aggravated and stressed over where he was going to or coming from. But this flight, with her by his side, explaining the routes, the airspace system, the radio aids and navigational aids, letting him take the yoke for a part of the trip, coaxed him out of his mind and into the present.

Much like with Hugh; she had thrown him into it and let him flail, understanding what he didn't know; that he was capable of more. That he would blossom with a little trust and a loosened rein. By the time they were making their descent and talking to Cheyenne Air Force Base on their way through, he couldn't stop smiling and feeling something deep inside that he was completely unfamiliar with. It took him a moment to understand that he was feeling wonder.

He'd never gotten to be a child. He'd never gotten to feel such innocent bliss. When he looked over at her as she adjusted their speed and the mixture of fuel for the altitude, his heart pulsed madly in his chest. Coming over the upper tail of the Rocky Mountains was breathtaking and shaky as the wind at their flight level picked up. The plane bounced a few hard times and Grant grabbed onto the sides of his seat with a nervous breath. Katelyn watched him with a knowing eye and started talking.

"That's Mitchell Peak. It's about 12,000 feet. My sisters, Elle and Laney and I would hike up there every summer when we were growing up. There's a great little lake near the top that you can skinny dip in." Grant forgot about crashing for a moment and looked over at her.

"What happens if there are people around?"

Katelyn laughed with the wild exuberance of youth that was unfettered with vanity or caring what other people thought.

"There aren't enough people in Wyoming to constitute a crowd much of anywhere, except maybe in War Memorial Stadium during the border wars." She put the plane into a descent as they cleared the mountain pass. The sound of the engine cutting in and out made him grip the seats tighter.

"What are you doing?"

"Getting ready to land," she said and pointed to the long but singular runway ten miles to the west, atop a high hill above a small town. A river snaked through the landscape, giving rise to pockets of cottonwoods and curved around the still-lush fields of hay and alfalfa of surrounding ranches.

"Ain't nothing like coming home," she whispered. Katelyn made a slightly rough touch-down into the wind and closed the flight plan while still parked on the tarmac. Grant looked around at the barren and unmanned airport.

"Are we just leaving the plane?" Grant asked as she grabbed a couple of bags from the back and locked the doors.

"Yep."

"But—"

"Don't worry, Tennyson. This isn't like any kind of town you've been in."

He looked around.

"Is there even a car rental here?"

"Nope," she said and walked towards the high chain-link fence and gate.

"But where are we staying? How will we get there?"

"You sure do like to worry about things," she said. He started to ask another question but was interrupted by a horn honking. A beat-up Ford pickup pulled through the gates with its lights on in the fading dusk. He stood back, his jacket in his hand, as Katelyn quickened her pace to the truck. A tall, lanky woman stepped out. She had short curly blonde hair and was smiling to light the night.

"Elle!" Katelyn shouted, and the woman pulled her in for a tight hug.

"Nice landing, kid! I saw it from the highway." Elle looked at the bags before picking one up with a shake of her head. "Did you not bother to pack clothes?"

"Who needs clothes?" Katelyn smiled and put her green bag and a small black suitcase in the seat. The women turned back and stared at Grant.

"Is this him?" Elle nodded at Grant. Katelyn smiled and offered a soft look at Grant.

"Suppose so." Elle walked over and extended her hand.

"Mr. Tennyson, I'm Eleanor O'Connor-Sullivan. Katelyn's sister."

"Mrs. O'Connor-Sullivan," he said morosely, vaguely remembering that she was married to the young man that had been raised by the family. Katelyn snorted.

"Well, don't get *too* formal with her. She milks goats for a living." Katelyn shoved Elle.

"You rub down horses! Hardly a step up," Elle teased back. Grant looked nervously between them.

"Well, you ready?" Katelyn asked. Grant stared down at her, and the way the western sunset was lighting her honey golden hair, coming loose from its ponytail in the wind.

"How could I deny such becoming ladies anything? Lead on," he said.

TWENTY

"No thank you," Grant stuttered and stepped away from the cooing, blue-eyed baby with wispy golden curls. "Children don't like me. I scare them." Emilee squealed with delight and blew a raspberry at him, her hands outstretched.

"Oh, yeah?" Elle laughed. "She looks terrified."

"*I'm* terrified," Grant grunted.

"Don't be a big baby. Here, I need both my hands for a minute." She handed the drooling, warm bundle into his arms and turned back to the kitchen sink. Grant froze. It was like holding a wriggling puppy, with less hair, and much more consequential if dropped.

"Mrs. O'Connor-Sulli—Elle—Eleanor, I dinna—" he began, until Emilee put her tiny fingers on his chin. One of her hands found the curls on the base of his neck and clung to them.

"Baba ship," she cooed, and Elle burst into laughter.

"What? What's so funny?" Grant asked, glowering over Emilee's head. Elle turned from the sink full of dishes and smiled at him, that beautiful Sullivan smile. Warm and teasing and utterly beguiling.

"Baa, baa, black sheep," she said. "You must remind her of a sheep. I imagine it's the thick hair." Grant scowled and looked down at the vibrant baby, now twining her tiny fingers in his curly brown locks, looking up at him with an innocent smile.

"Aw, ship, baa baa ship," she sang softly and nestled her head beneath his chin.

Grant's heart contracted in his chest. The smell of her, gentle and soft, and her tiny hand on the base of his neck. He knew suddenly, and beyond any shadow of doubt, that he would murder anyone who tried to hurt this baby. Something deep inside turned on; an instinct so paternal and singular that he could scarcely contain it with any reasonable thought. He closed his eyes and started murmuring the strains of a lullaby he didn't know he'd remembered. He whispered the words, haltingly, as if trying to pull the memory up through a thousand dark and painful layers that had buried it for so long.

"*Bonnie wee thing, cannie wee thing,*
lovely wee thing wer't thou mine,
I wad wear thee in my bosom, lest my jewel I should tine.
Wistfully, I look and languish in that bonnie face of thine
and my heart it stounds wi' anguish lest my wee thing be na
mine."

The melodic and low strains of his voice died away, and he hummed the melody again, his arms remembering the warmth of his mother's. For this moment, cradling the baby in his arms, he let go of his fearful world. He swayed and Emilee went soft and limp against his chest and the beat of his heart.

"Wow, you scared her right to sleep."

Grant turned in surprise, having forgotten there was anyone or anything in the room but him and Emilee. Elle and Katelyn stood, transfixed and soft-eyed, staring at him. Elle smiled.

"I'll put her to bed," she offered and stretched out her hands.

"Nay," he shook his head, afraid to wake her. "I'll do it, if you show me where."

Katelyn smiled. "Come on, you scary old man," she said and

led him up the stairs, to the second door on the right. Emilee's was
a pink and cream room with a simple white crib with a rocking
chair sat in the corner, decorated with pictures of goats, horses,
and farm life. Grant had to step over wooden farm animals and
stuffed bears before laying Emilee delicately down on the soft
sheets. He stared at her for a moment as Katelyn came to stand
beside him. He looked over at her, something new and distressed
in his eyes.

"Katie," he breathed.

"Yes?" she asked.

"Where are we sleeping?"

"Um, I think my sister has made up the guest room across the
—" But she didn't finish. Grant pulled her across the hallway to
the quiet and small room. Its warm, overstuffed bed was thick with
homemade quilts and clean, fresh sheets. He swung her around
and pushed her back towards the bed. His lips found hers with
desperation and hunger, devouring the warm taste of her. His
breath came in ragged gasps and he felt his whole world cleaved
into pieces.

The losses of his life, the anguished feelings of neglect and cold
familial ties seemed a foreign and ugly thing in this place. He
didn't know how to compensate for the dissonance. He didn't
know how to accept the wants of his heart and the vicious
whispers of his past. He wanted the life she had. He wanted to
have been raised with two spirited sisters and compassionate
parents who would take a neglected boy in and raise him with
love. He wanted a mother who worried over him. He wanted a
father who trusted him to do his best, but not scorn him for his
failures.

If he could just forget it all, for this moment, use her warmth
to take him away from the hard reckoning of all he wanted and all
he could not have, maybe it would give him some sense of peace.
Maybe if he could just pretend, here in this place, that this was his
life, and she was his. Maybe if he could pretend it was their love

filling cribs and falling asleep in his arms. He kissed her desperately for want of it.

"Grant, take it easy," Katelyn gasped, his teeth on her throat and his hands tearing at the buttons on her shirt. "What is this?" she asked, putting her hands on either side of his face.

"I want you." He dipped to kiss her again, but she dodged away.

"But something's different," she said, studying him. "What's on your mind?"

"I cannae," He paused, not meeting her eyes. "Nothing, it's nothing." His breath came hard, and she could see his control crumbling. He unfastened her pants, and she took them off.

"It's not nothing." Katelyn made him look at her. His eyes filled with tears and his teeth clenched.

"Just," he sobbed, and Katelyn pushed him back onto the bed. The metal frame squeaked under their weight and she pinned him down. "I just need this right now." He bit her neck, her chin, tearing her shirt open and finding her breasts with his hands. Grant couldn't put into words the aching need to fill this void or why he thought her body was the solution. He thought of the life he wanted. The feeling of warmth and safety that she embodied.

"This or me?" she whispered into his hair and pulled back.

"I need," his voice and body strained and he unzipped his pants. "I need—"

"What?" she said breathlessly, trying hard to read the pain in his eyes. "What do you need, Grant?"

"Love," he cried suddenly.

"Grant," she whispered. Her eyes were soft and understanding, and he couldn't hold on to the pain anymore. The flood gates opened and his body began to shake. He collapsed beneath her and she gently spread her legs, wrapping them around his waist and opening to him.

"I have it," she whispered into his hair. "I have so much of it." She guided him inside and he gasped and sobbed at the tight hold of her. "Take some of mine." She rolled him on top of her and whispered, "please, I love you so much."

She caressed the back of his head, his shoulders, the straining of his hips as he moved inside of her, so deeply and needful. She held onto him, matched his rhythm, and met his desire with her own. His tears wet her cheek and neck and she held him closer still.

Her warmth and softness, so accepting to his pain, caused Grant to slow and lean back to kiss and caress her face. She closed her eyes and her body responded to his desperation in a selfish and pleased way, until she climbed closer and closer over the edge.

"That's it, baby," she whispered. "Yes, all of it," she gasped, her voice rising in a pleased gasp as she crested, clinging to him and shaking. Grant drove into her, his whole world exploding. He yelled in the stillness and collapsed on top of her, still sobbing.

"It isna fair, it isna fair, it isna," he breathed over and over.

"Oh, darlin'," she said into his hair, gasping from the weight of his body and pain.

"You canna love me, he'll take you too. He'll destroy you. All of this. This heaven. That's what he does. Destroys goodness," he wept incoherently. "When he finds out what I've done—"

"Shh," she said and tugged at his hair. She wrapped her trembling legs around his waist, barely able to lock her ankles at his back for his size. "You haven't done anything wrong," she said.

"I have."

"What have you done?" She placed gentle kisses into his neck.

"Fallen, Katie. I've fallen and he'll find out."

"You don't worry about that tonight," she commanded softly. He pulled away to look down at her in the dim light. Her hair tangled beneath them, her cheeks pink and her body shaking and wet. She'd taken the brunt of his anger and stood up to his brooding without pity.

"What do I worry about then?"

"You worry about how you're going to keep your hands off me

long enough to get some sleep." She rolled him to lay below her and stripped away her shirt and her bra.

"You worry about how it feels to fall asleep next to me. You worry about learning how to milk goats and play with Emilee. You worry about what it's going to be like to ride a mangy pack of half-breed quarters. You worry about taxes, or chess, or what scotch to buy next. Or you worry about nothing, 'cause you've already done more than your fair share of worrying. But you sure as hell aren't gonna worry about Ian Tennyson in my bed. He's got no business being here."

"I can't love you," he whispered, his whole body weak; his eyes sore and heavy. His mind sunk into a strange sense of ease.

"I know you can't," she whispered and fell to his chest, resting her cheek against his heartbeat. "And it's okay. 'Cause, I've got enough for the both of us."

GRANT FELL ASLEEP WITH HER BODY SPREAD OVER HIM like a bandage. The sweet, warm weight of her, a pressure that stilled his chaotic mind and soothed every tense muscle into a deep calm. He dreamed, but not of Ian. He dreamed of Hugh, healed and strong, galloping across the open plains of the valley, Katelyn on his back, free from obligations and expectations.

He watched the stallion's mane blowing wild like a curtain of night, as she rode him bareback. Her smile lit the world and his heart rose and fell with every thundering hoof beat of their journey. He woke, startling, to the crow of a rooster outside.

"Goddamn Channing Tatum," Katelyn mumbled into his back where she spooned him.

"Have you forgotten my name, lass?" Grant chuckled in his sleep-rough voice.

"It's the fucking rooster. My sister got one in a batch of chicks and she can't stand to turn any animal out with her big ol' soft heart, so she kept him and named him Channing Tatum." She paused to nuzzle into his back. "Probably on account of his propensity for preening." Her sleep-low voice against his neck brought him a sense comfort and familiarity. Grant couldn't help but smile. He looked down at his hand locked around her arm and snuggled back in as the rooster crowed again.

"I guess I'd better get my lazy ass out of bed and help her," Katelyn sighed and stirred.

"Of all the arses in the world, yours is the least lazy I know," he disagreed.

"I feel pretty lazy right now." She kissed his warm skin.

"You're probably exhausted," he whispered.

"Oh?"

"Flying cross-country, introducing your family to a strange and grouchy old man that you'd kidnapped from an even stranger and grouchier man. Then, last night," he stopped as he remembered the hard and horrible feelings that had driven him with a desperation he'd never felt before.

"Mm, that was a bit of all right," she said and held him tighter when he moved to get up.

"I question your judgment still being here with me," he said, lying back down when the weakness in his muscles refused to fight with her strong hold.

"I question your questioning of my judgment," she said, still sleepy but defiant, and snuggled into his chest.

"I could—"

"Could what?" she said after a moment of silence.

"It's nothing." He shook his head, unable to tell her the truth that flooded him. That he could wake every morning to the sound of roosters crowing and babies mewing in the room down the hall and Katelyn's arms wrapped around him, her warm breath on his back. He could live without trust funds or multibillion-dollar business plans. He could live in the comfortable creaking of an old farmhouse, the smell of fresh biscuits and bacon coming up the stairs. He was, in short, happier than he ever remembered being.

That's usually when things went wrong.

"Must be something on your mind, cause your heart just started pounding like a jackrabbit." She sat up and smiled down at him, then swung her leg over his hips and sat up. The sweet weight of her pinned him to the bed, and his body grew hard. She pressed her cheek to his chest with a smile.

"Listen to that!" she said in mock surprise. "Now, I'd heard that you didn't have a heart, but there it is."

He meant to scowl at her when she sat up, but he couldn't. She was beautiful in her teasing, despite knowing the severity of his temper. So the frightening stare he would have normally given was lost, and he stared up at her in wonder as a painful smile started to spread.

"I have other more interesting parts you could attend to right now," he said in a quiet voice.

"You don't want me to help your heart?"

"I dinna think my heart could take much more, Katie love," he said and his eyes traveled down to her lips, her neck, the delicate line of her jaw and her shoulders where her golden hair spilled in the sunlight. "I think it's full."

His words were soft and sad in the morning light, and she couldn't bear to hear them. She lowered her body onto his, taking him inside with a gasp, and threw her head back. Grant arched beneath her in the soft bed and opened his eyes to watch the sunlight streaming in and bathing her in soft, golden light. This was all they could have. These moments before the storm of his father descended on the sweet and simple life. He wanted to lose himself to it, make believe that this was his life. Waking up with Katie, spending luxurious mornings between her thighs. Warm breakfasts, the laughter and comfort of hearth and home. His heart wanted it so badly, that even with her slow and steady pace, when she tightened around him, he lost control and came with her, enveloped in the fantasy of a different life.

"Well," she said breathlessly, collapsing on his chest. "I guess we'll just have to work on making more room in there." Grant threw his arms around her and held her close to his hammering heartbeat. He didn't want to speak and ruin the moment by bringing any sense of reality into it.

"Breakfast! You two crazy love birds! Disentangle before you pass out from exhaustion!" Elle called from downstairs.

"Walls are thin in an old farmhouse," Katelyn chuckled. Grant groaned and covered his eyes.

"Your family is going to think I'm a sex-starved maniac."

"I'm not complaining." Katelyn laughed, bit his neck, and slid off of him. She dressed quickly in jeans and a clean shirt and looked back to see him, languishing in the bed, propped up on his elbow to watch her.

"Don't worry about Elle, she's not the judgmental type." They heard the squeal of a baby from downstairs as the old screen door slammed and Blake came into the kitchen from outside.

"Daddy!" Emilee's excited scream floated up through the door and Blake's soft low voice followed.

"How's my beautiful baby girl?" Blake said. His daughter chattered in delight.

Grant couldn't pull himself out of the fantasy. How he wished Katelyn and he might someday—a cloud passed over the sun. He remembered her inability to have children. What had once comforted him, now filled him with sadness. Katelyn watched his face as he listened to the voices downstairs.

"Come on lazy bones, get up. Lots of work to do today." She nudged him with her knee and he shook himself out of his thoughts. He pinched her backside as she turned to leave. He hopped on one foot to get into his pants. He wasn't a man who normally wore jeans, but Katelyn said Jeffers had packed for him, insisting that he'd need something "rough and ready."

The truth was, he didn't really know much about the day-to-day work of a real ranch. He was management. He rode horses, but someone else always groomed and put them away. He didn't have the connection she did with animals, or the lifestyle. Grooming Hugh with her in the last months had been out of the ordinary for him. It had connected him in a way that his hours in the saddle had not. He put on the thin, flannel shirt—where had Jeffers even found a flannel shirt—and shook his head. He looked in the smoky antique mirror, hanging over the small vanity in the corner of the room, and hardly recognized himself. He looked like a hired hand. He looked like someone Katelyn Sullivan would take to bed.

He smiled and went downstairs, not missing his pressed pants one bit. Elle had laid a table full of delicious hot biscuits, fresh milk, butter, homemade jam, eggs, bacon and coffee. Grant paused in the doorway, his eyes growing big from the luscious spread.

"My god, woman, when did you get up?" he asked in his burr. Elle smiled over her coffee cup and shrugged.

"Sounded like we *all* got up early. I just made biscuits with my time." Her naughty smile made Grant blush and Blake cleared his throat.

"Sleep okay?" Blake asked, trying to spare Grant the embarrassment that the sisters were prone to put a new soul through.

"Like the dead, actually," Grant said and shot a quick glance at Katelyn, who was filling up a plate and sitting down. She smiled up at him and winked. His stomach grumbled.

"Well, come in and get yourself something to eat. You're going to need it. It's tagging day, and Blake wanted to do some work on the south pasture's irrigation. I told him you wouldn't mind," Katelyn said. Grant stared down at her and a small scowl threatened.

"Are you suddenly *my* boss?" he said.

"Baa baa!" shouted Emilee as she came out of her sticky-jam and biscuit haze and saw him in the doorway. Grant's frown fell off immediately.

"Hello my darlin' lass," he cooed and lost all sense of propriety as he plopped into the chair next to her. She reached her sticky fingers up to him and he let her smear strawberry jam into his stubble. Blake handed him a wet paper towel.

"Sorry about that," he said. Grant looked into Emilee's beautiful blue eyes, and back to Blake.

"'Tis no trouble. None at all." He smiled back at the baby. "And what will be done wi' you, my wee lassie? While we are mucking about today?" he asked, clucking her chin. She giggled and showed two tiny perfect pearls of teeth.

"Babababababa, gots."

"She'll come with us," Elle said, setting a cup of coffee in front of Grant.

"Outside? With the animals, and the equipment, and the dirt?" Grant looked at Katelyn with concern and she laughed.

"Of course. Where else would she go?"

"Well, with a nanny!" he said. Elle snorted.

"Sorry, my *au pair* has every third Saturday off," Elle retorted in an austere voice. The sisters laughed uproariously.

"We learned to toddle in cow pies and took our first steps in corrals. She's all the better for the fresh air and sunshine," Katelyn said. Grant cocked his head at her while she filled his plate. The thought was foreign. The idea was strange. Even his own mother had left him safely at home while she had gone to work. Ian had always had nannies or Jeffers care for him. He was never allowed out without supervision and certainly not to play while there were 'useful' activities to be forced upon him.

"Okay then. You two eat and we'll meet you outside," Blake said and nodded. He plucked Emilee gingerly out of her seat and stopped at the sink to wash her hands and face. Elle strapped on a child carrier and Blake slid Emilee inside, facing forward.

"Gots, gots!" Emilee shouted excitedly. Her legs kicked in the air as if she could drive her mother to go faster.

"That's right baby girl, we're off to feed the goats," Elle said.

Blake stopped after checking the straps and ran his long fingers through Elle's short curls. He looked at her with such deep affection, as if he'd never seen a woman so beautiful, as if his whole life depended on touching her just like this, in the warmth of a sunny kitchen with their baby babbling between them.

Then, to Grant's embarrassment and secret excitement, Blake kissed Elle and whispered something low to her. She blushed and bit his lip. Grant felt his chest and his groin tighten. Katelyn's hand gave his thigh a squeeze and brought his attention back to her.

"Okay?" she asked, licking butter from her finger. He watched the way it made her lips look supple and moist. God, he wanted her again. His stomach rumbled, and he shook his head and blushed. "Eat," she said softly.

They hadn't lied. The day was harder than Grant had been accustomed to. Days sitting behind a desk and crunching numbers, dealing with phone calls and management meetings, financial advisors, breeders, and the like were very mentally exhausting tasks, but by the time they'd called the day and headed back to the old white farmhouse, Grant was nearly dead on his feet. He shuffled beside Katelyn, whose steps were still lively and her smile nonplussed.

She swung her arms and tromped through the tall grass with Blake, and laughed as he told her about a bull that had escaped three ranches over and had copulated with most of the dude ranch's prize heifers before he was caught. Now they had a whole calving season wasted. One of the lawyers from back east had asked Blake if they didn't have some sort of morning-after pill to administer to the herd. Katelyn doubled over at this. She didn't seem upset. Grant scowled.

"That's a lot of money they've lost," he said. Katelyn looked sideways at him.

"Trust me, the Bar Nunn can stand to lose more than a few calves. They've been putting pressure on my parents to sell their land for years. It's no skin off my nose if they find themselves with forty 'sub-par' calves for one season."

Grant thought about a big ranch squeezing out her parents, making life harder for their family, and how the comical misfortunes of the conglomerate were a mere drop in the bucket for their bottom line. A mistake like that would have cost the Sullivan family their whole future. Then his thoughts turned to Ian, and what he could do to her family. They continued to walk to the house. Blake broke off to check on the chickens and change their water before night. Elle had left the field about an hour ago with a sleeping baby and had gotten dinner started. At the gate, the heavenly aroma of dinner wafted through the air at them.

"My god, that woman's an angel," Grant said, letting the smell of fried chicken, mashed potatoes, and bacon-wrapped green beans lead him to the door.

"She's a dream in the kitchen," Katelyn agreed.

"Don't you Sullivan women ever rest?" Grant asked as she climbed the porch steps. Katelyn looked back at him and paused with her hand on the screen door.

"There's an awful lot of living to get to," she responded, as if it were a silly question. On two steps below her, he was eye level. He reached a blistered hand out to hers, interlaced their fingers and his thumb caressed the back of her hand. Grubby, tired, dirty and sore, they stared at each other in the fading light of the day, on the porch steps where dinner and a soft bed waited.

"I wish I could take care of you," he whispered unexpectedly.

"What?" she chuckled.

"I mean, don't you ever wish you didn't have to work so hard? That they didn't have to work so hard?"

Katelyn turned to face him. She sighed and looked into his eyes.

"I know this isn't what you're used to. The work, the hours, the constant daily drudgery. But to see your own stock do well, your first set of foals coming into their talents, your land produce what you need, it just—" she paused, then shook her head. "Hell, yes. Yes! There are days when I wish I could just sit on my ass and do nothing. But after a while, I think it would just bore me to tears. Eating food I didn't cook, and looking out at pastures I didn't work. Watchin' other people train my horses?"

"I see. You don't approve of my lifestyle."

"I didn't say that. You work hard in other ways that I couldn't manage. I know you don't know any other way. But, I don't either." She shrugged. He wanted to kiss her, to beg her to teach him her way, to believe that he could handle the everyday 'drudgery' as she called it. But he was afraid he wasn't strong enough for the kind of life she lived. As he stared into her lavender-laced eyes, he felt his heart drop. It would never work, so posturing about changing his whole life was pointless. He was just having a vacation, wasn't he? They'd fly home tomorrow and life would resume just as always.

"You two gonna just stand there?" Elle called from inside. Blake, who'd finished with the hens, came up behind and shoved Katelyn out of the way playfully.

"Move, pipsqueak, I call dibs on the thighs!" he hooted with child-like enthusiasm.

"Elle's or the chicken's?" Katelyn yelled after him as the screen door slammed.

"Both!" Blake yelled back.

"Come on, my bonnie lad, you've never tasted heaven until you've had one of my sister's thighs," Katelyn said with a wink.

"Not interested in *her* thighs," he growled and pulled her in for a kiss. "But I'd give up the saints' souls to be between yours." He lifted her in his arms and groaned before setting her back down. "Or maybe a dozen paracetamol."

Katelyn laughed and caressed his cheek before pecking his lips.

"I've got a hot night of Advil and a bath all planned out for you, after dinner."

And that's just what Katelyn gave him. That and a feeling of sweet euphoria that he'd never had before in his life. From the warm and good food, the unpretentious company that made him laugh and feel accepted in a way he'd never felt before, to the warm Epsom salt bath and the clean sheets he sunk into. When she crawled in beside him and cuddled close, her warmth spread through him. His body was torn, wanting to make love to her, but needing the sleep.

"My darlin'," he whispered drowsily and ran his hand up her bare thigh. "I'm going to make love to you all night," he threatened, before yawning.

"Oh? Is that so?" she chuckled. "Sometimes the best love is made just holding each other."

"How'd you get so wise, so young," he murmured. His fingers traced up her back.

"I dunno. Grandma Em used to say I was an old soul," she said, lost in her own thoughts. His breathing evened out beneath her cheek as he fell into a deeper slumber.

WHAT WOULD SHE DO WITH THIS MAN SHE'D FALLEN SO hopelessly in love with? This man who wasn't free to love who he wanted to? She sighed and felt tears squeeze out from behind her closed eyelids. Would he take the chance at a happier life? Her brain ran itself in circles until the early hours of the morning. When she finally fell asleep, it was more from sheer exhaustion than from respite of the chaotic thoughts plaguing her mind.

Channing Tatum's call barely roused her. She was stuck in a dream, where she watched Ian push a girl with long chestnut hair over a cliff's edge, his gnarled hand at her back. She heard Grant yell for her and she startled when he moved beside her and kissed her shoulders. Grant paused, his warm hand on her thigh.

"Katie," he whispered. "What is it?" Katelyn took a moment to answer; her brain was foggy and the sound of the woman's scream was too haunting; it threatened to overpower the reality of his body pressed against hers.

"I'm fine," she stuttered. "I didn't sleep much last night.

That's all." Grant nuzzled her neck; his stubble scratched her delicate skin.

"Was I snoring? It's the curse of a grouchy, old man like myself." He smiled beneath her ear.

"No," she said quietly over her shoulder. "Just a lot on my mind, I think."

Grant stopped his kisses, but his fingers traced up her bare arm.

"What was it you told me, in this very bed not two days ago? That I'm not allowed to think of Ian Tennyson in your bed? That's a two-way street, Katie love."

"How do you know it was your father I was thinking of?" she said, turning in the bed to face him. He looked down at her, and studied the blue circles beneath her eyes, the worry just behind them.

"If it's one thing I can recognize, it's the way Ian frightens people. Causes even the strongest to cower."

Katelyn looked away. "I don't cower." The truth of the matter was that her mind was coming to terms with the horrible possibilities of what Ian could do to her if he found out what they'd done. She was suddenly afraid, for her family, for their land, for Grant. Grant swallowed, his eyes fell, and his jaw clenched.

"Katelyn?" Elle's voice floated up from downstairs. Katelyn shot out of bed and grabbed her shirt and pants, tumbling from bed to dress. Grant sat up in bed as he watched her smooth her hair into a ponytail before opening the door.

"What is it?" he asked, the sheet tucked into his bare middle.

"I don't know. I'll go see," she said, eager to get away. Katelyn bounced down the stairs and rounded into the kitchen where she was met with the sight of her mother and father standing in the kitchen.

"Hey Momma! Hey Dad!" Katelyn embraced them each in turn.

"Katie! We weren't expecting you to visit." Melissa kissed her forehead. "What's this I hear about a guest?"

"Uh, yeah, about that." Katelyn stammered, and her father cleared his throat. He lowered his eyes before squaring them on her.

"You know, was a time a young man had to sleep in a separate room if there wasn't a ring on the girl's hand," Warren said. Katelyn scowled.

"Well, thank God we don't live in a world where I have to guard my virginity like it's the only bargaining chip I have."

"Now, Katelyn, you know I don't really believe that old fuddy-duddy nonsense. I'm only teasing." Warren back-pedaled.

"Katelyn? Is everything all right?" came Grant's voice from the stairwell as he descended. He wore his normal clothes, looking sharp and every bit the rich-landowner part. The sight of him took her parents back, and Katelyn wished he had worn something less formal. Maybe he thought if there was trouble brewing, he should present his most powerful side. The problem was that Katelyn knew that it wasn't his true side. He was impressive, but cold in his eyes as he walked into the kitchen, expecting battle. She could see the recognition in his face when he studied her parents.

"Grant, these are my—"

"I can tell by your stunning beauty that you must be Katelyn's mother, Melissa." Grant interrupted and took Melissa's hand respectfully.

"Katelyn May, I'm not sure I like how smooth he is," Warren said.

"Only honest, sir. It's an honor to meet the man who's raised such a fine and hardworking young woman. Mr. Sullivan," he said and held out his hand to Warren.

"You must be Grant Tennyson. Can't say I've heard much about you from Katelyn, but your work over on the East Coast is something quite interesting." Warren said, and his eyes held Grant's. "I hear from a good friend that you're expecting a champion foal in the next few years. But I'm more interested in what business you have with my daughter."

"As you should be, sir. She's—"

"Dad!" Katelyn scolded and stepped up to the two of them. "I'm a grown ass woman, and you don't get to put your nose in my business."

"Well? Aren't you working for him?" Warren asked her, and Grant swung his head between them, sensing a tension he was all too familiar with.

"She's an independent contractor. She doesn't work for me. She's—"

"My own woman." Katelyn scowled at her dad.

"Katelyn invited me to come home with her."

"Grant, you don't need to explain anything." Katelyn tried to interrupt.

"Because she wanted to prove to me that families can be loving."

"Did you think otherwise?" Warren asked.

"If you knew my father, sir, you might understand," Grant said.

"And just what are your intentions with our daughter, Mr. Tennyson?" Warren asked and put his hands on his belt loops. There was a crackle of tension. This time Elle stepped in, pinching her dad on the back of his arm.

"Now stop it, you scraggly old fart! Grant is a guest here. He helped us irrigate all day yesterday, tagged the goats, helped me with the dishes, and your granddaughter is over the moon for him, so you leave him be! He's a good man. And Katie May is more than old enough to date who she wants."

Warren chuckled and rubbed his arm in mock hurt. He turned back to Grant.

"I'm just teasing you, son. Man, these women! No matter how amazing you think they are, they're nothin' more than a grouchy pack of bears when you pick on something of theirs." He shook

Grant's hand again and Katelyn saw Grant's expression changed at the implication that he was something of hers.

"You have every right to question my intentions. I assure you —" He looked down at Katelyn, who'd taken Emilee up from the floor to perch her on her hip. He swallowed hard. "I only have her best interests in mind."

After breakfast with the family and packing up their bags, along with a picnic hamper full of some of Elle's best homemade goodies, Blake drove them to the airport. Elle kissed Katelyn on the cheek, tugged at her ponytail and tried to staunch the tears that threatened.

"Don't do that, you'll see me soon enough." Katelyn rolled her eyes and pulled Elle's willowy frame in for a hug.

"You fly careful and you call me when you get there, goddamn it. No excuses."

"Yeah, yeah, yeah, I promise," Katelyn said. Blake shook Grant's hand.

"Nice to meet you, Grant. You're welcome anytime, so don't be a stranger now."

Something warm sprouted in Grant's chest at the young man's invitation. He thought back to the unreasonable way he'd once felt jealous over the mention of Blake. He couldn't imagine feeling anything of the sort now, having seen the love between Elle and Blake. "Thank you, Blake. I appreciate that."

While Katelyn readied the plane, walked around and inspected its soundness, Grant ducked his head in the open window of the truck and reached out to let Emilee take his finger in her tiny hand.

"You behave, wee lass. Be good to your ma, and dinna sass your dad." He winked and Emilee's smile turned into a gurgling chuckle. He tried to pull away, but she held him fast.

"No go, baba. No go." She shook her head and pursed her little lips. Grant nearly called off the whole rest of his life.

"Sorry, darlin', your Aunt Katie needs me," he whispered. "I fear there's a storm back home, an' I canna let her weather it alone." Fears that had hidden in his chest since their hushed conversation that morning sprang up when he talked to Emilee. She smiled with her curly head cocked at him.

"Aunt Kitty." She let go of his finger. "Bye bye, baba! Bye bye!" She waved and blew kisses.

"All right, you little charmer," Blake said from beside Grant. "Such a flirt."

"I blame that solely on you," Elle said from across the cab to Blake.

"Right you are," Blake nodded. He turned back to Grant. "Safe trip, keep that little shit outta trouble, would ya?" he said, and nodded towards where Katelyn was waving goodbye.

"I'll do my best," Grant said. He walked to the plane with his shoulders heavy. They sagged with the weight of leaving a world that had been so warm and welcoming. He didn't know if he felt better or worse for the trip, only more conflicted. He slid in beside Katelyn and put on his headset.

"You okay?" she said over the intercom. He nodded but didn't say anything in return. "Well, hang on then, I'll get you back before curfew," she said with a smile.

Grant didn't respond, and Katelyn studied him as they taxied out to the runway. He could tell she knew what was on his mind, but he wasn't ready to open up about it. She'd thrown him into a fire of emotional upheaval and made him question everything he thought about how life should be. But it wasn't her job to sway him one way or another. So, she focused on flying, and left him to his own thoughts.

Twenty-One

GRANT SHOULD HAVE EXPECTED THE RECKONING. HE'D dropped Katelyn off at the Sutters' on his way back to Tennyson Stables. When he pulled in, the high-end cars parked at the front of the house caused sweat to break all over his body. Ian was already home, and up to something.

The delicious calm that had lowered his shoulders and loosened his body for the past two days was now gone, and he felt every muscle in his body contract at once. His jaw clenched, and he hunched into his center. Adrenaline pulsed in his veins and he stormed from the truck, gripping his coat and bag with white knuckles. He entered the office, as he would have from any business trip, angry and exhausted, bee-lining for the bar in the corner. The gentlemen in his father's study looked up from their conversation and followed his livid entrance.

"There's the man of the hour!" Ian's voice froze the air between them.

"Aye," Grant returned in kind. He didn't offer any explanation as to where he'd gone, nor did he ask what was happening. He knew Ian had a show planned, and he wasn't going to jump in for a part.

"You've arrived just in time. I've gathered these fine gentlemen for the celebration," Ian said directly.

"And what, pray tell, are we celebrating this time, *Father*?" Grant swallowed the whisky and his heart hammered in his chest, fear pulsing in his blood.

"Well, I suppose it's a little bittersweet isn't it? After your less than successful business trip."

"I don't know what you're on about—"

"The potential merger you were sniffing into. Shame it fell through," Ian said.

"Fell through?" Of course Ian knew. He knew everything.

"No matter. We *both* knew it was a long shot. Besides, we're here to celebrate your upcoming nuptials." Ian clapped him on the back. Grant choked on the sip still in his mouth and coughed. Through the tears welled in his eyes, he saw Cecilia's father's pinched face, raising his glass to Grant's obvious discomfort.

"Glad you finally asked, Grant. Though I don't know what kind of idiot would take as long as you did," he said snidely.

"Yes, my son is an idiot." Ian stared at Grant with cold eyes. "But I think he's coming around to what's best for him."

"I did not—"

"*Will* not," Ian interrupted, "make any more mistakes," he finished under his breath. "Or I will make sure your 'interests' in that backwater little town of Sweet Valley will suffer. Immensely. Right down to their pathetic bakery and mangy quarter horses." Grant stared fiery daggers into his father's soul. The crystal glass cracked in his hand.

"You can't—"

"Hold your bloody tongue," Ian seethed, "or I will destroy that little harlot and everything she loves."

The tone, the menace, the malice of words that Grant knew were not empty threats, made his heart die inside of his chest. All of the warmth and love she'd given, Ian took. And if Grant dared to defy, Katelyn would suffer the consequences. That Ian knew the details of her family, their land and livelihood, made Grant sure that his threat was only a few signatures away from being put into action.

"You will discontinue that *merger*, immediately, and focus on your upcoming wedding," Ian insisted. "Or I'll have all their land and kick them into the dirty gutter where they belong." His voice was inaudible to the other men in the room.

Grant leaned away. The drink rose up his throat as he thought of her face, the eyes that would know him, know that he was lying when he told her. How she'd argue, how she'd fight. How she'd cause her own undoing, out of sheer stubborn insistence that she was right. And she was right.

But right didn't matter.

Only her safety, only the preservation of the family who had so lovingly taken him in. Emilee's blue eyes and blonde curls flashed in his mind and he stumbled backwards against the wall. Only her future mattered, and so that future could have nothing to do with him.

Grant searched the faces of the other men, who only half-understood the power play that was taking place, only half aware of the hell he'd lived in since the tender age of eight. Grant's eyes faltered when he saw Jeffers gathering up glasses on a tray. When the old butler looked at him, honest eyes moist, and stiff lip trembling, his whole world fell apart. Jeffers shook his head minutely, a silent plea for Grant's case in the matter that could not be defended by either of them.

Ian had won. Again.

———

THE NEXT DAY, KATELYN WOKE EARLY, DISAPPOINTED AT the empty bunk bed and missing him something awful. She dressed and did her chores for Jasmine with a spring in her step and a smile that couldn't be contained.

"Someone had a good couple of days break." Jasmine looked at her knowingly. "What young stable stud did you shack up with?" Katelyn threw her arm around Jasmine's shoulder and kissed her cheek on her way out the door.

"Oh, no one in particular."

"Liar! Jeremy told me you and Mr. Tennyson had a private ride the other afternoon. You wouldn't be fraternizing with the enemy would you?" She smiled. Grant was far from an enemy after his generosity to the family, but Katelyn appreciated being teased. It made her feel at home.

"Maybe a little bit."

"I don't think there's a 'little' bit about that man," Jasmine said. Katelyn laughed her way out the door and down the lane. She wondered if she should go straight to Grant's office. Or maybe, he'd be in the stable, more comfortable in the hay and dirt than in the lofty confines of his old job. She decided to try for Hugh's stall.

Katelyn walked through the stable with her heart in her throat and the other workers lowered their eyes as she passed. An arctic feeling settled in the air and preceded her approach towards the tall, thin man standing outside of Hugh's stall.

"Shit," Katelyn breathed before straightening her spine. "Mr. Tennyson," she began.

"Let's skip the pleasantries that neither one of us feels, shall we?"

"Not sure what you mean, but okay."

"I heard a very nasty rumor that one of my planes was stolen this weekend. A punishable offense to be sure."

Katelyn squared her shoulders. If the cat was out of the bag, she wasn't going to let him pretend that he had an upper hand in catching it.

"Really? That's a damn shame. You should probably vet your workers better. In any case, if Grant was in the plane at the time of its supposed theft, and he's listed as the owner, I don't think you'd have a case. Shame, if you're trying to get someone falsely arrested."

"Do you presume to think you're smarter than me, Miss Sullivan?" he growled.

"Well, I don't like to presume anything. I tend to deal in fact." She stood taller and feigned bravery that she did not feel. Katelyn recognized the look in his eyes, the one that Jane had surely faced herself. The one that had cowed Grant countless times. She took a deep breath, smiled at him wryly, and looked unflinching into his eyes.

"There are legal consequences for employees who engage in prohibited behavior at Tennyson Stables."

"I'm aware, Mr. Tennyson, that you are used to holding tight rein on your son and his business. I appreciate you being straightforward with me about the rules and expectations. However, he is no longer a minor ward under your care and can make his own decisions. As I've never signed a contract with or received a paycheck from Tennyson Stables, my time here is completely voluntary and I cannot be reprimanded as an employee for any breach of contract," Katelyn stated, countering his threat with fact. Ian faltered, leaned back, and disappointment furrowed his brow.

"It appears I have been deceived." Ian paced around her. He kept his hands clasped behind his back, studying the ground in thought, his lips thin with anger. She could tell he hadn't expected to be challenged or disempowered.

"I never claimed to be anything other than what I am," she said.

"That's a lie, Miss Sullivan. You assured me upon your arrival that you were here on business."

"I was. But situations, like people, evolve," Katelyn seethed.

"You've done damage, haven't you? Gotten your grubby little nails into him? I don't know what it is about you that's got him turned around, but you will, from this time on, cease all relations with my son."

"Oh, will I? Is that how things work around here? People obey when you command?"

"Yes," he answered and looked down his nose. Katelyn scowled.

"Well, I'm not one of your people."

"You'd rather cause Grant undue suffering for your own selfish gain than allow him his happiness?"

"My gain?" She came a step closer. "Just what do you think I'm gaining?"

Ian spread his arms wide open and gestured to the grand stables and shiny-coated horses, the green fields beyond, the austerity and name. "Tennyson Stables, of course! You simple-minded gold-digger. Thinking that you'd waltz in here, seduce my son, marry him away from his prearranged engagement and become heiress to the biggest and most respected thoroughbred program this side of the world?" It all came out in a strained breath, bit between his teeth. His sharp chin, so unlike Grant's, jutted out, as if to point at her accusingly. Katie's scowl deepened.

"So that's what it is? You think I'm here to con you out of your overpriced herd of inbred horses? That I want to steal your land? I don't give a shit about your stables, or those useless ribbons adorning your walls. If that's all you want, if that's all that matters to you, then keep them. Keep it all! All I want, all I ever wanted, was for Grant to be happy. For him to be the best person he can be. So, keep your damn land. Keep all your money and your precious bloodlines. Just let him be. You don't own him!"

"He's as much mine as the land and my 'inbred' herd. He is my son, and he will carry on my line as I see fit, or he won't get a dime."

"We don't need—"

"That's where you're wrong!" Ian interjected. "*You* don't need those things. *You're* perfectly happy living off of canned beans and government handouts."

"You uppity son-of-a-bitch."

"But Grant is accustomed to the life I've given him, and he's not going to give that up. Didn't he tell you why Jane killed herself? He refused to go back to living in squalor. He wouldn't for Jane, and he won't for you. The sooner you realize that and go back to your simple, insignificant life, the better."

"You can't tell me—"

"If you truly care for my son as you say you do, then you will leave," Ian said, but before she could answer he went on. "Don't make his life any harder than it has to be. Not when he's just proposed to Cecilia, and accepted the truth in his heart."

KATELYN WATCHED HIM GO, AND THE WORDS SUNK INTO her brain. She paced outside of the stall, one hand over her mouth, one on her hip. She tried to hold in the tears, but they snuck out. She wiped them on her sleeve and turned to pace another round.

Grant had proposed to Cecilia, right after they'd returned. Had he known he was going to do it the whole time they were in Sweet Valley? When he'd told her father that he only had her best interests at heart? She swallowed the sob in her throat.

She'd fallen too hard and too fast, and shut out good reason. She thought back to how he'd begged to be loved. How he'd seemed to absorb the acceptance and love as though he were a dry field taking first rain. Katelyn stopped at the large front doors of the stable and scowled at his office window, where the blinds had been pulled down.

Katelyn didn't believe it. She knew people. Grant wouldn't have asked Cecilia to be in the same room with him, let alone share the rest of his life. She huffed in a deep breath, squared her shoulders, and headed straight for the house. He was in the office, nursing what looked like a massive hangover. When she burst in, his face blanched as if he might throw up.

"Your father just came to see me."

"Not now," he barked and turned away.

"Yes, now Grant!" she demanded, and slammed the office door behind her. "He told me that you proposed to the viper."

"Katelyn, damn it! Just don't."

"No, Grant! You listen to m—"

"You knew!" His harsh tone caused Katelyn to falter backwards. "You knew from the beginning we couldn't do this."

"I thought—"

"No! Don't play dumb, Katelyn. It doesn't suit you. We're done here."

"What'n the hell do you mean?"

"I'm saying your position is terminated. My father has arranged for your flight. Here's a real paycheck for your time and efforts." He shoved an envelope at her without meeting her eyes.

"Grant," Katelyn's throat was tight and her eyes burned looking at his jaw set so resolutely; his eyes so cold. "Can't we just talk about this?"

"Your business with this facility is finished." His tone and temper rose and his hands shook as he held out the ticket and check.

"What about us? What about everything?"

"There is no *us*." He turned away.

"That's not true," she yelled and grabbed his arm.

"Dinna touch me!" he yelled back and tore his arm from her grasp. "Please leave the property or I will arrange to have you escorted." He shoved the envelope into her hand. Katelyn stared, disbelieving, as he moved around his desk, stuffed his paperwork into his briefcase, and took in a ragged breath. She studied him, putting aside her own confusion and sadness to observe. He swallowed thickly, as though his emotions were strangling him. His hands, with nerves of steel that had kept his body immobile through hardships, injuries, and battles, shook and fumbled with the locks on his case.

"He got to you," she said.

"What?"

Katelyn whispered in slight relief. "What did he threaten this time?" Grant sniffed, shut down his computer and turned away.

"I don't believe the conversations between my father and I are any of your business."

"It is my business when the man I love—"

"I'm not," He sighed with a broken breath. "I'm not the man you love. Whatever you may think or feel is just an overreaction of your naïve emotional experience."

"Love is not an overreaction. And I'm not naïve or emotional."

"Miss Sullivan. Please leave or I will be forced to call security."

"So, you let him make the choice for you. Was that easier?" She searched his downcast eyes. He looked up with a scowl.

"You dinna ken." His voice shook.

"Explain it to me, then. Help me understand!"

"There's nothing you need to understand, except that it's over. You're better off, Katelyn. Your family too. Please, just believe that and go," he said.

"Well, I *don't* believe that."

"You have to!" he interrupted with such desperation that she felt his fear as if it were her own. "You have to, please," he begged and his eyes filled.

"Please don't, Grant. Please don't ask me to do this. It isn't fair!"

"You'll discover, in time, Katelyn, that life is rarely fair," he said. His eyes locked on hers. "Please," he breathed. "If you know what's best for you."

"I do. I do know what's best for me!" she said and threw the envelope down on the desk. It slid across to his side, heavy with what she would not accept. "The real question, Grant, is do you?"

At his silence, she stormed out and walked straight to Hugh's stall. She undid the latch and locked herself inside. His soft grunt sounded from the back wall and she barely shut the door before she fell to a heap in the soft hay, sobbing. Grant was right; Ian always got what he wanted. He wanted a more suitable 'business merger,' and Grant had obeyed. Katelyn, Jane, even Grant's own mother had been nothing more than obstacles to Ian's endgame. Katelyn's pain turned to anger, as she sat with her arms around her knees, wiping her tears on the soft and well-worn jeans.

But Grant had let him. He'd chosen money over love. Because he'd had so little of each as a child, and at least money was predictable. It never faded or changed its agenda. Hugh came to her and bent his head to snuffle her hair, offering reassuring grunts. Katelyn threw her arms around his withers. He lifted her.

"What do you say, you old jackass. One more ride before I go?" She spoke into his neck and he leaned into her sadness. Katelyn wiped her nose against her sleeve and bridled him. He stood still while she led him from the stables and to the farthest green field, turned bright in the light of early morning. She swung onto his back.

Her legs tightened around his ribs, and Hugh listened. The age-old understanding and mutual respect between horse and rider, the give and take of a relationship, centuries old, bonded them. She felt his canter quicken, the desperation in her heart driving her to hunker down and press her weight into him. Every movement was a conversation, and she let her body meld to his. He responded, joyous to push faster across the emerald field. She wished they could just take flight and get away from this dark and insane world they'd been thrust into.

She watched the ground blur beneath them and wondered, at this speed, if she fell, would she survive the impact? Her fingers loosened, she shifted and Hugh, sensing the change, turned away, slowed and threw his head back.

No.

Katelyn wasn't sure if it was the wind she'd heard through the rhythmic beat of hooves and hearts or something else. The whisper brushed the hair from her forehead, closed her hands over the reins again and softly chuckled.

He'll never learn anything that way.

The Scottish lilt played in the wind, and Katelyn was sure her brain was taking a double gainer off of the high dive. She sat up and glanced around the empty field. The lights of the house in the distance caught her eye. Hugh followed the direction of her head and turned. The wind tugged at her free hair.

Hang in there, lass.

"I can't," Katelyn whispered back, voice ragged with tears.

You have to. Show him the strength I couldn't.

The whispering tall grass brushed against her feet and she felt her thighs tremble around Hugh. She tightened them, her heels gently digging into his sides, until he reared and took off towards the house at a breakneck speed. Katelyn rode from the voice, from the feeling that there was more to be gained from this lesson. She wasn't ready to hear it. She drove Hugh straight down the center of the field and leaned down.

GRANT HAD BARELY GOTTEN TO THE STUDY, A STIFF pour of scotch between his shaking fingers, when a soft knock startled him into turning around. He hoped it was her. He hoped it wasn't. His heart rose and fell with mania.

"Beg your pardon, *sir*." Jeffers cool voice was tinged with hints of defiance.

"What is it?" Equal anger met Jeffers as Grant's fingers closed over the drink.

"Mr. Parsons is here to see you," Jeffers bit back. "Has Katie left then?" he asked pointedly, his intelligent blue eyes boring into Grant.

"*Miss Sullivan* has left, aye," Grant said, but the tightness in his chest halted him and he felt weak against the knowing gaze of his ward.

"Haven't you learned anything?" Jeffers said softly.

"Aye, that my father is always right." Grant took a drink and

Jeffers came closer. Grant watched over the edge of his glass at the man who had raised him, comforted him after the loss of his mother, helped conspire with Katelyn to show him a different life.

"That's not what I mean, Grant." Jeffers eyes narrowed on him and Grant felt the truth in his heart. He shook his head.

"She's gone, so what does it matter?" he whispered. Jeffers face fell even as he nodded brusquely.

"Very good, sir."

"Is it?" Grant muttered. "Is it good?"

"I'll send Mr. Parsons in." Jeffers added a *bloody idiot* under his breath on his way out. A minute later, the roughened rancher came through the study door, brow creased and smile cocked up warily.

"Mr. Tennyson, I believe your butler is plotting mutiny."

"What?" Grant looked up from the floor.

"Having a rampant conversation with himself in the hall. Saying something about you needing a good cuffing, and that he thought he raised you better?"

"He's clearly senile," Grant yelled towards the hallway.

"Seemed lucid enough to me."

"What is it you want, Jim?"

"I actually came to talk to Katelyn about Hugh, but I hear she's no longer in your employ."

"It's hardly your business," he paused and tried to pull the veil of professionalism down. "She's fulfilled her duties here. You may direct any business concerning Hugh Dancy with me directly."

"I see." Jim sounded disappointed in a way that disturbed Grant. "She had asked me some questions about Hugh's future. Seems she heard that he'd be sent to a slaughterhouse if certain demands weren't met?" Jim's eyes leveled on Grant who took a long drink.

"There are conditions attached to everything under Ian's domain, aren't there?"

"Unfortunately, Ian does have a lot of power. But I wanted to propose a counter offer in the event of something like that happening. I was looking to talk to Katelyn first, as she'd been the one to approach me."

Grant stared at him blankly, his mind fogging with the drink and his heart pulling in opposite directions. She'd made plans to save his horse. To save him. And he'd thrown her out.

"She's left," he whispered lamely. Jim looked over Grant's shoulder and out the front window. A smile broke on his weathered face.

"You sure about that?" He nodded towards the window. Grant turned to see Katelyn riding Hugh across the pasture as if hell were on her heels. Her wild and free hair flew behind her and she gripped Hugh's bare back with her strong thighs. Her face was beautiful and furious. The speed at which she drove the magnificent animal, with no helmet, no saddle, across the roughened ground of the pasture, scared him senseless.

"What in God's name does she think she's doing?" He dropped the drink, bolted to the patio door, and ran outside with Jim close behind.

"She's a thing of beauty," Jim whispered in awe.

"She's going to crack her feckin skull open!" Grant said with anger and fear strangling him. Hugh followed the curve of the fence-line as they approached quickly, Hugh huffing and lathered, wild spirit in his eyes, and nostrils flaring.

"She's gonna jump the fence," Jim breathed.

"She cannae!" Grant demanded, as if she could hear his command. "He canna jump since the injury! She'll kill the both of them!" Grant stood paralyzed as she barreled ever closer. The thundering hooves vaulted into silence and Grant's world stood still for an instant as the image of horse and rider burned into his mind. Her, perfectly formed to the back of the sweaty and beautiful beast, Hugh's nostrils flared and teeth parting in an echoing cry that filled the static air.

They struck the ground, two perfectly-timed beats after

another, and landed with a powerful grace that continued as if the fence had never existed at all. She charged closer and drew Hugh up at the last moment with nothing but the minute signals of her shifting weight.

Hugh reared impressively in front of the two men. He pranced his feet down mere inches from Grant, who was gasping for breath. Hugh danced back and forth, to the side, throwing his head in an arrogant showing of pride. Not a stitch of injury apparent; not a hitch in his movements.

Katelyn jumped down and led him to Grant.

"Where I come from, we don't quit 'til the job's done. Looks like I fixed your horse, so I guess it's time that I go," she said, effectively taking away the power of either Grant or Ian telling her what to do. Hugh nickered and swayed against her. She tucked her head into his neck and whispered. "Take care of him, please."

"Of course I'll take care of him! He's my feckin horse!" Grant seethed, still panic-stricken and aching with the love he couldn't have.

"I wasn't talking to you," she said, and put the reins in Grant's hands without touching him. She walked to one of the company trucks, fired it up, and drove away as easily as she'd come. Grant's world fell away behind her.

Hugh huffed and panted. He turned his head to the departing truck and his ears perked in her direction. He whinnied after her, but Grant steadied him and leaned against the horse so he wouldn't crumple to the ground.

"Well?" Jim's voice cut through Grant's personal hell. Grant turned to the older man, tears in his eyes, and barely able to form words.

"What?" he choked.

"Well, aren't you going after her?" Jim demanded and gestured to the dust cloud. Grant watched the two-ton truck bounce down over the hill towards the Sutter Farm, and probably much farther away.

"I—I cannae." He felt defeated.

"You can't? What'n the hell do you mean you can't?" Jim argued.

"I mean I cannae. She—she has to go," Grant stuttered through the excuses and wanted to die.

"Son, you're either dumber than a bag of hammers or just a plain old coward."

Grant looked back at him angrily.

"If I go after her my father will—"

"Will what?" Jim demanded.

"He'll hurt her, to get to me. Her, her family, everything that's beautiful about Katelyn Sullivan will be destroyed. She's better off without me."

"Did you see her?" Jim pointed angrily at the truck, long gone. "Everything that's beautiful about Katie Sullivan is stronger than some old bastard's threats. And while you're right, she'll probably be just fine without you. She's asking you to be in her life."

"How is it any business of—"

"You want to protect her? Then you stand beside her. You stand up with her. Stop cowering from your father."

"I dinna ken how!" His voice broke desperately. He took Hugh by the reins and led him back to the stable, his head and heart fallen in shame.

Twenty-Two

KATELYN ARRIVED AT THE AIRPORT WITH FIFTEEN minutes to spare before the departing flight. She'd booked it while gathering her stuff from the Sutters' bunkhouse. With quick kisses and hugs, she'd lied and said the job was done and her parents needed her help. Jasmine looked at her sideways, not believing Katelyn's stone-like expression. But she'd shrugged, let her go, and sent her off with a hand-stitched lap quilt, and some of the photos off the fridge of Katelyn and the kids playing in the yard. Katelyn wouldn't dare look at them, already on the verge of tears, so she stuffed them in her pocket. She didn't want to blubber like an idiot in front of anyone.

She called Elle and asked if she or Laney could pick her up from the Laramie airport. Her voice, edged with calculating coldness, confused Elle. When she had pressed Katelyn for details about the sudden return, only the slightest waver in her voice was indicative of the heartache she felt.

"Job's done. Hugh's better. I'm coming home. I'm gonna help Dad in the clinic for the rest of the summer, then find something else to do. Somewhere else." Her future was easier to manage as an itinerary of facts, because the deeper truth of, *I fell in love with*

Grant Tennyson and he doesn't want me enough to give up his inheritance so now my heart's broke and I don't think it'll ever heal was too hard to say out loud.

"Are you serious? Katydid, what's happened?"

"My flight gets in at 10. I'll split the gas with you, or Laney, whoever."

"Katelyn May."

"I've gotta go Elle, they're boarding," Katelyn lied.

"Oh, okay," Elle stuttered.

"See you."

"See you. Love you, Katydid."

Katelyn hung up and hoisted her bag over her shoulder and Grant's words ran in a loop through her head. While she lined up at the gate. While she found her seat. While she sat back and ignored the other people jostling through the cabin. Her heart hurt and her stomach was sick. She'd known, all along, his future was already laid out for him.

But she hadn't known that future was coming so soon. She wondered, with a wave of nausea bubbling up in her throat, when he and Cecilia would get married. Would Grant do it without batting an eye? Callously marry the cold and unfeeling socialite in a faultless front-page ceremony, wherein she got the prestige of his estate and name in exchange for successfully producing an heir within the allotted time? Would her land become his; her herd his? Would that finally make his father proud? Would Grant find the peace he thought he'd have when Ian was finally appeased?

Katelyn swallowed back the bile in her throat. What would his obligation entail? Ovulation calculations and precise hormonal measurements followed by cold, impersonal sex until the desired result was achieved? Could Grant even have cold, impersonal sex? She supposed people who needed to survive were used to doing all kinds of horrible things.

A baby cried three rows back and Katelyn closed her eyes.

She'd never been disappointed to be barren. Motherhood

wasn't ever something she'd wanted. Having nieces was enough. But Cecilia could give him so much of what she couldn't. Prestige, wealth, Ian's approval, and a baby.

Would they love the baby, or would it only serve as a constant and bitter reminder of what they'd both done for money and out of fear? She felt heartsick for Grant's child. Would he hate it because it was the result of Ian's wishes? Would he emotionally abandon it, like his father before him? Katelyn thought of Grant with Emilee and how he'd sung to her, played with her, coddled her.

She felt the plane lift off from the runway and its speed pinned her to the seat. The man next to her cleared his throat, and she closed her eyes to the memory of Grant's nerves next to her in the tiny plane. She leaned against the window and fought the universe for control of her own mind. Her arms wrapped around her trembling middle.

Grant wouldn't punish the child. Even if Cecilia was more concerned with Belmont hat-buying and expensive tack to fill stables that she'd never clean herself, Grant would love their child. He would remember his own mother. He would remember Katelyn and her family, and the goodness he'd found in himself because of these things. He'd pass it on to his children. He'd end the cycle of control and manipulation that Ian had held over him for so long.

She felt more tears fill her eyes, and she pressed them away. She clung instead to the hope that, at the very least, knowing her and the time they'd had together, would allow Grant enough love in his heart to give it back and to be, in some way, healed.

Laney Sullivan was the oldest sister of the three; jaded without remorse, and tough as a box of nails. When Elle called and asked if she could pick Katelyn up from the airport, she didn't even have to think twice to say yes. But it was Elle's warning that made her blood boil. Something had gone wrong. A man had broken their baby sister's heart. Laney simmered her way through her last workshopping class for the session and picked up her children from day camp. Immediately, her oldest, Charlotte, could tell that her mother was on a war path.

"What's happened? Why's your mad on? Is it Sylvia because she caught a frog and was gonna keep it?"

A small *ribbit* erupted from what Laney now saw was a sopping wet backpack.

"What in the shit?" Laney returned her attention to traffic before she swerved into the curb. "No! Syl! Do you have a frog in there?"

"It's just a little one!" Sylvia argued.

"If it's not the frog, what is it?" Charlotte cut in.

"It's—I—" Laney checked her rearview and cut into the other lane headed west and towards the airport. "We have to go pick up Aunt Katelyn from the airport."

"Did she make you mad?"

"No, baby," Laney said. "But somebody was mean to her and made her run away."

"Aunt Katie doesn't run from nothin'!" Sylvia disputed from the back seat of the beat-up Isuzu. The frog croaked its assent at the known fact, and Laney closed her eyes with joy-laced frustration at life and the beautiful brilliance of her children.

"Sometimes, even the strongest of us get our asses kicked," she said quietly as they headed to the small airport.

Laney, Charlotte, and Sylvia waited anxiously as they saw the blinking lights of the beat-up commuter jet descend. Laney held a makeshift sign to her chest, colored with someone's crayons and a page from an old syllabus she'd found in her bag. When Katelyn stumbled into the small terminal, her tired eyes passed over it twice before a small smile tugged at her mouth.

"Butt Face, Jr.?" Katelyn looked up at her big sister with a scowl.

"Well, Butt Face, Sr. is already taken." She shrugged. When Katelyn looked back up at her sister's teasing grin; her nieces' bated and worried expressions, her cavalry here to catch her, her rational control broke open and she sobbed. She dropped her bag to the brown carpet, and Laney grabbed her up and cradled her close. She rocked her back and forth with loving and shushing sounds.

"Oh, honey. Oh, baby girl. It's gonna be all right. You'll be okay. It's all gonna be okay," she said softly. Katelyn clung to her for a long while, and Laney's patient and warm arms held her when her own strength failed. The girls circled her legs and waist and squeezed hard.

"He didn't want me," she sobbed. "He didn't want me enough." Pain rolled through and shook her body. The safety of being miles away from him and Ian, the warmth of being some place where she didn't have to pretend anymore, broke down her stoic walls.

"Oh, Katie May." Laney smoothed the hair away from her wet cheeks and sighed. "Then he just didn't deserve you. If he couldn't see the gift you are, then he's a goddamn moron."

"Then how come I still love him? Why does my heart still want somebody who doesn't want it?"

"Hearts are morons too." Laney shook her head. "Look, I don't know much about Grant Tennyson, but from what Elle and Dad said, I think he's spent his whole life hurt and confused. It's a pretty tall order to expect a person to change decades' worth of abuse in a few short weeks. You can't change people, Katydid. They have to change themselves."

Katelyn's eyes brimmed over again. "I know. I just can't understand why he'd want to stay someplace like that, where Ian holds everything over him, when he knows there's better. When he knows there's me."

"He's scared, Katelyn. He's scared of taking that leap. He's only ever known the fall," Laney said, and pressed her lips to Katelyn's forehead. "Come on, we're not going to solve this in the middle of the airport. Let's go find a bar," Laney said.

"We're going to a bar?" Sylvia said with delight. "Can I bring Lancelot?"

"Who in the hell is Lancelot?" The frog chirped from the backpack, now soaking her youngest's back.

"Never mind. I'll get you a drink at home. Come on, little cowpoke. You can stay with me tonight and tomorrow I'll take you over the mountain. Elle is worried sick, so you'll get plenty of fretting and food."

"I don't want anyone fretting." Katelyn began, but her throat closed off and she wished she could just be alone.

"I got you," Laney said. "We got you, baby girl." She reached for Katelyn's bag. Katelyn slumped; all drive conquered in her heart, and let Laney lift the bag over her shoulder. Her nieces held her hands as they walked to the car, but Katelyn couldn't feel anything but a cold numbness falling over her.

TWENTY-THREE

TENNYSON STABLES FELT THE DISSONANCE IN KATELYN'S absence. The Sutters, while better off in a hundred different ways, with a working farm, a steady income, and a newfound peace in their hearts, still felt the emptiness of the vacant bunkhouse. Jeffers felt it in the kitchen, where she'd popped in at least a few times a day to check on him, steal some food, and find a reason to make him smile. Jeffers felt it watching Grant either mope or rage in every task he set to. He'd not seen the boy so utterly miserable since his mother had passed away. Not even with Jane. He kept a closer eye on Grant.

A thick fog of loss and sadness seemed to settle in the paddocks, the fields, the arena, and tack rooms. The hired hands had seen a lot of specialists come and go, but none that had bothered to get to know them, none that had been as humble and hard-working as Katelyn. But perhaps the thickest quiet lay over the house, where both masters of the property kept their distance from one another, out of survival and the loss of will to fight.

Grant spent most of the first week on a steady diet of scotch and pipe tobacco, despite Jeffers' best efforts to follow Katelyn's request that he be taken care of in her absence. Grant would not take food. He would not sleep and, when he did, it was in half-hour stints at his desk or the couch in his office; anywhere she'd never stayed. When he wasn't working out deals on the newly healed Hugh, he was meeting property tax adjusters and agriculturalists, and hay market advisors. Vet visits were arranged, insurance inspections made, breeder meetings convened. All of it under the intense scrutiny of Ian's watchful gaze.

The work served a double purpose of avoiding both Ian's wrath and any wedding arrangements with Cecilia. He couldn't stand being within three feet of her, and had no idea how he'd manage to walk down the aisle with her, least of all bed her. Katelyn had asked that he marry anyone but her, and now the unfortunate opposite was happening.

Grant would occasionally look up from his computer when he'd catch Jeffers walking by the open door. His knowing eyes darted to Grant's with disappointment, as he took away another unfinished meal, and replaced it with a hopefully more successful attempt.

He couldn't sleep. Though the bedsheets had been changed and the room aired, he still felt her in every corner of the room. He couldn't bear looking at the bathtub; he didn't go into the kitchen or the study. It was like living with a ghost, only unlike Jane, he knew that Katelyn was still alive and carrying on without him. He hoped she was. He hoped she was back at her family's ranch, working long days in the sunshine, building callouses on her hands as well as her heart. Maybe she'd even find comfort with some younger man. The thought made him reach for the flask in his top drawer.

ONE WEEK TURNED INTO THREE.

·   ·   ·

ONE EVENING, NEARLY AT MIDNIGHT, HE STAGGERED, exhausted and drunk, to his room. He stripped down to nothing on his wandering path and littered the hallway with his three-day-old clothing. He smelled awful, but didn't see the point in bathing when it kept everyone a good distance away.

You idiot.

Jane's voice cut through the fog in his brain. He shook his head to rid it.

You heard me, Grant. You're a bloody idiot.

Grant looked around the empty bedroom, his eyes settled on the wardrobe in the corner. Before he could collapse into bed, he caught a shade of color that flashed through the barely-open doors. Grant scowled in the low light.

"There'll be no ghosts livin' with me!" He tore open the wardrobe doors. There in the bottom, gently touching the cuffs of his rugby shirt, was Katelyn's old tin cup. Grant straightened, turned the bedside lamp on, and walked cautiously back towards the wardrobe, as if he might startle the ghost who'd put it there. The cup reflected the lamp light and glowed warm in the cold room. Memories swept over him like the clanging of the cup against Hugh's bars. The water she'd thrown at the angry and hurt horse, to distract and disarm. Much like she'd distracted and disarmed him with her dripping wet body beside the lake. A piece of paper was tucked inside the cup. He recoiled.

Read it. Came the whisper. *Don't be a coward. Read it.* Grant reached tentatively for the note as if it were a snake poised to strike. His fingers shook as he unrolled it and squinted to read her neat and small writing.

GRANT—*I DON'T KNOW HOW LONG IT'LL TAKE YOU TO find this, but I told Jeffers to put it someplace you'd come to when you were ready. I don't know if you'll even read it. I hope you do, cause there's a few things you need to know before you marry the viper.*

1. You're an idiot. And I love you just the same.

2. The tragedy in your life is Ian's fault. Not yours. I reckon if you get rid of him, you'll get rid of it.

3. It took me 27 years to find you. I'm not afraid to wait a few more.

4. You're a good rider but you won't be if you don't get back on that horse, so you'd better be riding Hugh every chance you get.

5. If you can't overcome your stupidity, and you end up marrying the viper, then at least promise me you won't do it for Ian. You've given him enough.

6. Did I mention that I love you? I think I did, but it seems like you might need to be told more than once. Hell, if I had my way, I'd tell you every day, every minute, until you were tired of hearing it.

7. I love you, you big angry beast, and I won't ever give up on you.

GRANT FELL TO HIS KNEES, CLUTCHING THE NOTE. His hands shook, his mouth was dry, and the words blurred in and out of focus as his eyes filled. He was an idiot. The tragedies were Ian's. He'd given Ian enough. She'd wait a few more. She wouldn't give up on him. Don't marry the viper for him.

Don't marry the viper for Ian.

Don't marry the viper for Ian...

"Don't marry the viper *for* Ian," Grant whispered, and his sobs turned into fits of laughter. "Jeffers! Jeffers, damn you, where are you? I need you!" He laughed. Within moments, the bed-ready man shuffled through the door, glasses perched on the tip of his nose and he stared down at Grant, collapsed, naked, and sobbing in laughter on the floor.

"Sir?" he said when he noticed the cup and note in Grant's hands. "How may I be of assistance?"

"Jeffers, I've got a job for you."

"Sir?"

"Have all my contracts brought to the office first thing in the morning. All the employees' contracts, every horse's breeding rights, every box we've got in the safe. Bring it all up. I'll start at five."

"I'm afraid I don't understand—"

"That's all."

"Sir," Jeffers acquiesced, and his eyes turned soft watching Grant re-read the note he'd placed not hours before. "Are we going to do something rash?"

"We?"

"I'm at your service, sir. As always." The words, soft and filled with a warmth Grant only now recognized, made him look up into Jeffers' eyes.

"We are." He nodded. "I should get to bed. I need to sleep," Grant said suddenly and tucked the note into his hand. He smiled like a little boy to Jeffers.

"Yes sir, you should." Jeffers nodded and returned his smile.

"I've a big day tomorrow."

"Yes, sir. You do."

GRANT WAS ANTSY, AFTER HIS STRANGE AND TURBULENT night where he'd fallen asleep in his own bed, his body curled around her cup, the note tucked into his hand. He knew the work ahead of him. Knowing Ian as he did, the business as he did, it had taken him most of the week to finish the arrangements. Today a storm would come.

The cloud of Ian's presence heralded its arrival as he strode into Grant's office and began droning on about the engagement party set for next week. And when was he going to cut his damn hair? What was all this paperwork he'd been shuffling around to Jim Parsons? Why was he wearing that ridiculous rugby shirt, again? He'd better change before...

Grant stared, nonplussed, over Ian's head. His father's words seemed muffled against the virulent pounding of his heart in his ears. He felt the world go still.

"Did you hear me?" Ian's sharp tone broke through his haze.

"Did I?"

"God's sakes, Grant. Snap out of it. You've got to think about your schedule. I'm sending you into town today to go ring shopping with her and you'll put on every appearance that you are the happiest of couples. Now, I've already talked to the manager at Friedze and you'll have the viewing room to yourselves—" And on he went, until Grant had sunk back into the happy warmth that came from the note tucked in his pocket.

"Grant!" Ian yelled. "What is wrong with you? Pull your daft head out of your ass and answer me."

"Answer you?"

"Cecilia? The ring?"

"Oh, yes. Ring shopping," Grant said in a haze. "I've just been thinking of that."

Ian stopped to look at him sideways. "And? Will it be princess cut or square?"

"I think you should decide."

"What?"

"Well, she's your bride."

"What are you talking about? Stop being absurd."

"I'm saying, *Father*, that since you think she's the perfect match, perhaps you should marry her," Grant said matter-of-factly and smiled across the desk. He looked at the pile of contracts he'd successfully renegotiated to protect any and all horses and employees in the care of Tennyson Stables under the controlling clause of his position. The paper copies were relics now, as he'd digitized everything and had it sent to the lawyers not fifteen minutes before. With a bored lack of care, he pushed the pile off the edge and it scattered to the floor. Ian watched it as if he'd just seen a pig fly through the window.

"What did you just say to me?" Ian's voice seethed with indignation.

"I said," Grant responded with malice, "if you think Cecilia is the one you want to continue the Tennyson empire with, then *you* should marry her. Have an heir with her, another heir, a more suitable one. One that isn't a bastard. Cecilia's ready and has no need for wooing. If you're having mechanical difficulties, I'm sure you can arrange for the AI specialist to assist you."

"Are you insane?" Ian looked at Grant as though he had gone mad.

"You want an heir; she wants your empire. You get the added bonus of not having to worry about my mother's unworthy blood getting mixed into your line." Grant's voice lowered. Ian's face blanched, and he wavered, steading himself on the side of the desk.

"You're forgetting, *son*, that you will lose everything! Tennyson Stables, the horses, the hours of time and sweat you've put into this place will all disappear!"

"I won't lose anything that I cannot work to get on my own," He said and felt Katelyn in his heart. "Nothing you ever 'gave' me was worth having."

"I will dis—"

"Do it." Grant interrupted. "Disown me. Disinherit me. Please!" Grant yelled in the last rays of daylight that broke into the room and into his soul. Weight lifted off his shoulders with the few simple words. He laughed in a beautiful, rich way that caused Ian to stumble backwards. "*You* marry Cecilia. You've always been one to do away with the middleman anyway, and that's all I am."

"You're mad."

"Am I?" Grant laughed, and his thoughts turned to the strange elations of what life would be like without the man now cowering in front of him. With choices of his own to make. He paced from behind his desk. "Because I feel like this is the first sane thing I've done in years." With that, he slung his jacket over his shoulders, collected his bag with the old tin cup inside, knocking against his laptop, agricultural programs and plans, and a freshly printed resume. He grabbed the stable key ring and tossed it to Ian, who barely caught it in shaking fingers.

"Congratulations on your upcoming nuptials. Please don't invite me to the wedding."

"But you, you—" Ian sputtered as he stared at Grant's retreating back. "What about Hugh? What about your damn horse?" Ian yelled. "If you leave, I will sell him to the highest-bidding meat packing plant!" The ugly threat left his lips and Grant paused.

"I knew you might," Grant said, and a smile quirked his serious mouth. "Saved you the trouble." He rummaged through the haphazard papers on the floor and threw a copied packet at Ian's feet.

"Hugh's been bought, already. After he fulfills his 'obligations,' he will be taken from the property."

"By whom?" Ian yelled. "You had no right!"

"I had every right! You said it yourself, he was my feckin horse. Don't worry, Ian, he'll be well cared for."

"I demand to know where you're taking him."

"I'm not taking him. Jim Parsons is. He expressed an interest at a price that I couldn't refuse, and you'd already mentioned at the investor's party that he was getting past his prime. It will be better for business if you focus on the foals you have. Then again, you were never very good at doing the dirty work of managing your own business."

"Think about this, Grant. Think hard before you burn this bridge. You'll be out on the street within the week. You've no prospects here or abroad, I'll make sure of it. You'll be penniless, no better than the worthless gutter trash that I plucked from the refuse thirty-five years ago. You'll starve!" Ian's keystone threat struck the nerve that he knew would do most damage, desperate to change his son's course.

Grant took the words, into his heart, felt the worry turn to anger. Penniless, worthless, starving gutter trash. But before he could let them shackle him to the disastrous manipulations of his father, he heard Katelyn's soft voice over the ugliness. Something shuddering and true took Ian's echoing threat and covered it over, like dirt on a grave.

"Fuck you, Ian Tennyson," Grant said.

"What?" The unveiled rage spat from Ian. "What did you just say to me?"

Grant laughed. "Fuck you! I dinna need you. I willna starve. She won't let me. I'll never be without a home."

"What are you talking about? Have you gone mad?"

"I dinna need you, Ian. I have a family," Grant said, his laughter gone and his heart near to exploding.

"She? You can't possibly mean Katelyn Sullivan. If you think she'd ever take you back after the damage you've done to her, then you're a bigger fool than I thought. You destroyed her. She's broken, just like Jane. Just like your mother!" Ian's desperation peaked. Grant looked down at him.

"Poor Father, you really dinnae understand, do you?" Grant put his strong hand on Ian's brittle shoulder. "No one can break Katelyn Sullivan."

"If you leave this house now, I'll have nothing more to do with you." Ian clamored.

Grant, a changed and risen man, made Ian shrink into his own frailty, and years of questions filled his slack-aged face.

"That would be my sincerest hope." Grant clapped Ian on the back and left the room. In the hall, listening to the whole conversation, was Jeffers. He snapped to attention at the sight of Grant, his pressed shirt rolled up at the sleeves and a dishtowel over his shoulder. Grant smiled at him. He took one dish-wet hand in both of his large ones and pulled Jeffers in for a hug.

"Thank you, Jeffers, for everything. You've been the father I never had, and I couldna survived this long without you." Tears filled Jeffers' eyes.

"It has been my honor, sir," Jeffers responded, but before he could say more, Grant left.

He walked straight to the barn; taking in the scenery and the air of a place he'd spent far too much time cooped up behind a desk at. When he reached Hugh's stall, the horse seemed morose.

"Hey old man," he whispered and held his hand out. Hugh snuffled him and turned away to pace his stall. "I know, I miss her too. If I had a penny to my name, I'd take you with me and we'd go wait on her doorstep until she took us back," he said. Hugh came back to him and Grant touched his forehead to the horse's.

"Sounds like a man coming around." A voice came from behind. Grant looked back to see Jim Parsons.

"Jim! Uh, did you hear all that? I was just saying goodbye. I'm leaving."

"On business?"

"Forever, actually." Jim nodded, his lips curving up, and he looked down at his boots. "Thank you, by the way, for taking me up on my offer to buy Hugh. He's a fine horse."

"That he is, but the truth is that I don't really need another horse. At least that's what my wife keeps saying."

"Oh? What will you do with him?"

"Well, now that depends."

"On what?" Grant swallowed.

"On how much money you have in your pocket, right now."

"What?"

"Empty your pockets, Tennyson. Let's see." Grant was confused. He dropped his bag and shuffled through his pockets to find a few crumpled bills, some coins, and a hair tie of Katelyn's he'd found in bed.

"Well, I—that's it." He laughed, feeling light and stupid. "Ian was right, I am penniless. I've got about $3.52."

"Just so happens, that's two dollars and fifty-two cents more than I need." Grant looked at Jim and his brow furrowed.

"What are you saying?"

"I'm saying I'll sell Hugh back to you for a dollar. Throw in the rest, minus the hair tie, and I'll even deliver him for you."

"Deliver him?"

"Wherever you're headed."

"Well—" Grant blushed and cleared his throat. "Wyoming, I guess. I hope?"

"Funny, I was just headed there myself," Jim said, and shook Grant's hand.

GRANT STOOD OUTSIDE OF THE IRON-CLAD GATES OF Tennyson Stables. He'd been escorted from the premises, unsurprisingly, before he had a chance to even pack a bag. His father's goons hadn't even allowed him a chance to go back for his personal effects. His mother's photo. His favorite books. His pipe. He frowned; maybe it was best to leave behind all of these things and start over new. Jim had offered to take him on their way to Wyoming, but it would take three days and Grant needed to get to her today. If only he could fly, he'd kidnap himself.

How mad was he? Giving up everything and, thereby, not even having the means to get to her, let alone any assurances that she would take him back once he arrived. No assurances he or Hugh would have a place to live. Hell, after what he'd put her through, she could take Hugh and send him packing. Grant faltered against the gate. His freedom had come at an awful price, and maybe too late. Now all he had was hope to get him 1,700 miles across the country within the next twenty-four hours. He closed his eyes.

"What a damnable fool I am," he whispered.

"That you are, yet I can't seem to let you out of my sight," said the quiet voice beside him. Grant startled.

"Jeffers?" Grant turned, but the old man was nearly unrecognizable out of his normal uniform and in a traveling jacket and tam, a small suitcase in each hand. He stood complacently at

Grant's side. "What are you doing here?" Grant said, looking back at the house that seemed even further away now.

"Fulfilling a promise I made thirty years ago."

"What promise? What are you talking about?"

Jeffers handed him one of the bags and Grant looked inside to find his mother's picture, his books, his favorite whisky glass, his pipe, his diploma, and a binder full of Hugh's records, including those that Katelyn kept in her neat loopy writing.

"I made a promise your mother that I would watch over you as if you were my own," Jeffers said softly. "That I would see to it that you were cared for, fed, and given an ear to listen. To be the warmth she couldn't."

"That you have," Grant said softly, his mind and heart caught up in memories of the man who had taken him under his wing.

"I promised all three of them, actually. Your mother, Jane, and Miss Katelyn."

"Jeffers," Grant choked, tears in his throat.

"You didn't think I stayed all of these years for Ian's sake, did you?" Jeffers turned to look at him. "As long as I have breath, I am tied to that promise, and willingly so."

"God sakes, man." Grant pulled Jeffers into his arms with a sob. "You realize that you're tying your fate to a penniless fool."

"Wouldn't have it any other way, sir. I do wish you had left sooner, but like most stubborn asses, I knew you had to come to it on your own." He pulled away and Grant wiped at the tears. "And as it is, we never would have never met Miss Katelyn if you had."

"What'll we do, Jeffers?" Grant's heart filled with defeat. "How will I ever earn her forgiveness?"

"I find the best way is, often, simply to ask for it. Here's our ride now."

From behind of them, a dust cloud barreled down the road and Grant squinted into the afternoon light. Jeremy and Jasmine pulled to a stop beside them.

"Well, lookie here," Jasmine said from inside the cab. "Two vagrants loitering outside the Tennyson premises." Jeremy cleared his throat uncomfortably.

"Ah, Mrs. Sutter, would you be so kind?" Jeffers began, but she shook her head.

"Jeffers, I will take *you* anywhere, but *him*," she pointed at Grant accusingly. "I'm going to need answers first." She glared him down when he tried to look into her beautiful, fierce face. "Where are you heading and why?"

"Wyoming. To beg the woman I love to take me back."

She looked at him without softening. "Really?"

"Yes."

"And why did you let her go in the first place?"

"Because I was an absolute idiot," Grant grouched back.

"And now? Think you found enough of your balls to leave?"

"I've left. I'm no longer welcome on any of my father's properties."

"Well, well," Jasmine said, and shook her head. "Sounds like the kind of person I'd let in my truck. Hop in the back." She pointed to the bed. "Jeffers, you are welcome in the cab."

Jeffers chuckled. "I am much obliged, Mrs. Sutter. However, I will keep my young charge company. I can't let him do all the adventuring."

Grant, his heart and eyes opened to the man who'd spent his life taking care of him, took the suitcases from Jeffers' hands, placed them delicately into the bed of the truck and helped him up.

"Quite unnecessary," Jeffers began.

"Don't be senile," Grant said gruffly. "It's high time I started taking care of you."

"But—"

"We all do better when we watch out for one another," he said and grunted as he clambered into the back of the truck. Jeffers reached back over his shoulder and tapped the glass gently.

"To the airport, if you please, Mr. Sutter." He turned to Grant and smiled. "Always wanted to be the one directing the driver."

"Yessir," said Jeremy with a smile.

"The airport?" Grant said and clung to the strap of his bag. "But I don't have any money."

"Ian controlled your assets. He did no such thing with mine. I was properly paid for many years and lived those years quite modestly. And, now that we are both persona non grata at Tennyson Stables, I think you should know that ever since Jane's unfortunate death and the threats he made to you, I've been skimming off the top of several of Ian's accounts."

"Jeffers!"

"Well? Nothing that he didn't deserve, and certainly not more than I needed." Grant thought for a moment, a surprised smile stuck on his face.

"You've already done too much, Jeffers. I wouldn't be alive, if not for you. I wouldn't be the man I've become, the better man, if not for you. I'll not have you spending your money, no matter how justly obtained, to fix my mistakes."

"Well, perhaps I shall just hire you then."

"Hire me?"

"To carry my luggage, fetch my whisky, polish my boots, feed my horse."

"That's my horse," Grant said wryly.

"So it is, young Grant."

"And as for the rest," Grant huffed, "I'll do so gladly, for as long as you see fit to employ me."

"Fair enough, 'tis." Jeffers nodded. "Just in time, I've had my eye on a little piece of land near Sweet Valley Wyoming."

Grant smiled with tears in his eyes. "Have you now? Just so happens that's where I'm heading."

"Airport then," Jeremy confirmed as the truck drove farther away from the stables that had been part of the best and worst years of Grant's life.

"Yes, sir." Grant smiled all the way to the edge of the property and laughed out loud when they broke its bonds and the wild wind tossed his hair. The world lifted from his once-heavy shoulders.

Twenty-Four

Work.

Work was what she had. Lists and notes and calls to consult other therapists around the country. She hadn't counted on her name being spread far and wide as the therapist who had saved Hugh Dancy's career and Tennyson Stables' future. The phone rang at least twice a day with calls asking for her advice, for her to fly out, for her to come and work with an injured horse, a surly temperament, a problem that seemed above the talents of others who came before her. She'd become the goddamn horse whisperer. And yet she hadn't taken any of the jobs that would have made her leave home.

Coming back to her parents' house, her old room, her dad's clinic, her mom's stables, felt like a strange place that she barely recalled. She felt like there was a giant hole in the middle of all of it. A giant, Grant-sized, hole.

Her mom scolded her to eat. Her father quietly suggested she not work *all* the shifts at the clinic. Elle asked her to sleep more. Even Blake caught her in the middle of mucking out stables.

"You oughta take it easy, pipsqueak," he said, resting his lean form against the frame of the stable where she pitched hay. "You're gonna burn out."

"Shut up, Blake," she scowled back. "What the fuck you know about anything? You've got the easy life." She grunted as shafts of hay flew and dispersed into the light shining through the large doors.

"Sure, elbows deep in calf turning, every day. I'm living the goddamn dream," he chuckled. "You know, you could be a veterinarian yourself, easy."

"Town only needs *one* know-it-all," she grumbled. "I'm fine here. You can leave, I'll take care of the littles in recovery."

"I think you should go home."

"What home?" Her voice shook, and she turned away from him. "Just get on and go now. Go be with that baby, and my sister who's—who's probably missing you."

"Katelyn."

"Blake. I—" She sniffed and wiped her nose on her sleeve. "I'm okay, okay? Just go." Blake didn't believe it for even a minute. He knew a struggling Sullivan when he saw one. He'd been part of their family since he was eight, and though he'd lost his way for a while, he never stopped being Katelyn's big brother.

"No. You're not okay. You're *gonna* be okay. But you're not there yet," he said resolutely, and Katelyn turned back around with tears in her eyes.

"I don't know if that's true. I don't think I'm ever gonna feel better about this," she confessed and threw the pitchfork into the pile with surprising strength for a girl who couldn't seem to sit down for a meal. Blake caught her round the shoulders and pulled her tiny and shaking frame into his arms.

"You will. I know you will. Katie May Sullivan don't run, and she don't quit," he said softly into her hair and kissed the crown of her head. "You don't know it yet. You don't know how strong you are, because you got knocked down, lower than you've ever been. Lower than I ever seen you. And you're hurt. And I'm so sorry,"

Blake said and held her even tighter. "If I could murder the son-of-a-bitch, you know I would."

Katelyn's muffled protest was lost in his shoulder.

"But he's got enough to deal with. And so do you. You have to worry about getting back up, short stack. It ain't gonna happen overnight and it will always hurt."

"Is this supposed to be a pep talk? Because you suck at it."

"You'll come up stronger, Katelyn. You'll come up so goddamn strong that only the person who deserves to be with you will have to rise to your level."

She sniffed and pulled away. "That person never existed. I shouldn't have ever bothered to think he did." She stopped, shook her head, and stormed out of the barn.

"Katelyn."

"I'll close up. Go home," she said over her shoulder, and Blake could do nothing but scowl in frustration as Katelyn stormed through the clinic doors.

LATER THAT EVENING, LANEY CAME INTO TOWN WHILE her girls were spending the weekend with her ex. She'd swung up, in her beat-up Isuzu, and kidnapped an unwilling Katelyn from filing paperwork at the clinic. Now they were in Sweet Valley's oldest hotel and bar, Belle's.

"All right, kiddo. What's the story?" Laney asked as they sat at the bar. Jim Travers, who'd been tending bar there for at least a hundred years, set a glass of red wine in front of Laney and looked to Katelyn. Katelyn didn't look up. She was exhausted, and the only reason she sat here now was because her sister had physically dragged her out. Katelyn didn't go to bars. She didn't drink. She couldn't stomach much with the sour ache so heavy in her heart.

"Uh," Katelyn shook her head without acknowledging the man. "I don't want anything."

"She'll have a double Basil Hayden on the rocks, please Jim," Laney countered. Jim raised his brow.

"That kind of night, huh? Who's the asshole that broke our little Katelyn's heart?" he said morosely. Laney looked to her sister.

"A man who didn't want to, I reckon."

"What the hell, Laney?" Katelyn stuttered indignantly and swung her head towards her sister. "Since when do you know anything about it?" Katelyn shook her head and turned her attention to the drink Jim set in front of her. Harsh sadness hit her gut, mixed with the burn of the bourbon, and she settled back into checking the emails from a rehabilitation center in North Dakota. Laney took the phone from her and pocketed it.

"Listen, short stack, there's only room in this family for one bitter old maid, and I'm tenured there. And, whether you want to agree or not, I know about love. Or at least, I like to think I do. Elle filled me in on Grant's trip here."

Katelyn blanched, took a hearty swallow, and coughed with the searing heat of it.

"Walls are pretty thin in an old farmhouse." Laney smirked and took a sip of wine. "He wanted to be loved. You gave him that love," she said softly.

"Yeah? And look where that got me." Katelyn wheezed and took a smaller sip.

Laney nodded. "I know. That first fall? Shit, it's rough. It changes you in the deep layers."

Laney's words made Katelyn finish her drink and nod to Jim for another. The gray haze that settled into her brain seemed to numb every neuron that was lit up thinking about Grant, and the night he'd begged her for love, only to turn her out not a week later.

"I don't want to talk about my layers. I'm fine," Katelyn grouched and took her phone from Laney.

"You are not fine, look at you. The unsinkable Katelyn May,

moping around like a goddamn character in a book? And don't get me started on how hard you've been working."

"I am not moping." Katelyn argued. "I just finally opened my eyes." She gestured vaguely towards the direction of the man who was all at once the cause for such light and dark in her life. "Love is uneven, and unfair and it can't exist in the world without cost. I would have paid anything, but he wouldn't. I can't change a man, Laney."

"I'm not saying you should. I think you did it without even realizing."

"What in the hell are you talking about?" Katelyn took another swallow and swooned in her seat. "I didn't change him. I even wrote him a pitiful and stupid girly note and left it for him, and he probably didn't even read it."

They sat in silence for a moment. Laney watched Katelyn sink into the seat, tears in her eyes.

"You wrote him a note?" she pried.

"Don't make fun of me!"

"I'm not! I think that's, well, shit you know me, I think that's beautiful."

"Yeah, well, he didn't. 'Cause I'm still here alone." Katelyn clinked her second nearly finished drink to Laney's barely-touched glass and tossed back the rest.

They sat in silence for a whole minute before a preening young man settled into the chair beside Katelyn. He smelled like too much fraternity cologne. Nothing like peat and pipe tobacco. Nothing like stable dust and hay. Scotch and sunlit lakes, tucked away in forested oases. Nothing like anything she wanted or needed.

"Doesn't seem fair, a pretty mouth like yours frowning that way," he said and flashed a perfect smile, no wrinkles to be found. A boy, looking for instant gratification. Laney cleared her throat and leaned back to get a better look at him.

"Listen, friend, you probably want to just move along," she said with a scowl.

"I don't think it's right to leave a pretty girl sad," he crooned. Katelyn didn't turn to either of them. Her brain was back in North Carolina.

Grant should have found her note by now; should have had enough time to change his mind, if he'd really wanted her. Now, as she sat next to the faceless peacock in blinged-out jeans, all she could think about was her heartfelt letter and her grandmother's lucky tin cup in some trash bin in the austere house.

"Wanna talk about what's right?" Katelyn grumbled. "Let's talk about how you've got two choices of women here and you picked me to use your one good line on. Now take my gorgeous sister here—" Laney snorted and nodded to Jim.

"And that's Jenga, she's had enough." Laney pulled out her wallet.

"Well," the man cleared his throat and looked at Laney. "I've never been with an older woman, but I'm game."

"Oh, for fuck's sake," Laney scowled. Katelyn laughed.

"You probably wanna just walk away before she takes a piece outta your hide," Katelyn advised.

"You can do whatever you want to me, if it puts a smile back on those lips," he said. Katelyn groaned and buried her head in her hands. She wished Grant were here. She wished he was puffed up and angry, looking at the other man with hatred and possessiveness in his eyes. She never wished for anyone else to solve her problems. But she was tired and her heart was heavy.

"What do you say, babe?" he purred.

"My name is Katelyn, not babe. Go find instant gratification someplace else," she growled and stood up. She threw some cash on the bar before storming out. Laney followed, muttering apologies to Jim.

"Katelyn!" Laney yelled as she ran after her sister.

"I appreciate you trying to help me, but I didn't ask," she said.

"I just want you to know you're not alone, Katie. And I'll sit beside you while you wait."

"Wait for what?" Katelyn yelled angrily.

"For it to stop hurting so bad."

"Does that ever happen?" Katelyn wavered.

"Katie? You okay?" Laney's voice seemed muffled and far away.

"Goodnight, Lane," Katelyn mumbled, wobbled on one boot before quickly righting herself. She felt dizzy and stupid. She felt like she wasn't worth the gutter beneath her feet. She felt hopeless. Like the sun would never find its way to her again. She felt bereft of reason and purpose. Barren.

The word sunk into her bones and made her knees tremble. She felt the world spin. Saw the concrete coming up to meet her face. The stab of pain to her forehead was the last thing she felt before falling into blissful, dark nothingness.

DEHYDRATED...MAYBE A SLIGHT CONCUSSION. SHE NEEDS plenty of bed rest...no work. The words echoed as she fell in and out of dreams. Tennyson Stables, Hugh, and Grant, shepherd's pie and sun-dazzled lakes. Katelyn opened one eye, and pain shot through her forehead. She groaned and started to sit up, but vertigo washed over her and she fell back against the pillows.

Her father and mother were there, and had told her, in no uncertain terms, that she wasn't allowed to work in the clinic for the next week at least.

"Y'all are overreacting." she grouched.

"We'll find something to keep you busy," Warren said.

"I'm not allowed in the clinic. I can't ride. I can't work. What at the fuck am I gonna do?"

"You're gonna start by watching your mouth, young lady." Melissa reprimanded and kissed her forehead. "You're going to rest."

So, there she was, waking up with a headache, feeling wobbly in her knees, and angry at herself for letting it get so bad that she couldn't even do the things that kept her sane.

Elle brought her a box of baked goods, and Laney came to read chapters from her latest novel, a thriller set in the South. By day three, Katelyn was about to die from boredom. When her sisters offered to sneak her out of the house for a gentle ride around their parents' land, she readily agreed. Like any terrible patient and good sisters would, they waited until their parents had left for the clinic, and Katelyn tip-toed downstairs, donned her boots, and snuck into the stables with Elle and Laney.

Katelyn knew that riding would help. She hadn't been able to take Dakota out for months, and the horse had missed it nearly as much as she had. Laney's insistence that they follow the property lines of the back forty with Elle was strange. Katelyn would have preferred to go out by herself and think about how miserable she was. She suspected her sisters knew this, and weren't going to put up with her brooding alone after her fall. She sighed, scowled, and trotted ahead of Elle and Lottie, and the mismatched pair of Laney and Goliath. Goliath reminded her of Scotty and Grant's first time back in the saddle.

Everything reminded her of Grant. Her stomach felt sick; she wanted to throw up.

"Hold your horses, little lady!" Laney yelled from the back as Katelyn picked up speed. "This is supposed to be a leisurely cruise. You gotta watch your head."

"You watch *your* head, professor," Katelyn grumbled back quietly.

"Ooo, I'm gonna tell her you said that," Elle laughed from behind. Katelyn turned and scowled from below her tipped down cap.

"You know I *could* do this on my own."

"Oh, I know," Elle nodded and caught Katelyn in her tough, blue gaze. "But we don't let the ones we love alone when they're hurt."

"I'm fine."

"No, you aren't," Laney gasped, coming up from behind with the great heralding hoofbeats of the Clydesdale, who nipped at Lottie's flank, causing her to startle and Elle to let out a whoop.

"Kindly control your horse." Elle grouched.

"What's the matter? Afraid you might get dumped off?"

"Don't say dumped," Elle whispered. Katelyn blanched.

"Why don't you both just shut up," she grumbled and faced forward. They traveled in silence along the fence line, the early July morning quiet and hot. The sun lent an orange glow over the prairie, and Katelyn's eyes fell to the distant horizon, where a rider and horse appeared, tall shadows along the far hill. She squinted.

"Who's that? A new hired hand for the Bar?" she whispered; Bar Nunn's property bordered the Sullivan's. No one answered, and she didn't expect them to. "Why's he on our side of the fence?" she said louder as the roan stallion cantered ever closer.

"I dunno," Elle said. "Maybe, he's not on the wrong side."

"What?" Katelyn looked over her shoulder to both sisters, whose faces didn't look surprised at the stranger on their land.

"Ride ahead, see what he wants." Laney nodded.

"What? Why me?"

"We're right behind you," Elle said and tilted her head towards the horseman. Katelyn huffed.

"You two are being weird. Fine. I'll go chase off the trespasser. Great way to treat the invalid," she grouched and took off, nudging Dakota's sides with her booted heels and jumping into a gallop.

The wind in her hair, the thundering hoof and heartbeats below her filled her chest with something she'd been missing. Something undeniably her, and she smiled with the rush of it. Cresting the small hill where the rider had descended, she looked down.

.   .   .

HE CLIMBED UP TOWARDS HER. THE WIND BLEW HIS shirt tight across his chest and tangled Hugh's mane with its updraft. The rays of sun lit on the bronze of Grant's hair and she squinted with the tears that sprung up, unwanted, while her heart fell out of her chest. Hugh whinnied loudly and Dakota startled back with a nervous grunt. Katelyn patted her reassuringly and turned her in a circle until he approached.

"There's a fine lass, riding into the fray."

"I must have hit my head harder than I thought."

"Aye, maybe."

"What in the hell are you doing here?"

"I told your sisters you shouldn't be out of bed yet," he said simultaneously.

"*You* don't tell *me* what to do, Grant Tennyson. This is my land!" she yelled and immediately regretted how her head split in two. When she faltered and pressed her hand to her forehead, Grant urged Hugh closer. Dakota backed up under the shift of Katelyn's pressure.

"Now, see? You dinna get to yell at me," he said softer, but when he tried to pull up next to her, Dakota skirted away. His eyes followed her body, attuned to the beautiful mare beneath her. She was too thin, but she was every bit as tough as the afternoon she'd walked away from him. The words came out easily. "I love you."

"Bullshit."

Grant laughed. "Let me explain."

"The viper kick you out or something? Did your husbandly duty and decide to find something on the sly? Why the hell did you have to drag Hugh into it?" No breaths came between the accusations and questions. "You can just leave him here and be on your merry way."

"God sake's, lass, you're mean," he chuckled. "Let me say a word."

"No! Not a goddamn one!" Dakota startled beneath her and she moved to gallop back to where her sisters were waiting on the next rise behind them. Hugh rounded the sagebrush and stood firmly in front of them both. "You don't belong here," she yelled.

"Aye, I do. This is my land."

"What? What in the hell are you talking about?" Katelyn stopped.

"Your father agreed to let Jeffers and I buy this small plot and all the way down to the river."

"You son-of-a-bitch. You can't bring Ian's dirty money into my life. And how dare you involve Jeffers when that man did nothing but love you your whole life."

"I didn't buy it with Ian's money. I bought it with mine. Well, Jeffers' and mine. And it was Jeffers brilliant idea by the way. But none of the paperwork has even a fingerprint of Ian's."

Katelyn stared at him, the way his chest rose and fell with every desperate gasp.

"And Hugh? What in the hell is Hugh doing here? Did you," she paused to huff, "Did you horsenap him? And don't you laugh at me!"

"Oh, Katie love," he said, and the endearment softened her eyes. "No, I didn't steal him. He's been paid for." Katelyn looked at him suspiciously. Grant's eyes never left hers while Hugh danced, nervously aware of Dakota but anxious to greet his Katelyn.

"You can't just come runnin' out here every time the viper gets overbearing. I'm not gonna be some side piece of tail, Grant."

"You most certainly will *not* be my mistress," he barked.

"But you married her."

"I did not marry Cecilia. I would not. I will not. Not ever!" Hugh skirted from his harsh tone, but Grant's body read his movements and they redirected into a circle around Dakota. Katelyn watched the ease with which he fit into Hugh's movements. The bond that had been healed.

"But, your inheritance? Ian's plans?"

"If I want to marry, no one but *you* will be my wife, Katelyn.

All others are less, and I will not have you as some belittled 'side piece'. You will be my all, wife or not. Only you will wake me up to help with the chores, only you will mend my rough and readies—"

"Now, hang on! I don't even sew—"

"I will make you shepherd's pie and you'll bring me my whisky and I'll give you my lap and a lifetime worth of kisses. You'll share your bed and I'll share my bath. I'll take your name, proudly. If you'll be mine, Katelyn, my partner, my solid ground, *I will be yours*. And absolutely nothing less. We can work our own land and train our own horses. I'm here to stay, and I canna be anywhere else." He said it all in a single breath and took Katelyn's away. She wavered on the dusty hill while the sound of Hugh snuffling and Dakota grunting in response mimicked their own negotiations.

"I left it all behind. I dinna care if I live in a barn as long as you're there in the sweet hay beside me, I just, I canna live—" He choked back a sob. "I canna live without you, Katie, lass. I'd be a poor man indeed."

"Grant," she said, tears in her eyes and rooted in place. Her fists tight on the reins, the emotions rushing through her. The need, the confusion, the worry.

"The night I found your note, ah, Katie, I was such a damnable mess without you." He sniffed; eyes full of tears. "Saying you loved me, that you'd wait for me?" He choked and wiped his eyes with his shirt sleeve.

"I did say those things."

Grant stopped, pulled Hugh up, and dismounted.

"I knew I'd rather die than live without you another day. So, I started making plans. As for the contract and his heir, well, it was actually your idea that solved the problem."

"My idea? How the hell do you figure?" Katelyn scowled, continuing to circle them.

"You told me not to marry the viper *for* Ian. Sure'n let him marry the horrible harpy himself." Grant smiled up at her. Katelyn stared down at him and pulled Dakota up. Her resolve faltered next to the man she couldn't ever stop loving.

"Grant Lachlan Blackwood," Katelyn whispered, and hopped down. She came at him, grabbed the front of his shirt, and pulled him to her. She kissed him, hard and angry and with all the desperate longing that had filled her since the day she'd walked away from him. Grant wrapped his arms around her and lifted her up in a rush of joy. She found his soft curls, and threading them through her fingers. He nuzzled into her warm body, inhaled her, and sighed.

"Do you love me? Still, Katie, after lying that I didn't love you, and mistakes and hurt? My stupidity? Could you, somehow—"

"Shut up," she whispered and sniffed. "Shut up and kiss me, you stupid, stubborn beast, before I throw a cup at you." The words were laced with a smile and broken with happy sobs. Grant set her down and kissed her fervently, with every lost day to pay for. His mouth was warm and delicious, and she was surrounded in his heat and strength. She felt dizzy and was glad for his arms.

"Aye, but you'll have to get it back from me first," he chuckled into her lips. "Ah, Katie love." He nuzzled her nose with his own. From behind them a loud whinny broke through their embrace. Dakota was nipping at Hugh's flank and chasing him in circles.

"He's gonna have to learn the pecking order," Katelyn said with a smile. Finally, when Dakota had asserted her authority, Hugh came to softly nuzzle into Katelyn's neck, sandwiching her between Grant and himself. She'd never been so happy to be surrounded.

"All right, you impatient bastard," Katelyn laughed and caressed his long nose before pressing her forehead to his. He grunted soothingly. "Soon as I can, you and I'll sneak out to the river. Don't tell Dad." Grant's laugh rumbled through her ribs.

"Aye, and dad will be watching from the bushes, while his little water nymph disrobes." Katelyn felt Grant's reaction pressing against her body. She leaned into it, her nails against his chest.

"I'm not supposed to do anything too jarring," she whispered, but began kissing her way up his strong jaw line all the same. Grant groaned.

"I only have the land, but what I'd give for a bed."

"Well, I guess we'll just have to work for that. Maybe even some walls to go around it," she teased and nudged him beneath the ear.

"I'm not afraid to work for it, Katelyn. You taught me that."

"You've always known it, Grant. I just reminded you." He smiled into her mouth as his hand slipped beneath her shirt to find the hard peak of her breast. She gasped, threw her head back, and he bit her neck.

"I want to take you back to the house, but I know how your father feels about unwed couples sharing a bed," he groaned. "But I feel if I don't have you soon, I might just die."

"Well, I dinna want you to die. Least not anymore," she teased, causing him to laugh heartily.

"I can wait, a little longer."

"Well, I can't," she argued and scowled up at him.

"You two gonna try going at it in the sagebrush? 'Cause it is tick season and Lyme disease is no joke." Laney's laughter came from behind, where she and Elle had taken the other two horses by the reins before they could go off frolicking in the fields, flirting with the new idea of unsanctioned breeding. Grant looked up at her smiling sisters.

"Thanks for bringing her," he said.

"You cagey, untrustworthy assholes." Katelyn shook her head.

"I prefer *wing women*," Elle said.

"I love it when a good romance comes together," Laney sighed.

"And you don't have to stay in the field. We have a broken-in bed until it gets settled." Elle smiled coyly. Grant blushed.

"Aye, that would be fine," he said sweetly and scooped up Katelyn, no longer in need of daydreaming what life would be like.

"Aye," she said and kissed the lips she had long missed.

Rate and Review

We hope you've enjoyed *Granting Katelyn* by S.E. Reichert. Please take a moment to rate and review as each review helps our authors reach more readers.

Rate and Review: Granting Katelyn

MEET THE AUTHOR

Sarah Reichert (S.E. Reichert) is a novelist, poet, and blogger. She owns and operates The Beautiful Stuff Blog, a website for writing advice, poetry, and inspiration for living a more balanced, realistic life.

Currently, she is a full-time mom of two creative and talented teenage girls, and a full-time writer of both fiction and poetry, and the Youth Coordinator for Writing Heights Writers Association. She is a terrible cat wrangler and her rescue pit bull steals all her cookies. Her garden is passionately planted every spring, and quietly neglected for most of the summer, in favor of getting lost in the wild gardens of the Rocky Mountains.

OTHER TITLES FROM
5 PRINCE PUBLISHING

www.ingramcontent.com/pod-product-compliance
Lightning Source LLC
Chambersburg PA
CBHW030345020726
47493CB00003B/698